Maybe it was the sight of Mitch with his tie tugged off and the first few buttons of his white shirt opened.

Maybe it was her reaction to the black chest hair peeking out. Maybe she thought about all he'd done for her.

Maybe, for just a short time, she gave in to the thought that she might *need* a protector. She only knew thoughts weren't running through her brain as fast as heat was flashing through her body.

Lily wasn't thinking at all when she leaned forward.

Rather, she was feeling and wishing and hoping and remembering what it had felt like to be held in a man's arms.

Twins for Christmas

ALISON ROBERTS

&

USA TODAY BESTSELLING AUTHOR

KAREN ROSE SMITH

Previously published as *Sleigh Ride with the Single Dad*
and *Twins Under His Tree*

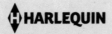

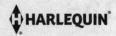

ISBN-13: 978-1-335-41883-8

Twins for Christmas

Copyright © 2021 by Harlequin Books S.A.

Sleigh Ride with the Single Dad
First published in 2017. This edition published in 2021.
Copyright © 2017 by Harlequin Books S.A.

Twins Under His Tree
First published in 2010. This edition published in 2021.
Copyright © 2010 by Karen Rose Smith

Special thanks and acknowledgment are given to Alison Roberts
for her contribution to the Christmas in Manhattan series.

This edition published by arrangement with Harlequin Books S.A.

For questions and comments about the quality of this book,
please contact us at CustomerService@Harlequin.com.

Harlequin Enterprises ULC
22 Adelaide St. West, 40th Floor
Toronto, Ontario M5H 4E3, Canada
www.Harlequin.com

Printed in U.S.A.

PLEASE RECYCLE
THIS PRODUCT IS RECYCLABLE

Recycling programs
for this product may
not exist in your area.

CONTENTS

Alison Roberts is a New Zealander, currently lucky enough to be living in the South of France. She is also lucky enough to write for the Harlequin Medical Romance line. A primary school teacher in a former life, she is now a qualified paramedic. She loves to travel and dance, drink champagne, and spend time with her daughter and her friends.

Books by Alison Roberts

Harlequin Medical Romance

Royal Christmas at Seattle General

Falling for the Secret Prince

Medics, Sisters, Brides

Awakening the Shy Nurse
Saved by Their Miracle Baby

Rescue Docs

Resisting Her Rescue Doc
Pregnant with Her Best Friend's Baby
Dr. Right for the Single Mom

Hope Children's Hospital

Their Newborn Baby Gift

Visit the Author Profile page at
Harlequin.com for more titles.

Sleigh Ride with the Single Dad

ALISON ROBERTS

Chapter 1

As an omen, this wasn't good.

It could have been the opening scene to a horror movie, in fact.

Grace Forbes, in her crisp, clean set of scrubs—her stethoscope slung around her neck along with the lanyard holding her new Manhattan Mercy ID card—walking towards Charles Davenport who, as chief of Emergency Services, was about to give her an official welcome to her new job.

An enormous clap of thunder rolled overhead from a storm that had to be directly on top of central New York and big enough for the sound to carry into every corner of this huge building.

And then the lights went out.

Unexpectedly, the moment Grace had been bracing herself for became an anti-climax. It was no longer im-

portant that this was the first time in more than a decade that her path was about to cross with that of the
man who'd rocked her world back in the days of Harvard Medical School. Taking control of a potential crisis in a crowded emergency room was the only thing
that mattered.

In the brief, shocked silence that followed both the
clap of thunder, a terrified scream from a child and the
startling contrast of a virtually windowless area bathed
in bright, neon lighting being transformed instantly into
the shadowed gloom of a deep cave, Charles Davenport
did exactly that.

'It's just a power outage, folks.' He raised his voice but
still sounded calm. 'Stay where you are. The emergency
generators will kick in any minute.'

Torch apps on mobile phones flickered on like stars
appearing in a night sky and beams of light began to
sweep the area as people tried to see what was going on.
The noise level rose and rapidly got louder and louder.
Telephones were ringing against the backdrop of the buzz
of agitated conversations. Alarms sounded to warn of the
power disruption to medical equipment. Staff, including
the administrative clerks from the waiting area, triage
nurses and technicians were moving towards the central
desk to await instructions and their movements triggered
shouts from people desperate for attention.

'Hey, come back…where are you going?'

'Help… I need *help*.'

'Nurse…over *here*…please?'

'I'm scared, Mommy… I want to go *home*…'

Grace stayed where she was, her gaze fixed on
Charles. The dramatic change in the lighting had soft-
ened the differences that time had inevitably produced

and, for a heartbeat, he looked exactly as he had that night. Exactly like the haunting figure that had walked through her mind and her heart so often when sleep had opened portals to another time.

Tall and commanding. Caring enough to come after her and find out what was wrong so he could do something about making it better...

Which was pretty much what he was doing right now. She could see him assessing the situation and dealing with the most urgent priorities, even as he took in information that was coming at him from numerous directions.

'Miranda—check any alarms coming from cardiac monitors.'

'Get ready to put us on bypass for incoming patients. If we don't get power back on fast, we'll have a problem.'

'Put the trauma team on standby. If this outage is widespread, we could be in for a spate of accidents.'

Sure enough, people manning the telephones and radio links with the ambulance service were already taking calls.

'Traffic lights out at an intersection on Riverside Drive. Multi-vehicle pile-up. Fire service called for trapped patients. Cyclist versus truck incoming, stat.'

'Fall down stairs only two blocks away. Possible spinal injury. ETA two minutes.'

'Estates need to talk to you, Dr Davenport. Apparently there's some issue with the generators and they're prioritising Theatres and ICU...'

Charles nodded tersely and began issuing orders rapidly. Staff dispersed swiftly to cover designated areas and calm patients. A technician was dispatched to find extra batteries that might be needed for backup for equipment like portable ultrasound and X-ray machines. Flashlights were found and given to orderlies, security personnel and even patients' relatives to hold. Finally, Charles had an instruction specifically directed to Grace.

'Come with me,' he said. 'I need someone to head the trauma team if I have to troubleshoot other stuff.' He noticed heads turning in his direction. 'This is Dr Grace Forbes,' he announced briskly. 'Old colleague of mine who's come from running her own emergency department in outback Australia. She probably feels right at home in primitive conditions like this.'

A smile or two flashed in Grace's direction as her new workmates rushed past to follow their own orders. The smile Charles gave her was distinctly wry. Because of the unusual situation she was being thrown into? Or was it because he knew that describing her as an old colleague was stretching the truth more than a little? It was true that she and Charles had worked in the same hospital more than once in that final year of medical school but their real relationship had been that of fierce but amicable rivals for the position of being the top student of their year. The fact that Charles knew where she'd been recently, when he hadn't been present for the interview she'd had for this job, was another indication that he was on top of his position of being head of this department. No wonder he'd won that final battle of the marks, even though it had only been by a small margin.

'Welcome to Manhattan Mercy, Grace... Trauma One is this way...'

It was hardly the best way to welcome a new member of staff but maybe it was better this way, with so many things to think about that Charles couldn't allow any flashes of memory to do more than float past the edges of his conscious mind.

He hadn't seen Grace since he'd noticed her in the audience when he'd walked onto the stage to accept the trophy for being the top student of their graduation party from medical school.

He hadn't spoken to her since…since *that* night…

'Warn people that waiting times are going to go through the roof for anything non-urgent,' he told the senior member of the administrative team as he passed her. 'But don't push them out the door. By the sound of this storm, it's not safe out there.'

A flicker in the ambient light filtering into the department suggested a flash of lightning outside and another roll of thunder could be heard only a second later so they were still right underneath it. Fingers crossed that the worst of the storm would cross the central city quickly but how long would it be before the power disruption was sorted? And how many problems would it cause?

The weather alone would give them a huge spike in traffic accidents. A sudden plunge into darkness could cause all sorts of trauma like that fall down stairs already on its way. And what about the people on home oxygen who could find themselves in severe respiratory distress with the power outage cutting off their support? They needed to be ready for anything in the ER and he needed to clear space for the potential battleground of dodging unexpected missiles of incoming cases and whatever ambush could be in store with equipment that might not be functioning until power came back on.

He hadn't faced a challenge like this for a long time but he had learned way back how to multi-task when the proverbial was hitting the fan and Charles knew he could function effectively on different levels at the same time.

Like knowing which patients could be sidelined for observation well away from centre-stage and directing staff members to transfer them as he passed their ed cubicles at the same time as fending off a request from a television crew who happened to be in the area and wanted to cover the fallout from what was apparently a record-breaking storm.

'Keep them out of here,' he growled. 'We're going to have more than enough to deal with.'

It never took long for the media to get their teeth into something, did it? Memories of how much damage had been done to his own family all those years ago had left Charles with a mistrust bordering on paranoia. It was a time of his life he had no desire to revisit so it was perhaps unfortunate that the arrival of Grace Forbes in his department had the ability to stir those memories.

And others...

A glance over his shoulder showed him that Grace was following his slightly circuitous route to Trauma One as he made sure he knew what was happening everywhere at the moment. The expression on her face was serious and the focus in those dark grey eyes reminded him of how capable he knew she was. And how intelligent. He'd had to fight hard back at medical school to keep his marks on the same level as Grace and, while they'd never moved in the same social circles, he'd had enormous respect for her. A respect that had tipped into something very different when he'd discovered that she had a vulnerable side, mind you, but he wasn't going to allow the memory of that night to surface.

No way. Even if this situation wasn't making it completely unacceptable to allow such a personal distraction, he wouldn't go there. It was in the same, forbidden territory that housed flirting and he had never been tempted to respond to opportunities that were only becoming more blatant as time crept on.

No. He couldn't go there. It would still feel like he was being unfaithful…

Nobody could ever accuse Charles Davenport of being less than totally loyal. To his family and to his work.

And that was exactly where his entire focus had to be right now. It didn't matter a damn that this was a less than ideal welcome to a new staff member. Grace would have to jump into the deep end and do her bit to get Manhattan Mercy's ER through this unexpected crisis.

Just as he was doing.

Other staff members were already in the area assigned to deal with major trauma, preparing it for the accident victims they had been warned were on their way. A nurse handed Grace a gown to cover her scrubs and then a face mask that had the plastic eye shield attached.

'Gloves are on the wall there. Choose your size.'

Someone helpfully shone a torch beam over the bench at the side of the area so that Grace could see the 'M' for medium on the front of the box she needed. She also caught a glimpse of an airway cart ready for business, an IV cart, a cardiac monitor, ventilator and portable ultrasound machine.

Okay. She could work with this. Even in semi-darkness she had what she needed to assess an airway, breathing and circulation and to do her best to handle whatever emergencies needed to be treated to stabilise a critically injured patient. And she wasn't alone. As the shadowy figures of paramedics surrounding a gurney came rapidly towards them, Charles was already standing at the head of the bed, ready to take on the most important role of managing an airway.

'Male approximately forty years old,' one of the paramedics told them. He was wearing wet weather gear but his hair was soaked and he had to wipe away the water that was still trickling into his eyes. 'Hit by a truck and thrown about thirty feet to land on the hood of an approaching car. GCS of twelve, blood pressure ninety on palp, tachycardic at one-thirty. Major trauma to left arm and leg.'

The man was semi-conscious and clearly in pain. Despite wearing a neck collar and being strapped to a back board, he was trying to move and groaning loudly.

'On my count,' Charles directed. 'One, two…*three*…'

The patient was smoothly transferred to the bed.

'I need light here, please,' Charles said. He leaned close to their patient's head as someone shone a beam of light in his direction. 'Can you hear me?' He seemed to understand the muffled change to the groan coming from beneath an oxygen mask. 'You're in hospital, buddy. We're going to take care of you.'

A nurse was cutting away clothing. Another was wrapping a blood pressure cuff around an arm and a young, resident doctor was swapping the leads from an ambulance monitor to their own. Grace was watching, assessing the injuries that were becoming apparent. A mangled right arm and a huge wound on the left thigh where a snapped femur had probably gone through the skin and then been pulled back again. The heavy blood loss was an immediate priority. She grabbed a wad of dressing material and put it on the wound to apply direct pressure.

'We need to get back out there,' the lead paramedic told them. 'It's gone crazy. Raining cats and dogs and visibility is almost zero.'

'How widespread is the power cut?'

'At least sixteen blocks from what we've heard. Lightning strike on a power station, apparently. Nobody knows how long it's gonna be before it's back on.'

Charles nodded. 'Thanks, guys.' But his attention was on assessing his patient's breathing. He had crouched to put his line of sight just over head level and Grace knew he was watching the rise and fall of the man's chest to see whether it was symmetrical. If it wasn't, it could indicate a collapsed lung or another problem affecting his breathing.

She was also in a direct line for the steady glance and she saw the shift, when Charles was satisfied with chest movement and had taken on board what she was doing to control haemorrhage and his gaze flicked up to meet her own. For a split second, he held the eye contact and there was something in his gaze that made her feel... what? That he had confidence in her abilities? That she was already a part of the team?

That he was pleased to see her again?

Behind that emotional frisson, there was something else, too. An awareness of how different Charles looked. It shouldn't be a surprise. Thirteen years was a very long time and, even then, they had been young people who were products of their very different backgrounds. But everyone had known that Charles Davenport had the perfect life mapped out for him so why did Grace get the fleeting impression that he looked older than she would have expected? That he had lines in his face that suggested a profound weariness. Sadness, even...

'Blood pressure eighty on forty.' The resident looked up at the overhead monitor. 'And heart rate is one-thirty. Oxygen saturation ninety-four percent.'

'Is that bleeding under control, Grace?'

'Almost. I'd like to get a traction splint on asap for definitive control. It's a mid-shaft femoral fracture.'

Another nod from Charles. 'As soon as you've done that, we need a second line in and more fluids running. And I want an abdominal ultrasound as soon as I've intubated. Can someone ring through to Theatre and see what the situation is up there?'

The buzz of activity around the patient picked up pace and the noise level rose so much that Grace barely noticed the arrival of more paramedics and another patient being delivered to the adjoining trauma room, separated only by curtains. Working conditions were difficult, especially when some of the staff members were directed to the new arrival, but they were by no means impossible. Even with the murky half-light when a torch wasn't being directed at the arm she was working on, Grace managed to get a wide-bore IV line inserted and secured, attaching more fluids to try and stabilise this patient's blood pressure.

With the airway and breathing secured by intubation and ventilation, Charles was able to step back and oversee everything else being done here. He could also watch what was happening on the neighbouring bed, as the curtain had been pulled halfway open. As Grace picked up the ultrasound transducer and squeezed some jelly onto her patient's abdomen, she got a glimpse of what was happening next door.

Judging by the spinal board and the neck collar immobilising the Spanish-looking woman, this was the 'fall down stairs' patient they had been alerted to. What was more of a surprise was that Charles was already in position at the head of this new patient. And he looked... fresher, somehow. Younger...?

No... Grace blinked. It wasn't Charles.

And then she remembered. He'd had a twin brother who'd gone to a different medical school. Elijah? And hadn't their father been the chief of emergency services at a prestigious New York hospital?

This hospital. Of course it was.

Waiting for the image to become readable on her screen as she angled the transducer, Grace allowed herself a moment to think about that. The dynasty was clearly continuing with the Davenport family front and centre in Manhattan Mercy's ER. Hadn't there been a younger sister who was expected to go into medicine as well? It wouldn't surprise her if there was yet another Davenport on the staff here. That was how rich and powerful families worked, wasn't it—sticking together to become even more powerful?

A beat of something like resentment appeared. Or was it an old disappointment that she'd been so insignificant compared to the importance of family for Charles? That she'd become instantly invisible the moment that scandal had erupted?

Whatever. It was easy to push aside. Part of a past that had absolutely nothing to do with the present. Or the future.

'We've got free fluid in the abdomen and pelvis,' she announced. 'Looks like it's coming from the spleen.'

'Let's get him to Theatre,' Charles ordered. 'They've got power and they've been cleared to only take emergencies. He's stable enough for transfer but he needs a medical escort. Grace, can you go with him, please?'

The metallic sounds of brakes being released and side-bars being raised and locked were almost instant. Grace only had time to ensure that IV lines were safe from snagging before the bed began moving. This was an efficient team who were well used to working together and following the directions of their chief. Even in the thick of what had to be an unusually stressful shift for this department, Grace could feel the respect with which Charles was regarded.

Behind her, as she stayed close to the head of the bed to monitor her patient's airway and breathing en route to Theatre, Grace could hear Charles moving onto a new task without missing a beat.

'Any signs of spinal injury, Elijah? Want me to see if the CT lab is clear?'

And then she heard his voice change. 'Oh, my God… *Maria?*'

He must know this patient, she realised. And he was clearly horrified. She could still hear him even though she was some distance on the other side of the curtain now.

'What happened? Where are the boys?'

A break from the barely controlled chaos in a badly lit emergency department was exactly what Grace needed to catch her breath but it was a worry how crowded the corridors were. And a glimpse into the main waiting area as they rushed past on their way to the only elevators being run on a generator suggested that the workload wasn't going to diminish any time soon.

This was a different planet from the kind of environment Grace had been working in for the last few years and the overall impression was initially overwhelming. Why on earth had she thought she could thrive with a volume of work that was so fast-paced? In a totally new place and in a huge city that was at the opposite end of the spectrum from where she'd chosen to be for such a long time.

Because her friend Helena had convinced her that it was time to reconnect with the real world? Because she had become exhausted by relying solely on personal resources to fight every battle that presented itself? Because the isolation of the places she had chosen to practise medicine had finally tipped the balance from being a welcome escape to a bone-deep loneliness that couldn't be ignored for ever?

Like another omen, lights flickered overhead as neon strips came alive with a renewed supply of power. Everybody, including the porters and nurses guiding this bed towards Theatre, looked up and Grace could hear a collective sigh of relief. Normal life would be resumed as soon as the aftermath of this unexpected challenge was dealt with.

And she could cope, too. Possibly even thrive, which had been the plan when she'd signed the contract to begin work in Manhattan Mercy's ER. This was a new beginning and Grace knew better than most that to get the best out of new beginnings you had to draw a line under the past and move on. And yes…some things needed more time to heal but she had taken that time. A lot more time than she had anticipated needing, in fact.

She was ready.

Having stayed longer than the rest of the transfer team so that she could give the anaesthetist and surgeons a comprehensive handover, Grace found that she needed to find her own way back to the ER and it turned out to be a slightly more circuitous route than before. Instead of passing the main reception area, she went past an orthopaedic room where casts were being applied, what looked like a small operating theatre that was labelled for minor surgery and seemed to have someone having a major laceration stitched and then a couple of smaller rooms that looked as if they had been designed for privacy. Were these rooms used for family consultations, perhaps? Or a space where people could be with a loved one who was dying?

A nurse was peering out of one of the doors.

'Oh, thank goodness,' she said, when she saw Grace approaching. 'I'm about to *burst*... Could you please, please stay with the boys in here for two minutes while I dash to the bathroom?'

The young nurse, whose name badge introduced her as 'Jackie', certainly looked desperate. Having had to grab a bathroom stop herself on her way back from Theatre, Grace could sympathise with the urgency. She was probably already later in her return to the ER than might have been expected so another minute or two wouldn't make any difference, would it?

'Sure,' she said. 'But be as quick as you can?'

Jackie sped off with a grateful smile and vigorous nod without giving Grace the chance to ask anything else— like why these 'boys' were in a side room and whether they needed any medical management.

She turned to go through the door and then froze.

Two small faces were filling the space. Identical faces.

These two children had to be the most adorable little boys she had ever seen. They were about three years old, with tousled mops of dark hair, huge curious eyes and small button noses.

There was something about twins...

For someone who'd had to let go of the dream of even having a single baby, the magic of twins could pack a punch that left a very physical ache somewhere deep inside Grace.

Maybe she wasn't as ready as she'd thought she was to step back into the real world and a new future…

Chapter 2

'Who are you?'

'I'm Grace. I'm one of the doctors here.'

It wasn't as hard as she'd expected to find a smile. Who wouldn't smile at this pair? 'Who are *you*?'

'I'm Cameron,' one of the boys told her. 'And he's Max.'

'Hello, Max,' Grace said. 'Hello, Cameron. Can I come into your room?'

'Why?' Cameron seemed to be the spokesman for the pair. 'Where's Jackie gone?'

'Just to the bathroom. She'll be back in a minute. She asked me to look after you.'

'Oh… 'Kay…'

Grace stepped into the room as the children turned. There was a couch and two armchairs in here, some magazines on a low table and a box of toys that had been emptied.

'Are you waiting for somebody?' Grace asked, perching on the arm of the couch.

'Yes. Daddy.' Cameron dropped to his knees and picked up a toy. His brother sat on the floor beside him. 'Here…you can have the fire truck, Max. I'm going to have the p'lice car, 'kay?'

Max nodded. But as he took hold of the plastic fire truck that had been generously gifted with both hands, the back wheels came off.

'Oh…no…' Cameron sounded horrified. 'You *broke* it.'

Max's bottom lip quivered. Grace slid off the arm of the couch and crouched down beside him.

'Let me have a look. I don't think it's very broken. See…?' She clipped the axle of the wheels back into place. 'All fixed.'

She handed the truck back with a smile and, unexpectedly, received a smile back. A delicious curve of a wide little mouth that curled itself instantly right around her heart.

Wow…

'Fank you,' Max said gravely.

'You're so welcome.' Grace's response came out in no more than a whisper.

Love at first sight could catch you unawares in all sorts of different ways, couldn't it? It could be a potential partner for life, or a gorgeous place like a peaceful forest, or a special house or cute puppy. Or it could be a small boy with a heartbreaking smile.

Cameron was pushing his police car across the top of the coffee table and making muted siren noises but Max stayed where he was, with the mended fire truck in his arms. Or not quite where he was. He leaned, so that his head and shoulder were pressed against Grace's arm. It was impossible not to return this gesture of acceptance and it was purely instinctive to shift her arm so that it slid around the small body and let him snuggle more comfortably.

It would only be for a moment because Nurse Jackie would be back any second. Grace could hear people in the corridor outside. She could feel the draught of air as the door was pushed open behind her so she closed her eyes for a heartbeat to help her lock this exquisite fraction of time into her memory banks. This feeling of connection with a precious small person…

'Daddy…' Cameron's face split into a huge grin.

Max wriggled out from under Grace's arm, dropping the fire truck in his haste to get to his feet, but Grace was still sitting on the floor as she turned her head. And then astonishment stopped her moving at all.

'Charles?'

'Grace…' He sounded as surprised as she had. 'What on earth are you doing in here?'

She felt as guilty as a child caught with her hand in a forbidden cookie jar. 'It was only for a minute. To help out…'

'Jackie had to go to the bathroom.' Cameron had hold of one of his father's hands and he was bouncing up and down.

'She fixed the truck,' Max added, clearly impressed with the skills Grace had demonstrated. 'The wheels came off.'

'Oh…' Charles scooped Cameron up with one arm. Max was next and the ease with which two small boys were positioned on each hip with their arms wrapped around their father's neck suggested that this was a very well-practised manoeuvre. 'That's all right, then…'

Charles was smiling, first at one twin and then the other, and Grace felt her heart melt a little more.

She could feel the intense bond between this man and his children. The power of an infinite amount of love.

She'd been wrong about that moment of doubt earlier, hadn't she? Charles *did* have the perfect life.

'Can we go home now? Is Maria all better?'

Grace was on her feet now. She should excuse herself and get back to where she was supposed to be but something made her hesitate. To stand there and stare at Charles as she remembered hearing the concern in his voice when he'd recognised the new patient in ER.

He was shaking his head now. 'Maria's got a sore back after falling down the stairs. She's going to be fine but she needs to have a rest for a few days.'

He looked up, as if he could feel the questions buzzing in Grace's head.

'Maria is the boys' nanny,' he said. 'I'll be taking a few days' leave to look after them until she's back on her feet. Fortunately, it was only a sprain and not a fracture.'

That didn't stop the questions but Grace couldn't ask why the head of her new department would automatically take time away to care for his children. Where was their mother? Maybe she was another high-achieving medic who was away—presenting at some international conference or something?

Whatever. It was none of her business. And anyway, Jackie the nurse had come back and there was no reason for her to take any more time away from the job she was employed to be doing.

'I'd better get back,' she said. 'Do you still want me to cover Trauma One?'

'Thanks.' Charles nodded. 'I'll come with you. Jackie,

I just came to give you some money. The cafeteria should be up and running again now and I thought you could take the boys up for some lunch.'

Planting a kiss on each small, dark head, he deposited the twins back on the floor.

'Be good,' he instructed. 'And if it's not still raining when we go home, we'll stop in the park for a swing.'

He led Grace back towards the main area of the ER.

'It's still crazy in here,' he said. 'But we've got extra staff and it's under control now that we've got power back on.'

'I'm sorry I took so long. I probably shouldn't have stopped to help Jackie out.'

'It's not a problem.'

'They're gorgeous children,' Grace added. 'You're a very lucky man, Charles.'

The look he gave her was almost astonished. Then a wash of something poignant crossed his face and he smiled.

A slow kind of smile that took her back through time instantly. To when the brilliant young man who'd been like royalty in their year at med school had suddenly been interested in her as more than the only barrier he had to be a star academically and not just socially. He had cared about what she had to say. About who she was...

'Yes,' he said slowly. 'I am.'

He held open one of the double doors in front of them. 'How 'bout you, Grace? You got kids?'

She shook her head.

'Too busy with that exciting career I was reading about in your CV? Working with the flying doctors in the remotest parts of the outback?'

Her throat felt tight. 'Something like that.'

She could feel his gaze on her back. A beat of silence—curiosity, even, as if he knew there was a lot being left unspoken.

And then he caught up with her in a single, long stride. Turned his head and, yes…she could see the flicker of curiosity.

'It's been a long time, Grace.'

'It has.'

'Be nice to catch up sometime…'

People were coming towards them. There were obviously matters that required the attention of the chief and Grace had her own work to do. She could see paramedics and junior staff clustered around a new gurney in Trauma One but she took a moment before she broke that eye contact.

A moment when she remembered that smile from a few moments ago. And so much more, from a very long time ago.

'Yes,' she said quietly. 'It would…'

The rest of that first shift in Manhattan Mercy's emergency department passed in something of a blur for Grace. Trauma related to the storm and power outage continued to roll in. A kitchen worker had been badly burned when a huge pot of soup had been tipped over in the confusion of a crowded restaurant kitchen plunged into darkness. A man had suffered a heart attack while trapped in an elevator and had been close to the end of the time window for curtailing the damage to his cardiac muscle by the time he'd been rescued. A pedestrian had been badly injured when they'd made a dash to get across a busy road in the pouring rain and a woman who relied on her home oxygen supply had been brought to the ER in severe respiratory distress after it had been cut off.

Grace was completely focused on each patient that spent time in Trauma One but Charles seemed to be everywhere, suddenly appearing where and when he was most needed. How did he do that?

Sometimes it had to be obvious, of course. Like when the young kitchen worker arrived and his screams from the pain of his severe burns would have been heard all over the department and the general level of tension rocketed skywards. He was so distressed he was in danger of injuring himself further by fighting off staff as they attempted to restrain him enough to gain IV access and administer adequate pain relief and Grace was almost knocked off her feet by a flying fist that caught her hip.

It was Charles who was suddenly there to steady her before she fell. Charles who positioned security personnel to restrain their patient safely. And it was Charles who spoke calmly enough to capture a terrified youth's attention and stop the agonised cries for long enough for him to hear what was being said.

'We're going to help you,' he said. 'Try and hold still for just a minute. It will stop hurting very soon...'

He stayed where he was and took over the task of sedating and intubating the young man. Like everyone else in the department, Grace breathed a sigh of relief as the terrible sounds of agony were silenced. She could assess this patient properly now, start dressing the burns that covered the lower half of his body and arrange his transfer to the specialist unit that could take over his care.

She heard Charles on the phone as she passed the unit desk later, clearly making arrangements for a patient who'd been under someone else's initial care.

'It's a full thickness inferior infarct. He's been trapped in an elevator for at least four hours. I'm sending him up to the catheter laboratory, stat.'

The hours passed swiftly and it was Charles who reminded Grace that it was time she went home.

'We're under control and the new shift is taking over. Go home and have a well-deserved rest, Grace. And thanks,' he added, as he turned away. 'I knew you would be an asset to this department.'

The smile was a reward for an extraordinarily testing first day and the words of praise stayed with Grace as she made her way to the locker room to find her coat to throw on over her scrubs.

There were new arrivals in the space, locking away their personal belongings before they started their shift. And one of them was a familiar face.

Helena Tate was scraping auburn curls back from her face to restrain with a scrunchie but she abandoned the task as she caught sight of Grace.

'I hear you've had quite a day.'

Grace simply nodded.

'Do you hate me—for persuading you to come back?'

She shook her head now. 'It's been full on,' she said, 'but you know what?'

'What?'

Grace felt her mouth curving into a grin. 'I loved it.'

It was true, she realised. The pace of the work had left no time for first day nerves. She had done her job well enough to earn praise from the chief and, best of all, the moment she'd been dreading—seeing Charles again—had somehow morphed into something that had nothing to do with heartbreak or embarrassment or even resentment. It almost felt like a reconnection with an old friend. With a part of her life that had been so full of promise because she'd had no idea of just how tough life could become.

'Really?' Helena let out a huff of relief. 'Oh, I'm so happy to hear that.' She was smiling now. 'So it wasn't weird, finding that someone you went to med school with is your boss now?'

Grace had never confessed the real reason it was going to be awkward seeing Charles Davenport again. She had never told anybody about that night, not even her best friend. And certainly not the man she had married. It had been a secret—a shameful one when it had become apparent that Charles had no desire to remember it.

But today it seemed that she had finally been able to move past something that had been a mere blip of time in a now distant past life.

'Not really,' she told Helena. 'Not that we had time to chat. I did meet his little boys, though.'

'The twins? Aren't they cute? Such a tragic story.' Helena lowered her voice. 'Nina was the absolute love of Charles's life and she died minutes after they were born. Amniotic embolism. He'll never get over it...'

Shock made Grace speechless but Helena didn't seem to notice. The hum of voices around them was increasing as more people came in and out of the locker room. Helena glanced up, clearly refocusing on what was around her. She pulled her hair back again and wound the elastic band around her short ponytail. 'I'd better get in there. You can tell me all about it in the morning.'

The door of her locker shut with a metallic clang to reveal the figure arriving beside her to open another locker. Charles Davenport glanced sideways as Helena kept talking.

'Have my bed tonight,' she told Grace. 'I'll be home

so late, a couple of hours on that awful couch won't make any difference.'

And then she was gone. Grace immediately turned to look for her own locker because she didn't want to catch Charles's gaze and possibly reveal that she had just learned something very personal about his life. She turned back just as swiftly, however, as she heard him speak.

'You're sleeping on a couch?'

'Only until I find my own place.' Grace could see those new lines on his face in a different light now and it made something tighten in her chest. He'd suffered, hadn't he?

She knew what that was like…

'It's a bit of a squash,' she added hurriedly. 'But Helena's an old friend. Do you remember her from Harvard?'

Charles shook his head and Grace nodded a beat later. Why would he remember someone who was not only several years younger but, like her, had not been anywhere near the kind of elite social circles the Davenports belonged to? Her own close friendship with Helena had only come about because they'd lived in the same student accommodation block.

'She was a few years behind us. We've kept in touch, though. It was Helena who persuaded me to apply for the job here.'

Charles took a warm coat from its hanger and draped it over his arm. 'I'll have to remember to thank her for that.' He pulled a worn-looking leather satchel from his locker before pushing the door shut. He looked like a man in a hurry. 'I'd better go and rescue my boys. Good luck with the apartment hunting.'

'Thanks. I might need it. From what I've heard, it's a

bit of a mission to find something affordable within easy commuting of Central Manhattan.'

'Hmm.' Charles turned away, the sound no more than a sympathetic grunt. But then his head turned swiftly, his eyes narrowed, as if he'd just thought of something important. 'Do you like dogs?'

The random question took Grace by surprise. She blinked at Charles.

'Sorry?'

He shook his head. 'It's just a thought. Might come to nothing but…' He was pulling a mobile phone from the pocket of his scrubs and then tapping on the screen. 'Give me your phone number,' he said. 'Just in case…'

What had he been thinking?

Was he really intending to follow through with that crazy idea that had occurred to him when he'd heard that the newest member of his department was camping in another colleague's apartment and sleeping on an apparently uncomfortable couch?

Why would he do that when his life had suddenly become even more complicated than it already was?

'It's not raining, Daddy.' Zipped up inside his bright red puffer jacket, with a matching woolly hat covering his curls, Cameron tugged on his father's hand. 'Swing?'

Max's tired little face lit up at the reminder and he nodded with enthusiasm. 'I want a swing, too.'

'But it's pouring, guys.' Charles had to smile down at his sons. 'See? You're just dry because you're under my umbrella.'

A huge, black umbrella. Big enough for all of them to be sheltered as they walked beneath dripping branches of the massive trees lining this edge of Central Park, the pavement plastered with the evidence of the autumnal leaf fall. Past one of the more than twenty playgrounds for children that this amazing space boasted, currently empty of any nannies or parents trying to entertain their young people.

'Aww...'

The weight of two tired small boys suddenly increased as their steps dragged.

'And it's too dark now, anyway,' Charles pointed out. 'We'll go tomorrow. In the daytime. We can do that because it's Sunday and there's no nursery school. And I'm going to be at home to look after you.'

'Why?'

'Because Maria's got a sore back.'

'Because she fell down the stairs?'

'That's right, buddy.'

'It went dark,' Cameron said.

'I was scared,' Max added. 'Maria was *crying...*'

'Horse was barking and barking.'

'Was he?'

'I told Max to sit on the stair,' Cameron said proudly. 'And Mr Jack came to help.'

Jack was the elderly concierge for their apartment block and he'd been there for many years before Charles had bought the penthouse floor. He was almost part of the family now.

And probably more willing to help than his real family would be if he told them about the latest complication in his home life.

No, that wasn't fair. His siblings would do whatever they could but they were all so busy with their own lives and careers. Elijah would have to step up to take his place as Chief of Emergency in the next few days. His sister Penelope was on a much-needed break, although she was probably on some adrenaline-filled adventure that involved climbing a mountain or extreme skiing. The youngest Davenport, Zachary, was back from his latest tour of duty and working at the Navy Academy in Annapolis and his half-sister, Miranda, would try *too* hard, even if it was too much. Protecting his siblings had become second nature to Charles ever since the Davenports' sheltered world had imploded all those years ago.

And his parents? Hugo Davenport had retired as Chief of Emergency to allow Charles to take the position but he'd barely had time for his own children as they were growing up and he would be at a complete loss if he was left with the sole responsibility of boisterous twin almost three-year-olds. It would be sole responsibility, too, because Vanessa had led an almost completely separate life ever since the scandal, and playing happy grandparents together would never be added to her agenda.

His mother would rush to help, of course, and put out the word that she urgently needed the services of the best nanny available in New York but Charles didn't want that. He didn't want a stranger suddenly appearing in his home. His boys had to feel loved and totally secure at all times. He'd promised them that much when they were only an hour old—in those terrible first minutes after their mother's death.

His grip tightened on the hand of each twin.

'You were both very brave in the dark,' he told them. 'And you've both been a big help by being so good when you had to stay at Daddy's work all day. I'm very, very proud of you both.'

'So we can go to the park?'

'Tomorrow,' he promised. 'We'll go to the park even

if it's still raining. You can put your rubber boots on and jump in all the puddles.'

They could take some time out and make the outside world unimportant for an hour or two. Maybe he would be able to put aside the guilt that he was taking emergency leave from his work and stop fretting that he was creating extra pressure for Elijah or that his other siblings would worry about him when they heard that he was struggling as a single parent—yet again. Maybe he could even forget about the background tension of being part of a family that was a far cry from the united presence they could still display for the sake of a gala fundraising event or any other glittering, high-society occasion. A family whose motto of 'What happens in the family stays in the family' had been sorely tested but had, in recent years, regained its former strength.

A yellow taxi swooped into the kerb, sending a spray of water onto the pavement. Charles hurried the twins past a taco restaurant, souvenir shop, a hot dog stand and the twenty-four-seven deli to turn into the tree-lined avenue that was the prestigious address for the brownstone apartment block they called home.

And it was then that Charles recognised why he'd felt the urge to reach out and try to help Grace Forbes.

Like taking the boys to the park, it felt like he had the opportunity to shut the rest of the world out to some extent.

Grace was part of a world that had ceased to exist when the trauma of the family trouble had threatened everything the Davenport family held dear. It had been the happiest time of Charles's life. He had been achieving his dream of following in his father's footsteps and becoming a doctor who could one day be in charge of the

most challenging and exciting place he had ever known—
Manhattan Mercy's ER. The biggest problem he'd had
was how to balance a demanding social life with the drive
to achieve the honour of topping his class, and the only
real barrier to that position had been Grace.

He'd managed to succeed, despite the appalling pressure
that had exploded around him in the run-up to final exams,
by focusing only on the things that mattered the most—
supporting his mother and protecting his siblings from the
fallout of scandal and passing those exams with the best
possible results. He had been forced to dismiss Grace, along
with every other social aspect of his life. And he'd learned
to dismiss any emotion that could threaten his goals.

But he had never forgotten how simple and happy his
life at medical school had been up until that point.

And, if he was honest, he'd never forgotten that night
with Grace...

He could never go back, of course, but the pull of even
connecting with it from a distance was surprisingly compelling. And what harm could it do? His life wasn't about
to change. He had his boys and he had his job and that
was all he needed. All he could ever hope for.

But Grace had been special. And there was something about her that made him think that, perhaps—like
him—life hadn't quite turned out the way she'd planned.
Or deserved?

'Shall we stop and say hello to Horse before we go
upstairs?'

'*Yes...*' The tug on his hands was in a forward direction now, instead of a reluctant weight he was encouraging to follow him. 'Let's *go*, Daddy...'

Chapter 3

'So here's the thing...'

'Mmm?' Grace was still trying to get her head around hearing Charles Davenport's voice on a phone for the first time ever.

The twang of a New York accent had probably been mellowed by so many years at exclusive, private schools but his enunciation was crisp. Decisive, even. It made her think of someone in a suit. Presenting a killer summary in a courtroom, perhaps. Or detailing a take-over bid in the boardroom of a global company.

She was sitting cross-legged on the couch in Helena's apartment, a take-out container of pad Thai on her lap and a pair of chopsticks now idle in her hands. She was in her pyjamas already, thanks to getting soaked in the tail end of the storm during her long walk home from the nearest subway station.

Was her attire partly responsible for hearing that slightly gravelly edge to Charles's voice that made her think that he would sound just like that if his head was on a pillow, very close to her own?

'Sorry…did you say your neighbour's name was *Houston*? As in "Houston, we have a problem"?'

The chuckle of laughter came out of the phone and went straight for somewhere deep in Grace's chest. Or maybe her belly. It created a warmth that brought a smile to her face.

'Exactly. It's their dog that's called Houston and they chose the name on the first day they brought him home as a puppy when they found what he'd left in the middle of their white carpet.'

The bubble of her own laughter took Grace by surprise. Because it felt like the kind of easy laughter that she hadn't experienced in such a long time? The kind that made her think of a first date? Or worse, made her remember *that* night. When Charles had found her, so stressed before the start of their final exams that she was in pieces and he'd tried to reassure her. To distract her, by talking to her rather like this. By making her laugh through her tears and then…

And then there'd been that astonishing moment when they couldn't break the eye contact between them and the kiss that had started everything had been as inevitable as the sun rising the next morning.

It was an effort to force herself to focus on what Charles was actually saying as he kept talking.

'The boys call him Horse, because they weren't even two when he arrived and they couldn't pronounce Houston but he's quite big so that seemed to work, too.'

Grace cleared her throat, hoping her voice would come

out sounding normal. How embarrassing would it be if it was kind of husky and betrayed those memories that refused to stay where they should be. Buried.

'What sort of dog is he?'

'A retro doodle. Half poodle, half golden retriever. One of those designer, hypo-allergenic kind of dogs, you know? But he's lovely. Very well behaved and gentle.'

Grace closed her eyes for a moment. This was *so* weird. She hadn't seen Charles Davenport in more than a decade but here they were chatting about something completely random as if they were friends who caught up every other week. And they'd never been *friends*, exactly. Friend*ly*, certainly—with a lot of respect for each other's abilities. And they'd been passionate—so briefly it had always seemed like nothing more than a fantasy that had unexpectedly achieved reality. But this?

Thanks to the memories it was stirring up, this was doing Grace's head in.

On top of that, her noodles were getting cold and probably wouldn't appreciate another spin in the microwave.

The beat of an awkward silence made her wonder if this apparently easy chatting was actually just as weird for Charles.

'Anyway... I'm sorry to disturb your evening but it occurred to me that it could be a win-win situation.'

'Oh?'

'Houston's parents are my neighbours on the ground floor of this block—which, I should mention, is about two minutes' walk to Central Park and ten at the most to Manhattan Mercy.'

'Oh...' How good would that be, not to have to battle crowds in the subway and a long walk at the end of the commute?

'Stefan's an interior designer and his husband, Jerome, is an artist. They're heading off tomorrow for a belated honeymoon in Europe and they'll be gone for about six weeks. They're both fretting about Houston having to go into kennels. I suggested they get a dog-sitter to live in but...' Charles cleared his throat as if he was slightly embarrassed. 'Apparently Houston is their fur child and they couldn't find someone trustworthy enough. When I got home this evening, I told them about you and they seem to be very impressed with the recommendation I gave them.'

'Oh...?' Good grief, she was beginning to sound like a broken record. 'But... I work long hours. I couldn't look after a dog...'

'Houston has a puppy walker that he loves who would come twice a day on the days that you're working. That's another part of his routine that Stefan and Jerome are worried about disrupting because he gets to play with his dog friends who get taken out at the same time. Even more importantly, if he was still in his own home, he wouldn't miss his dads so much. And I thought that it could give you a bit of breathing space, you know? To find your feet in a new city and where you want to be.'

Not just breathing space. Living space. Sharing a tiny apartment, even with a good friend, was a shock to the system for someone who had guarded their privacy so well for so long.

'I know it's all very last minute with them being due to drop Houston at the kennels in the morning but they're home this evening and they'd love to meet you and have a chat about it. Stefan said he'd be delighted to cover your taxi fares if you were at all interested.' Charles paused and Grace could hear something that sounded like a weary sigh. 'Anyway... I've only just got the boys to bed and I need to have a hunt in the fridge and see if I can find something to eat that isn't the boys' favourite packet mac and cheese.'

Again, Grace was aware of that tightness in her chest. Empathy? Charles might have the blessing of having two gorgeous children but he had lost something huge as well. Something that had changed his future for ever—the loss of a complete family.

They had a lot more than he realised in common.

Her new boss had also had a very difficult day, coping with a crisis in his department and the added blow of having to deal with a personal crisis with his nanny being put out of action. And yet he'd found the time to think about her and a way to possibly help her adjust to a dauntingly huge change in her life?

How astonishing was that?

'Thank you so much, Charles.' Grace dropped the chopsticks into the plastic bowl and put it onto the coffee table as she unfurled her legs. It didn't matter that she would have to get dressed again and then head out into this huge city that never slept. Despite so much going on in his own life, Charles had made a very thoughtful effort on her behalf and she knew exactly how she needed to show her appreciation.

There was something else prompting her, too. A niggle that was purely instinctive that was telling her not to miss this unexpected opportunity. That it might, somehow, be a signpost to the new path in life that she was seeking. The kind of niggle that had persuaded her, in the end, to come to New York in the first place.

'Let me grab a pen. Give me the address and I'll get there as soon as I can.'

* * *

'Morning, Doc.'

'Morning, Jack. How's the weather looking out there?' Not that Charles needed to ask. The view from his penthouse apartment over Central Park and the Manhattan skyline had shown him that any residual cloudiness from the storm of a few days ago had been blown well clear of the city. It was a perfect October day. But discussing the weather was a ritual. And it gave him the chance to make sure that the twins were well protected from the chill, with their jackets fastened, ears covered by their hats and twenty little fingers encased in warm mittens.

'It's a day for the park, that's fo' sure.' Jack had a passion for following meteorology and spent any free time on door duty surfing weather channels. 'High of sixteen degrees, thirty-two percent clear skies and twenty-one percent chance of light rain but that won't happen until after two p.m.'

'Perfect. Nice change, isn't it?' As usual, Cameron's mittens were hanging by the strings that attached them to his jacket sleeves. Charles pulled them over the small hands. 'That was some storm we had the other day.'

'Sure was. Won't forget that in a hurry. Not with poor Maria crashing down the stairs like that.' Jack shook his head. 'How's she doin'?'

'Good, but I don't want her coming back to work too soon. She won't be up to lifting small boys out of trouble for a while.' Charles tugged Max's hat down over his ears. 'You guys ready?'

'Can we say "hi" to Horse?'

Charles glanced behind the boys, to the door that led to one of the two ground-floor apartments. He'd been tempted to knock on that door more than once in the last few days—ever since he'd heard the news that Grace had taken on the dog-sitting gig—but something had held him back.

Something odd that felt almost like shyness, which was ridiculous because hanging back had never been an attribute that anyone would associate with the Davenport family.

Maybe he was just waiting for it to happen naturally so that it didn't seem like he was being pushy? He was her boss, after all. Or he would be, as soon as he got back to work properly. There were boundaries here and maybe Grace didn't want to cross them, either. That might explain why she hadn't knocked on *his* door.

He turned, holding out his hands. 'Let's go. Or you'll be wanting a hotdog before we even get to the playground.'

Jack was holding open the front door, letting sunlight stream in to brighten the mosaic tiles of the entrance foyer, but the boys weren't moving to take their father's hands. They were going in the opposite direction, as the door behind Charles swung open.

'Horse...'

The big woolly dog looked as pleased to see the twins as they were to see him. He stood there with what looked like a grin on his face, the long plume of his tail waving, as Cameron and Max wrapped their arms around his neck and buried their faces in his curls.

Grace was grinning as well, as she looked down at the reunion.

'Oh, yeah...cuddles are the best way to start the day, aren't they, Houston?'

She was still smiling as she looked up. The black woollen hat she was wearing made a frame that seemed to accentuate the brightness of that smile. A smile that went all the way to her eyes and made them sparkle.

'We're off to the park,' she said. 'It's my first day off so I'm on dog-walking duty today.'

'We're going to the park, too,' Cameron shouted. 'You can come with us.'

'I want to throw the ball for Horse.' Max nodded.

'I think he has to stay on his lead,' Grace said. 'I've been reading the rules this morning.'

Charles nodded. 'And he's not allowed in the playgrounds. But we can walk with him for a while.'

Grace's smile seemed to wobble, as if a shadow was crossing her face, and Charles had the impression that this was a bigger deal than he would have expected.

'If Grace doesn't mind the extra company, that is,' he added.

'I'd love it,' Grace said firmly. She was clipping the dog's lead onto his harness so Charles couldn't see if she really meant that but then she straightened and caught his gaze.

'You can show me the best places to walk. I don't know anything about Central Park.'

Her smile was strong again and he could see a gleam in her eyes that he remembered very well. He'd seen it often enough in the past, usually when they were both heading in to the same examination.

Determination, that was what it was.

But why did she need to tap into that kind of reserve for something that should be no problem? A pleasure, even…

It was puzzling.

'Have you never been to New York before?' Juggling two small children and a dog on the busy pavement meant that Charles had to wait until they were almost at the gates of the park to say anything more to Grace.

'Never. I was born in Australia and then my family moved to Florida when my dad got a job with NASA.' She was smiling again. 'He thinks it's hilarious that I've got a job looking after a dog called Houston. Anyway... coming here was always a plan once I got to medical school in Boston but there never seemed to be enough time. I was too busy studying...' The glance Charles received was mischievous. 'Trying to keep up with you.'

'I think it was the other way round.' Charles kept a firm grip on small mittened hands, as he paused to wait until a horse-drawn carriage rolled past, carrying tourists on a relaxed tour of the park, but he was holding Grace's gaze as well. They would have to part company very soon and it felt...disappointing?

'Okay...we have two favourite playgrounds close to here but...'

'But dogs aren't allowed, I know. When I looked on the map, there was a track called the Bridle Path? That sounds like a nice place to walk.'

'It is. Come with us as far as the playground and I'll show you which direction to take to find it. Next time, I'll bring the boys' bikes and we can all go on the Bridle Path.'

The way Grace's eyes widened revealed her surprise, which was quite understandable because Charles was a little surprised himself that the suggestion had emerged so casually. As if this was already a thing—this walking in the park together like a...like a *family*? A whole family, with two parents and even a dog.

And her surprise quickly morphed into something else. Something softer that hadn't been fuelled by determination. Pleasure, even? Was she enjoying their company as much as he was enjoying hers?

Charles was silent the rest of the way to the playground. Not that anybody seemed to notice because Cameron and Max were making sure that Grace didn't miss any of the important attractions.

'Look, Gace…it's a *sk-wirrel*…'

'Oh, yes… I *love* squirrels.'

'Look at all the leafs. Why are they all on the ground?'

'Because it's autumn. The trees get undressed for winter. Like you do when you're getting ready for bed. Aren't they pretty?'

Why had it felt so natural up until now, Charles wondered, to add feminine and canine company to his little troupe when it could be seen as potentially disturbing? He and his boys didn't need extra people in their lives. Against quite a few odds, he had managed perfectly well up until now and his children were happy and healthy and safe…

At least things would go back to normal any second now. Grace would continue her dog walk and he'd stand around with the other parents, watching the children run and climb and shout, until he was summoned to push the swings.

But when they got to the wrought-iron fence surrounding the playground, it seemed that his boys wanted a larger audience for their exploits.

'I want Horse to watch me on the slide,' Cameron said.

'And Gace,' Max added. His face was serious enough to let them know that this was important. 'Gace can push me on the swing.'

'Um…' Grace hadn't missed the slightly awkward edge to the atmosphere in the last minute or two because it had left her feeling just a bit confused.

She'd been happy to have company on her first walk to Central Park because it was always so much easier to go somewhere new with somebody who knew the way. And because it had been so good to see the twins again. Especially Max. Cameron's smile was identical, of course, but there was something a little more serious about Max that pulled her heartstrings so hard it was too close to pain to be comfortable. That was why, for a heartbeat back at the apartment block, she had wondered if it wasn't a good idea to share even a part of this walk. But she'd pushed aside any deeply personal misgivings. Maybe it did still hurt that she would never be part of her own family group like this, but surely she could embrace this moment for what it was? Being included, instead of watching from a distance?

Having Houston walking by her side helped a lot. In fact, the last few days had been a revelation. Due to her work hours and never settling in one place for very long, Grace had never considered adopting a dog and getting to know Houston had been a joy. She wished she'd learned years ago that a companion like this could make you feel so much less alone in the world.

Charles's company was surprisingly good, too. When she'd told him of her father's amusement about the dog's name, the appreciative glint in his eyes made her remember how easy that telephone conversation the other night had been. How close to the surface laughter had felt. He'd caught her memory of how focused life had been back in medical school, too, but twisted it slightly, to make it sound as if he'd been a lot more aware of her than she had realised.

And then he'd made that comment about them all coming to the park again together, as if this was the start of something that he'd expected to happen all along? That was when the awkwardness had sprouted.

Had he somehow heard the alarm bells sounding in her own head or did he have a warning system of his own?

Maybe she should just say goodbye and head off with Houston to explore the park and leave Charles to have time with his boys.

Except…it felt like it would suddenly be less interesting. A bit lonely, even?

And the way Max was looking up at her, with those big, blue eyes, as if her being here was the most important thing in the world to him. He had eyes just like his father, she realised. That amazingly bright blue, made even more striking by the darker rim around the irises.

'I have to stay here, on this side of the fence. To look after Horse.' She smiled at Max. 'But I could watch Daddy push you?'

Houston seemed perfectly happy to sit by her side and Grace was grateful for the dog's warmth as he leaned against her leg. She watched Charles lift the little boys into the bucket seats of the swings, side by side, and then position himself between them so that he could push a swing with each hand. She could see the huge grins on the children's faces and hear the peals of their laughter as the arc of movement got steadily higher. And Charles finally looked exactly as she'd remembered him. Happy. Carefree. Enjoying all the best things in life that automatically came his way because he was one of life's golden people that always had the best available.

Except she knew better now. Charles might have had a very different upbringing from her solid, middle-class existence, but he hadn't been protected from the hard things in life any more than she had. His world had been shattered, maybe as much as hers had been, but he was making the best of it and clearly fatherhood was just as important to him as his work. More important, perhaps. He hadn't hesitated in taking time off when his children needed him.

That said a lot about who he was, didn't it? About his ability to cherish the things that were most important in life?

A beat of something very poignant washed through Grace as she remembered those whispered words in the locker room.

'Nina was the absolute love of his life...he'll never get over it...'

The death of his wife was utterly tragic but how lucky had they both been to find a love like that? She certainly hadn't been lucky enough to find it in her marriage and she wasn't about to stumble across it any time soon.

Grace closed her eyes for a heartbeat as she let her breath escape in a sigh. How good was this kind of weather, when she could snuggle beneath layers of warm clothes and a lovely, puffy jacket? Nobody would ever guess what she was hiding.

Charles was smiling again as he came back towards her. He hadn't bothered with a hat or gloves and he was rubbing his hands together against the chill of the late autumn air. The breeze was ruffling his hair, which looked longer and more tousled than Grace remembered. Maybe he didn't get much time for haircuts these days. Or maybe how he looked wasn't a priority. It would be ironic if that was the reason, because the tousled look, along with that designer stubble, actually made him look way more attractive.

'That's my duty done. Now I get to watch them run

around and climb things until they either get hungry or need to go to the toilet. Probably both at the same time.'

'I should get going. Horse isn't getting the exercise I promised him.'

'Wait a bit? The boys won't forgive me if you disappear before they've had a chance to show off a bit.'

'Sure.'

With the bars of the fence between them and Charles's attention back on his children, it felt curiously safe to be standing this close to him. It was safe anyway, Grace reminded herself. The last thing Charles Davenport would want would be another complication in his life and nobody could take the place of the twins' mother, anyway. With another wash of that empathy, the words came out before Grace thought to filter them.

'You must miss their mom so much…'

The beat of silence between them was surprisingly loud against the backdrop of happy shrieks and laughter from the small crowd of children swarming over the playground attractions. She couldn't miss the way Charles swallowed so carefully.

'So much,' he agreed. 'I can only be thankful that the boys will never feel that loss.'

Grace was silent but she could feel her brow furrowing as Charles slid a brief glance back in her direction.

'Oh, they'll know that something's missing from their life as they get older and notice that all the other kids have moms but they never knew Nina. She didn't even get to hold them.'

'I'm so sorry, Charles,' Grace said quietly. 'I had no idea until Helena mentioned it the other day. I can't even imagine how awful that must have been.'

'We had no warning.' His voice sounded raw. 'The

pregnancy had gone so well and we were both so excited about welcoming the twins. Twins run in the family, you know. My brother Elijah is my twin. And we knew they were boys.'

Grace was listening but didn't say anything. She couldn't say anything because her treacherous mind was racing down its own, private track. Picking the scab off an old, emotional wound. Imagining what it would be like to have an enormous belly sheltering not one but *two* babies. She could actually feel a wash of that excitement of waiting for the birth.

'The birth was textbook perfect, too. Cameron arrived and then five minutes later Max did. They were a few weeks early but healthy enough not to need any intervention. I had just cut Max's umbilical cord and was lifting him up to put him in Nina's arms when it happened. She suddenly started gasping for breath and her blood pressure crashed. She was unconscious even before the massive haemorrhage started.'

'Oh… *God*…' Grace wasn't distracted by any personal baggage now. She was in that room with Charles and his two newborn sons. Watching his wife die right in front of his eyes. Her own eyes filled with tears.

'Sorry…' Charles sucked in a deep breath. 'It's not something I ever talk about. I feel…guilty, you know?'

'What? How could you possibly feel *guilty*? There was nothing you could have done.'

'There *should* have been.' There was an intensity to his voice that made the weight of the burden Charles carried very clear. 'It was my job to protect her. I was a doctor, for God's sake. I should have seen something. Some warning. She could have had a medically controlled birth. A Caesarean.'

'It could still have happened.' Grace could hear an odd intensity in her own voice now. Why did it seem so important to try and convince Charles that he had nothing to feel guilty about? 'A C-section might not have made any difference. These things are rare but they happen—with no warning. Sometimes, you lose the babies as well.' She glanced away from Charles, her gaze drawn to the two happy, healthy little boys running around in the playground. 'Look at them,' she said softly. 'Feel blessed... not guilty...'

Charles nodded. 'I do. Those boys are the most important thing in my life. They *are* my life. It's just that it gets harder at this time of year. It sucks that the anniversary of losing Nina is also the twins' birthday. They're old enough to know about birthdays now and that they're supposed to be happy. And it's Halloween, for heaven's sake. Every kid in the country is getting dressed up and having fun.'

'That's next week.'

'Yeah.' Charles pushed his fingers through his hair as he watched Max follow Cameron through a tunnel at the base of the wooden fort. 'And, thanks to their little friends at nursery school, they're determined to go trick or treating for the first time. And they all wear their costumes to school that day.'

Clearly, it was the last thing Charles wanted to think about. The urge to offer help of some kind was powerful but that might not be something Charles wanted, either. But, he'd opened up to her about the tragedy, hadn't he? And he'd said that he never talked about it but he'd told her. Oddly, that felt remarkably special.

Grace bit her lip, absently scratching Houston's ear as he leaned his head against her leg.

'I wonder if they do Halloween costumes for dogs,' she murmured.

Clearly, Charles picked up on this subtle offer to help make this time of year more fun. More of a celebration than a source of painful memories. His startled glance reminded her of the one she'd received the other day when she'd told him what a lucky man he was to have such gorgeous children. As if he was unexpectedly looking at something from a very different perspective.

If so, he obviously needed time to think about it and that was fine by Grace. Maybe she did, too. Offering to help—to become more involved in this little family—might very well be a mistake. So why did it feel so much like the right thing to do?

Charles was watching the boys again as they emerged from the other end of the tunnel and immediately ran back to do it all over again.

'Enough about me,' he said. 'I was trying to remember the last time I heard about you and it was at a conference about ten years ago. I'm sure someone told me that you'd got married.'

'Mmm.'

Charles was leaning against the wrought-iron rails between them, so that when he turned his head, he seemed very close. 'But you're not married now?'

'No.'

He held her gaze. He'd just told her about the huge thing that had changed his life for ever. He wasn't going to ask any more questions but he wanted to know her story, didn't he?

He'd just told her about his personal catastrophe that he never normally told anyone. She *wanted* to tell him about hers. To tell him everything. To reveal that they had a connection in grief that others could never understand completely.

But it was the recognition of that connection that prevented her saying anything. Because it was a time warp. She was suddenly back in that blip of time that had connected them that first time. Outside, on a night that had been almost cold enough to freeze her tears.

She could hear his voice.

'Grace? Oh, my God...are you crying? What's wrong?'

He hadn't asked any more questions then, either. He'd known that it didn't actually matter what had gone wrong, it was comfort that she'd needed. Reassurance.

'Come with me. It's far too cold to be out here...'

He could see that there was something huge that had gone wrong now, too. And maybe she wouldn't need to say anything. If that rail wasn't between them, maybe Charles would take her in his arms again.

The way he had that night, before he'd led her away to a warm place.

His room.

His bed.

It was a very good thing that that strong rail was there. That Charles couldn't come through the gate when he had to be in that playground to supervise his children.

Even though she knew it couldn't happen, Grace still pulled her layers of protective clothing a little more tightly around her body. She still found herself stepping back from the fence.

'I really should go,' she said. 'It's not fair to make Houston wait any longer for his walk.'

Charles nodded slowly. His smile said it was fine.

But his eyes told her that he knew she was running away. That he could see a lot more than she wanted him to.

He couldn't see the physical scars, of course. Nobody got to see those.

Grace had been confident that nobody could see the emotional scars, either.

Until now…

Chapter 4

It might well have been the two cops standing outside a curtained cubicle that attracted his attention as he walked past.

If he'd had any inclination to analyse it, though, Charles would probably have realised that it was the voice on the other side of the curtain that made him slow down.

Grace's voice.

'Looks like we've got an entrance wound here. And… an exit wound here. But it's possible that they're two entrance wounds. We need an X-ray.'

One of the cops caught his gaze and responded to the raised eyebrow.

'Drive-by shooting,' he said. 'He's lucky. It was his arm and not his head.'

With a nod, Charles moved on. Grace clearly had things under control. She always did, whenever he noticed her in the department and that was almost every day now that he had adjusted his hours to fit around nursery school for the twins. More than once a day, too. Not that he went out of his way to make their paths cross or anything. It just seemed to happen.

Okay, maybe he was choosing to do some necessary paperwork at one side of the unit desk instead of tucked away in his office but that was because he liked to keep half an eye on how the whole department was functioning. He could see the steady movement of people and equipment and hear phone calls being made and the radio link to the ambulance service. If anybody needed urgent assistance, he could be on his feet and moving in an instant.

It had nothing to do with the fact that Grace would be in this area before too long, checking the X-rays that would arrive digitally on one of the bank of departmental computer screens beside him.

He had a sheaf of statistics that he needed to review, like the numbers and types of patients that were coming through his department and it was important to see how they stacked up and whether trends were changing. Level one patients were the critical cases that took the most in the way of personnel and resources, but too many level four or five patients could create barriers to meeting target times for treatment and patient flow.

Grace Forbes certainly wasn't wasting time with her patients. It was only minutes later that she was logging in to a computer nearby, flanked by two medical students and a junior doctor. As they waited to upload files, she glanced sideways and acknowledged Charles with a smile but then she peered intently at the screen. Her colleagues leaned in as she used the cursor to highlight what she was looking at.

'There… Can you see that?'

'Is it a bone fragment?'

'No. Look how smooth the edges of the humerus are. And this is well away from it.'

'So it's a bullet fragment?'

'Yes. A very small one.'

'Do we need to get it out?'

'No. It's not clinically significant. And we were right that it's only one entrance and an exit wound but it was also right to check.'

'Want me to clean and dress it, then?' The junior doctor was keen to take over the case. 'Let the cops take him in to talk to him?'

'Yes. We'll put him on a broad-spectrum antibiotic as well. And make sure he gets a tetanus shot. Thanks, Danny. You're in charge now.' Grace's attention was swiftly diverted as she saw an incoming stretcher and she straightened and moved smoothly towards the new arrival as if she'd been ready and waiting all along.

'Hi, honey.' The girl on the stretcher looked very young, very pale and very frightened. 'My name's Grace and I'm going to be looking after you.'

Charles could hear one of the paramedics talking to Grace as they moved past to a vacant cubicle.

'Looks like gastro. Fever of thirty-nine point five and history of vomiting and diarrhoea. Mom called us when she fainted.'

'BP?'

'Eighty systolic. Couldn't get a diastolic.'

'I'm not surprised she fainted, then…'

The voices faded but Charles found himself still

watching, even after the curtain had twitched into place to protect the new patient's privacy.

His attention was well and truly caught this time.

Because he was puzzled.

At moments like this, Grace was exactly the person he would have predicted that she would become. Totally on top of her work. Clever, competent and confident. She got along well with all her colleagues, too. Charles had heard more than one report of how great she was to work with and how generous she was with her time for staff members who were here to learn.

Thanks to the challenge that had been thrown at her within the first minutes of her coming to work here, Charles already knew how good Grace was at her job and how well she coped with difficult circumstances. That ability to think on her feet and adapt was a huge advantage for someone who worked in Emergency and she demonstrated the same kind of attitude in her private life, too, didn't she—in the way she had jumped on board, under pressure, to take on the dog-sitting offer.

But…and this was what was puzzling Charles so much…there was something very different about her personality away from work.

Something that felt off-key.

A timidity, almost. Lack of confidence, anyway.

Vulnerability? The way she'd shrunk away from him at the park yesterday. When he'd ventured onto personal ground by asking her about her marriage. He'd been puzzled then and he hadn't been able to shake it off.

He didn't want to shake it off, in fact. It was quite nice having this distraction because it meant he could ignore the background tension he always had at this time of year when he was walking an emotional tightrope between celebrating the joy of the twins' birth and being swamped by the grief of losing Nina, which was a can of mental worms that included so many other things he felt he should have done better—like protecting his family during the time of that scandal.

A nurse appeared from behind the curtain, with a handful of glass tubes full of blood that were clearly being rushed off for testing. He caught a glimpse of Grace bent over her patient, with her stethoscope in her ears and a frown of concentration on her face.

Grace had understood that grief so easily. He could still see those tears shimmering in her eyes when she'd been listening to him. Perhaps he'd known that she would understand on a different level from anybody else and that was why he had chosen to say more to her than he would have even to members of his own family.

But how had he known that?

And why was it that she did understand so clearly?

Who had she lost? Her husband, obviously, but the tone of her limited response to his queries had made him think that it was a marriage that simply hadn't worked out, not one that had been blown apart by tragedy, as his had been.

He wanted to know, dammit.

More than that, and he knew that it was ridiculous, but he was a bit hurt by being shut out.

Why?

Because—once upon a time—she had fallen into his arms and told him everything she was so worried about? That the pressure of those final exams was doing her head in? That it was times like this that she felt so lonely because it made her miss the mother she'd lost more than ever?

He'd had no intention of revisiting the memories of

that night but they were creeping back now. The events that threatened to derail his life that had crashed around him so soon after that night had made it inevitable that it had to be dismissed but there was one aspect he'd never completely buried.

That sense of connection with another person.

He'd never felt it before that night.

He'd been lucky enough to find it again—with Nina—but he'd known that any chance of a third strike was out of the question. He wasn't looking because he didn't want to find it.

But it was already there with Grace, wasn't it? It had been, from the moment he'd taken her into his arms that night to comfort her.

And he'd felt it again at the park, when he'd seen her crying for his loss.

She'd been crying that night, too…

'You okay?'

'Huh?' Charles blinked as he heard the voice beside him. 'I'm fine, thanks, Miranda.'

'Okay…' But his half-sister was frowning at him. 'It's not like you to be sitting staring into space.'

Her frown advertised concern. A closeness that gave Charles a beat of something warm. Something good. Because it had been hard won? Miranda had come into their family as a penniless, lonely and frightened sixteen-year-old who was desperately missing her mother who had just died. It had been Charles who'd taken on the responsibility of trying to make her feel wanted. A little less lonely. Trying to persuade her that the scandal hadn't been *her* fault.

'I was just thinking.' About Grace. And he needed to stop because he was still aware of that warmth of something that felt good but now it was coming from remembering something Grace had said. The way she had tried to convince him that he had no valid reason to feel guilty over Nina's death—as if she really cared about how he felt.

Charles tapped the pile of papers in front of him. 'I'm up to my eyeballs in statistics. What are you up to?'

'I need a portable ultrasound to check a stab wound for underlying damage. It looks superficial but I want to make absolutely sure.' Miranda looked around. 'They seem to have gone walkabout.'

Charles glanced towards the glass board where patient details were constantly updated to keep track of where people were and what was going on. Who could be currently using ultrasound to help a diagnosis?

'It could be in with the abdo pain in Curtain Two.'

'Thanks. I'll check.' Miranda turned her head as she moved away. 'How are the party plans going? Do we get an invitation this year?'

Charles shook his head but offered an apologetic smile. 'I'm keeping it low-key. I'm taking them to visit the grandparents the next day for afternoon tea and I'm sure you'll be invited as well, but my neighbours have said they'd be delighted to have an in-house trick or treat happen on the actual birthday and that's probably as much excitement as two three-year-olds can handle.'

Miranda's nod conveyed understanding of the need to keep the celebration private. She'd seen photographs of the Davenport extravaganzas of years past, before she'd become a part of the family—when there had been bouncy castles, magicians and even ponies or small zoos involved.

Buying into Halloween was a big step forward this

year but there was going to be a nursery school parade so the costumes were essential. Charles found himself staring again at the curtain that Grace was behind. Hadn't she said something about finding a costume for Houston? Maybe she'd found a good costume shop.

And maybe Houston could join in the fun? The boys loved that dog and he could be an addition to the private party that would delight them rather than overwhelm them, like a full-on Davenport gathering had the potential to do.

Grace would have to be invited, too, of course, but that wasn't a big deal. Somehow, the intrigue about what had happened to change her had overridden any internal warning about spending time with her. He wanted an answer to the puzzle and getting a little closer was the only way he was going to solve the mystery. Close enough to be friends—like he and Miranda had become all those years ago—but nothing more. And that wouldn't be a problem. The barrier to anything more was so solid he wouldn't have the first idea how to get past it.

And he didn't want to. Even the reminder that that barrier was there was enough to send him back to safe territory and Charles spent the next fifteen minutes focused on the graphs he needed to analyse.

But then Grace appeared from the cubicle and headed straight to the computer closest to where he was sitting. It was tempting to say something totally inappropriate, like asking her whether she might be available for a while in two days' time, to go trick or treating but this wasn't the time or place. It was a bit of a shock, in fact, that the urge was even there. So out of character that it wasn't at all difficult to squash.

'Looking for results?'

'Yep. White blood count and creatinine should be available by now. I've got cultures, throat swabs and urine pending.'

'More than a viral illness, then?'

Grace didn't seem surprised that he was aware of which patient she was dealing with.

'I think she's got staphylococcal toxic shock syndrome. Sixteen years old.'

Charles blinked. It was a rare thing to see these days, which meant that it could be missed until it was late enough for the condition to be extremely serious.

'Signs and symptoms?'

'High fever, vomiting and diarrhoea, muscle aches, a widespread rash that looks like sunburn. She's also hypotensive. Seventy-five over thirty and she's onto her second litre of fluid resus.' Grace flicked him a glance. 'She also finished her period two days ago and likes to leave her tampons in overnight.'

Charles could feel his mouth twisting into a lopsided smile. An impressed one. That was the key question that needed to be asked and could be missed. But not by Grace Forbes, apparently.

'Any foreign material left? Had she forgotten to take a tampon out?'

'No, but I still think I'm right.' Grace clicked a key. 'Yes… Her white count's sky high. So's her creatinine, which means she's got renal involvement. Could be septic shock from another cause but that won't change the initial management.'

'Plan?'

'More fluids, vasopressor support to try and get her BP up. And antibiotics, of course.'

'Flucloxacillin?'

'Yes. And I'll add in clindamycin. There's good evidence that it's effective in decreasing toxin production.' Grace looked past Charles to catch the attention of one of the nursing staff. 'Amy, could you see if there's a bed available in ICU, please? I've got a patient that's going to need intensive monitoring for a while.'

'On it, Dr Forbes.' The nurse reached for the phone.

Grace was gone, too, back to her patient. Charles gave up on the statistics. He would take them home and do his work later tonight, in those quiet hours after the boys were asleep. He was due to go and collect them soon, anyway.

Maybe he should give up on the idea of inviting Grace and Houston to join their party, too. He could give his boys everything they needed. He could take them out later today and let them choose the costumes they wanted themselves.

A sideways glance showed that Amy had finished her urgent arrangements for Grace's patient. She noticed his glance.

'Anything you need, Dr Davenport?'

He smiled at her. 'Not unless you happen to know of a good costume shop in this part of town?'

It seemed like every shop between Manhattan Mercy and home had decorated their windows for Halloween and it made Grace smile, despite her weariness after a couple of such busy days at work, to see the jack-o'-lanterns and ghosts and plastic spiders hanging on fluffy webs.

She'd missed this celebration in Australia.

As she turned towards the more residential area, there were groups of children already out, too, off to do their trick or treating in the late afternoon. So many excited little faces peeping out from beneath witches' hats or lions' ears, dancing along in pretty dresses with fairy wings on their backs or proudly being miniature superheroes.

What a shame that Charles hadn't taken her up on her subtle offer to share Halloween with him and his boys. She'd been thinking about him all day, and wondering just how difficult it had been for him when he had to be reliving every moment of this day three years ago when the twins had been born and he'd lost the love of his life.

Her heart was aching for Charles all over again, as she let herself into the apartment building, so it came as a surprise to hear a peal of laughter echoing down the tiled stairway with its wrought-iron bannisters.

The laughter of small people. And a deeper rumble of an adult male.

Grace paused in the foyer, looking upwards, and was rewarded by a small face she recognised instantly, peering down through the rails. His head was covered by a brown hood that had small round ears.

'*Gace*… Look at *us*…'

'I can't see you properly, Max.'

The face disappeared but she could still hear him.

'Daddy… *Daddy*…we have to visit Gace now…'

And there they were, coming down the stairs. Charles had hold of each twin's hand to keep them steady. In their other hands, the boys clutched a small, orange, plastic bucket shaped like a pumpkin. She could see plenty of candy in each bucket.

The brown hoods were part of a costume that covered them from head to toe.

'You're monkeys.' Grace grinned. 'But…where are your tails?'

The twins gave her a very patient look.

Charles gave her a shadow of a wink. 'Curious George doesn't have a tail,' he explained.

'Oh…'

'Trick or treat!' Cameron shouted. He bounced up and down on small padded feet. 'We want *candy*…'

'Please,' Charles admonished. 'Where are your manners, buddy?'

'Please!' It was Max who was first to comply.

'Grace might not have any candy. Maybe we could just say "hi" to Horse?'

'Actually, I *do* have some candy.' Grace smiled at Charles. 'I have a personal weakness for M&M'S. Would they be suitable?'

'A very small packet?' Charles was smiling back at her but looking slightly haunted. 'We already have enough candy to last till Christmas.'

'They're tiny boxes.' Grace pulled her keys from her bag. 'Come on in. Horse will be so happy to see you.'

Charles had probably been in this apartment before, visiting Stefan and Jerome, but he hadn't come in since Grace had taken over and it felt like a huge step forward somehow. The huge, modern spaces had felt rather empty and totally not her style, although she was slowly getting used to them. With two small boys rolling around on the floor with Houston and Charles following her into the kitchen, it suddenly felt far more like a home.

'Let me open the French doors so that Houston can get out into the garden. It's been an hour or two since Kylie took him out for his last walk.' Grace headed for the pantry next, where she knew the big bag still had plenty of the small boxes of candy-covered chocolate she kept for an after-dinner treat.

She had a bottle of wine in the fridge, too. Would it be a step too far to offer one to Charles? She wanted to ask how the day had gone because she knew that she would be able to see past any cheerful accounts and know how hard it had really been. But she could see that anyway. Charles was looking tired and his smile didn't reach his eyes.

And she wasn't about to get the chance to say anything, because his phone was ringing. He took the call, keeping an eye on the children, who were now racing around the garden with the dog, as he listened and then started firing questions.

'Who's there? How long ago did you activate Code Red?'

Grace caught her breath. 'Code Red' was a term used in Manhattan Mercy's ER to indicate that the level of patient numbers was exceeding the resources the department had to deal with them. Like a traffic light that was not functioning correctly, a traffic jam could ensue and, with patients, it meant that urgent treatment could be delayed and fatalities could result.

He listened a moment longer. 'I'll be there as soon as I can.'

'I can go back,' Grace offered as he ended the call. She could get there in less than ten minutes and she was still in her scrubs—she wouldn't even need to get changed.

But Charles shook his head. 'It's the administrative side that needs management. I'll have to go in.' He looked out at the garden. 'I can take the boys.'

This time, it was Grace who shook her head. 'Don't be daft. I'll look after them.'

Charles looked stunned by the offer. 'But...'

'But, nothing. I'll take them back up to your apartment. That way I can feed them. Or get them to bed if you end up being late. Is it okay if I take Houston up, too?'

'Of course…but…are you sure, Grace? They're going to get tired and cranky after the day they've had.'

Grace held his gaze. 'Go,' she said quietly. 'And don't worry about them. They'll be safe.'

For a heartbeat, she saw the shadows on his face lift as his smile very definitely reached his eyes.

'Thank you,' was all Charles said but it felt like she was the one who was being given something very special.

Trust?

Chapter 5

If it hadn't been for her small entourage of two little boys and one large, fluffy dog, Grace might have felt like she was doing something wrong, stepping into Charles Davenport's private life like this.

How weird was it that just a few hours of one's lifetime, over a decade ago, could have had such an impact that it could make her feel like...like some kind of *stalker*?

It was her own fault. She had allowed herself to remember those hours. Enshrine them, almost, so that they had become a comfort zone that she had relied on, especially in the early days of coming to terms with what had felt like a broken and very lonely life. In those sleepless hours when things always seemed so much worse, she had imagined herself back in Charles's arms. Being held as though she was something precious.

Being made love to, as if she was the only woman in the world that Charles had wanted to be with.

She could have had a faceless fantasy to tap into but it had seemed perfectly safe to use Charles because she had never expected to see him again. And it had made it all seem so much more believable, because it *had* happened.

Once…

And, somewhere along the way, she had allowed herself to wonder about all the things she didn't know about him. What kind of house he lived in, for example. What his favourite food was. Whether he was married now and had a bunch of gorgeous kids.

She probably could have found out with a quick internet search but she never allowed those secret thoughts any head space in daylight hours. And, as soon as she'd started considering working at Manhattan Mercy, she had shut down even the familiar fantasy. It was no more than a very personal secret—a rather embarrassing one now.

But…entering his private domain like this was…

Satisfying?

Exciting?

Astonishing, certainly.

For some reason, she had expected it to be like the apartment she was living in on the ground floor of this wonderful, old building with its high ceilings and period features like original fireplaces and polished wooden floors. She had also expected the slightly overwhelming aura of wealth and style that Stefan and Jerome had created with their bespoke furniture and expertly displayed artworks.

The framework of the apartment with the floors and ceilings was no surprise but Grace's breath was taken away the moment she stepped through the door to face floor-to-ceiling windows that opened onto a terrace looking directly over Central Park. The polished floors didn't have huge Persian rugs like hers and the furniture looked like it had once been in a house out in the country somewhere. A big, old rambling farmhouse, maybe.

The couch was enormous and so well used that the leather looked crinkled and soft. There were picture books scattered over the rustic coffee table, along with crayons and paper and even the curling crust of an abandoned sandwich. There were toys all over the place, too—building bricks and brightly coloured cars, soft toy animals and half-done jigsaw puzzles.

It looked like…*home*…

The kind of home that was as much of a fantasy for Grace as being held—and loved—by someone totally genuine.

She had to swallow a huge lump in her throat.

And then she had to laugh, because Houston made a beeline for the coffee table and scoffed the old sandwich crust.

'I'm hungry,' Cameron announced, as he spotted the dog licking its lips.

'Me, too.' Max nodded.

Cameron upended his pumpkin bucket of candy onto the coffee table. Grace gave Houston a stern look that warned him to keep his nose out. Then she extracted the handfuls of candy from Cameron's fists.

'You can choose *one* thing,' she told him. 'But you can't eat it until after your dinner, okay?'

Cameron scowled at her. 'But I'm *hungry*.'

'I know.' Grace was putting the candy back into the bucket. 'Show me where the kitchen is and I'll make you some dinner. You'd better show me where the bathroom is, too.'

The twins led her into a spacious kitchen with a walk-in pantry.

'I'll show you,' Max offered.

He climbed onto a small step and wobbled precariously as he reached for something on a shelf. Grace caught him as he, and the packet he had triumphantly caught the edge of, fell off the step. For a moment, she stood there with the small, warm body in its fluffy monkey suit in her arms. She could smell the soft scent of something that was distinctly child-like. Baby shampoo, maybe?

Max giggled at the pleasure of being caught and, without thinking, Grace planted a kiss on his forehead.

'Down you go,' she said. 'And keep those monkey paws on the floor, where they're safe.'

She stooped to pick up the packet as she set him down.

'Mac and cheese? Is that what you guys want to eat?'

'Yes…*yes*…mac and cheese. For Horse, too…'

Houston waved his plume of a tail, clearly in agreement with the plan, but Grace was more dubious. She eyed the fruit bowl on the table in the kitchen and then the big fridge freezer. Could she tempt them to something healthier first—like an apple or a carrot? Were there some vegetables they might like in the freezer to go with the cheese and pasta? And packet pasta? *Really?* If she could find the ingredients, it wouldn't be hard to throw a fresh version in the oven. Cooking—and baking—were splinter skills she had enjoyed honing over the years.

The twins—and Horse—crowded around as she checked out what she might have to work with. There wasn't much in the way of fresh vegetables but the freezer looked well stocked.

'What's this?' The long cylindrical object was unfamiliar.

'Cookie dough,' Cameron told her. 'Maria makes us cookies.'

'Can you make cookies, Gace?' Max leaned forward so that he could turn his head to look up at her as she crouched. 'I *like* cookies.' Again, she had to catch him before he lost his balance and toppled into the freezer drawer.

'I don't see why not,' she decided. 'You can help. But only if you both eat an apple while I'm getting things ready. And we won't use the frozen sort. If there's some flour in the pantry and butter in the fridge, we'll make our own. From scratch.'

Over an hour later, Grace realised that the grand plan might have been ill-advised. This huge kitchen with its granite and stainless-steel work surfaces looked like a food bomb had been detonated and the sink was stacked with dirty pots and bowls. A fine snowstorm of flour had settled everywhere along with shreds of grated cheese and dribbles of chocolate icing. Houston had done his best to help and there wasn't a single crumb to be found on the floor, but he wasn't so keen on raw flour.

Whose idea had it been to make Halloween spider cookies?

The boys were sitting on the bench right now, on either side of the tray of cookies that had come out of the oven a short time ago. They had to be so tired by now, but they both had their hands clasped firmly in front of them, their eyes huge with excitement as they waited patiently for Grace to tell them it was safe to touch the hot cookies. It was so cute, she had to get her phone out and take a photo. Then she took a close-up of the cookies. The pale dough had made a perfect canvas for the iced chocolate spiders that had M&M eyes. She'd used a plastic bag to make a piping tool and had done her best to guide three-year-old hands to position spider legs but the results were haphazard. One spider appeared to be holding its eyes on the ends of a very fat leg.

Should she send one of the photos to Charles?

A closer glance at the image of his sons made her decide not to. Still in their monkey suits, the boys now had chocolate smears on their faces and the curls of Max's hair that had escaped his hood had something that looked like cheese sauce in it. Her own hair had somehow escaped its fastenings recently and she was fairly sure that she would find a surprise or two when she tried to brush it later.

Hopefully, she would have time to clean up before their father got home but the children and the kitchen would have to take priority. Not wanting to look a wreck in front of Charles was no excuse to worry about her own appearance. She was still in her work scrubs, for heaven's sake—what did it matter?

She prodded one of the cookies.

'Still too hot, guys,' she said. 'But our mac and cheese has cooled down. You can have some of that and then the cookies will be ready for dessert.'

She lifted one twin and then the other off the bench. 'Do you want to take your monkey suits off now?'

'No. We want to be George.'

'And *watch* George,' Max added, nodding his agreement.

'Okay. Do you eat your dinner at the table?'

'Our table,' Cameron told her. 'With TV.'

'Hmm. Let's wash those monkey paws.'

Grace wasn't sure that eating in front of the television was really the norm but, hey…they were all tired now and it was a birthday, after all. She served bowls of the homemade pasta bake on the top of a small, bright yellow table that Cameron and Max dragged to be right in front of the widescreen television. The chairs were different primary shades and had the boys' names painted on the back. Fortunately, it was easy to see how to use the DVD player and an episode of *Curious George* was already loaded.

The smell of the mac and cheese made Grace realise how hungry she was herself. She knew she should tackle the mess in the kitchen but it wouldn't hurt to curl up on the couch with a bowl of food for a few minutes, would it?

The yellow table, and the bowls, were suspiciously clean when Grace came in later with the platter of cookies and Houston had an innocent air that looked well practised. She had to press her lips together not to laugh out loud. She needed some practice of her own, perhaps, in good parenting?

The thought caught her unawares. She'd been enjoying this time so much it hadn't occurred to her to realise that she was living a fantasy. But that was good, wasn't it? That day at the park, she had wanted to able to embrace a special moment for what it was and not ruin it by remembering old pain. She had done that with bells on with this unexpected babysitting job.

The laughter had evaporated, though. And her smile felt distinctly wobbly. It was just as well that Cameron turned his head to notice what she was carrying.

'Cookies…'

Max's chair fell over backwards in his haste to get up and Houston barked his approval of the new game as they all rushed at Grace. She sat on the couch with a bump and held the platter too high to be reached by all those small fingers.

'One each,' she commanded. 'And none for Horse, okay?'

They ended up having two each but they weren't overly big cookies. And the crumbs didn't really matter because a leather couch would be easy enough to clean. Not that Grace wanted to move just yet. She had two small boys nestled on either side of her and they were all mesmerised by what Curious George was up to on the screen.

'He's a very naughty monkey, isn't he? Look at all that paint he's spilling everywhere!'

The boys thought it was hilarious but she could feel their warm bodies getting heavier and heavier against her own. Houston was sound asleep with his head pillowed on her feet and Grace could feel her own eyes drooping. Full of comfort food and suddenly exhausted by throwing herself so enthusiastically into what would undoubtedly become an emotionally charged memory, it was impossible not to let herself slip into a moment of putting off the inevitable return to reality.

She wouldn't let herself fall asleep, of course. She would just close her eyes and sink into this group cuddle for a minute or two longer…

It was the last thing Charles had expected to see when he let himself quietly into his apartment late that evening.

He knew his boys would have crashed hours ago and he had assumed they would be tucked up in their shared bedroom, in the racing car beds that had been last year's extravagant gift from their grandparents.

They were, indeed, fast asleep when he arrived home after his hectic troubleshooting in a stretched emergency department, but they weren't in their own beds. Or even in their pyjamas. Still encased in their little monkey suits, Cameron and Max were curled up like puppies on either side of Grace, who was also apparently sound asleep on the couch. Houston had woken at the scratch of the key in the lock, of course, but he wasn't about to abandon the humans he was protecting. He didn't budge from where he was lying across Grace's feet but he seemed to be smiling up at Charles and his tail was twitching in a muted wag.

It might have been a totally unexpected sight, but it was also the cutest thing Charles had ever seen. He gazed at the angelic, sleeping faces of his sons and could feel his heart expanding with love so much it felt like it was in danger of bursting. They were both tucked under a protective arm. Grace had managed to stay sitting upright in her sleep but her head was tilted to one side. He had never seen her face in slumber and she looked far younger than the thirty-six years he knew she shared with him. Far more vulnerable than she ever looked when she was awake.

Maybe it was because she was a single unit with his boys at the moment that she was automatically included in this soft wash of feeling so protective.

So…blessed?

But then Charles stepped closer. What was that in Grace's hair? And smeared on her cheek?

Chocolate?

A closer glance at the twins revealed unexplained substances in odd places as well. Charles could feel his face crease into a deep frown. What on earth had been going on here? Walking quietly, he went through the sitting room towards the kitchen and it wasn't long before he stopped in his tracks, utterly stunned.

He'd never seen a mess like this.

Ever...

His feet were leaving prints in the layer of flour on the floor. The sink was overflowing with dirty dishes. There was a deep dish half-full of what looked like mac and cheese and a wire rack that was covered with cookies. Cookies that were decorated with...good grief...what were those strange blobs and squiggles with chocolate candies poked amongst them?

Ah...there was one with a recognisable shape.

A spider...

And then it hit Charles. Grace had been making Halloween cookies with the boys and clearly she had let them do most of the decorating themselves.

Suddenly, the appalling mess in the kitchen ceased to matter because Charles had glimpsed a much bigger picture. One that caught his heart in a very different way to seeing his boys sleeping so contentedly.

This was a kind of scene that he had never envisaged in the lives of his precious little family. Because it was a dimension that only a woman would think of including?

A *mother*?

Somehow, it wrapped itself into the whole idea of a home. Of a kitchen being the heart of the house. Of putting up with unnecessary mess because that was how children learned important things. Not just about how to make cookies but about...about *home*.

About being safe. And loved.

For a moment, the feeling was overwhelming enough to bring a lump to his throat and a prickle to the back of his eyes that brought all sorts of other sensations in their wake.

Feelings of loss.

And longing…

He had to cradle his forehead between his thumb and finger and rub hard at his temples to stop himself falling into a complete wreck.

It was too much. On top of such an emotionally charged day riding that roller-coaster between remembered grief and the very real celebration of his boys' lives, topped off with an exhausting few hours of high-powered management of a potentially dangerous situation, it was no wonder this was overwhelming.

It was too much.

But it was also kind of perfect.

It was the gentle extraction of a small body from beneath her arm that woke Grace.

For a moment, she blinked sleepily up at Charles, thinking that she was dreaming.

That *smile*…

She had never seen anything quite so tender.

He was smiling at her as if he loved her as much as she knew he loved his children.

Yep. Definitely a dream.

But then Max gave a tiny whimper in his sleep as he was lifted. And the warm weight on her feet shifted as Houston got up and then it all came rushing back to Grace.

'Oh, my God…' she whispered. 'I fell asleep. Oh, Charles, I'm *so* sorry…'

'Don't be.'

'But the *mess*. I was going to clean it all up before you got home.'

'Shh…' Charles was turning away, a still sleeping Max cradled in his arms. 'I'll put Max down and then come back for Cameron. Don't move, or you might wake him up.'

That gave Grace all the time she needed to remember exactly what state she'd left this beautiful apartment in. It was bad enough in here, with the television still going, scattered toys and dinner dishes where they'd been left, but the kitchen…

Oh, help… She'd been given total responsibility and she had created a complete disaster.

But Charles didn't seem to mind. He lifted Cameron with a gentleness that took her breath away. Maybe because his hands brushed her own body as he slid them into place and she could feel just how much care he was taking not to wake his son. His gaze caught hers as she lifted her arm to make his task easier and, amazingly, he was still smiling.

As if he didn't actually care about the mess.

Grace cared. She got to her feet and any residual fuzziness from being woken from a deep sleep evaporated instantly as she went back to the kitchen.

It was even worse than she'd remembered.

Should she start with that pile of unwashed dishes or find a broom and start sweeping the floor?

Reaching out, she touched a puddle of chocolate icing on the granite surface of the work bench. It had hardened enough that it would need a lot more than a cloth to wipe it clean. Where were the cleaning supplies kept? Grace pushed her hair back from her face as she looked around and, to her horror, she found a hard lump that had glued a large clump of hair together. Hard enough to suggest it was more chocolate icing.

She was still standing there, mortified, when Charles came to find her.

For a long moment, she couldn't think of anything to say that could encompass how embarrassed she was. Finally, she had to risk making eye contact. He had to be furious, surely, even if he'd been doing a superb job of hiding it so far.

He caught her gaze and held it firmly. Grace couldn't look away.

Yes…there was something stern enough there to let her know he knew exactly how major the clean-up job would be. That he knew how carried away she'd been in her attempt to keep the twins entertained. That she'd surprised him, to say the very least.

But there was something else there as well.

A…twinkle…

Of amusement, laced with something else.

Appreciation maybe.

No…it was deeper than that. Something she couldn't identify.

'What?' she heard herself whisper. 'What are you thinking? That you'll never leave me in charge of your kids again?'

One corner of his mouth lifted into a smile that could only be described as poignant.

'I'm thinking,' he said quietly. 'That I've spent the last three years trying to be both a father and a mother to my kids and keep their lives as predictable and safe as I can and then someone comes in and, in the space of a few hours, wrecks my house and shows me exactly what I didn't realise was missing.'

Grace's brain had fixed on the comment about wrecking his house.

'I'm sorry,' she murmured.

Charles's gaze shifted a fraction. Oh, help…was he staring at the lump of chocolate icing in her hair?

'I've never even thought of making cookies with the boys,' he said. 'I wouldn't know where to start. I know Maria makes them sometimes, but all that's involved there is slicing up a frozen roll and sticking them in the oven. I'm surprised you even found a bag of flour in the pantry. Not only that, you let them draw spiders on the top.'

'Oh…' Grace could feel her lips curve with pleasure. 'You could tell what they were, then?'

'Only after I spotted one that you probably did. Some of them seem to have eyes on their legs.'

'Helps to see round corners,' Grace suggested. Her smile widened.

Charles was smiling back at her and that twinkle in his eyes had changed into something else.

Something that was giving her a very distinctive shaft of sensation deep in her belly.

Attraction, that's what it was.

A very physical and very definite attraction.

Maybe Charles was feeling it, too. Maybe that was why he lifted his hand to touch her hair.

'Chocolate,' he told her.

'I know…' Grace made a face. 'You might find you need to wash the boys' hair in the morning as well.'

'It's not a problem.' Charles was touching her cheek now, his finger feather-light. 'You've got some here, too.'

Grace couldn't say anything. She was shocked by the touch and the electricity of the current it was producing that flashed through her body like a lightning bolt to join the pool of sensation lower down.

The smile on Charles's face was fading fast. For another one of those endless moments, they stared at each other again.

Fragments of unformed thoughts bombarded Grace. Memories of another time when they'd looked at each other just like this. Before Charles had kissed her for the very first time. Snatches of the conversation they'd just had. What had he meant when he'd said that she'd shown him what he hadn't realised was missing in his life?

Surely he didn't mean *her*?

Part of her really wanted that to have been the meaning.

The part that held his gaze, willing him to make the first move…

He was still touching her cheek but his finger moved past any smear of chocolate, tracing the edge of her nose and then out to the corner of her mouth and along her bottom lip.

And then he shut his eyes as he bent his head, taking his finger away just before his lips took its place.

Another shock wave of unbearably exquisite pleasure shot through Grace's body and she had to close her own eyes as she fell into it.

Dear Lord…she had relived a kiss from this man so many times in her imagination but somehow the reality had been muted over the years.

Nobody else had ever kissed her like this.

Ever…

It was impossible not to respond. To welcome the deepening of that kiss. To press herself closer to the remembered planes of that hard, lean body. It wasn't until his hand shifted from her back to slide under her ribs and up onto her breast that Grace was suddenly blind-sided by reality.

By what Charles was about to touch.

She could feel the adrenaline flood her body now, her muscles tensing instantly in a classic fight-or-flight re-flex, in the same moment that she jerked herself back.

Charles dropped his hand instantly. Stepped back from the kiss just as swiftly.

And this time there was a note of bewilderment in his eyes. Of horror, even…

They both looked away.

'Um…' Grace struggled to find her voice. And a rea-son to escape. 'I… I really need to take Houston down-stairs. He must be a bit desperate to get out by now.'

'Of course.' Was it her imagination or did Charles seem grateful for an excuse to ignore what had just hap-pened? 'He needs his garden.'

'I can't leave you with this mess, though.'

'My cleaner's due in the morning. It really isn't a prob-lem.'

No. Grace swallowed hard. They had another problem now, though, didn't they?

But she could feel the distance between them accel-erating. She wasn't the only one who needed to escape, was she?

They hadn't just crossed a barrier here. They had smashed through it with no consideration of any reper-cussions.

And maybe they were just as big for Charles as they were for herself.

But Grace couldn't afford to feel any empathy right now. The need to protect herself was too overwhelming.

With no more than a nod to acknowledge her being excused from cleaning up the mess she had created, Grace took her leave and fled downstairs with Houston.

She had no mental space to feel guilty about escaping.

Besides, Charles had created a bit of a mess himself, hadn't he? By kissing her like that.

That was more than enough to deal with for the moment.

Chapter 6

'Oh, my...' Vanessa Davenport looked slightly appalled as she peered more closely at what was being held up for her admiration. 'What *are* they?'

'Cookies, Grandma.' Cameron was using that patient tone that told adults they were being deliberately obtuse. 'We *made* them.'

'And Gace,' Max added.

'Gace?' Vanessa was looking bewildered now but Charles didn't offer an explanation.

He was kicking himself inwardly. He should have known exactly what his mother's reaction would be to the less than perfect cookies, but he couldn't forgive the slap to his boys' pride that had prompted them to insist on bringing their creations to the family afternoon tea.

It was the complete opposite end to the spectrum that Grace was also on. She'd been just as proud of the boys at the results of their efforts. This morning, she'd sent him the photo she'd taken of them sitting on the bench, their hands clasped and eyes shining with the tray of cookies between them. It even had Horse's nose photo-bombing the bottom of the image and Charles had been so taken with it, he'd thought of using it for his Christmas cards this year.

Maybe not, if his mother was going to look like this.

'Let's give them to Alice.' Vanessa was an expert in ignoring anything that she didn't approve of. 'She can put them in the kitchen.'

Alice was hovering in the background, ready to help with hanging coats up in the cloakroom, but she moved swiftly when there was another knock on the massive front door of the Davenport mansion. His father, Hugo, was coming into the foyer at the same time and the twins' faces brightened.

'Look, Grandpa…look what we made.'

'Wow…cookies…they look delicious.'

'Did I hear someone mention cookies?'

Charles turned towards the door. 'Miranda. Hey… I'm glad you could make it.'

His half-sister had two brightly wrapped parcels under her arm and the twins' eyes got very round.

'Presents, Daddy. For us?'

But Charles had been distracted by someone who had followed Miranda into the house. He hadn't seen his youngest brother, Zachary, for such a long time.

'Zac… What are you doing here?'

'I heard there was a birthday celebration happening.'

'But I thought you were in Annapolis.'

'I was. I am. I'm just in town for the day—you should know why…'

Charles had to shake his head but there was no time to ask. The shriek of excitement behind him had to mean that Miranda had handed over the parcels and, turning his head, he could see his mother already moving towards the main reception lounge.

'For goodness' sake,' she said. 'Let's go somewhere a little more civilised than the doorstep, shall we?'

Charles saw the glance that flashed between Zac and Miranda. Would there ever come a day when Vanessa actually welcomed Miranda into this house, instead of barely tolerating her?

His father was now holding the platter of cookies.

'Shall I take those to the kitchen, sir?' Alice asked.

'No…no…they have to go on the table with all the other treats.'

Charles felt a wash of relief. Families were always complicated and this one a lot more than most but there was still a thread of something good to be found. Something worth celebrating.

He scooped up Cameron, who was already ripping the paper off his gift. 'Hang on, buddy. Let's do that in the big room.'

Zac had parcels in his hands, too. And when the door swung open behind him to reveal Elijah with a single, impressively large box in his arms, Charles could only hope that this gathering wasn't going to be too overwhelming for small boys. He thought wistfully of the relatively calm oasis of their own apartment and, unbidden, an image of the ultimately peaceful scene he'd come home to last night filled his mind.

The one of Grace, asleep on the couch, cuddled up with the boys and with a dog asleep on her feet.

So peaceful. So…perfect…?

'I can't stay,' Elijah said, as they all started moving to the lounge. 'I got someone to cover me for an hour at work. I'll be getting a taxi back in half an hour.'

'Oh…' Miranda was beside him. 'Could I share? My shift starts at five but it takes so long on the Tube I'd have to leave about then, anyway.'

'Flying visit,' Zac murmured. 'It's always the way with us Davenports, isn't it? Do your duty but preferably with an excuse to escape before things get awkward?'

'Mmm.' The sound was noncommittal but Charles put Cameron down with an inward sigh. This vast room, with a feature fireplace and enough seating for forty people, had obviously been professionally decorated. Huge, helium balloons were tethered everywhere and there were streamers looping between the chandeliers and a banner covering the wall behind the mahogany dining table that had been shifted in here from the adjoining dining room. A table that was laden with perfectly decorated cakes and cookies and any number of other delicious treats that had been provided by professional caterers.

Cameron, with his half-unwrapped parcel in his arms, ran towards the pile of other gifts near the table, Max hot on his heels. A maid he didn't recognise came towards the adults with a silver tray laden with flutes of champagne.

'Orange juice for me, thanks,' Elijah said. Miranda just shook her head politely and went after the twins to help them with the unwrapping.

'So what's with your flying visit?' he asked Zac. 'And why should I know about it?'

'Because I'm here for an interview. I've applied for a job at Manhattan Mercy that starts next month.'

'Really? Wow…' Charles took a sip of his champagne.

'That's great, man. And there I was thinking you were going to be a navy medic for the rest of your life.'

Zac shrugged. 'Maybe I'm thinking that life's short, you know? If I don't get around to building some bridges soon, it's never going to happen.'

Charles could only nod. He knew better than anyone how short life could be, didn't he? About the kind of jagged hole that could be left when someone you loved got ripped from it.

But that hole had been covered last night, hadn't it? Just for a moment or two, he had stepped far enough away from it for it to have become invisible. And it had been that perfect family scene that had led him away. His two boys, under the sheltering arms of someone who had looked, for all the world, like their mother. With a loyal family pet at their feet, even.

But now Zac had shown him the signpost that led straight back to the gaping hole in his life.

And Elijah was shaking his head. 'I hope you're not harbouring any hope of this lot playing happy families any time soon.'

They all turned their gazes on their parents. Hugo and Miranda were both down on the floor with the twins. Miranda's gifts of a new toy car for Cameron and a tractor for Max had been opened and set aside and now the first of the many parcels from the grandparents were being opened. It looked like it was a very large train set, judging by the lengths of wooden rails that were appearing. The level of excitement was increasing and Charles needed to go and share it. Maybe that way, the twins wouldn't notice the way their grandmother was perched on a sofa at some distance, merely watching the spectacle.

'Anyone else coming?' Zac asked. 'Where's Penny?'

'Still on holiday. Skiing, I think. Or was it sky-diving?'

'Sounds like her. And Jude? I'd love to catch up with him.'

'Are you kidding?' Elijah's eyebrows rose. 'Being a cousin is a perfect "get out of jail" card for most of our family get-togethers.'

Charles moved away from his brothers. It was always like this. Yes, there were moments of joy to be found in his family but the undercurrents were strong enough to mean that there was always tension. And most of that tension came from Vanessa and Elijah.

You had to make allowances, of course. It was his mother who'd been hardest hit by the scandal of learning that her husband had been having an affair that had resulted in a child—Miranda. That knowledge would have been hard enough, but to find out because Miranda's mother had died and her father had insisted on acknowledging her and bringing her into the family home had been unbearable for Vanessa.

Unbearable for everyone. The difference in age between himself and his twin might have been insignificant but Charles had always known that he was the oldest child. The firstborn. And that came with a responsibility that he took very seriously. That turbulent period of the scandal had been his first real test and he'd done everything he could to comfort his siblings—especially Elijah, who'd been so angry and bitter. To protect the frightened teenager who had suddenly become one of their number as well. And to support his devastated mother, who was being forced to start an unexpected chapter in her life.

Like the authors of many of the gossip columns, he'd expected his mother would walk away from her marriage but Vanessa had chosen not to take that option. She'd claimed that she didn't want to bring more shame on the Davenport family but they all knew that what scared her more would have been walking away from her own exalted position in New York society and the fundraising efforts that had become her passion.

To outward appearances, the shocking changes had been tolerated with extraordinary grace. Behind closed doors, however, it had been a rather different story. There were no-go areas that Vanessa had constructed for her own protection and nobody, including her husband, would dream of intruding on them uninvited.

Charles had always wondered if he could have done more, especially for Elijah, who had ended up so bitter about marriage and what he sarcastically referred to as 'happy families'. If he could have done a better job as the firstborn, maybe he could have protected his family more successfully, perhaps by somehow diverting the destructive force of the scandal breaking. It hadn't been his fault, of course, any more than Nina's death had been. Why didn't that lessen the burden that a sense of responsibility created?

But surely enough time had passed to let them all move on?

Charles felt tired of it all suddenly. The effort it had taken to try and keep his shattered family together would have been all-consuming at any time. To have had it happen in the run-up to his final exams had been unbelievably difficult. Life-changing.

If it hadn't happened, right after that night he'd shared with Grace, how different might his life have been?

Would he have shut her out so completely? Pretended that night had never happened because that was a factor he had absolutely no head space to even consider?

To his shame, Charles had been so successful in shutting it out in that overwhelmingly stressful period, he had never thought of how it might have hurt Grace.

Was *that* why she'd pretty much flinched during that kiss last night? Why she'd practically run away from him as hard and fast as she could politely manage?

Receiving that photo this morning had felt kind of like Grace was sending an olive branch. An apology for running, perhaps. Or at least an indication that they could still be friends?

The effect was a swirl of confusion. He had glimpsed something huge that was missing from his life, along with the impression that Grace was possibly the only person who could fill that gap. The very edges of that notion should be stirring his usual reaction of disloyalty to Nina that thoughts of including any other woman in his life usually engendered.

But it wasn't happening…

Because there was a part of his brain that was standing back and providing a rather different perspective? Would Nina have wanted her babies to grow up without a mom?

Would *he* have wanted them to grow up without a dad, if he'd been the one to die too soon?

Of course not.

He had experienced the first real surge of physical desire in three long years, too. That should be sparking the guilt but it didn't seem to be. Not in the way he'd become so accustomed to, anyway.

He wouldn't have inflicted a life of celibacy on Nina, either.

Maybe the guilt was muted by something more than a different perspective. Because, after the way she had reacted last night, it seemed that going any further down that path was very unlikely?

The more he thought about it, the more his curiosity about Grace was intensifying.

She had felt the same level of need, he knew she had. She had responded to that kiss in a way that had inflamed that desire to a mind-blowing height.

And then she'd flinched as though he had caused her physical pain.

Why?

It wasn't really any of his business but curiosity was becoming a need to know.

Because, as unlikely as it was, could the small part he had played in Grace's life in the past somehow have contributed to whatever it was?

A ridiculous notion but, if nothing else, it seemed like a legitimate reason to try and find out the truth. Not that it was going to be easy, mind you. Some people were very good at building walls to keep their pain private. Like his mother. Thanks to that enormous effort he'd made to try and keep his family together during the worst time of that scandal breaking, however, he had learned more than anyone about exactly what was behind Vanessa Davenport's walls. Because he'd respected that pain and had had a base of complete trust to work from.

He could hardly expect Grace to trust him that much. Not when he looked back over the years and could see the way he'd treated her from her point of view.

But there was something there.

And, oddly, it did *feel* a bit like trust.

Stepping over train tracks that his father was slotting together, smiling at the delight on his sons' faces as they unwrapped a bright blue steam engine with a happy face on the front, Charles moved towards the couch and bent to kiss Vanessa's cheek.

'Awesome present, Mom,' he said with a smile. 'Clever of you to know how much the boys love Thomas the Tank Engine.'

That kiss had changed everything.

Only a few, short weeks ago Grace had been so nervous about meeting Charles Davenport again that she had almost decided against applying for the job at Manhattan Mercy.

What had she been so afraid of? That old feelings might resurface and she'd have to suffer the humiliation of being dismissed so completely again?

To find that the opposite had happened was even scarier. That old connection was still there and could clearly be tapped into but… Grace didn't want that.

Well…she *did*…but she wasn't ready.

She might never be ready.

Charles must think she was crazy. He must have sensed the connection at the same moment she had, when they'd shared their amusement about the spiders that had eyes on their legs, otherwise he wouldn't have touched her like that.

And he must have seen that fierce shaft of desire because she had felt it throughout her entire body so why wouldn't it have shown in her eyes?

Just for those few, deliciously long moments she had been unaware of anything but that desire when he'd kissed her. That spiralling need for more.

And then his hand had—almost—touched her breast and she'd reacted as if he'd pulled a knife on her or something.

It had been purely instinctive and Grace knew how over the top it must have seemed. She was embarrassed.

A bit ashamed of herself, to be honest, but there it was. A trigger that had been too deeply set to be disabled.

The net effect was to make her feel even more nervous about her next meeting with Charles than she had been about the first one and he hadn't been at work the next day so her anxiety kept growing.

She had sent out mixed messages and he had every right to be annoyed with her. How awkward would it be to work together from now on? Did she really want to live with a resurrection of all the reasons why she'd taken herself off to work in the remotest places she could find?

No. What she wanted was to wind back the clock just a little. To the time before that kiss, when it had felt like an important friendship was being cemented. When she had discovered a totally unexpected dimension in her life by embracing a sense of family in her time with Charles and his sons and Houston.

So she had sent through that photo she had taken of Max and Cameron waiting for the cookies to cool. Along with another apology for the mess they had all created. Maybe she wanted to test the waters and see just how annoyed he might be.

He had texted back to thank her, and say that it was one of the best photos of the boys he'd ever seen. He also said that they were going to a family birthday celebration that afternoon and surprised her by saying he didn't think it would be nearly as much fun as baking Halloween cookies.

A friendly message—as if nothing had changed.

The relief was welcome.

But confusing.

Unless Charles was just as keen as she was to turn the clock back?

Of course he was, she decided by the end of that day, as she took Houston for a long, solitary walk in the park. He had as big a reason as she did not to want to get that close to someone. He had lost the absolute love of his life under horrifically traumatic circumstances. Part of him had to want to keep on living—as she did—and not to be deprived of the best things that life had to offer.

But maybe he wasn't ready yet, either.

Maybe he never would be.

And that was okay—because maybe they could still be friends and that was something that could be treasured.

Evidence that Charles wanted to push the 'reset' button on their friendship came at increasingly frequent intervals over the next week or two. Now that his nanny, Maria, had recovered from her back injury enough to work during week days, he was in the emergency room every day that Grace was working.

He gave her a printed copy of the photograph, during a quiet moment when they both happened to be near the unit desk on one occasion.

'Did you see that Horse photobombed it?'

Grace laughed. 'No… I thought I'd had my thumb on the lens or something. I was going to edit it out.'

She wouldn't now. She would tuck this small picture into her wallet and she knew that sometimes she would take it out and look at it. A part of her would melt with love every time. And part of her would splinter into little pieces and cry?

She avoided looking directly at Charles as she slipped the image carefully into her pocket.

'Did your cleaning lady resign the next day?'

'No. She wants the recipe for your homemade mac and cheese.'

It was unfortunate that Grace glanced at Charles as he stopped speaking to lick his lips. That punch of sensation in her belly was a warning that friendship with this man would never be simple. Or easy. That it could become even worse, in fact, because there might come a time when she was ready to take that enormous step into a new life only to find that Charles would never feel the same way.

'I'd like it, too.' He didn't seem to have noticed that she was edging away. 'I had some later that night and it was the most delicious thing ever. It had *bacon* in it.'

'Mmm… It's not hard.'

'Maybe you could show me. Sometime…'

The suggestion was casual but Grace had to push an image from her mind of standing beside Charles as she taught him how to make a cheese sauce. Of being close enough to touch him whilst wrapped in the warmth and smells of a kitchen—the heart of a home. She could even feel a beat of the fear that being so close would bring and she had to swallow hard.

'I'll write down how to do it for you.'

Charles smiled and nodded but seemed distracted now. He was staring at the patient details board. 'What's going on with that patient in Curtain Six? She's been here for a long time.'

'We're waiting for a paediatric psyche consult. This is her third admission in a week. Looks like a self-inflicted injury and I think there's something going on at home that she's trying to escape from.'

'Oh…' His breath was a sigh. 'Who brought her in?'

'Her stepfather. And he's very reluctant to leave her alone with staff.'

'Need any help?'

'I think we're getting there. I've told him that we need to run more tests. Might even have to keep her in overnight for observation. I know we've blocked up a bed for too long, but…'

'Don't worry about it.' The glance Grace received was direct. Warm. 'Do whatever you need to do. I trust you. Just let me know if you need backup.'

Feeling trusted was a powerful thing.

Knowing that you had the kind of backup that could also be trusted was even better and Grace was particularly grateful for that a couple of mornings later with the first case that arrived on her shift.

A thirteen-month-old boy, who had somehow managed to crawl out of the house at some point during the night and had been found, virtually frozen solid, in the back yard.

'VF arrest,' the paramedics had radioed in. 'CPR under way. We can't intubate—his mouth's frozen. We've just got an OPA in.'

Grace had the team ready in their resuscitation area.

'We need warmed blankets and heat packs. Warmed IV fluids. We'll be looking at thoracic lavage or even ECMO. Have we heard back from the cardiac surgical team yet?'

'Someone's on their way.'

'ECMO?' she heard a nurse whisper. 'What's that?'

'Extra corporeal membrane oxygenation,' she told them. 'It's a form of cardiopulmonary bypass and we can warm the blood at the same time. Because, like we've all been taught, you're not—'

'—dead until you're warm and dead.'

It was Charles who finished her sentence for her, as he appeared beside her, pushing his arms through the sleeves of a gown. He didn't smile at her, but there was a crinkle at the corners of his eyes that gave her a boost of confidence.

'Thought you might like a hand,' he murmured. 'We've done this before, remember?'

Grace tilted her head in a single nod of acknowledgement. She was focused on the gurney being wheeled rapidly towards them through the doors. Of course she remembered. It had been the only time she and Charles had worked so closely together during those long years of training. They had been left to deal with a case of severe hypothermia in an overstretched emergency department when they had been no more than senior medical students. Their patient had been an older homeless woman that nobody had seemed to want to bother with.

They had looked at each other and quietly chanted their new mantra in unison.

'You're not dead until you're warm and dead.'

And they'd stayed with her, taking turns to change heat packs and blankets while keeping up continuous CPR for more than ninety minutes. Until her body temperature was high enough for defibrillation to be an effective option.

Nobody ever forgot the first time they defibrillated somebody.

Especially when it was successful.

But this was very different. This wasn't an elderly woman who might not have even been missed if she had succumbed to her hypothermia. This was a precious child who had distraught members of his family watching their every move. A tiny body that looked, and felt, as if it was made of chilled wax as he was gently transferred to the heated mattress, where his soaked, frozen nappy was removed and heat packs were nestled under his arms and in his groin.

'Pupils?'

'Fixed and dilated.'

Grace caught Charles's gaze as she answered his query and it was no surprise that she couldn't see any hint of a suggestion that it might be too late to help this child. It was more an acknowledgement that the battle had just begun. That they'd done this before and they could do it again. And they might be surrounded by other staff members but it almost felt like it was just them again. A tight team, bonded by an enormous challenge and the determination to succeed.

Finding a vein to start infusing warmed IV fluids presented a challenge they didn't have time for so Grace used an intraosseous needle to place a catheter inside the tibia where the bone marrow provided a reliable connection to the central circulation. It was Charles who took over the chest compressions from the paramedics and initiated the start of warmed oxygen for ventilation and then it was Elijah who stepped in to continue while Charles and Grace worked together to intubate and hook the baby up to the ventilator.

The cardiac surgical team arrived soon after that, along with the equipment that could be used for more aggressive internal warming, by direct cannulation of major veins and arteries to both warm the blood and take over the work of the heart and lungs or the procedure of infusing the chest cavity with warmed fluids and then draining it off again. If ECMO or bypass was going to be used, the decision had to be made whether to do it here in the department or move their small patient to Theatre.

'How long has CPR been going?'

'Seventy-five minutes.'

'Body temperature?'

'Twenty-two degrees Celsius. Up from twenty-one on arrival. It was under twenty on scene.'

'Rhythm?'

'Still ventricular fibrillation.'

'Has he been shocked?'

'Once. On scene.' Again, it was Charles's gaze that Grace sought. 'We were waiting to get his temperature up a bit more before we tried again but maybe…'

'It's worth a try,' one of the cardiac team said. 'Before we start cannulation.'

But it was the nod from Charles that Grace really wanted to see before she pushed the charge button on the defibrillator.

'Stand clear,' she warned as crescendo of sound switched to a loud beeping. 'Shocking now.'

It was very unlikely that one shock would convert the fatal rhythm into one that was capable of pumping blood but, to everyone's astonishment, that was exactly what it did. Charles had his fingers resting gently near a tiny elbow.

'I've got a pulse.'

'Might not last,' the surgeon warned. 'He's still cold enough for it to deteriorate back into VF at any time, especially if he's moved.'

Grace nodded. 'We won't move him. Let's keep on with what we're doing with active external rewarming and ventilation. We'll add in some inotropes as well.'

'It could take hours.' The surgeon looked at his watch.

'I can't stay, I'm afraid. I've got a theatre list I'm already late for but page me if you run into trouble.'

Charles nodded but the glance he gave Grace echoed what she was thinking herself. They had won the first round of this battle and, together, they would win the next.

There wasn't much that they could do, other than keep up an intensive monitoring that meant not stepping away from this bedside. Heat packs were refreshed and body temperature crept up, half a degree at a time. There were blood tests to run and drugs to be cautiously administered. They could let the parents come in for a short time to see what was happening and to reassure them that everything possible was being done but they couldn't be allowed to touch their son yet. The situation was still fragile and only time would give them the answers they all needed.

His name, they learned, was Toby.

It wasn't necessary to have two senior doctors present the whole time but neither Charles nor Grace gave any hint of wanting to be anywhere else and, fortunately, there were enough staff to cover everything else that was happening in the department.

More than once, they were the only people in the room with Toby. Their conversation was quiet and professional, focused solely on the challenge they were dealing with and, at first, any eye contact was that of colleagues. Encouraging. Appreciative. Hopeful…

It was an odd bubble to be in, at the centre of a busy department but isolated at the same time. And when it was just the two of them, when a nurse left to deliver blood samples or collect new heat packs, there was an atmosphere that Grace could only describe as…peaceful?

No. That wasn't the right word. It felt as though she was a piece of a puzzle that was complete enough to see what the whole picture was going to be. There were only a few pieces still to fit into the puzzle and they were lying close by, waiting to be picked up. It was a feeling of trust that went a step beyond hope. It was simply a matter of time.

So perhaps that was why those moments of eye contact changed as one hour morphed into the next. Why it was so hard to look away, because that was when she could feel it the most—that feeling that the puzzle was going to be completed and that it was a picture she had been waiting her whole life to see.

It felt like…happiness.

Nearly three hours later, Toby was declared stable enough to move to the paediatric intensive care unit. He was still unconscious but his heart and other organs were functioning normally again. Whether he had suffered any brain damage would not be able to be assessed until he woke up.

If he woke up?

Was that why Grace was left with the feeling that she hadn't quite been able to reach those last puzzle pieces? Why the picture she wanted to see so badly was still a little blurred?

No. The way Charles was looking at her as Toby's bed disappeared through the internal doors of the ER assured Grace that she had done the best job she could and, for now, the outcome was the best it could possibly be. That he was proud of her. Proud of his department.

And then he turned to start catching up with the multitude of tasks that had accumulated and needed his attention. Grace watched him walking away from her and that was when instinct kicked in.

That puzzle wasn't really about a patient at all, was it?

It was about herself.

And Charles.

Chapter 7

'Bit cold for the park today, isn't it, Doc? They're sayin' it could snow.'

'I know, but the boys are desperate for a bike ride. We haven't been able to get outside to play for days.'

Jack brightened at the prospect of leaving the tiny space that was his office by the front door of this apartment block.

'Stay here. I'll fetch those bikes from the basement. Could do with checkin' that the rubbish has been collected.'

'Oh, thanks, Jack.' It was always a mission managing two small boys and their bikes in the elevator. This way, he could get their coats and helmets securely fastened without them trying to climb on board their beloved bikes.

As always, he cast more than one glance towards the door at the back of the foyer as he got ready to head outside. He remembered wanting to knock on it when Grace had first moved in and that he'd been held back by some nebulous idea of boundaries. He didn't have any problems with it now.

They'd come a long way since then. Too far, perhaps, but they'd obviously both decided to put that ill-advised kiss behind them and focus on a friendship that was growing steadily stronger.

And Charles had news that he really wanted to share.

So he knocked on Grace's door. He knew she had a day off today because he'd started taking more notice of her name on the weekly rosters.

'Charles… Hi…' Was it his imagination or was there a glow of real pleasure amidst the surprise of a morning caller?

He could certainly feel that glow but maybe it was coming from his own pleasure at seeing *her*. Especially away from work, when she wasn't wearing her scrubs, with her hair scraped back from her face in her usual ponytail. Today, she was in jeans tucked into sheepskin-lined boots and she had a bright red sweater and her hair was falling around her face in messy waves—a bit like it had been when he'd come home to find her sound asleep on his couch.

Horse sneaked past her legs and made a beeline for the boys, who shrieked with glee and fell on their furry friend for cuddles.

'I have something I have to tell you,' Charles said.

Her eyes widened. 'Oh, no…is it Miranda? Helena texted me to say she was involved in that subway tunnel collapse—that she'd been trapped under rubble or something.'

Charles shook his head. 'She's fine. She didn't even

need to come into the ER. A paramedic took care of her, apparently. No, it's about Toby. I just had a call from PICU.'

He could hear the gasp as Grace sucked in her breath. 'Toby?'

'Yes. He woke up this morning.'

'Oh…it's been forty-eight hours. I was starting to think the worst… Is he…? Has he…?'

'As far as they can tell, he's neurologically intact. They're going to run more tests but he recognises his parents and he's said the few words he knows. And he's smiling…'

Grace was smiling, too. Beaming, in fact. And then she noticed Jack as the elevator doors opened and he stepped out with a small bike under each arm.

'Morning, Jack.'

'Morning, Miss Forbes.' His face broke into a wide grin. 'Yo' sure look happy today.'

'I am…' There was a sparkle in her eyes that looked like unshed tears as she met Charles's gaze again. 'So happy. Thanks so much for coming to tell me.'

'Can Horse come to the park?' Max was beside his father's legs. 'Can he watch us ride our bikes?'

The glance from Grace held a query now. Did Charles want their company?

He smiled. Of course he did.

'Wrap up warm,' Jack warned. 'It's only about five degrees out there. It might snow.'

'Really?' Grace sounded excited. 'I can't wait for it to snow. And I'm really, really hoping for a white Christmas this year.'

'Could happen.' Jack nodded. 'They're predicting

some big storms for December and that's not far off. It'll be Christmas before we know it.'

Charles groaned. 'Let's get Thanksgiving out of the way before we start talking Christmas. We've only just finished Halloween!'

Except Halloween felt like a long way in the past now, didn't it? Long enough for this friendship to feel like it was becoming something much more solid.

Real.

'Give me two minutes,' Grace said. 'I need to find my hat and scarf. Horse? Come and get your harness on.'

The boys had trainer wheels on their small bikes and needed constant reminding not to get too far ahead of the adults. Pedestrians on the busy pavement had to jump out of the way as the boys powered towards the park but most of them smiled at the two identical little faces with their proud smiles. Charles kept a firm hand on each set of handlebars as they crossed the main road at the lights but once they were through the gates of Central Park, he let them go as fast as they wanted.

'Phew… I think we're safe now. I'm pretty sure the tourist carriages don't use this path.'

'Do they do sleigh rides here when it snows?'

'I don't know. I've seen carriages that look like sleighs but I think they have wheels rather than runners. Why?'

Grace's breath came out in a huff of white as she sighed. 'It's always been my dream for Christmas. A sleigh ride in a snowy park. At night, when there's sparkly lights everywhere and there are bells on the horses and you have to be all wrapped up in soft blankets.'

Charles smiled but he felt a squeeze of something poignant catch his heart. The picture she was painting was ultimately romantic but did she see herself alone in that sleigh?

He couldn't ask. They might have reached new ground with their friendship, especially after that oddly intimate case of working to save little Toby, but asking such a personal question seemed premature. Risky.

Besides, Grace was still talking.

'Christmas in Australia was so weird. Too hot to do anything but head for the nearest beach or pool but lots of people still want to do the whole roast turkey thing. Or dress up in Santa suits.' She rubbed at her nose, which was already red from the cold. 'It feels much more like a proper Christmas when it snows.'

The boys were turning their bikes in a circle ahead of them, which seemed to be a complicated procedure. And then they were pedalling furiously back towards them.

'Look at us, Gace! Look how fast we can go.'

Grace leapt out of Cameron's way, pulling Houston to safety as Cameron tried, and failed, to slow down. The bike tilted sideways and then toppled.

'Whoops...' Charles scooped up his son. 'Okay, buddy?'

Cameron's face crumpled but then he sniffed hard and nodded.

'Is it time for a hotdog?'

'Soon.' He was climbing back onto his bike. 'I have to ride some more first.'

'He's determined,' Grace said, watching him pedal after his brother. 'Like his daddy.'

'Oh? You think I'm determined?'

'Absolutely. You don't give up easily, even if you have a challenge that would defeat a lot of people.'

'You mean Toby? You were just as determined as I was to save him.'

'Mmm. But I'd seen that look in your eyes before, remember? I'm not sure if I would have had the confidence to try that hard when I had absolutely no experience, like you did back when we were students.' She shook her head. 'I still don't have that much experience of arrest from hypothermia. That old woman that we worked on is the only other case I've ever had. Bit of a coincidence, isn't it?'

'Meant to be,' Charles suggested lightly. 'We're a good team.'

'It's easier to be determined when you're part of a team,' Grace said quietly. 'I think you've coped amazingly with challenges you've had to face alone. Your boys are a credit to you.'

He might not know her story yet but he knew that Grace had been through her own share of tough challenges.

He spoke quietly as well. 'I have a feeling you've done that, too.'

The glance they shared acknowledged the truth. And their connection. A mutual appreciation of another person's strength of character, perhaps?

And Charles was quite sure that Grace was almost ready to tell him what he wanted to know. That all it would take was the right question. But he had no idea what that question might be and this was hardly the best place to start a conversation that needed care. He could feel the cold seeping through his shoes and gloves and he would need to take the boys home soon.

'Come and visit later, if you're not busy,' he found

himself suggesting. 'The boys got a train set from my parents for their birthday and they'd love to show it to you.'

The twins were on the return leg of one of the loops that took them away from their father and then back again.

'What do you think, Max?' he called out. 'Is it a good idea for Grace to come and see your new train?'

Later, Charles knew he would feel a little guilty about enlisting his sons' backup like this but right then, he just wanted to know that he was going to get to spend some more time with Grace.

Soon.

It seemed important.

'*Yes*,' Max shouted obligingly, his instant grin an irresistible invitation. 'And Horse.'

'And mac and cheese,' Cameron added.

But Max shook his head. 'Not Daddy's,' he said sadly. 'It comes in a box. I don't like it…'

Charles raised an eyebrow. 'This is your fault, Grace. I have at least half a dozen boxes of Easy Mac 'n' Cheese in my pantry—my go-to quick favourite dinner for the boys—and they're useless. Even when I try adding bacon.'

'Oh, dear…' Grace was smiling. 'Guess I'd better teach you how to make cheese sauce, then?'

His nod was solemn. 'I think so. You did promise.'

Her cheeks were already pink from the cold but Charles had the impression that the colour had deepened even more suddenly.

'I think I promised to write it down for you.'

'Ah…but I learn so much better by doing something. Do you remember that class we did on suturing once? When we had that pig skin to practise on?'

'Yes… It was fun.'

'Tricky, though. I'd stayed up the night before, reading all about exactly where to grasp a needle with the needle driver and wrapping the suture around it and then switching hand positions to make the knots. I even watched a whole bunch of videos.'

'Ha! I knew you always stayed up all night studying. It was why I had so much trouble keeping up with you.'

'My point is, actually doing it was a completely different story. I felt like I had two left hands. You were way better at it.'

'Not by the end of the class. You aced it.'

'Because I was doing it. Not reading about it, or watching it.'

Why was he working so hard to persuade her to do something that she might not be comfortable with? Because it felt important—just like the idea of spending more time with her?

There was something about the way her gaze slid away from his that made him want to touch her arm. To tell her that this was okay. That she could trust him.

But maybe he managed to communicate that, anyway, in the briefest glance she returned to, because her breath came out in a cloudy puff again—the way it had when she'd sighed after confessing her dream of having a Christmas sleigh ride in the snow. Her chin bobbed in a single nod.

'I'll pick up some ingredients on my way home.'

'We don't want to go home, Daddy,' Cameron said. 'We want to go to the playground.'

With their determined pedalling efforts, their feet probably weren't as cold as his, Charles decided. And with some running and climbing added in, they were going to be very tired by this evening. They'd probably fall asleep as soon as they'd had their dinner and…and that would be the perfect opportunity to talk to Grace, wouldn't it?

Really talk to Grace.

He smiled at his boys. 'Okay. Let's head for the playground.'

'And Gace,' Max added.

But she shook her head. 'I can't, sorry, sweetheart. I have to take Horse home now.'

'Why?'

'Because Stefan and Jerome are going to Skype us and talk to him, like they do every Sunday. And he needs his hair brushed first. Oh… I've just had an idea.' She held the dog's lead out to Charles. 'Can you stand with the boys? I'll take a photo I can send them, so they can see that he's been having fun in the park today.'

It took a moment or two to get two small boys, two bikes, a large fluffy dog and a tall man into a cohesive enough group to photograph. And then a passer-by stopped and insisted on taking the phone from Grace's hands.

'You need one of the whole family,' he said firmly.

Grace looked startled. And then embarrassed as she caught Charles's gaze.

It reminded him of Davenport family photos. Where everyone had to look as though they were a happy family and hide the undercurrents and secret emotions that were too private to share. The kind of image that would be taken very soon for their annual Thanksgiving gathering?

Charles was good at this. He'd been doing it for a very long time. And he knew it was far easier to just get it over with than try and explain why it wasn't a good idea.

So he smiled at Grace and pulled Houston a bit closer to make a space for her to stand beside him, behind the boys on their bikes.

'Come on,' he encouraged. 'Before we all freeze to death here.'

Strangely, when Grace was in place a moment later, with Charles's arm draped over her shoulders, it didn't feel at all like the uncomfortable publicity shots of the New York Davenports destined to appear in some glossy magazine.

It was, in fact, surprisingly easy to find the 'big smile' that the stranger requested.

It wasn't a case of her heart conflicting with her head, which would have been far simpler to deal with.

This was more like her heart arranging itself into two separate divisions on either side of what was more like a solid wall than a battle line.

There were moments when Grace could even believe there was a door hidden in that wall, somewhere, and time with Charles felt like she was moving along, tapping on that solid surface, waiting for the change in sound that would tell her she was close.

Moments like this, as she stood beside Charles in his kitchen, supervising his first attempt at making a cheese sauce.

'Add the milk gradually and just keep stirring.'

'It's all lumpy.'

'It'll be fine. Stir a bit faster. And have faith.'

'Hmm…okay…' Charles peered into the pot, frowning. 'How did your Skype session go?'

'Houston wasn't terribly co-operative. He didn't want to wake up. I showed them the photo from the park, though, and they said to say "hi" and wish you a happy Thanksgiving.'

'That's nice.' Charles added some more milk to his sauce. 'Where are they going to be celebrating? Still in Italy?'

'Yes. They're fallen head over heels in love with the Amalfi coast. They've bought a house there.'

'What? How's that going to work?'

'They've got this idea that they could spend six months in Europe and six months here every year and never have winters.'

'But what about Houston?'

'I guess he'll have to get used to travelling.' Grace pointed at the pot. 'Keep stirring or lumps will sneak in. You can add the grated cheese now, too.'

Charles was shaking his head. 'I don't think Houston would like summers in Italy. It'd be too hot for a big, fluffy dog.'

'Mmm…' Grace looked over her shoulder. Not that she could see into the living area from here but she could imagine that Houston hadn't moved from where the boys had commanded him to stay—a canine mountain that they were constructing a new train line around. From the happy tooting noises she could hear, it seemed like the line was up and running now.

'I'd adopt him,' Charles said. 'Max and Cameron think he's another brother.'

'I would, too.' Grace smiled. 'I love that dog. I don't think you ever feel truly lonely when you're sharing your life with a dog.'

The glance from Charles was quick enough to be sharp. A flash of surprise followed by something very warm, like sympathy. Concern…

She was stepping onto dangerous territory here, inadvertently admitting that she was often lonely.

'Right…let's drain that pasta, mix in the bacon and you can pour the sauce over the top. All we need is the breadcrumbs on top with a bit more cheese and it can go in the oven for half an hour.'

The distraction seemed to have been successful and Grace relaxed again, helping herself to a glass of wine when Charles chased the boys into the bathroom to get clean. She had to abandon her drink before their dinner was ready to come out of the oven, though, in order to answer the summons to the bathroom where she found Charles kneeling beside a huge tub that contained two small boys, a flotilla of plastic toys and a ridiculous amount of bubbles.

'Look, Gace. A snowman!'

'Could be a snow woman,' Charles suggested. 'Or possibly a snow dog.'

He had taken off the ribbed, navy pullover he'd been wearing and his T-shirt had large, damp patches on the front. There were clumps of bubbles on his bare arms and another one on the top of his head and the grin on his face told her that, in this moment, Charles Davenport was possibly the happiest man on earth.

Tap, tap, tap…

Would she be brave enough to go through that door if she *did* find it?

What if she opened her heart to this little family and then found they didn't actually want her?

'Nobody's ever going to want you again… Not now…'

That ugly voice from the past should have lost its power long ago but there were still moments. Like this one, when she was smiling down at two, perfect, beautiful children and a man that she knew was even more gorgeous without those designer jeans and shirt.

Even as her smile began to wobble, though, she was saved by the bell of the oven timer.

'I'll take that out,' she excused herself. 'Dinner will be ready by the time you guys have got your jimjams on.'

The twins were just as cute in their pyjamas as they had been in their monkey suits for Halloween but another glass of wine had made it easier for Grace. The pleasant fuzziness reminded her that it was possible to embrace the moment and enjoy this for simply what it was—spending time with a friend and being included in his family.

Because they were real friends now, with a shared history of good times in the past and an understanding of how hard it could be to move on from tougher aspects in life. Maybe that kiss had let them both know that anything other than friendship would be a mistake. It was weeks ago and there had been no hint of anything more than a growing trust.

Look at them…having a relaxed dinner in front of a fire, with an episode of *Curious George* on the television and a contented dog stretched out on the mat, and the might-have-beens weren't trying to break her heart. Grace was loving every minute of it.

Okay, it was a bit harder when she got the sleepy cuddles and kisses from the boys before Charles carried them off to bed but even then she wasn't in any hurry to escape. This time, she wasn't going to go home until she had cleaned up the kitchen. She wasn't even going to get off this couch until she had finished this particularly delicious glass of wine.

And then Charles came back and sat on the couch

beside her and everything suddenly seemed even more delicious.

Tap, tap, tap...

For a heartbeat, Grace could actually hear the sound. Because the expression on Charles's face made her wonder if he was tapping at a wall of his own?

Maybe it was her own heartbeat she could hear as it picked up its pace.

He hadn't forgotten that comment about being lonely at all, had he?

'Have you got any plans for Thanksgiving tomorrow, Grace? You'd be welcome to join us, although a full-on Davenport occasion might be a bit...' He made a face that suggested he wasn't particularly looking forward to it himself. 'Sorry, I shouldn't make assumptions. You've probably got your own family to think about.'

Her own family. A separate family. That wall had just got a lot more solid.

Grace didn't protest when Charles refilled her glass.

'I had thought of going to visit my dad but I would have had to find someone to care for Houston and I didn't have enough of a gap in my roster. It's a long way to go just for a night or two. He might come to New York for Christmas, though.'

'And you lost your mum, didn't you? I remember you telling me how much you missed her.'

Good grief...he actually remembered what she'd said that night when she'd been crying on his shoulder as a result of her stress about her final exams?

'She died a couple of years before I went to med school. Ovarian cancer.'

'Oh...that must have been tough.'

'Yeah...it was. Dad's never got over it.' Grace fell silent. Had she just reminded Charles of his own loss. That he would never get over it?

The silence stretched long enough for Charles to finish his glass of wine and refill it.

'There's something else I should apologise for, too.'

'What?' Grace tried to lighten what felt like an oddly serious vibe. Was he going to apologise for that kiss? Explain why it had been such a mistake? 'You're going to send me into the kitchen to do the dishes?'

He wasn't smiling.

'I treated you badly,' he said quietly. 'Back in med school. After…that night…'

Oh, help… This was breaking the first rule in the new book. The one that made that night a taboo subject.

'I don't know how much you knew of what hit the fan the next day regarding the Davenport scandal…'

'Not much,' Grace confessed. 'I heard about it, of course, but I was a bit preoccupied. With, you know… finals coming up.'

And dealing with the rejection…

He nodded. 'The pressure was intense, wasn't it? And I was trying to stop my family completely disintegrating. The intrusion of the media was unbelievable. They ripped my father to shreds, which only made us all more aware of how damaged our own relationship with him was. It tarnished all the good memories we had as a family. It nearly destroyed us.

'We'd always been in the limelight as one of the most important families in New York,' he continued quietly. 'A perfect family. And then it turns out that my father had been living a lie. That he'd had an affair. That there was a half-sister none of us knew about.'

He cleared his throat. 'I was the oldest and it was down

to me to handle the media and focus on what mattered and the only way I could do that was to ignore how *I* felt. My only job was to protect the people that mattered most to me and, at that time, it had to be my family. It hit my mother hardest, as you can probably imagine, but they went to town on Miranda's mother, too. Describing her as worthless was one of the kinder labels. I didn't know her and I probably wouldn't have wanted to but I did know that my new half-sister was just a scared kid who had nobody to protect her. She was as vulnerable as you could get...'

Grace bit her lip. Charles couldn't help himself, could he? He had to protect the vulnerable. It had been the reason why they'd been together that night—he'd felt the need to protect *her*. To comfort her. To make her feel strong enough to cope with the world.

That ability to care for others more than himself was a huge part of what made him such an amazing person.

And, yes...she could understand why his attention had been so convincingly distracted.

Could forgive it, even?

'By the time things settled down, you were gone.'

Grace shrugged. Of course she had gone. There had been nothing to stay for. Would it have changed things if she'd known how difficult life was for Charles at that time?

Maybe.

Or maybe not. It was more likely that she would have been made much more aware of how different his world was and how unlikely it would have been that she could have been a part of it.

'I can't imagine what it must have been like. Life can be difficult enough without having your privacy invaded like that. I couldn't think of anything worse...' Grace shook her head. 'I get that a one-night stand would have fallen off your radar. You don't need to apologise.'

But it was nice that he had.

'It was a lot more than a one-night stand, Grace.' The words were quiet. Convincing. 'You need to know that. And I asked about you, later—every time I came across someone from school at a conference or something. That was how I found out you'd got married.'

Grace was silent. He'd been asking about her? Looking for her, even? If she had known that, would she have taken her relationship with Mike as far as marrying him?

Possibly not. She had thought she'd found love but she'd always known the connection hadn't been as fierce as the one she'd found with Charles that night.

'It was just after that that I met Nina,' he continued. There was a hint of a smile tugging at his lips. 'Even then, I thought, well...if you could get married and live happily ever after, I'd better make sure I didn't get left behind.'

The silence was very poignant this time.

'I'm sorry,' Grace whispered. 'Everybody knows how much you loved her. I'm so sorry you didn't get your happily ever after.'

'I got some wonderful memories. And two amazing children. You reminded me just how lucky I am, on your first day at work.' Charles drew in a deep breath and let it out slowly. 'I hope you have things to feel lucky about, too.'

'Of course I do.'

'Like?'

Grace swallowed hard. She was leaning against that wall in her heart now, as if she needed support to stay upright.

But maybe she needed more than that. To hear someone agree that she was lucky?

'I'm alive,' she whispered.

She could feel his shock. Did he think she was making a reference to Nina? Grace closed her eyes. She hadn't intended saying more but she couldn't leave it like that.

'I found a lump in my breast,' she said slowly, into the silence. 'I'd been married for about a year by then and Mike was keen to start a family. The lump turned out to be only a cyst but, because of my mother, they ran a lot of tests and one of them was for the genetic markers that let you know how much risk you have of getting ovarian or breast cancer. Mine was as high as it gets. And some people think that pregnancy can make that worse.'

'So you decided not to have kids?'

Grace shook her head, glancing up. 'No. I decided I'd have them as quickly as possible and then have a hysterectomy and mastectomy. Only…it didn't work out that way because they found another lump and that one wasn't a cyst. So… I decided to get the surgery and give up any dreams of having kids.'

She had to close her eyes again. 'Mike couldn't handle that. And he couldn't handle the treatment—especially the chemo and living with someone who was sick all the time. And later, my scars were just a reminder of what I'd taken away from him. A mother for his children. A woman he could look at without being…' her next word came out like a tiny sob '…disgusted…'

Maybe she had known how Charles would react.

Maybe she had wanted, more than anything, to feel his arms around her, like this.

To hear his voice, soft against her ear.

'You're gorgeous, Grace. There are no scars that could ever take that away.'

She could hear the steady thump of his heart and feel the solid comfort of the band of his arms around her.

'You're strong, too. I fought external things and I'm not sure that I did such a great job but you…you fought a battle that you could never step away from, even for a moment. And you won.'

Grace's breath caught in a hitch. She *had* won. She would never forget any one of those steps towards hearing those magic words…

Cancer-free…

'Your courage blows me away,' Charles continued. 'You not only got through that battle with the kind of obstacles that your jerk of a husband added but you took yourself off to work in places that are as tough as they get. You didn't let it dent your sense of adventure or the amazing ability you have to care for others.' His arms tightened around her. 'You should be so proud of yourself. Don't ever let anything that he said or did take any of that away from you.'

Grace had to look up. To make sure that his eyes were telling her the same thing that his words were. To see if what she was feeling right now was something real. That she could be proud of everything she'd been through. That she could, finally, dismiss the legacy that Mike's rejection had engraved on her soul. That she was so much stronger now…

How amazing was this that Charles could make her feel as if she'd just taken the biggest step ever into a bright, new future?

That she'd found someone who made it possible to

take the kind of risk that she'd never believed she would be strong enough to take again?

And maybe she had known what would happen when they fell into each other's eyes again like this.

As the distance between them slowly disappeared and their lips touched.

That door in the wall in her heart had been so well hidden she hadn't even realised she was leaning right against it until it fell open with their combined weight.

And the other side was a magic place where scars didn't matter.

Where they could be touched by someone else. Kissed, even, and it wasn't shameful. Or terrifying.

It was real. Raw. And heartbreakingly beautiful.

No. It wasn't 'someone else' who could have done this.

It could only have been Charles.

Chapter 8

The soft trill advertising an incoming text message on his phone woke Charles.

It could have been from anyone. One of his siblings, perhaps. Or a message from work to warn him that there was a situation requiring his input.

But he knew it was from Grace.

He just *knew*...

And, in that moment of knowing, there was a profound pleasure. Excitement, even. An instant pull back into the astonishing connection they had rediscovered last night that was still hovering at the edges of his consciousness as he reached sleepily for the phone on his bedside table.

Okay, he'd broken rule number one, not only by allowing female companionship to progress to this level but by allowing it to happen under his own roof and not keeping it totally separate from his home life—and his children.

And he'd broken an even bigger, albeit undefined, rule, by doing it with someone that he had a potentially important emotional connection to.

Had he been blindsided, because that connection had already been there and only waiting to be uncovered and that meant he hadn't been able to make a conscious choice to back off before it was even a possibility?

Maybe his undoing had been the way her story had touched his heart. That someone as clever and warm and beautiful as Grace could have been made to believe that she didn't deserve to be loved.

Whatever had pushed him past his boundaries, it had felt inevitable by the time he'd led Grace to his bed. And everything that had happened after that was a blurred mix of sensation and emotion that was overwhelming, even now.

Physically, it had been as astonishing as that first time. Exquisite. But there had been more to it this time. So much more. The gift of trust that she'd given him. The feeling that the dark place in his soul had been flooded with a light he'd never expected to experience again after Nina had died. Had never wanted to experience again because he knew what it was like when it got turned off?

It was early, with only the faintest suggestion of the approaching day between the gap of curtains that had been hastily pulled. Grace would be at work already, though. Her early shift had been the reason she hadn't stayed all night and Charles hadn't tried to persuade her. The twins might be far too young to read anything into finding Grace and Horse in their apartment first thing in the morning but what if they dropped an innocent bombshell in front of their grandparents, for instance, during the family's Thanksgiving dinner tonight?

He wasn't ready to share any of this.

It was too new—this feeling of an intimate connection, when you could get a burst of pleasure from even the prospect of communication via text.

He wasn't exactly sure how he felt about it himself yet, so he certainly didn't want the opinions of anyone else— like his parents or his siblings. This was very private.

There was only one other person on the planet who could share this.

Can't believe I left without doing the dishes again. I owe you one. xx

For a moment Charles let his head sink into his pillow again, a smile spreading over his face. He loved Grace's humour. And how powerful two little letters could be at the end of a message. Not one kiss, but two…

Powerful letters.

Even more powerful feelings.

They reminded him of the heady days of falling in love with Nina, when they couldn't bear to be apart. When they were the only two people in the world that mattered.

Was that what was happening here?

Was he falling in *love* with Grace?

His smile faded. The swirling potentially humorous responses to her text message vanished. He'd known that he would never fall in love again. He'd known that from the moment Nina's life had ebbed away that terrible day and he hadn't given it a second thought since. That part of his life had simply been dismissed as he'd coped with what had been important. His babies. And his work.

It had been a very long time before his body reminded him that there were other needs that could be deemed of importance. That was when rule number one had been considered and then put into place.

And he'd broken it.

Without giving any thought to any implications.

The jarring sound of his phone starting to ring cut through the heavy thoughts pressing down and suffocating the pleasure of any memories of last night. His heart skipped a beat with what felt like alarm as he glanced at the screen.

But it wasn't Grace calling. It was his mother.

At this time of the day?

'Mom…what's up? Is everything all right?'

'Maybe you can tell me, Charles. Who is she?'

'Sorry?'

'I'm reading the *New York Post*. Page six…'

Of course she was. Anyone who was anyone in New York turned to page six first, either to read about someone they knew or about themselves. It was a prime example of the gossip columns that Charles hated above everything else. The kind that had almost destroyed his family once as people fed on every juicy detail that the Davenport scandal had offered. The kind that had made getting through the tragedy of losing his wife just that much harder as the details of their fairy-tale romance and wedding were pored over again. The kind that had made him keep his own life as private as possible ever since in his determination to protect his sons.

'Why now?' Vanessa continued. 'Really, Charles. We could do without another airing of the family's dirty laundry. Especially today, with it being Thanksgiving.'

He was out of bed now, clad only in his pyjama pants as he headed into the living area. His laptop was on the dining table, already open. It took only a couple of clicks to find what his mother was referring to.

The photograph was a shock. How on earth had a journalist got hold of it when it had been taken only yesterday—on Grace's phone?

But there it was. The boys on their bikes on either side of Houston. Himself with his arm slung over Grace's shoulders. And they were all grinning like the archetypal happy family.

His brain was working overtime. Had that friendly stranger actually been a journalist? Or had Grace shared the photograph on social media? No… But she had shared it with Stefan and Jerome and they had many friends who were the kind of celebrities that often graced page six. Easy pickings for anyone who contributed to this gossip column, thanks to a thoughtless moment on his behalf.

'She's a friend, Mom. Someone I went to med school with, who happens to be living downstairs at the moment. Dog-sitting.'

'That's not what's getting assumed.'

'Of course it isn't. Why do you even read this stuff?' He scanned the headline.

Who is the mystery woman in Charles Davenport's life?

'And why are they raking over old news? It's too much. Really, Charles. Can't you be more careful?'

Speed-reading was a skill he had mastered a long time ago.

It's been a while since we caught up with the New York Davenports. Who could forget the scandal of the love child that almost blew this famous family apart? Where is she now, you might be asking? Where are any of them, in fact?

Moving on with their lives, apparently. Dr Charles Davenport is retired, with his notoriously private firstborn son taking over as chief of the ER at Manhattan Mercy in the manner of the best dynasties. He's become something of a recluse since the tragic death of his wife but it looks as though he's finally moving on. And isn't it a treat to get a peek at his adorable twin sons?

We see his own twin brother Elijah more than any of the family members, with his penchant for attending every important party, and with a different woman on his arm every time. Their sister Penelope is a celebrated daredevil and the youngest brother, Zachary, is reportedly returning to the family fold very soon, in more ways than one. He has resigned from the Navy and will be adding his medical skills to the Davenport team at Manhattan Mercy. Watch this space for more news later.

And the love child, Miranda? Well...she's so much a part of the family now she's also a doctor and it's no surprise that she's working in exactly the same place.

Are the New York Davenports an example of what doesn't kill you makes you stronger? Or is it just window dressing...?

Charles stopped reading as the article went on to focus on Vanessa Davenport's recent philanthropic endeavours. His mother was still talking—about a fundraising luncheon she was supposed to be attending in a matter of hours.

'How can I go? There'll be reporters everywhere and intrusive questions. But, if I don't go, it'll just fuel speculation. *Everybody* will be talking about it.'

'Just ignore it,' Charles advised. 'Keep your head high, smile and say "No comment". It'll die down. It always does.'

He could hear the weary sigh on the other end of the line.

'I'm so sick of it. We've all been through enough. Haven't we?'

'Mmm.' Charles rubbed his forehead with his fingers. 'I have to go, Mom. The boys are waking up and we need to get ready. It's the Macy's Thanksgiving parade today and we'll have to get there early to find a good place to watch. I'll see you tonight.'

It should have been such a happy day.

Some of Charles's earliest memories were of the sheer wonder of this famous parade. Of being in a privileged viewing position with his siblings, bundled up against the cold, jumping up and down with the amazement of every new sight and adding his own contribution to the cacophony of sound—the music and cheers and squeals of excitement—that built and built until the finale they were all waiting for when Santa Claus in his sleigh being pulled by reindeer with spectacular gilded antlers would let them know that the excitement wasn't over. Christmas was coming...

This was the first year that Cameron and Max were old enough to appreciate the spectacle and not be frightened by the crowds and noise. They were well bundled up in their coats and mittens and hats and their little faces were shining with excitement. They found a spot on Central Park West, not far from one of their favourite playgrounds, and Charles held a twin on each hip, giving them a clear view over the older children in front of them.

The towering balloons sailed past. Superman and Spiderman and Muppets and Disney characters. There was a brass band with its members dressed like tin soldiers and people on stilts that looked like enormous candy canes with their striped costumes and the handles on their tall hats. There were clowns and jugglers and dancers and they kept coming. Charles's arms began to ache with the weight of the twins and their joyous wriggling.

He wasn't going to put them down. This was his job. Supporting his boys. Protecting them. And he could cope. The three of them would always cope. The happiness that today should have provided was clouded for Charles, though. He could feel an echo that reminded him of his mother's heavy sigh earlier this morning.

That it was starting again. The media interest that could become like a searchlight, illuminating so many things that were best left in the shade now. Things that were nobody else's business. Putting them out there for others to speculate on only made things so much harder to deal with.

He could still feel the pain of photographs that had been put on public display in the aftermath of the family scandal breaking. Of the snippets of gossip, whether true or not, that had been raked over. The fresh wave of interest in the days after Nina's death had been even worse as he'd struggled to deal with his own grief. Seeing that photograph that had been taken at their engagement party, with Nina looking so stunning in her white designer gown, proudly showing off the famed Davenport, pink diamond ring, had been like a kick in the guts.

What if that photograph surfaced again now, with gossip mills cranking up at the notion that he'd found a new partner? Grace was nothing like Nina, who'd been part of the kind of society he'd grown up in. Nina had been well used to being in the public eye. Grace was someone who kept herself in the background, working as part of a team in her job where the centre stage was always taken by the person needing her help.

Or making two small boys happy by baking cookies and trashing his kitchen...

She would be appalled at any media interest. She'd as much as told him how she wouldn't be able to cope.

'I can't imagine what it must have been like. Life can be difficult enough without having your privacy invaded like that. I couldn't think of anything worse...'

The cloud settled even more heavily over Charles as the real implications hit him.

He knew her story now. That she had been broken by the reaction of the man who had been her husband to the battle she'd had to fight. That she'd actually hidden herself from the world to come to terms with being made to feel less than loveable. Ugly, even...

He hadn't even noticed her scars last night. Not as anything that detracted from her beauty, anyway. If anything, they added to it because they were a mark of her astonishing courage and strength.

But he knew exactly how vulnerable she could still be, despite that strength.

As vulnerable as his younger siblings had been when the 'love child' scandal had broken. He'd learned how to shut things down then, in order to protect them.

Maybe he needed to call on those skills again now.

To protect Grace. He could imagine the devastating effect if the spotlight was turned on her. If someone thought to find images of what mastectomy scars looked like, perhaps, and coupled it with headline bait like *Is this why her husband left her?*

He couldn't let that happen.

He *wouldn't* let that happen.

He had to protect his boys, too.

They weren't just old enough to appreciate this parade now. They knew—and loved—the new person who had come into their lives. Someone who was as happy as he was to stand in the cold and watch them run and climb in a playground. Who baked cookies with them and fell asleep on the couch with them cuddled beside her.

He wouldn't be the only one to be left with a dark place if she vanished from their lives.

What about that different perspective he'd found the day after the twins' birthday, when he'd known that he wouldn't want his boys growing up without a dad, if the tragedy had been reversed? That he wouldn't have wanted Nina to have a restricted, celibate life?

It was all spiralling out of control. His feelings for Grace. How close they had suddenly become. The threat of having his private life picked over by emotional vultures, thanks to media interest and having important things damaged beyond repair.

Yes. He needed to remember lessons learned. That control could be regained eventually if things could be ignored. He had done this before but this time he could do it better. He was responsible and he was old enough and wise enough this time around not to make the same mistakes.

He had to choose each step with great care. And the first step was to narrow his focus to what was most important.

And he was holding that in his arms.

'Show's almost over, guys. Want to go to the playground on the way home?'

'There's something different about you today.' Helena looked up as she finished scribbling a note in a patient file on the main desk in the ER. 'You look…happy.'

Grace's huff was indignant. 'Are you trying to tell me I usually look miserable?'

'No…' Helena was smiling but she still had a puzzled frown. 'You never look *miserable*. You just don't usually look… I don't know…*this* happy. Not at this time of the morning, anyway.'

Grace shrugged but found herself averting her gaze in case her friend might actually see more than she was ready to share.

She'd already seen too much.

This happiness was seeping out of every cell in her body and it was no surprise it was visible to someone who knew her well. It felt like she was glowing. As if she could still feel the touch of Charles's hands—and lips—on her body.

On more than her body, in fact. It felt like her soul was glowing this morning.

Reborn.

Oh, help… She wasn't going to be as focused on her work today as she needed to be if she let herself get pulled back into memories of last night. That was a pleasure that needed to wait until later. With a huge effort, Grace closed the mental door on that compelling space.

'I have a clown in Curtain Three,' she told Helena.

Helena shook her head with a grimace. 'We get a lot of clowns in here. They're usually drunk.'

'No…this is a real clown. He was trying to do a cartwheel and I've just finished relocating his shoulder that couldn't cope. I want to check his X-ray before I discharge him. He has a clown friend with him, too. Didn't you see them come in? Spotty suits, squeaky horns, bright red wigs—the whole works.'

But Helena didn't seem to be listening. She was staring at an ambulance gurney that was being wheeled past the desk. The person lying on the gurney seemed to be a life-sized tin soldier.

'Oh…of course…' she sighed. 'It's the Macy's Thanksgiving parade today, isn't it?'

'Chest pain,' one of the paramedics announced. 'Query ST elevation in the inferior leads.'

'Straight into Resus, thanks.' Grace shared a glance with Helena. This tin soldier was probably having a heart attack. 'I can take this.'

Helena nodded. 'I'll follow up on your clown, if you like.' She glanced over her shoulder as if she was expecting more gurneys to be rolling up. 'We're in for a crazy day,' she murmured. 'It always is, with the parade.'

Crazy was probably good, Grace decided as she followed her tin soldier into Resus.

'Let's get him onto the bed. On my count. One, two… *three*.' She smiled at the middle-aged man. 'My name's Grace and I'm one of the doctors here at Manhattan Mercy. Don't worry, we're going to take good care of you. What's your name?'

'Tom.'

'How old are you, Tom?'

'Fifty-three.'

'Do you have any medical history of heart problems? Hypertension? Diabetes?'

Tom was shaking his head to every query.

'Have you ever had chest pain like this before?'

Another shake. 'I get a bit out of puff sometimes. But playing the trumpet is hard, you know?'

'And you got out of breath this morning?'

'Yeah. And then I felt sick and got real sweaty. And the pain…'

'He's had six milligrams of morphine.' A paramedic was busy helping the nursing staff to change the leads that clipped to the electrodes dotting Tom's chest so that he was attached to the hospital's monitor. His oxygen tubing came off the portable cylinder to be linked to the overhead supply and a different blood pressure cuff was being wrapped around his arm.

'How's the pain now, Tom?' Grace asked. 'On a scale of zero to ten, with ten being the worst?'

'About six, I guess.'

'It was ten when we got to him.'

'Let's give you a bit more pain relief, then,' Grace said. 'And I want some bloods off for cardiac enzymes, please. I want a twelve-lead ECG, stat. And can someone call the cath lab and check availability?'

Yes. Crazy was definitely good. From the moment Tom had arrived in her care to nearly an hour later, when she accompanied him to the cardiac catheter laboratory so that he could receive angioplasty to open his blocked artery, she didn't have a spare second where her thoughts could travel to where they wanted to go so much.

Heading back to the ER was a different matter.

Her route that took her back to bypass the main waiting area was familiar now. The medical staff all used it because if you went through the waiting area at busy times, you ran the risk of being confronted by angry people who didn't like the fact that they had to wait while more urgent cases were prioritised. If Helena was right, this was going to be a very busy day. Which made sense, because they were the closest hospital to where the parade was happening and the participants and spectators would number in the tens of thousands.

Had Charles taken the boys to see the parade?

Was that why he hadn't had the time to answer her text message yet?

Grace's hand touched the phone that was clipped to the waistband of her scrub trousers but she resisted the urge to bring the screen to life and check that she hadn't missed a message.

She wasn't some love-crazed teenager who was holding her breath to hear from a boy.

She'd never been that girl. Had never dated a boy that had had that much of an impact on her. She'd been confident in her life choices and her focus on her study and the career she wanted more than anything.

But she'd turned into that girl, hadn't she? After that first night with Charles Davenport. The waiting for that message or call. The excitement that had morphed into anxiety and then crushing disappointment and heartbreak.

And humiliation…

Grace dropped her hand. They were a long way from being teenagers now. Charles was a busy man. Quite apart from his job, he was a hands-on father with two small boys. History was not about to repeat itself. Charles understood how badly he had treated her by ignoring her last time. He had apologised for it, even. There was no way he would do that again.

And she was stronger. He'd told her that. He'd made her believe it was true.

Walking past the cast room, Grace could see an elderly woman having a broken wrist plastered. There were people in the minor surgery area, too, with another elderly patient who looked like he was having a skin flap replaced. And then she was walking past the small rooms, their doors open and the interiors empty, but that couldn't stop a memory of the first time she had walked past one of them. When she'd seen those two small faces peering out and she had met Cameron and Max.

It couldn't stop the tight squeeze on her heart as she remembered falling in love with Max when he'd smiled at her and thanked her for fixing his truck and then cuddled up against her. He was more cuddly than his brother but she loved Cameron just as much now.

And their father?

Oh… Grace paused for a moment to grab a cup of water from the cooler before she pushed through the double doors into the coal face of the ER.

It hadn't been love at first sight with Charles.

But it had been love at first *night*.

That was why she'd been so nervous about working with him again. He'd surprised her by calling her that night about the dog-sitting possibility by revealing that he'd been thinking about her.

And he'd made her laugh. Made her drop her guard a little?

She'd realised soon after that that the connection was still there. The way he'd looked at her that day at the park—as if he really wanted to hear her story.

As if he really cared.

Oh, and that *kiss*. In that wreck of a kitchen still redolent with the smells of grilled cheese and freshly baked cookies. Even now, Grace could remember the fear that had stepped in when he'd been about to touch her breast. As though the lumpy scars beneath her clothing had suddenly been flashing like neon signs.

Crumpling the empty polystyrene cup, she dropped it into the bin beside the cooler, catching her bottom lip between her teeth as if she wanted to hide a smile.

They hadn't mattered last night, those scars. She'd barely been aware of them herself…

She was back in the department now and she could see a new patient being wheeled into Resus.

So many patients came and went from that intensive diagnostic and treatment area but some were so much more memorable than others.

Like the first patient she had ever dealt with here. That badly injured cyclist who'd been a casualty of the power cut when the traffic lights had gone out. And the frozen baby that she and Charles had miraculously brought back to life. Yep… Grace would never forget that one.

That time with just the two of them when it had seemed as if time had been somehow rewound and that there was nothing standing between herself and Charles. No social differences that had put them on separate planets all those years ago. No past history of partners who had been loved and lost. No barriers apart from the defensive walls they had both constructed and maybe that had been the moment when Grace had believed there might be a way through those barriers.

She'd been right. And Helena had been right in noticing that there was something different about her today.

The only thing that could have made her even happier would be to feel the vibration against her waistband that would advertise an incoming text message.

But it didn't happen. Case after case took her attention during the next few hours. An asthmatic child who had forgotten his inhaler in the excitement of heading to watch the parade and suffered an attack that meant an urgent trip to the nearest ER. A man who'd had his foot stepped on by a horse. A woman who'd been caught up in the crowd when the first pains of her miscarriage had struck.

Case after case and the time flew by and Grace focused on each and every case as if it was the only thing that mattered. To stop herself checking her phone? It was well past lunchtime when she finally took a break in a deserted staffroom and sat down with a cup of coffee and could no longer ignore the weight and shape of her phone. No way to avoid glancing at it. At a blank screen that had no new messages or missed calls flagged.

Anxiety crept in as she stared at that blank screen. Was Charles sick or injured or had something happened to one of the twins? She could forgive this silence if that was the case but it would have to be something major like that because to treat her like this again when he knew how it would make her feel was…well, it was unforgiveable. All he'd had to do was send a simple message. A stupid smiley face would have been enough. Surely he would understand that every minute of continuing silence would feel like hours? That hours would actually start to feel like days?

But if something major like that had happened, she would have heard about it. Like she'd heard about Miranda being caught up in that tunnel collapse. A thread of anger took over from anxiety. How could she have allowed herself to get into a position where everything she had worked so hard for was under threat? She had come to New York to start a new life. To move on from so much loss. The loss of her marriage. The loss of the family she'd dreamed of having. The loss of feeling desirable, even.

Charles had given her a glimpse of a future that could have filled all those empty places in her soul.

This silence felt like a warning shot that it was no more than an illusion.

That the extraordinary happiness she had brought to work with her was no more than a puff of breath on an icy morning. The kind she had been making as she'd walked to Manhattan Mercy this morning in a haze of happiness after last night.

Last night?

It was beginning to feel like a lifetime ago. A lifetime in which this scenario had already played out to a miserable ending.

Anxiety and anger both gave way to doubt.

Had she really thought that history couldn't repeat itself? This was certainly beginning to feel like a re-run.

Maybe it had only been in her imagination that her scars didn't matter.

Maybe having a woman in his bed had opened old wounds for Charles and he was realising how much he missed Nina and that no one could ever take her place.

Maybe it had been too much, too soon and everything had been ruined.

For a moment, Grace considered sending another message. Just something casual, like asking whether they'd been to the parade this morning or saying that she hoped they were all having a good day.

But this new doubt was strong enough to make her hesitate and, in that moment of hesitation, she knew she couldn't do it.

Her confidence was starting to ebb away just as quickly as that happiness.

Chapter 9

Another hour went past and then another…and still nothing.

Nothing…

No call. No text. No serendipitous meeting as their paths crossed in the ER, which was such a normal thing to happen that its absence was starting to feel deliberate.

Grace knew Charles had finally come to work this afternoon because the door to his office was open and she'd seen his leather laptop bag on his desk when she'd gone past a while back. She'd heard someone say he was in a meeting, which wasn't unusual for the chief of emergency services, but surely there weren't administrative issues that would take hours and hours to discuss? Maybe it hadn't actually been that long but it was certainly beginning to feel like it.

She thought she saw him heading for the unit desk

when she slipped through a curtain, intending to chase up the first test results on one of her patients.

Her heart skipped a beat and started racing.

She'd know, wouldn't she? In that first instant of eye contact, she'd know exactly what was going on. She'd know whether it had been a huge mistake to get this close to Charles Davenport again. To be so completely in love and have so many shiny hopes for a new future that were floating around her like fragile, newly blown bubbles.

She'd know whether she was going to find herself right back at Square One in rebuilding her life.

Almost in the same instant, however, and even though she couldn't see his face properly, she knew it wasn't Charles, it was his twin, Elijah. And she knew this because the air she was sucking into her lungs felt completely normal. There was none of that indefinable extra energy that permeated the atmosphere when she was in the same space as Charles. The energy that made those bubbles shine with iridescent colours and change their shape as if they were dancing in response to the sizzle of hope.

'Dr Forbes?'

The tone in her migraine patient's voice made her swing back, letting the curtain fall into place behind her.

'I'm going to be sick…'

Grace grabbed a vomit container but she was too late. A nurse responded swiftly to her call for assistance and her gaze was sympathetic.

'I'll clean up in here,' she said. 'You'd better go and find some clean scrubs.' Pulling on gloves, she added a murmur that their patient couldn't overhear. 'It's been one of *those* days, hasn't it?'

Helena was in the linen supply room.

'Oh, no…' She wrinkled her nose. 'You poor thing…'

'Do we have any plastic bags in here? For super-soiled laundry?'

'Over there. Want me to guard the door for a minute so you can strip that lot off?'

'Please. I'm starting to feel a bit queasy myself.'

'Do you need a shower?'

'No. It's just on my scrubs.' Grace unhooked her stethoscope and then unclipped her phone and pager from her waistband. She put them onto a stainless-steel trolley and then peeled off her tunic. 'What are you doing in here, anyway?'

'We were low on blankets in the warmer and everyone was busy. I'm due for a break.' Helena was leaning against the closed door, blocking the small window. 'Past due to go home, in fact. We both are.' Her smile was rueful. 'How come we were among the ones to offer to stay on?'

'We were short-staffed and overloaded. It was lucky Sarah Grayson could stay on as well.'

'I know. Well, I've hardly seen you since this morning. You okay?' She wrinkled her nose. 'Sorry—silly question. Crazy day, huh?'

'Mmm.' Grace was folding the tunic carefully so she could put it into the bag without touching the worst stains. 'I certainly wouldn't want another one like this in a hurry.'

Not that staying on past her rostered hours had bothered her, mind you. Or the patient load. She loved a professional challenge. It was the personal challenge she was in the middle of that was a lot less welcome.

'What are you doing after work? There's a group going out for Thanksgiving dinner at a local restaurant that sounds like it might be fun. I know you'd be more than welcome.'

But, again, Grace shook her head. 'I can't abandon my dog after being at work so much longer than expected. And I need to Skype my dad. I haven't spoken to him for a while and it's Thanksgiving. Family time.'

'Ah…' Helena's gaze was mischievous. 'And there was me thinking you might be going to some glitzy Davenport occasion.'

Pulling on her clean scrub trousers, Grace let the elastic waist band go with more force than necessary. 'What?'

'You and Charles…?' Helena was smiling now. 'Is *that* why you were looking so happy first thing this morning? Everybody's wondering…'

A heavy knot formed in Grace's gut. People were gossiping about her? And Charles? Had he said something to someone else when he hadn't bothered talking to her? Or had someone seen something or said something to remind Charles that he would never be able to replace his beloved wife? Maybe *that* was why he was ignoring her.

'I have no idea what you're talking about,' she said. 'We're just friends.'

'That's what he said, too.'

'What?' Grace fought the shock wave that made it difficult to move. *'When?'*

'There was someone here earlier this afternoon. A journalist pretending to be a patient and she was asking for you. You'd taken a patient off for an MRI, I think. Or maybe you were finally having a late lunch. Anyway… Charles told her she was wasting her time. That you were nothing more than a colleague and friend. And never would be.'

Was it simply the waft of soiled laundry that was making Grace feel a little faint? She secured the top of the plastic bag and shoved it into the contaminated linen sack.

So she didn't need to make eye contact with Charles to know that the truth was every bit as gut wrenching as she had suspected it would be.

'I don't understand,' she murmured. 'Why was he even saying anything?'

'It's because of the gossip column. That photo. Any Davenport news is going to be jumped on around here. They're like New York royalty.'

'What gossip column? What *photo*?'

'You don't know?' Helena's eyes widened. 'Look. I can show you on my phone. I have to admit, you do look like a really happy little family...'

Focus, Charles reminded himself. Shut out anything irrelevant that's only going to make everything worse.

He had responsibilities that took priority over any personal discomfort.

His boys came first. He'd been a little later for work this afternoon, after getting home from the parade, because he'd needed to brief Maria about the renewed media interest in his life and warn her not to say anything about his private life if she was approached by a journalist. He was going to keep the boys away from nursery school for a day or two, as well, for the same reason.

He'd assumed that he'd see Grace at work and be able to have a quiet word and warn her that she might be faced with some unwelcome attention but she hadn't been in the department when he'd arrived. Instead, he'd been confronted with the reality that interest in the Davenport family's private lives was never going to vanish. How had someone found out that Grace worked here? Had it helped to deal so brusquely with that journalist who had been masquerading as a patient or had he protested too much?

At least Grace hadn't been there to hear him dismissing her as someone who would never be anything more significant than a friend but the echo of his own words was haunting him now.

It wasn't true. He might have no idea how to handle these unexpected emotions that were undermining everything in his personal life that he'd believed would never change but the thing he could be certain of was that his own feelings were irrelevant right now.

He was in a meeting, for heaven's sake, where his push for additional resources in his department was dependent on being able to defend the statistics of patient outcomes and being able to explain anomalies in terms of scientific reasoning that was balanced by morality and the mission statements of Manhattan Mercy's emergency room.

He had to focus.

One meeting merged into the next until it was late in the day and he was still caught up in a boardroom. The detailed report of how his department and others had coped in the power cut last month was up for discussion with the purpose of making sure that they would be better prepared if it should ever happen again.

It was hard to focus in this meeting as well. The day of the power cut had been the day that Grace Forbes had walked back into his life in more than a professional sense. It seemed like fate had been determined to bring her close as quickly as possible. How else could he explain the series of events that had led her to meet his sons and remind him of how lucky he actually was? That had been when his barriers had been weakened, he realised.

When that curiosity about Grace had put her into a different space than any other woman could have reached.

The kind of determination to focus that was needed here was reminiscent of one of the most difficult times of his life—when he'd had to try and pass his final exams in medicine while the fallout of the Davenport scandal had been exploding around him. How hard that had been had been eclipsed by the tragedy of Nina's death, of course, but he'd somehow coped then as well.

And he could cope now.

'We can't base future plans on the normal throughput of the department,' he reminded the people gathered in this boardroom. 'What we have to factor in is that this kind of widespread disruption causes a huge spike in admissions due to the accidents directly caused by it. Fortunately, it's a rare event so we can't resource the department to be ready at all times. What we can do is have a management plan in place that will put us in the best position to deal with whatever disaster we find on our doorstep. And haven't there been predictions already for severe snow storms in December? If it's correct, that could also impact our power supply and patient numbers.'

By the time his meeting finished, a new shift was staffing the department and Grace was nowhere to be seen.

He could knock on her door when he got home, Charles decided, but a glance at his watch told him that he'd have to be quick. He was due to take the boys to their grandparents' house for Thanksgiving dinner tonight and he was already running late.

Was she even at home? He'd heard about the staff dinner at a restaurant being planned and, when there was no response to his knock other than a warning bark from Houston, he hoped that was exactly where she was.

Out having fun.

More fun than he was likely to have tonight, with his mother still stressed about renewed media interest in the family and the necessity of trying to keep two three-year-old boys behaving themselves at a very formal dining table.

Maria had got the boys dressed and said she didn't mind waiting while he got changed himself. A quick shower was needed and then Charles found his dinner jacket and bow tie. The formality was a family tradition, like getting the annual Davenport photograph that would be made available to the media to remind them that this family was still together. Still strong enough to survive anything.

Charles rummaged in the top drawer of his dresser, to find the box that contained his silver cufflinks. He didn't know how many of the family members would be there tonight but hopefully the table would be full. Elijah would definitely be there. And Zac, who was about to start his new job at Manhattan Mercy.

His fingers closed around a velvet box and he opened it, only to have his breath catch in his throat.

This wasn't the box that contained his cufflinks. It was the box that contained the Davenport ring. The astonishing pink diamond that Nina had accepted when she had accepted his proposal of marriage. A symbol of the continuation of the Davenport name. A symbol of their position in New York society, even, given the value and rarity of this famous stone.

As the oldest son, it had been given to Charles for his

wife-to-be and there was only one person in the world who could have worn it.

Nina.

Shadows of old grief enclosed Charles as he stared at the ring. He could never give it to anyone else.

It wouldn't even suit Grace...

Oh, help...where had *that* come from?

Memories of how he'd felt waking up this morning came back to him in a rush. That excitement. The pleasure.

The...longing...

And right now, those feelings were at war with remnants of grief. With the weight of all the responsibilities he had been trying so hard to focus on.

The battle was leaving him even more confused.

Drained, even.

He left the ring in its opened box on top of the dresser as he found and inserted his cufflinks and then slipped on his silk-lined jacket.

He closed the box on the ring then, and was about to put it back where he'd found it but his hand stopped in mid-air.

He had no right to keep this ring shut away in a drawer when he had no intention of ever using it again himself. It could be hidden for decades if he waited to hand it on to his firstborn, Cameron.

He should give it to the next Davenport in line. Elijah.

Charles let his breath out in a sigh. He knew perfectly well how his twin felt about marriage. With his bitterness about the marriage of their parents and scepticism about its value in general, he wouldn't want anything to do with the Davenport ring.

He couldn't give it to Penelope, because it was traditional for it to go to a son who would be carrying on the family name. Miranda was out of the question, even if she hadn't been another female, because of the distress that could cause to his mother, given her reluctance to absorb his half-sister into the family.

Zac. Was that his answer? The youngest Davenport male in his own generation. Okay, Zac had always had a tendency to rebel against Davenport traditions but he was making an effort now, wasn't he? Coming back into the fold. Trying to rebuild bridges? Was it possible that could even extend to taking an interest in Dr Ella Lockwood, the daughter of family friends and the woman who everyone had once expected Zac to marry? Though he'd noticed Ella hadn't seemed too pleased to learn that Zac was joining the team, so maybe not. But whatever happened, he hoped his youngest brother would find the happiness he deserved.

Yes. Charles slipped the ring box into his pocket. Even if Zac wasn't ready to accept it yet, he would know that it would be waiting for him.

He'd have a word with Elijah, first, of course. And then Zac. Maybe with his parents as well. If he could handle it all diplomatically, it could actually be a focus for this evening that would bring them all a little closer together and distract them from directing any attention on his own life. It would also be a symbol that he was moving on from his past, too. For himself as much as his family.

Yes. This felt like the next step in dealing with this unexpected intrusion into their lives. And maybe it would help settle the confusing boundaries between his responsibilities and his desires. Between the determination to protect everyone he had cared about in his life so far and the longing to just be somewhere alone with the new person in his life that he also wanted to protect?

Grace heard the knock on her door.

But what could she do? Her father had just answered her Skype call and he was so delighted to see her.

If there'd been a second knock, she might have excused herself for a moment but, after a single bark, Houston came and settled himself with his head on her feet. There was obviously no one on the other side of the door now. Maybe it had been someone else who lived in this apartment block. After all, Charles had had an entire day in which he could have called or texted her. Or he could have found her at work this afternoon because she'd certainly hung around long enough.

And he hadn't.

History was clearly repeating itself.

She had offered him everything she had to give and he had accepted it and then simply walked away without a backward glance.

'Sorry—what was that, Dad?'

'Just saying we hit the national high again today. Blue skies and sunshine here in Florida. How's it looking in the big smoke?'

'Grey. And freezing. They're predicting snow tomorrow. It could be heavy.'

Her father laughed. 'We have hospitals in this neck of the woods, you know. You don't have to suffer!'

'Maybe I'll see what's being advertised.'

The comment was light-hearted but, as they chatted about other things, the thought stayed in the back of her mind.

She could walk away from New York, couldn't she? She didn't *have* to stay here and feel…rejected…

Grace had to swallow a sudden lump in her throat. 'I feel a long way away at the moment. I miss you, Dad.'

'Miss you, too, honey.' Her father's smile wobbled a bit. 'So tell me, what are you doing for Thanksgiving dinner? Have you got yourself some turkey?'

'No. Work's been really busy and, anyway, it seemed a bit silly buying a turkey for one person.'

'I'll bet that dog you're living with could have helped you out there.'

Grace laughed but her brain was racing down another track. It couldn't have been Charles knocking at her door because wasn't he going to some big Davenport family dinner tonight? A dinner that he had suggested she could also go to but then he'd made a face as if the idea was distasteful.

Why? Did he not enjoy the family gathering himself or was it more the idea that she would hate it because she wouldn't fit in?

Of course she wouldn't. As Helena had reminded her so recently, the Davenports were New York royalty and she wasn't even American by birth. She was a foreigner. A divorced foreigner. A divorced foreigner with a scarred body who wasn't even capable of becoming a mother.

Oh, help… Going down this track any further when she had a night alone stretching out in front of her was a very bad idea.

'Have you got some wine to go with your turkey, Dad?'

'Of course. A very nice Australian chardonnay.'

'Well… I've got something in the fridge. Prosecco, I think. Why don't we both have a glass together and we can tap the screen and say cheers.' It was hard to summon up a cheerful smile but Grace gave it her best shot.

She could deal with this.

She had, in fact, just had a very good idea of exactly how she could deal with it. When she had finished this call with her dad, and had had a glass or two of wine, she was going to do something very proactive.

It was ironic that it had been Charles who'd pointed out how far she had come from being someone vulnerable enough to be easily crushed. How strong she was now.

Ironic because she was going to write her resignation letter from Manhattan Mercy. And, tomorrow, as soon as she started her shift, it would be Charles Davenport's desk that she would put that letter on.

Chapter 10

'Thanks ever so much for coming home, Dr Davenport.'

'It's no problem, Maria. You need to get to this appointment for the final check on that back of yours. I hope you won't need the brace any more after this.'

'I shouldn't be more than a couple of hours. I'll text you if there's any hold-up.'

'Don't worry about it. I've got more than enough work that I can do from home.'

His nanny nodded, wrapping a thick scarf around her neck. 'The boys are happy. They're busy drawing pictures at the moment.'

A glance into the living area showed a coffee table covered with sheets of paper and scattered crayons. Two tousled heads were bent as the twins focused on their masterpieces. Charles stayed where he was for a moment, pulling his phone from his pocket and hitting a rapid-dial key.

'Emergency Room.'

Charles recognised the voice of one of the staff members who managed the phone system and incoming radio calls.

'Hi, Sharon. Charles Davenport here. I'm working from home for a few hours.'

'Yes, we're aware of that, Dr Davenport. Did you want to speak to the other Dr Davenport?'

'No. I actually wanted to speak to Dr Forbes. Is she available at the moment?'

'Hang on, I'll check.'

Charles could hear the busy sounds of the department through the line but it sounded a little calmer than it had been earlier today. When he'd gone to his office to collect his briefcase after the latest meeting, there'd been security personnel and police officers there but Elijah had assured him that everything was under control and he was free to take the time he needed away.

Right now, the voices close by were probably doctors checking lab results or X-rays on the computers. Would one of them be Grace, by any chance?

He hadn't seen her when he'd been in at work earlier and this was getting ridiculous. It was well into the second day after their night together and they hadn't even spoken. His intention to protect everyone he cared about by ignoring the potential for public scrutiny on his private life had been so strong, it was only now that it was beginning to feel like something was very wrong.

No. Make that more than 'feel'. He knew that he was in trouble.

He'd met the Australian dog walker, Kylie, in the foyer on his way in, minutes ago. The one that looked after Houston when Grace was at work.

She'd introduced herself. Because, she explained, she might be in residence for a while—if Grace left before Houston's owners were due to return.

But Stefan and Jerome had been planning to come back in less than a couple of weeks as far as Charles was aware.

Why would Grace be thinking of leaving before then?

It had only been just over a day since he'd seen her. How could something that huge have changed so much in such a short space of time?

He needed to speak to her. To apologise for not having spoken to her yesterday. At the very least, he had to arrange a time when they could talk. To find out what was going on.

To repair any damage he had the horrible feeling he might be responsible for? He'd tried so hard to do things perfectly this time—to think through each step logically so that he could avoid making a mistake.

But he'd missed something. Something that was seeming increasingly important.

Sharon was back on the line.

'Sorry, Dr Davenport. Dr Forbes is in CT at the moment. We had a head injury patient earlier who was extremely combative. We had to call Security in to help restrain him while he got sedated and intubated.'

'Yes, I saw them there when I was leaving.'

'He was Dr Forbes's patient. She's gone with him to CT and may have to stay with him if he needs to go to Theatre so I have no idea how long she'll be. Do you want me to page her to call you back when she can?'

'Daddy... *Daddy*...' Cameron was tugging on his arm, a sheet of paper in his other hand. 'Look at *this*.'

'No, thanks, Sharon. She's busy enough, by the sound of things. I'll catch up with her later.'

He ended the call. Was he kidding himself? He'd been trying to 'catch up' with her from the moment he'd arrived at work yesterday and it hadn't happened. And suddenly he felt like he was chasing something that was rapidly disappearing into the distance.

'Daddy? What's the matter?'

The concern in Max's voice snapped Charles back to where he was. He crouched down as Max joined his brother.

'Nothing's the matter, buddy.'

'But you look sad.'

'No-o-o…' Charles ruffled the heads of both his boys. 'How could I be sad when I get to spend some extra time with you guys? Hey…did you really draw that picture all by yourself?' He reached out for the paper to admire the artwork more closely but, to his surprise, Max shook his head and stepped back.

'It's for Gace,' he said solemnly.

'So's mine,' Cameron said. 'But you can look.'

The colourful scribbles were getting more recognisable these days. A stick figure person with a huge, crooked smile. And another one with too many legs.

'It's Gace. And Horse.'

'Aww…she'll love them. You know what?'

'What?'

'I'll bet she puts them in a frame and puts them on her wall.'

The boys beamed at him but then Max's smile wobbled.

'And then she'll come back?'

Why hadn't it occurred to him how much the twins

were already missing Grace? How much they loved her as well as Horse. He hadn't factored that in when he'd chosen to distance himself enough to keep his family temporarily out of the spotlight, had he? When he'd left her text unanswered and had told that journalist that they were nothing more than friends.

And never would be.

How many people had overheard that comment? Passed it on, even?

Could *that* have been enough to persuade Grace that she didn't want to be in New York any more?

The sinking sensation that had begun with that chance meeting with Kylie gained momentum and crashed into the pit of Charles's stomach but he smiled reassuringly and nodded.

It was tantamount to a promise, that smile and nod. A promise that Grace would be back. Now he just had to find a way to make sure he didn't let his boys down.

'You guys hungry? Want some cookies and milk? And *Curious George* on TV?'

'*Yes!*'

At least three-year-old boys were easily distracted.

Or maybe not.

'*Spider* cookies,' Cameron shouted. 'They're the best-est.'

'I think we've run out of spider cookies,' he apologised.

'That's okay, Daddy.' Max patted his arm. 'I'll tell Gace and we'll help her make some more.'

He had to sit down with the boys and supervise the milk drinking but Charles wasn't taking any notice of the monkey's antics on the screen that were sending the twins into fits of giggles.

His mind was somewhere else entirely, carried away by the echo of his son's words. The tone of his voice.

That confidence that everything would be put to rights when he'd had the chance to explain what was wrong to Grace.

It hadn't even occurred to either of his boys to suggest that *he* make them some more homemade cookies. It might be only a superficial example but it symbolised all those things a mother could do that perhaps he couldn't even recognise as being missing from their lives.

And that longing in Max's voice.

And then she'll come back?

It touched something very deep inside Charles. Opened the door he'd shut in his head and heart that was a space that was filled with the same longing. Not just for a woman in his life or for sex. That need was there, of course, but this longing—it was for Grace.

He had to do a whole lot more than simply apologise for leaving her text unanswered when he spoke to her. He had to make her understand how important she'd become to his boys. How much they loved her.

And…and he had to tell her that he felt the same way.

That *he* loved her.

That the idea of life without her had become something unthinkable.

There was a painful lump in his throat that he tried to clear away but that only made Max look up at him with those big, blue eyes that could often see so much more than you'd expect a small boy to see.

'You happy, Daddy?'

'Sure am, buddy.' Man, it was hard work to sound as though he meant it. 'You finished with that milk?'

He took the empty cups back to the kitchen. He

glanced at his phone lying on the table beside his laptop on his return.

Was it worth trying to find out if Grace was available?

There was a sense of urgency about this now. What if she really was planning to leave? What if she was actually planning to leave New York? Surely she wouldn't do that without telling him?

But why would she?

He hadn't spoken to her since they'd spent the night together. He hadn't even answered her text message.

Okay, stuff had happened and events had conspired to prevent him seeing her the way he'd assumed he'd be able to, but the truth was there was no excuse for what the combination of things had produced. Without any intention of doing so, he had allowed history to repeat itself. He'd made love to Grace and then seemingly ignored her. Pushed her out of his life because something else had seemed more important.

So why wouldn't she just walk away?

He'd thought he was protecting her by not giving any journalists a reason to pry into her life when there were things that he knew she would prefer to keep very private.

Those same things that had made her so vulnerable to allowing herself to get close to another man.

Why had he assumed that she needed his protection anyway? As he'd reminded her himself, she was a strong, courageous woman and she had dealt with far worse things in her life than the threat of having her privacy invaded.

She had been courageous enough to take the risk of letting *him* that close.

And somehow—albeit unintentionally—he'd repeated the same mistake he'd made the first time.

He'd made everything worse.

He hadn't even been protecting his boys in one sense, either. He'd created the risk of them losing someone they loved. Someone they needed in their lives.

Charles rubbed the back of his neck, lifting his gaze as he tried to fight his way through this mess in his head. The view from the massive windows caught his attention for a blessed moment of distraction. It was beginning to snow heavily. Huge, fat flakes were drifting down, misting the view of the Manhattan skyline and Central Park.

Charles loved snow. He'd never quite lost that childish excitement of seeing it fall or waking up to find his world transformed by the soft, white blanket of a thick covering. But there wasn't even a spark of that excitement right now. All he could feel was that lump-inducing longing. A bone-deep need to be close to Grace.

He'd never thought he'd ever feel like this again. He'd never wanted to after Nina had died because the grief had been crippling and he never wanted to face another loss like that. He didn't want his boys to have to face that kind of loss, either.

But it had happened. He had fallen in love. Maybe it had always been there, in an enforced hibernation after that first night they'd been together, thanks to the life events that had happened afterwards.

And here he was, possibly facing the loss of this love and, in a way, it would be worse than losing Nina because Grace would still be alive. If she wasn't actually planning on leaving Manhattan Mercy, and was only thinking of finding a new place to live, he'd see her at work and see that smile and hear her voice and know that being together could have been possible if he'd done things differently.

There had to be some way he could fix this.

If Grace had feelings for him that were anything like as powerful as the ones he had finally recognised, surely there was a way to put things right.

But how?

A phone call couldn't do it.

Even a conversation might not be enough.

Charles took a deep inward breath and then let it out very slowly as he watched the flakes continuing to fall. This was no passing shower. This snow would settle. Maybe not for long. It would probably be slush by the morning if the temperature lifted but for the next few hours at least it would look like a different world out there.

A world that Grace had been so eager to see.

An echo of her voice whispered in his mind.

'It's always been my dream for Christmas. A sleigh ride in a snowy park. At night, when there's sparkly lights everywhere and there are bells on the horses and you have to be all wrapped up in soft blankets.'

He could have given her that. But how likely was it to be possible now? Christmas was weeks away and maybe she wouldn't even be here.

He needed a small miracle.

And as he stood there, watching the snow fall, Charles became aware of the spark that had been missing. Excitement about the snow?

Maybe.

Or maybe it was just hope.

The letter was still in her pocket.

Grace could feel it crinkle as she sat down on the chair beside her elderly patient's bed.

She could have gone in and put it on Charles Davenport's desk first thing this morning but she hadn't.

Because he'd been in the office. Sitting at his desk, his head bent, clearly focused on the paperwork in front of him. And it had been just too hard to know what it would be like to meet his eyes. To explain what was in the sealed envelope in her hands. To have the conversation that might have suggested they were both adults and surely they could continue working together. To be friends, even?

Nope. She didn't think she could do that. Okay, maybe it was cowardly to leave a letter and run away. She was going to have to work out her notice and that meant that they would be working in the same space for the next couple of weeks but she would cope with that the same way she was going to cope today. By immersing herself in her work to the exclusion of absolutely everything else.

And fate seemed set to help her do exactly that, by providing an endless stream of patients that needed her complete focus.

Like the guy this morning. A victim of assault but it was highly likely he'd started the fight himself. The huge and very aggressive man had presented a danger to all staff involved with his care, despite the presence of the police escort who'd brought him in. Security had had to be called and it had been a real challenge to sedate this patient and get him on a ventilator. Due to his size, the drugs needed to keep him sedated were at a high level and Grace had needed to monitor their effects very closely. Knowing what could happen if his levels dropped meant that she'd had to stay with him while he went to CT and then to Theatre so the case had taken up a good part of her morning.

Charles was nowhere to be seen when she was back in the ER but, even if he had been there, she could have kept herself almost invisible behind the curtains of various cubicles or the resuscitation areas. Patient after patient came under her care. A man with a broken finger who'd needed a nerve block before it could be realigned and splinted. A stroke victim. Two heart attacks. A woman who'd slipped on the snow that was apparently starting to fall outside and had a compound tib and fib fracture and no circulation in her foot.

And now she was in a side room with a very elderly woman called Mary who had been brought in a couple of hours ago in severe respiratory distress from an advanced case of pneumonia. Mary was eighty-six years old and had adamantly refused to have any treatment other than something to make her more comfortable.

'It's my time,' she'd told Grace quietly. 'I don't want to fight any more.'

Grace had called up her patient's notes. Mary had had a double mastectomy for breast cancer more than thirty years ago and only a few weeks back she had been diagnosed with ovarian cancer. She had refused treatment then as well. While it was difficult, as a doctor, to stand by and not provide treatment that could help, like antibiotics, it was Mary's right to make this decision and her reasoning was understandable. Very much of sound mind, she had smiled very sweetly at Grace and squeezed her hand.

'You're a darling to be so concerned but please don't worry. I'm not afraid.'

'Do you have any family we can call? Or close friends?'

'There was only ever my Billy. And he's waiting for me. He's been waiting a long time now...'

Helena had been concerned that Grace was caring for this patient.

'I can take her,' she said. 'I know how hard this must be for you. Your mum died of ovarian cancer, didn't she?'

Grace nodded, swallowing past the constriction in her throat. 'I sat with her at the end, too. Right now it feels like it was yesterday.'

'Which is why you should step back, maybe. We'll make her as comfortable as possible in one of the private rooms out the back. It could take a while, you know. I'll find a nurse to sit with her so she won't be alone.'

'She knows me now. And I don't care how long it takes, as long as you can cope without me in here?'

'Of course. But—'

'It's because of my mum that I'm the right person to do this,' Grace said softly. 'Because of how real it feels for me. I want to do this for Mary. I want her to know that she's with someone who really cares.'

So, here they were. In one of the rooms she had noticed on her very first day here when she had wondered what they might be used for. It might even be the room next door to the one that she had stayed in with the twins and fixed Max's fire truck but this one had a bed with a comfortable air mattress. It was warm and softly lit. There was an oxygen port that was providing a little comfort to ease how difficult it was for Mary to breathe and there was a trolley that contained the drugs Grace might need to keep her from any undue distress. The morphine had taken away her pain and made her drowsy but they had talked off and on for the last hour and Grace knew that her husband Billy had died suddenly ten years ago.

'I'm so glad he didn't know about this new cancer,'

Mary whispered. 'He would have been so upset. He was so good to me the first time…'

She knew that they had met seventy years ago at a summer event in Central Park.

'People say that there's no such thing as true love at first sight. But we knew different, Billy and me…'

She knew that they'd never had children.

'We never got blessed like that. It wasn't so hard…we had each other and that was enough…'

In the last half an hour Mary had stopped talking and her breathing had become shallow and rapid. Grace knew that she was still aware of her surroundings, however, because every so often she would feel a gentle squeeze from the hand her own fingers were curled around.

And finally that laboured breathing hitched and then stopped and Mary slipped away so quietly and peacefully that Grace simply sat there, still holding her hand, for the longest time.

It didn't matter now that she had tears rolling down her cheeks. She wasn't sad, exactly. Mary had believed that she was about to be reunited with her love and she had welcomed the release from any more suffering. She hadn't died alone, either. She had been grateful for Grace's company. For a hand to hold.

And she'd been lucky, hadn't she?

She had known true love. Had loved and been loved in equal measure.

Or maybe she *was* sad.

Not for Mary, but for herself.

Grace had come so close to finding that sort of love for herself—or she'd thought she had. But now, it seemed as far away as ever. As if she was standing on the other side of a plate-glass window, looking in at a scene that she couldn't be a part of.

A perfect scene.

A Christmas one, perhaps. With pretty lights on a tree and parcels tied up with bows underneath. A fire in a grate beneath a mantelpiece that had colourful stockings hanging from it. There were people in that scene, too. A tall man with dark hair and piercing blue eyes. Two little mop-topped, happy boys. And a big, curly, adorable dog.

It took a while to get those overwhelming emotions under control but the company of this brave old woman who had unexpectedly appeared in her life helped, so by the time Grace alerted others of Mary's death, nobody would have guessed how much it had affected her. They probably just thought she looked very tired and who wouldn't, after such a long day?

It took a while after that to do what was necessary after a death of a patient and it was past time for Grace's shift to finish by the time she bundled herself up in her warm coat and scarf and gloves, ready for her walk home.

She walked out of the ER via the ambulance bay and found that it had been snowing far more than she'd been told about. A soft blanket of whiteness had cloaked everything and the world had that muted sound that came with snow when even the traffic was almost silent. And it was cold. Despite her gloves, Grace could feel her fingers tingling so she shoved her hands in her pockets and that was when she felt the crinkle of that envelope again.

Thanks to her time with Mary, she had completely forgotten to put it on Charles's desk.

Perhaps that was a good thing?

Running away from something because it was difficult wasn't the kind of person she was now.

Charles had told her how courageous she was. He had made her believe it and that belief had been enough to push her into risking her heart again.

And that had to be a good thing, too.

Even if it didn't feel like it right now.

She had almost reached the street now where the lamps were casting a circle of light amidst a swirl of snowflakes but she turned back, hesitating.

She hadn't even looked in the direction of Charles's office when she'd left. Maybe he was still there?

Maybe the kind of person she was now would actually go back and talk about this. Take the risk of making herself even more vulnerable?

And that was when she heard it.

Someone calling her name.

No. It was a jingle of bells. She had just imagined hearing her name.

She turned back to the road and any need to make a decision on what direction she was about to take evaporated.

There was a sleigh just outside the ambulance entrance to Manhattan Mercy.

A bright red sleigh, with swirling gold patterns on its sides and a canopy that was rimmed with fairy lights. A single white horse was in front, its red harness covered with small bells and, on its head—instead of the usual feathery plume—it had a set of reindeer antlers.

A driver sat in the front, a dark shape in a heavy black coat and scarf and top hat. But, in the back, there was someone else.

Charles…

'Grace…?'

Her legs were taking her forward without any instruction from her brain.

She was too stunned to be thinking of anything, in fact. Other than that Charles was here.

In a *sleigh*?

Maybe she'd got that image behind the plate-glass window a little wrong earlier.

Maybe *this* was the magic place she hadn't been able to reach.

Just Charles. In a sleigh. In the snow.

And he was holding out his hand now, to invite her to join him under the canopy at the back. Waiting to help her reach that place.

Grace was still too stunned to be aware of any coherent thoughts but her body seemed to know what to do and she found herself reaching up to take that hand.

She had been on the point of summoning the courage to go and find Charles even if it meant stepping into the most vulnerable space she could imagine.

Here she was, literally stepping into that space.

And it hadn't taken as much courage as she'd expected.

Because it felt…right…

Because it was Charles who was reaching out to her and there was no way on earth she could have turned away.

Chapter 11

Heart-wrenching…

That look on Grace's face when she'd seen him waiting for her in the sleigh.

He'd expected her to be surprised, of course. The sleigh might not be genuine but the sides had been cleverly designed to cover most of the wheels so it not only looked the part but was a pretty unusual sight on a New York street. Along with the bells and fairy lights and the reindeer antlers on the horse, he had already been a target for every phone or camera that people had been able to produce.

For once, he didn't mind the attention. Bundled up in his thick coat and scarf, with a hat pulled well down over his head, Charles Davenport was unrecognisable but the worry about publicity was a million miles from his mind, anyway. The sight of this spectacle—that had taken him most of the day to organise—didn't just make people want to capture the image. It was delighting them, making them point and wave. To smile and laugh.

But Grace hadn't smiled when she saw him.

She'd looked shocked.

Scared, almost?

So, so vulnerable that Charles knew in that instant just how much damage his silence had caused.

And how vital it was to fix it.

The sheer relief when Grace had accepted his hand to climb up into the carriage had been so overwhelming that perhaps he couldn't blame the biting cold for making his eyes water. Or for making it too hard to say anything just yet. How much courage had it taken for her to accept his hand?

He loved her for that courage. And for everything else he knew to be true about her.

And nothing needed to be said just yet. For now, it was too important to make sure that Grace was going to be warm enough. To pull one faux fur blanket after another from the pile at his feet, to wrap them both in a soft cocoon. A single cocoon, so that as soon as he was satisfied there was no danger of hypothermia, he could wrap his arms around Grace beneath these blankets and simply hold her close.

Extra protection from the cold?

No. This was about protecting what he knew was the most important thing in his life at this moment. Grace. So important in his boys' lives as well. The only thing he wasn't sure of yet was how important it might be in her life.

The steady, rocking motion of the carriage was like a slow heartbeat that made him acutely aware of every curve in the body of the woman he was holding and, as the driver finished negotiating traffic and turned into the lamplit, almost deserted paths of Central Park, he could feel the tension in Grace's body begin to lessen. It was under the halo of one of those antique streetlamps that Grace finally raised her head to meet his gaze and he could see that the shock had worn off.

There was something else in her gaze now.

Hope?

That wouldn't be there, would it? Unless this was just as important to her as it was to him?

Again, the rush of emotion made it impossible to find any words.

Instead, Charles bent his head and touched Grace's lips gently with his own. Her lips parted beneath his and he felt the astonishing warmth of her mouth. Of her breath.

A breath of life…

Maybe he still didn't need to say anything yet. Or maybe he could say it another way…

For the longest time, Grace's brain had been stunned into immobility. She was aware of what was around her but couldn't begin to understand what any of it meant.

Her senses were oddly heightened. The softness of the furry blankets felt like she was being wrapped inside a cloud. The motion of the carriage was like being rocked in someone's arms. And then she *was* in someone's arms. Charles's. Grace didn't want to think about what this meant. She just wanted to feel it. This sense of being in the one place in the world she most wanted to be. This feeling of being protected.

Precious…

Finally, she had to raise her head. To check whether

this was real. Had she slipped in the snow and knocked herself out cold, perhaps? Was this dream-come-to-life no more than an elaborate creation of her subconscious?

If it was, it couldn't have conjured up a more compelling expression in the eyes of the man she loved.

It was a gaze that told her she was the only thing in the world that mattered right now.

That she was loved…

And then his lips touched her own and Grace could feel how cold they were, which only intensified the heat that was coming from inside his body. From his breath. From the touch of his tongue.

She wasn't unconscious.

Grace had never felt more alive in her life.

It was the longest, most tender kiss she had ever experienced. A whole conversation in itself.

An apology from Charles, definitely. A declaration of love, even.

And on her part? A statement that the agony of his silence and distance since they'd last been together didn't matter, perhaps. That she forgave him. That nothing mattered other than being together, like this.

They had to come up for air eventually, however, and the magic of the kiss retreated.

Actions might speak a whole lot louder than words, but words were important, too.

Charles was the first to use some.

'I'm so sorry,' he said. 'It's been crazy…but when Kylie told me this morning that you were thinking of leaving, I got enough of a shock to realise just how much I'd messed this up.'

'You didn't even answer my text message,' Grace

whispered, her voice cracking. 'The morning after we'd… we'd…'

'I know. I'm sorry. I woke up that morning and realised how I felt about you and…and it was huge. My head was all over the place and then my mother rang. She'd seen something in the paper that suggested we were a couple. That photo of us all in the park.'

Grace nodded. 'Helena showed it to me. She said that there'd been a reporter in the department pretending to be a patient. That you'd told her we were just colleagues. Friends. That it would never be anything more than that.'

She looked away from Charles. A long, pristine stretch of the wide pathway lay ahead of them, the string of lamps shining to illuminate the bare, snow-laden branches of the huge, old trees guarding this passage. The snow was still falling but it was gentle now. Slow enough to be seen as separate stars beneath the glow of the lamps.

'I'd thought I would be able to find you as soon as I got to work. That I could warn you of the media interest. I thought…that I was protecting you from having your privacy invaded by putting them off the scent. And…and it didn't seem that long. It was only a day…'

Grace squeezed her eyes shut. 'It felt like a month…'

'I'm sorry…'

The silence continued on and then she heard Charles take a deep breath.

'I can't believe I made the same mistake. For the same reasons.'

'It's who you are, Charles.' Grace opened her eyes but she didn't turn to meet his gaze. 'You're always going to try and protect your family above everything else.'

She was looking at the fountain they were approaching. She'd seen it in the daytime—an angel with one hand held out over a pond. The angel looked weighed down now, her wings encrusted with a thick layer of snow.

Their carriage driver was doing a slow circuit around the fountain. Grace felt Charles shift slightly and looked up to see him staring at the angel.

'She's the Angel of the Waters, did you know that?'

'No.'

'The statue was commissioned to commemorate the first fresh water system for New York. It came after a cholera outbreak. She's blessing the water, to give it healing powers.'

He turned to meet her gaze directly and there was something very serious in his own. A plea, almost.

For healing?

'I do understand,' Grace said softly. 'And I don't blame you for ignoring me that first time. But it hurt, you know? I really didn't think you would do it again…'

'I didn't realise I was. I went into the pattern that I'd learned back then, to focus on protecting the people that mattered. My mother was upset. It was Thanksgiving and the family was gathering. The worst thing that could happen was to have everything out there and being raked up all over again.'

Grace was silent. Confused. He had gone to goodness only knew how much trouble to create this dream sleigh ride for her and he'd kissed her as if she was the only person who mattered. And yet he had made that same mistake. Maybe it hadn't seemed like very much time to him but it had felt like an eternity to her.

'What I said to that reporter was intended to protect you, Grace, as much as to try and keep the spotlight off my family. I had the feeling that you never talk about what you've been through. That maybe I was the only person who knew your story. I didn't want someone digging through your past and making something private public. You'd told me that that was the worst thing you could imagine happening. Especially something that was perhaps private between just *us*—that made it even more important to protect.'

He sighed as the carriage turned away from the fountain and continued its journey.

'I needed to talk to you somewhere private and it just wasn't happening. I couldn't get near you at work. There was the family Thanksgiving dinner and I was running late. I knocked on your door but you weren't home.'

'I was Skyping my dad. I couldn't answer the door.' And she could have made it easier for him, couldn't she? If she'd only had a little more confidence. She could have texted him again. Or made an effort to find him at work instead of waiting for him to come and find her.

He hadn't been put off by her scarred body. He'd been trying to protect her from others finding out about it. It made it a secret. One that didn't matter but was just between them. A private bond.

'I know that you don't actually need my protection,' Charles said slowly. 'That you're strong enough to survive anything on your own, but there's a part of me that would like you to need it, I guess. Because I want to be able to give it to you.'

They were passing the carousel now, the brightly coloured horses rising and falling under bright lights. There were children riding the horses and they could hear shrieks of glee.

'The boys are missing you,' Charles added quietly. 'They were drawing pictures for you this morning and

I said that you'd love them and probably put them in a frame and Max said…he asked if you'd come back then.'

'Oh…' Grace had a huge lump in her throat.

'We need you, Grace. The boys need you. *I* need you.'

He took his hands from beneath the warmth of the blankets to cradle her face between them.

'I love you, Grace Forbes. I think I always have…

The lump was painful to swallow. It was too hard to find more than a single word.

'Same…'

'You were right in what you said—I will always protect my family above everything else. But you're part of my family now. The part we need the most.'

They didn't notice they had left the carousel behind them as they sank into another slow, heartbreakingly tender kiss.

When Grace opened her eyes again, she found they were going past the Wollman skating rink. Dozens of people were on the ice, with the lights of the Manhattan skyline a dramatic backdrop.

'I thought I had to ignore how I felt in order to protect the people around me,' Charles told her. 'But now I know how wrong I was.'

He kissed her again.

'I want everybody to know how much I love you. And I'm going to protect that love before everything else because that's what's going to keep us all safe. You. Me. The boys…' He caught Grace's hand in his own and brought it up to his lips. 'I can't go down on one knee, and I don't have a ring because I'd want you to choose what's perfect just for you, but…will you let me love you and protect you for the rest of our lives—even if you don't need it and even if I don't get it quite right sometimes? Will you…will you marry me, Grace?

'Yes…' The word came out in no more than a whisper but it felt like the loudest thing Grace had ever said in her life.

This sleigh ride might have been a dream come true but it was nothing more than a stage set for her *real* dream. One that she'd thought she'd lost for ever. To love and be loved in equal measure.

To have her own family…

She had to blink back the sudden tears that filled her eyes. Had to clear away the lump in her throat so that she could be sure that Charles could hear her.

'Yes,' she said firmly, a huge smile starting to spread over her face. 'Yes and yes and *yes*…'

Epilogue

It was a twenty-minute walk from the apartment block to the Rockefeller Center but the two small boys weren't complaining about the distance. It was too exciting to be walking through the park in the dark of the evening and besides, if they weren't having a turn riding on Daddy's shoulders, they got to hold hands with Grace.

'Look, Daddy…look, Gace…' It was Max's turn to be carried high on his father's shoulders. 'What are they doing?'

'Ice skating,' Charles told him. 'Would you like to try it one day soon?'

'Is Gace coming, too?'

'Yes.' Grace grinned up at the little boy, her heart swelling with love. One day maybe he would call her 'Mummy' but it really didn't matter.

'Of course she is,' Charles said. 'Remember what we

talked about? Grace and I are going to be married. Very soon. Before Christmas, even. We're a family now.'

'And Gace is going to be our *mummy*,' Cameron shouted.

Max bounced on Charles's shoulders as a signal to be put down. 'I want to hold my mummy's hand,' he said.

'She's *my* mummy, too.' Cameron glared at his brother.

'Hey… I've got two hands. One each.' Grace caught Charles's gaze over the heads of the boys and the look in his eyes melted her heart.

Mummy.

It *did* matter.

Not the name. The feeling. Feeling like the bond between all of them was unbreakable.

Family.

A branch of the Davenport family of New York— something which she still hadn't got used to—but their own unique unit within that dynasty.

Charles had shown her the Davenport ring last week, after that magical sleigh ride in the park.

'I've told Zac it's waiting for him, if he ever gets round to needing it. It belongs to the past and, even before you agreed to marry me, I knew it wouldn't suit you.'

'Because it's so flashy?'

'Because it represents everything that is window dressing in life, not the really important stuff.'

'Like love?'

'Like love. Like what's beneath any kind of window dressing.'

He'd touched her body then. A gentle reminder that what her clothes covered was real. Not something to be ashamed of but a symbol of struggle and triumph. Something to be proud of.

So she had chosen a ring that could have also made its way through struggle and triumph already. An antique ring with a simple, small diamond.

'We're almost there, guys.' Charles was leading them through the increasingly dense crowds on the Manhattan streets. 'Let's find somewhere we'll be able to see.'

Grace could hear the music now. And smell hotdogs and popcorn from street stalls. People around them were wearing Santa hats with flashing stars and reindeer antlers that made her remember the horse that had pulled her sleigh so recently on the night that had changed her life for ever.

They couldn't get very close to the Rockefeller Center in midtown Manhattan but it didn't matter because the huge tree towered above the crowds and the live music was loud enough to be heard for miles. Charles lifted Cameron to his shoulders and Grace picked up Max to rest him on her hip. He wrapped his arms around her neck and planted a kiss on her cheek.

'I love you, Mummy.'

'I love you, too, Max,' she whispered back.

A new performance was starting. If it wasn't Mariah Carey singing, it was someone who sounded exactly like her. And it was *her* song: 'All I Want for Christmas Is You'.

Grace leaned back against the man standing protectively so close behind her. She turned her head and smiled up at him.

'That's so true,' she told him. 'It's now officially my favourite Christmas song, ever.'

'Mine, too.'

When the song finished, the countdown started and

when the countdown finished, the magnificent tree with its gorgeous crystal star on the top blazed into life.

The Christmas season had officially begun.

And Grace had all she had ever wanted. All she would ever want.

The tender kiss that Charles bent to place on her lips right then made it clear that they both did.

* * * * *

USA TODAY bestselling author **Karen Rose Smith** has written over ninety novels. Her passion is caring for her four rescued cats, and her hobbies are gardening, cooking and photography. An only child, Karen delved into books at an early age. Even though she escaped into story worlds, she had many cousins around her on weekends. Families are a strong theme in her novels. Find out more about Karen at karenrosesmith.com.

Books by Karen Rose Smith

Harlequin Special Edition

The Montana Mavericks: The Great Family Roundup

The Maverick's Snowbound Christmas

Fortunes of Texas: All Fortune's Children

Fortune's Secret Husband

The Mommy Club

The Cowboy's Secret Baby
A Match Made by Baby
Wanted: A Real Family

Reunion Brides

Riley's Baby Boy
The CEO'S Unexpected Proposal
Once Upon a Groom
His Daughter...Their Child

Visit the Author Profile page at Harlequin.com for more titles.

Twins Under His Tree

KAREN ROSE SMITH

To my father-in-law, Edgar S. Smith, who served in World War II in Patton's army. We miss you.

For all servicemen who strive to keep us safe.

Thanks to Captain Jay Ostrich, Pennsylvania National Guard, who so readily and patiently answered my questions. I couldn't have developed my hero's character so deeply without his input.

Chapter 1

Late February

Dr. Lily Wescott stood at the podium, peering through the spotlight into the sea of faces in the hotel ballroom. Many grinned and waved as she prepared to accept the Medical Professional Woman of the Year Award.

She brushed tears away, stunned and totally overwhelmed. These days, she blamed the rise and fall of her emotions on her pregnancy, though memories of the husband she'd lost in Afghanistan were never far from her heart.

Suddenly an odd sensation gripped her back and a cramp rippled through her stomach. As best she could, she fought to keep her shoulders back and a smile on her face. She couldn't go into labor now! She was only at thirty-three weeks.

But she was an ob/gyn—and she knew all too well that her twins would come when *they* were ready. Lily could only hope for the best....

"Thank you," she said into the microphone. "I never imagined I'd win this award." She'd really expected one of her friends at the table to win. After all, they were all baby experts at the Family Tree Health Center in Lubbock, Texas. She went on, "At the Family Tree Fertility Center, we strive to help women who—"

A second cramp squeezed Lily's side and she caught the wooden podium for support. Out of the corner of her eye, she saw her friend and colleague, Dr. Mitch Catega, jump to his feet, concern on his face. He rushed to the stage and up the steps.

As she managed to suck in a gulp of air, hot liquid washed down her leg. *Oh, God—I am in labor!*

She was *not* going to panic. She was *not* going to crumple to the floor. She was *not* going to be embarrassed.

At her side now, Mitch's arm curled around her waist...his injured arm. *The one he never let anyone see,* she thought, needing something other than the pain to concentrate on. His arm was always covered, tonight by a well-cut black tuxedo that made his shoulders seem even broader than usual. She'd noticed that tonight...and it wasn't the first time...

"Can you walk?" he asked, his breath warm at her ear.

A murmur swept through the audience.

She turned, the side of her cheek brushing his chin. "I'm not sure."

Mitch's angular jaw tightened, his almost-black gaze held hers with...something she couldn't define. But then it was replaced by the empathy and compassion she'd felt from him many times before. "The twins are our main priority. Hold on to me if you can't stand on your own."

She really thought she could. The cramp faded away. If it weren't for the wetness between her legs, she could deny what was happening.

With Mitch's arm still around her, she took a couple of steps. Maybe she could even give the rest of her acceptance speech—

The lance of pain that pierced her back stole her breath and weakened her knees. She exhaled, "Mitch…"

And he was there…lifting her into his arms…carrying her down the dais steps.

"I'm driving her to the hospital myself," Mitch said, as Lily's friends and colleagues rushed toward him. "It will be quicker than waiting for an ambulance."

"And more economical," Lily realized aloud, trying to think practically. But that was difficult with Mitch's cologne reminding her of the last time he'd held her so close on the day she'd discovered she was having twins. His grip felt safe now as it had then…as if no harm could come to her while she was in his arms.

She must be delusional.

"I'll ride with you," Jared Madison offered as he jogged alongside Mitch and pushed open the ballroom door. "I'll be handy if the twins won't wait, since Lily's doctor is at a conference."

Jared had his own obstetrical practice at Family Tree but took turns covering with the doctors in *her* practice. Lily knew and liked Jared and felt comfortable with him. Still, she murmured, "They'd darn well better wait. It's too early. They'll be too small!" Her last words almost caught in her throat and her bravado deflated.

In the middle of the hotel lobby, Mitch stopped. Looking her directly in the eye, he said, "If you panic, Lily, you won't help the babies. Take calming breaths. You can do this."

Her heart felt lighter, as if Mitch was really part of this pregnancy, too. Not just because her husband had asked him to watch over her but because he *cared*. "If I'd taken the childbirth classes this month instead of next—" She'd been putting them off, maybe trying to deny the inevitable—that yet again, her life would be altered in an earth-shattering way.

"The twins would still come early," he reminded her. "They apparently want to meet their mom *now*."

Yes, they did. And she wanted to meet *them*. She couldn't wait to hold them and tell them how much she loved them. How much their daddy would have loved them...

Mitch's expression was gentle, as if he could read her thoughts, but his gaze didn't waver. His arms were so strong. For a moment, she felt a little trill of excitement in her chest. But that was because of the babies—wasn't it?

"Let's go," she whispered, shaken by the emotions she didn't understand.

Mitch paced the maternity floor waiting room and stopped when he saw Lily's friends watching him peculiarly. He didn't like the worried expressions on their faces. Raina, Gina and Tessa were all baby experts. Along with them, he knew premature babies often had problems—thirty-three weeks was iffy.

Trying to loosen up the tight feeling in his shoulder, arm and hand—injuries that reminded him all too often of his service in Iraq—Mitch flexed them, then sank down on one of the vinyl chairs.

Moving forward on the sofa, Tessa said gently, "It really hasn't been that long."

What was worrying Mitch was that they hadn't heard anything in the hour they'd been here. Closing his eyes, he remembered the day Lily had learned she was having twins. It had been the week before Thanksgiving. One of the techs in the office had performed the ultrasound. Mitch had just finished discussing fertility procedure options with a couple. As his clients had headed for the reception area, he'd noticed Lily exit the exam room, her complexion almost sheet-white, her blue eyes very bright.

"The ultrasound go okay?" he'd asked.

"Oh, Mitch, I'm having *twins!*"

He hadn't been able to tell if she was totally elated or totally terrified.

Clasping her hand, he'd pulled her into the office he'd just vacated. "What's going through your head?"

She'd stood at the chair in front of his desk, holding on to it for support. "The obvious. I'll be a single mom. My friends all say they'll help, but these babies will be *my* responsibility."

"Twins will always have each other," he pointed out. "They won't grow up lonely. They'll be able to play together." He hoped Lily could see the upside of this monumental news. "Girls or boys?"

"They're girls."

"Our techs are pretty good at distinguishing the difference."

Lily had actually blushed a little. Until he'd met her, he didn't think women blushed anymore. But she was blonde with fair skin and all of her emotions seemed to show in her complexion. Major ones had played over her face over the past few months—grief, fear, determination and the sheer loss of her husband.

"Troy would be so proud," she'd said, tears beginning to run down her face.

That's when Mitch had done something he *never* should have done. He'd taken her into his arms. She'd laid her head on his shoulder, crying. And he'd felt desire that had no place in that room.

Mitch had met Troy—at that time Troy and Lily had been engaged—when the Family Tree staff had planned a dinner to welcome Mitch into the practice. Since he'd once served in the Army National Guard and Troy still had, they'd developed an immediate rapport, becoming friends. After Troy and Lily married, Troy had even asked Mitch to watch over Lily while he'd served overseas.

But then Troy had been killed in action, leaving Lily pregnant and alone.

When Lily had finally looked up at him, Mitch hadn't been sure *what* he'd seen there. Yet he'd known damn well it hadn't been interest. Gratitude, maybe?

She'd pulled away, wiped her eyes and mumbled an awkward apology, and they'd gone their separate ways. They'd gone back to being colleagues. She hadn't really confided in him again.

That was okay. Being merely colleagues was safer for both of them.

Now, however, it was the last week in February and she was in labor. When he'd seen her double over on that dais, he'd felt panic twist his gut.

"Mitch!" A male voice called his name.

When he opened his eyes, he saw Jared, gesturing from the hall.

He stood immediately. "What's going on?"

"She wants you."

"What do you mean, she wants me?"

"She's in labor, and she wants you to coach her."

Her friends all glanced his way. He knew they were wondering why and so was he. But he wasn't going to ask Jared his questions. He was going to ask Lily.

"Suit up," Jared advised him. "When you're ready, she's in delivery room two."

Five minutes later, Mitch had pulled sterile garb over his clothes. It would feel strange being back in an operating-room setting, even though he had to admit a delivery room wasn't *exactly* that. When he'd rushed through the ER with Lily, one of the nurses had waved at him. Years ago, she'd worked with him in trauma surgery.

Sometimes he itched to be doing that kind of work again. Reflexively, he bent his fingers, most of them not responding well. But he'd gotten used to limited use of his right hand, as well as insomnia and nightmares. At least the stiffness in his shoulder and leg could be relieved with the right amount of exercise. He was damn lucky he'd left Iraq with his life. There was no point in complaining about what might have been. Changing his specialty to endocrinology had saved his sanity.

When he pushed open the door of the delivery room, he forgot about whether he should or shouldn't be there. Seeing Lily on the table, her face flushed, her hands clenched tight on the sheet, a protective urge took over. She was hooked up to monitors that measured the frequency and intensity of contractions as well as the babies' heart rates. She looked small and frightened...and fragile. Yet he knew she was the strongest woman he'd ever known. She'd proved that since her husband had died.

He strode to the bed, hooked a stool with his foot and positioned it beside her. Glancing at Emily Madison, Jared's wife and a professional midwife, he asked, "Don't you want Emily to coach you?"

Lily pushed damp hair behind her ear. "She's assisting Jared."

He knew why he was fighting being here. Witnessing a woman in labor, watching a birth, was an intimate experience. Right now, bonding with Lily would be foolish.

He could see a contraction gearing up in intensity. Maybe she just wanted him here instead of one of her friends because he might be more detached yet professional about the births.

With a mental kick that he hoped would push him toward that detachment, he took hold of her hand, felt the softness and warmth of it.

Suddenly she squeezed his fingers so hard he lost any feeling he *did* have left. But the pressure reminded him he had a job to do. If he concentrated on coaching, maybe he wouldn't notice how her chin quivered or how her eyes grew shiny with emotion.

When the contraction eased, he admitted, "I'm not sure how best to help you."

"You worked with men in the field. You helped them. Help me the same way. Just help me *focus* on something."

She was right. He had helped men before and after surgeries, with mortar blasts exploding, with rocket-propelled grenades shattering the air. Finally he really did understand why she wanted him here.

Realizing what he had to do, he smoothed his thumb over the top of her hand, telling himself his need to touch her was simply for her comfort. "Watch my nose," Mitch ordered Lily.

She looked at him as if he was crazy. "You're kidding, right?"

"I'm not. Use it as your focal point and listen to the sound of my voice."

She focused on his eyes instead of his nose. He saw so many emotions there—worry, hope and grief…the resoluteness he'd admired as she'd exhibited it each day, ready to go on with her life and care for her twins.

Mitch saw her tense and turned to the monitor. With another contraction coming, he squeezed her hand. "You can do this."

She was still looking into his eyes instead of at his nose. He felt as if his heart was going to jump out of his chest. He felt as if…he *shouldn't* be here. Again, he warned himself that he couldn't make such an intimate connection. He should just be watching over her.

But how could he watch over her without getting involved?

At this moment, he wished he'd never made that promise to Troy.

At the foot of the bed, Emily said, "Lily, you can start pushing now."

At that moment, neonatologist Francesca Fitzgerald came into the room with two nurses behind her.

Lily gasped, "Francesca."

The doctor patted Lily's arm and summed up the situation with a quick assessment. "My team's here. You do your part and we'll take care of the rest."

Lily's contraction peaked and her cry of pain sliced through Mitch.

Jared encouraged her. "Good one, Lily. Come on. I want this baby out."

"You can do this," Mitch reminded her. He held her

hand as the tension built in her body again. Her face reddened and she gave another fantastically effort-filled push.

All at once he heard Jared say, "I've got one!"

"Is she all right?" Lily asked. "Please tell me she's all right."

A light infant cry came from the area where Francesca was standing. It was very soft, but it *was* a cry.

"She's a beauty," Jared told her. "We might have a few minutes now. I want to get her sister out, as quickly as I can."

"I don't think I have a few minutes," Lily gasped. "It's starting again." She practically sat up with the strength and pain of the contraction.

"Use it," Mitch said. "Go with it."

"Just one more push," Emily encouraged her. "She's your youngest. You're going to have to coax her a little harder."

Mitch realized Lily wasn't focusing on him anymore. She was breathing when she had to, breathing any way she could. She needed a different type of support, physical as well as emotional. Knowing exactly what he had to do, Mitch stood, went to the head of the birthing table and wrapped his arm around her shoulders. He warned himself he was only a substitute for Troy. But he didn't feel like a substitute. His arms around Lily, he knew he was doing this for himself as well as his friend.

Tears swept down her cheeks. Her bangs were plastered to her forehead. She pushed her shoulder-length hair away from her face and stared straight ahead.

As her contraction built, her body curved into it, curved around it. Mitch held her as she delivered a second little girl.

Jared announced, "And here's princess number two."

Again he passed the infant to Francesca who worked at clearing her airway, cleaning her eyes, checking her lungs, hooking her up to the ventilator to help her breathe. When Mitch saw that, a lump rose in his throat.

"I've got them," Francesca reassured Lily. "I'll be around to give you a report as soon as I can." Then she pushed the babies away, out another door before Lily even glimpsed them.

Reluctantly, Mitch released Lily as she collapsed onto the bed, murmuring, "Maybe I should have quit work sooner and stayed in bed. It's often recommended with twins. But I rested the past two weeks. I kept my feet up as much as I could."

Mitch knew he had to keep Lily calm after her ordeal. "You did everything you thought was best. That's all you could do."

Lily surprised him when she caught his hand again and held it tight. "Troy should have been here. He should have seen his girls born. He should have helped me name them. He should have…he should have…"

"He should have never died," Mitch filled in.

Lily bowed her head and finally let the tears fall unchecked. Mitch did the only thing he could—he held her in his arms until she simply couldn't cry anymore.

Lily had been settled in her hospital room for at least two hours and was growing anxious. Why hadn't Francesca come yet? Wouldn't they have told her if something had happened to either of the babies?

Her gaze landed on Mitch, who was standing at the window. He was as calm as she was agitated. Where did that calm come from after what he'd been through?

He'd been presented a Combat Medical Badge, awarded a Silver Star and a Purple Heart, though he never spoke of them. All Troy had told her was that Mitch had been involved in an IED explosion.

"How do you do it?" she asked, following the train of thoughts in her head.

Minus his jacket and tie, his tuxedo shirt was rumpled. He turned to look at her. "Do what?"

"Stay calm under any circumstances."

He shot her a wry half smile. "It's a learned technique."

Interested in anything that would keep her mind off what was going on down the hall, she asked, "Like meditation?"

Even though she'd worked with Mitch for more than two and a half years, she didn't know much about him. Just the little Troy had told her. She knew he was forty-five, had been born in Sagebrush—the small town where they both lived about fifteen minutes outside Lubbock—but he had no family there. He'd been deployed to Iraq, injured and changed specialties—from trauma surgery to endocrinology—because he'd lost the fine motor co-ordination in his hand that he needed to perform surgery. But that was about the extent of her knowledge of his background.

"I learned several techniques," he replied, running his hand through his jet-black hair. "Meditation was one. Guided imagery was another."

Her gaze went to his hand and the ragged scars there. She wanted to ask if he'd learned the techniques when he'd been hurt. Had they been his method of recovering? But that was such personal territory. If he didn't mention Iraq himself, she knew better than to jump into it.

In spite of herself, she still remembered gazing into his eyes rather than looking at his nose while he'd coached her. Every time since the day she'd told him she was having twins, she'd felt such an intense…

She wasn't sure what it was she felt. Mitch knew things. He'd *felt* things. She could just instinctively sense that. The compassion he showed her seemed personal, but maybe he was that way with everyone.

"You know, your friends wanted to stay," he said.

Yes, they did. But they all had children and husbands and practices to see to. "I told them there was nothing they could do here. I'm going to call them as soon as we find out about the babies. Oh, Mitch, what's taking so long?"

Leaving his pensive position at the window, he crossed to her bed. He was so tall…confident…strong.

She remembered being held in his arms—in the exam room at the practice, on the dais, in the delivery room. His cologne had wrapped around her as he'd given her his strength. That's why she'd needed him with her through the delivery—because he was so strong. Now when she looked at him she could hardly swallow.

With one push of his booted foot, the comfortable chair by the nightstand now sat beside her bed. He sank down into the chair. It was well after 1:00 a.m. and she knew he had to be tired after a full day of work. She should tell him to go home, too. But he seemed willing to see her through this and she felt she needed him here.

Though she realized her body was ready for a good long rest, she couldn't relax. Adrenaline was still rushing through her because she was so concerned about her twins.

In the labor room, Mitch had taken her hand. Now he didn't.

Why should it matter? she wondered. She quickly decided it didn't. After all, she was still in love with Troy. At times, she thought she heard him in the next room. Other times, she expected his booming voice to announce that he was home. She fought back sudden emotion.

Mitch's deep, even voice reassured her. "I have a feeling Francesca will only come to you after the babies are stabilized…after she can tell you something for certain."

"You're so honest," Lily blurted out. "I wanted you to say she probably had another emergency and that's why it was taking her so long."

"Do you believe that?"

His expression wasn't stern. His lean cheeks and high cheekbones just made him appear that way sometimes. As his black brows drew together just a little, he looked expectant…as if he knew she couldn't lie to herself.

"It's possible," she murmured.

"Yes, it's possible," he agreed.

"Talk to me about something," she pleaded. "Anything."

She knew she might be asking for a lot. Mitch communicated, but only when he had something to say. Chitchat didn't seem to be in his nature. But now she would be glad for anything her mind could latch on to.

"When is Raina McGraw's baby due?"

Lily smiled, picturing her friend with her rounding stomach. "June fifth. Talk about having a lot on your plate."

"I understand Shep adopted three children before she married him."

"They're still in the process with Manuel, their two-

and-a-half-year-old. Shep had started adoption proceedings, but then he and Raina married. It was almost like starting over. Their housekeeper, Eva, is wonderful, but Raina could be running from morning to night once the baby's born. I think she's going to take a leave from her practice."

"Have you decided yet how long you're going to stay out?"

"I'll make up my mind soon. Everything about my life is in flux right now."

"You don't have to decide right away. You might have to consider getting help with the twins."

"No, I won't need it. My roommate Angie—Gina's sister—says she'll help me. She's a nurse, away right now on the disaster relief team. But she should be back soon. Besides, there are lots of moms who take care of two babies."

"Not necessarily at the same time." His tone held a warning note that maybe she was being a little too Pollyanna-ish.

"I can handle it, Mitch. You'll see."

She was contemplating the idea of breast-feeding both babies when the door pushed open and Francesca walked in. She seemed surprised to see Mitch there, but didn't comment.

Lily hadn't known Francesca very long. But one evening, the women who'd lived in the Victorian house on a quiet street in Sagebrush had gathered there and just enjoyed a ladies' night of chatting and sharing backgrounds. All of them were connected in so many ways—through their professions, friendships or family ties.

Lily had felt so alone after Troy had died, but that

night all of the women had made her feel as if she had a support network.

"Tell me," Lily said to Francesca.

"Your older daughter weighs four point two pounds, is seventeen inches long, and needs a little time to put on weight. We're giving her CPAP treatment. She's breathing on her own and is definitely a crier when she's unhappy."

The continuous positive airway pressure would help the infant breathe but not breathe for her. Lily's heart swelled with love for this tiny baby although she hadn't even laid eyes on her yet. "And my youngest?" Lily's voice shook a little bit when she asked.

"She weighs four pounds, is sixteen and a half inches and had trouble breathing." Francesca immediately held up both hands. "Now, don't panic. We have her stabilized. She's on a ventilator for now—"

"Oh my God!" Lily's chest felt so tight she could hardly breathe.

"I mean it, Lily. Don't panic. We'll wean her off it. Her lungs need to develop and, of course, she needs to gain weight, too, before she can go home."

"When can I see them?"

Francesca sighed. "I shouldn't allow it, but I know you're not going to rest or get any sleep until I let you visit them."

Lily nodded. She was happy, afraid and plain exhausted. But she had to see them.

"All right. I'll find a wheelchair. But you can only have a few minutes with them, and then I need to tuck you in. Childbirth is natural, but it's traumatic, too, and you need time to recover."

"I know," Lily said. "When do you think I'll be discharged?"

"You'll have to ask Jared that, but my guess is you'll be here until Sunday morning."

At least she'd be here so she could visit her babies. *Her babies.* Everything about their birth came rushing back, especially Mitch's presence and support. "Can Mitch come, too?"

Francesca hesitated and looked from one of them to the other. "This is just for a few minutes. You both have to wear masks and sterile gowns. I'll be right back."

Mitch looked troubled. "Are you sure you want me there, Lily?"

"You helped me bring them into the world. Of course, I want you there."

Maybe it was because of the letter Troy had left for her. In it, he'd told her he'd asked Mitch to look after her if anything happened to him. He'd trusted Mitch, and that made it easy for her to trust him, too. He'd certainly come through for her tonight.

Ten minutes later, Lily and Mitch were in the NIC unit, staring at her two precious little girls. The babies absolutely snatched Lily's breath away.

Mitch stood behind her, his hand on her shoulder. "Have you considered names?"

"Now that I see them, I can name them." She pointed to her firstborn, saying lightly, "Sophie, I'd like you to meet Mitch. He helped me bring you into this world."

Her baby opened her eyes, seemed to gaze at them both for a few seconds before she closed them again.

Lily's heart overflowed with love as her focus turned to her youngest, who needed help to breathe.

Mitch's fingers tightened on Lily's shoulder and she was so grateful for his quiet strength, his stalwart caring.

"And this tiny angel is—" Lily's voice caught. Finally she managed to say, "Her name is Grace."

Mitch crouched down beside Lily so he could see her children from her vantage point. The slant of his jaw almost grazed her cheek as he reassured her, "They're going to gain weight and strength each day."

When Mitch turned to her instead of the twins, Lily's heart beat faster. "Thank you," she said simply.

"You're welcome," Mitch returned with a crooked smile. Just for tonight she'd let Mitch Cortega be her rock. Just for tonight, she'd depend on him.

Then she'd stand on her own two feet and raise her babies alone.

Chapter 2

Mitch stood in Lily's hospital room on Sunday afternoon. She was ready to go home and be a mom, but her babies couldn't go home with her. At least, not for a few weeks, and only then if no further problems developed. She didn't want to leave them, but she had no choice. She also couldn't drive herself home. Gina was in Houston again. Angie was still away, helping flood victims. And Raina, six months pregnant with a new husband and three boys to think about, had enough on her plate.

So Mitch had offered to drive Lily home, and she'd accepted. In fact, the thought of being with him again had made her feel…less worried. But now that he was standing in the room, dressed in jeans and a dark-green V-neck sweater, her pulse was speeding faster. She told herself she was just excited about leaving the hospital.

However, she snuck another peek at him and felt her stomach flutter.

Maybe she should have just paid taxi fare from Lubbock to Sagebrush instead of accepting his assistance so readily.

He seemed to read some of her thoughts. "I know you want to be independent, Lily, but I'm only giving you a ride home. You'll be driving again soon."

She did have to put this in perspective. "I just never expected to be going home without my babies and without—" She abruptly stopped.

"And without Troy," he filled in, not afraid to say it.

Blinking very fast she zipped the overnight case that Raina had dropped off for her. "I'm ready to get out of here and finish decorating the nursery. Everything needs to be perfect when my girls come home."

Mitch came up behind her, gently took her by the shoulders and turned her around. "You don't have to hide what you're feeling."

"I have to get *over* what I'm feeling, Mitch. I have two babies to take care of, to support. I can't think about Troy not being here and do what I have to do."

"You can't deny it, either. That will only bring you more heartache in the end."

Gazing into his deep brown eyes, she felt that unsettled sensation in the pit of her stomach again.

"I'm ready to go," she said firmly. She'd cry at night when she was too tired to do anything else. In the meantime, she was going to put a life together for her children.

Mitch dropped his hands from her shoulders and picked up her overnight case. "Then let's get you home."

Their fifteen-minute drive from Lubbock to the small Texas town of Sagebrush was quiet for the most part. Mitch didn't seem to feel the need to talk and stared straight ahead as he drove. She had too many thoughts

buzzing through her mind to want to be involved in conversation—including her unsettling awareness of the
black-haired, broad-shouldered, protective man sitting
beside her. Before her labor, hadn't she looked at Mitch
as the person he was? Had she just seen him merely as
a colleague? Simply a friend of Troy's? A person on the
outskirts of her life but not really *in* her life?

He pulled into the driveway in front of the detached
garage at the large blue Victorian-style house with yellow shutters, then turned to her with questions in his
eyes, voicing one of them. "Who's going to be staying
with you?"

"No one's staying with me."

Silence fell over the SUV as wind buffeted it.

"Isn't Angie back yet?" Mitch asked.

"No. When she's called away on the disaster relief
team, there's no knowing how long she'll be gone."

"What about Raina?"

"I can't expect her to come over here and sit with
me with all her responsibilities. Besides, I don't need a
babysitter."

"As soon as you walk into that house, you're going to
be surprised by how tired you feel. You can't stay here
alone tonight."

Lily suddenly felt panicked without knowing exactly
why. "What are you suggesting?"

"I'm not suggesting anything. I'm going to give you
two options. One, I can take you home with me and you
can stay there for the night."

She was shaking her head already.

"Or, two, I can sleep on your couch."

She was still shaking her head.

"Is your refrigerator stocked?"

"I don't know."

"Do you feel like cooking supper?"

Though she didn't want to admit it, she did feel really tired. "I can make myself an egg."

"I seem to remember Jared ordering you to go home and rest today, for what's left of it, and turn in early tonight."

"He's just being cautious."

Mitch unbuckled his seat belt and shifted behind the wheel to face her. "I know as doctors we make the worst patients, but you've got to be sensible. When those babies come home in a few weeks, you have to be ready *physically* as well as emotionally. So, at least for today, accept help without argument."

Was she being unreasonable? *Was* she trying to be too strong? Why was that? Because she didn't want anyone helping her…or she suddenly didn't want *Mitch* helping her? The thought of him sleeping on her couch tonight made her stomach do something more than flutter. She felt as if she'd gone over the top of a Ferris wheel.

But she certainly wasn't going to Mitch's place. The gossips in Sagebrush would have a field day.

"Let's go inside and you can curl up on the sofa," he suggested. "I'll get you something to drink and we'll go from there."

"Don't you have other things to do today?"

"Repairing winter's damage to the patio? Sweeping out my garage?" He gave her one of his rare smiles.

Ever since Mitch had started with the practice, she'd noticed the long hours he worked, longer than any of the other physicians. He even scheduled consultations on Saturdays. He had rarely taken off work in the time she'd known him. Didn't he have a life outside of the fertility lab? Did he have friends other than the service buddies Troy had once mentioned? Mitch was an enigma, a puzzle she couldn't solve—one she shouldn't be interested in at all.

She nibbled on her lower lip for a couple of seconds and then asked, "Do you know how to cook?"

When he chuckled, she liked the sound of it. "I do. My mother taught me the basics," he said with fond remembrance. "I do all right."

The air in his SUV seemed stifling. She was relieved they were separated in the bucket seats because being physically close to Mitch now seemed...dangerous.

She asked in a low voice, "Why are you doing this, Mitch?"

"I made a promise to Troy. I keep my promises."

That's what she thought. This was duty for Mitch. He was a man who knew duty and honor well.

She let out a long breath. "All right, you can sleep on my couch. But just tonight. That's it. Tomorrow I'm on my own again."

"Deal," he agreed.

Even though he said it, she saw a considering flicker in his eyes. How long would his promise to Troy hold?

Minutes later they were escaping the blustery weather outside and walking into the old house that Lily now thought of as home. Last September she'd moved out of the apartment she'd shared with Troy because the memories there had been too painful.

She breathed in the scent of cinnamon emanating from the potpourri dish beside the Tiffany lamp in the foyer. Angie had filled it before Christmas. Her housemate had understood how difficult the holidays would be for Lily and had included her in her family's celebrations. So had

Gina and, of course, Raina. They'd kept Lily too busy to think if not feel. At night, alone in her room, she'd faced her loss and spoken to her unborn babies about their dad and about what their first Christmas the following year might bring. She had to look toward the future.

"Where would you like your overnight case?" Mitch asked, stepping in behind her.

"Upstairs on my bed would be great."

"The steps won't be a problem?"

"Not at all. But I'll only do them once today."

"Which room is yours?"

A jolt of reality hit when she realized Mitch would be standing in her bedroom in a few minutes. He'd see the baby catalogs and magazines splayed across the chest at the foot of the bed, as well as the photo of Troy on her dresser. What else would he notice?

And why was the idea of Mitch standing in her bedroom so unnerving?

"What's wrong?" he asked.

"Nothing. My bedroom's the second one on the right. It's the one with the yellow rose wallpaper."

"Got it," he said with the flash of a smile that made her breath hitch a little.

Confused, she decided she was just tired from the trip home and worried about her babies. She wasn't reacting to Mitch as a man. She absolutely wasn't.

When Mitch returned downstairs, she was pulling greens and carrots from the refrigerator.

He came up beside her and took them out of her hands. "Stop. Today you're not doing a thing. Wouldn't you be more comfortable in the living room in an easy chair?"

He was a doctor, too. He knew what her body had been through, though she was trying to deny it.

"Don't you have a good book you want to read?" he teased.

She supposed humor was better than anything else. Maybe it would make this jumpy feeling she had when she was around him go away. "I'm sure I can find something to read."

When she took a last glance around, he said, "Relax and trust me."

Trust him. That was the tall and short of it. She did. And trusting him formed a bond that she just didn't want right now. She'd trusted Troy because he was her husband. But now he was gone, and she shouldn't be able to simply turn around and trust another man so easily.

Should she?

"What's going on in your head?" Mitch asked with gentle persuasion.

Nothing he'd want to know about. Her doubts and questions and issues were all hers. None of it had anything to do with him. "I'm just...wired and tired at the same time."

He set the greens and carrots on the counter. Then he nudged her around and walked her toward the living room. He was a good six inches taller than she was and she felt petite beside him.

The heat of his palm on her shoulder seeped through her knit top. She should have worn a sweater. This old house could be drafty. If she'd worn a sweater, she wouldn't feel the warmth of his hand at all...or remember him holding hers as Sophie was born.

He released her as they reached the sofa. Then he stood there and waited and she realized he wanted her to sit. He definitely was a commanding male. Why would that change simply because he was trying to be her friend?

Men in the military had a particular bearing, a straightness of their backs, a tautness of their shoulders, that made them seem *more* than ordinary men. Not that anything about Mitch today seemed military. His jeans, sweater and even his leather boots looked comfortable. She couldn't remember ever seeing him dressed so casually before.

She sank down onto the sofa.

"Put your legs up," he ordered.

She didn't usually take orders well. "I'll be bored," she muttered.

While he pulled the afghan from the back of the sofa and spread it over her, he asked, "Don't you knit or something?"

"Crochet," she corrected automatically, then pointed to the tapestry bag beside the easy chair. She knew if she made a move to get it, he wouldn't let her.

When he stooped to pick up the bag, she noticed the play of his shoulder muscles, the length of his upper torso, his slim hips. A tingle that she relegated to post-birth pangs rippled through her belly. Looking away, she pulled the afghan up higher.

He brought the bag to her and settled it in her lap. "What are you making?"

After opening the Velcro closure, she extracted a pink sweater that sported one sleeve. "I didn't know whether to make these both pink or not. You know, stereotypes and all. But then I thought, two baby girls. What could be cuter than matching pink sweaters?"

He laughed. "I'm sure Sophie and Grace will agree."

She turned the sweater over in her hands and then admitted, "I was an only child. I wanted a sister desperately. Sophie and Grace will always have each other."

She looked up at him again. "Do you have brothers or sisters?" She really didn't know anything about Mitch's background or his childhood.

"Nope. No brothers or sisters."

"Troy and his sister Ellie were close," Lily said in a low voice.

"He talked about her often," Mitch responded, in the way he had ever since Troy had been killed. She was grateful he made it all right for her to speak about her husband and anything connected to him.

"She's in a tough situation right now," Lily said to Mitch. "She had a small store where she sold her own line of baby clothes. But her area of Oklahoma was hard hit by the economic downturn and she had to close the store."

"What's she doing now?"

"She's trying to take her business to the internet."

"Is she coming for a visit?"

"Ellie and Troy's mom, Darlene, both want to visit after the babies come home." She'd always gotten along well with Ellie and Darlene...with all of Troy's family. She knew he'd moved to Texas because the construction market had been thriving around Lubbock, unlike Oklahoma. She'd often wished his family wasn't so far away.

An odd expression crossed Mitch's face, one she couldn't decipher. He said, "You'll have a lot of people to help with the babies. That's just what you need."

"*Is* that what I need, Mitch? I'm their mom. I want to take care of them myself."

"Sure you do. But twins are a lot of work. There was a kid in my neighborhood when I was growing up. His mother had twins. She was always run ragged. And when you go back to work, you're definitely going to need child care."

"I have to go back," she said. "Insurance money and savings will only go so far."

"You'll have Troy's benefits," Mitch reminded her.

"That money is going into a trust fund for the twins."

He didn't contradict her, or try to convince her otherwise. She wanted to give her girls the advantages she'd had growing up. Yet, most of all, she wanted them to appreciate the people around them who loved them. When she'd lost her parents, she'd realized how little material possessions actually meant, and she'd grown up quickly.

"Did you grow up here in Sagebrush?" she asked Mitch, curious about his childhood.

"Yes, I did."

Frustrated he wasn't more expansive, she prompted, "But you don't have family here."

"No, I don't."

"Mitch," she said, letting her frustration show.

"What do you want to know, Lily? Just ask."

Studying his collar-length black hair, his chiseled features, she let the question pop into her head. *Are you just here out of duty or do you care?* Instead she replied, "I *am* asking. But you're not telling me much."

"And why is this suddenly important?"

That was a good question. "I'm not sure. I guess talking about Ellie, thinking about how I'm going to raise the twins— It just made me wonder, that's all. At least give me something to think about while I rest and twiddle my thumbs."

"Crochet," he pointed out.

"Same difference."

The silence in the living room enveloped them for a few moments until Mitch said, "Your background and mine are very different."

"How do you know about mine?"

"Troy shared some of it when we played pool."

Lily's husband and Mitch had gone out and shared an evening of guy stuff now and then, the same way she shared time with her friends.

"Just what did he tell you?"

Mitch's shrug told her he was attempting to make the conversation casual. "That your father was a respected scientist and professor at Stanford. That your mother was a pharmacist who developed her own line of cosmetics and did quite well with them. Something about after your father died, she sold the formula to provide you with a college education."

"Yes, she did," Lily murmured, mind-traveling back to a time that was filled with bittersweet memories. "Daddy died of a massive coronary when I was in high school. My mom died of breast cancer when I was in college. Losing them both made me want to find a profession that gave life."

"If your father taught at Stanford, how did you end up *here?*"

"My mom had a friend who lived in Lubbock, so we moved here. But she and my dad had always planned I'd go to their alma mater. I was at Stanford when she got sick. I flew home as often as I could, but then took off a semester when we called in hospice."

"You've had a lot of loss."

"The people I love leave me." She stared at her hands when she said it, but then she raised her gaze to his. "I know. I know. I shouldn't believe that. If nothing else, I should think positive to change the pattern. But this negative pattern is awfully fresh again and it's hard not to wonder."

"You have two little girls now to love."

"I do. And you can bet, I *will* be an overprotective mom."

"I don't think there's anything wrong with that."

Somehow the conversation had rolled back to Lily again. Mitch was so good at deflecting. Why had she never realized that? But she was also determined to delve below the surface.

Hiking herself up higher against the sofa arm, she nodded toward the space at the end of the couch where her feet had been. "Tell me how you grew up."

He looked as reluctant to sit on her couch as she was to have him sleep there tonight. But in the end, he decided she wouldn't rest until he gave her something. So he sat on the sofa, his thigh brushing one of her stockinged feet. He looked terrifically uncomfortable. "There's not much to it."

She waited, her gaze on his rugged profile.

With a grimace, he finally said, "My father married my mother because she was pregnant when they were both eighteen."

She knew Mitch was probably going to need some prompting, so she asked, "Did it last?"

Mitch's brows drew together as he, obviously reluctant, answered, "He stuck around for a year, then took off on his motorcycle and bailed. She went to business school and became a medical transcriber, but she couldn't always find work. Other times she held two jobs, cleaned offices at night and saved for when times were thin again. I was determined to make life better for both of us."

"Did you always want to be a doctor?"

"Do you mean was it a lifelong wish from childhood?

No. Actually, at first I thought I might become a stock-broker or an investment banker."

Lily couldn't help but smile. She couldn't imagine Mitch as either of those. She didn't know why. She just couldn't. "So why aren't you working on Wall Street?"

"I was good at sports...basketball. I won a scholarship to college. But during my sophomore year my mother got sick and didn't tell me. She didn't have insurance so she didn't go to the doctor. She developed pneumonia and died."

"Oh, Mitch. I'm sorry. That had to be awful for you."

Again he looked uncomfortable revealing this part of his past. "She'd been my motivator. After she died, I took a nosedive. I'd been a good student, but my grades tanked. Then one day, after a few months of drinking into the night and sleeping too late to get up for class, I looked out the dorm window and knew that campus wasn't *real* life. Guys hooking up with girls, frat parties, learning to play teachers for better grades. I thought about my mom's life, how hard it had been and how it ended, and I decided to make a difference. I wanted to help patients who didn't have much of a chance. I wanted to give life when it was hardly there any longer. So I juggled two jobs, got my B.S., and went on to med school. I decided on trauma surgery. In my last year of residency, September 11th happened."

Lily thought of Raina and her first husband, a fire-fighter, who had lost his life that day. Her knowledge of Mitch's character and her intuition where he was concerned urged her to ask, "And that's when you signed up for the Army National Guard?"

"Yes."

"When did you go to Iraq?"

"Two years later."

They were both quiet for a few moments.

Mitch flexed his hand and moved his fingers as she often saw him do, and she knew he was remembering something he never talked about…something that caused those deep fatigue lines around his eyes some mornings.

To break the heavy silence, she asked, "Are you happy being part of our fertility practice?" She and two other doctors had been in unanimous agreement, voting him into their partnership.

"You mean would I rather be performing surgery? Sure. But I like what I do. You and me, Jon and Hillary… we give the seeds of life a chance, as well as at-risk pregnancies. That's rewarding. What I miss is not being part of the Guard, no longer having that unique camaraderie and sense of spirit. Before deployment, it was tough trying to be a doctor as well as a guardsman. But it was what I wanted to be doing."

Abruptly he stood, his body language telling her that this conversation was over. He already knew Lily was the type who wanted to know more, who would ask questions until she got her answers. He was cutting that off before it could go any further. To her surprise, she already missed his presence at the end of the sofa.

"I checked your refrigerator and you have a couple of choices," he said with a forced smile. "Scrambled eggs, scrambled eggs with asparagus and bacon on the side, or… I think I saw sausage in there that I could turn into sausage and pasta of some kind, maybe with canned tomatoes."

"Are you kidding me?" Her eyes were open wide and she was staring at him as if she really didn't know him.

"I told you my mom taught me the basics. But in college I had an apartment with two other guys. I couldn't stomach pizza every night, so I cooked. I borrowed a cookbook or two from the library and they kept me going for the year."

"You're just full of surprises," Lily said, laying her head back against the arm of the sofa, suddenly tired and feeling weak.

"Is the adrenaline finally giving out?" he asked her.

"If you mean do I feel like a wet noodle, yes. Are you happy now?"

The corner of his mouth turned down. "Seeing you tired doesn't make me happy. But knowing that because of it you'll get some rest does." He took hold of the afghan and pulled it above her breasts. He made sure she was covered from there to her toes. Then he gave it a little tuck under her hip so it wouldn't fall away.

Mitch's fingers were strong and long. She felt heat from them with just that quick touch. He'd used his left hand. From what she'd heard, he didn't have much feeling in the fingers of his right hand.

She caught his arm before he moved away.

His gaze crashed into hers and they stared at each other for a few moments.

"Thank you for bringing me home."

"No problem," he responded, as if it was no big deal.

But it was a big deal to Lily. She'd never forget his friendship with Troy. She'd certainly never forget his kindness to her. But something about that kindness and her acceptance of it unsettled her. She had to figure out why it bothered her so much that Mitch would be sleeping on her couch tonight.

Chapter 3

Lily stared at the TV that evening, not really focused on the newsmagazine show that was airing. She was too aware of Mitch rattling the back screen door, fixing loose weather stripping.

Over supper they'd talked about the house and former tenants, needing dispassionate conversation. When they didn't stay on neutral territory, they seemed to wander into intensity…or awkwardness that came from being alone together. It was odd, really. For the past two and a half years while working with Mitch, she'd found him easy to be with. Now…

The phone rang and Lily picked up the cordless from the end table. When she saw Gina's number on caller ID, she breathed a sigh of relief.

"Hi," Gina said. "How are you and Sophie and Grace?"

"I called the hospital a little bit ago. They're doing okay. And I'm…good. I'm at home."

"So you said in your message. I'm sorry I just got it. My plane had a delay taking off. It was a whirlwind trip, leaving yesterday and coming back today. But I didn't want to be away from Daniel and Logan any longer than I had to be."

A baby development expert, Gina had received an offer from a Houston hospital to start her Baby Grows center there, too. Lily was sure Gina would someday not only have an additional Baby Grows center in Houston but many all around the country.

"So Mitch is keeping you company? How's that going?"

"It's okay. It's just…he's hovering. He insists I shouldn't be alone today. He gave me the option to sleep over at his place, or his sleeping on my couch. So he's sleeping here on my couch tonight."

"Are you okay with that?"

"Sure." But Lily knew her voice didn't sound sure. A man who wasn't her husband sleeping under her roof. Is that what was bothering her? Or was there more to it?

"Do you want me to come over?"

"No," Lily was quick to answer. "You need to be with your family."

"I was going to take off work tomorrow. Why don't I drive over first thing? Then Mitch can go to Family Tree."

"Are you sure you don't have other things you have to do?"

"I don't," Gina replied. "Tomorrow we can talk about Sophie and Grace, possibly visit them, and maybe I can get some things ready for you."

Seeing her twins. Baby talk. Girl talk. That sounded great to Lily. "I really appreciate this."

"No problem. Have you heard from Angie?"

Angie was Gina's sister, and Lily knew Gina worried about her when she worked on the team. "No. Have you?"

"No, not since she reached the Gulf. But the disaster relief team really doesn't have time for anything but helping the victims." After a short pause, she asked, "Why don't I stop at the bakery and pick up croissants on my way over?"

"I'm supposed to be losing weight, not gaining it."

"You don't have that much to lose. Besides, if you're going to pump milk and then breast-feed, you need some extra calories."

"The croissants sound good. That way I can convince Mitch he doesn't have to make breakfast."

"Did he make supper?"

"He did. And now he's doing some minor repairs on the house."

It must have been her tone of voice when she said it that made Gina ask, "That bothers you?"

"I don't want to be indebted to him. Do you know what I mean?"

"Oh, I know. But remember, Troy asked him to watch over you. That's what he's doing."

Last fall, Lily had shared Troy's letter with Gina, Angie and Raina. They also knew Mitch was simply fulfilling a promise. She should be grateful instead of uncomfortable.

Lily had just ended the call when Mitch strode into the living room. She told him, "Gina's coming over early tomorrow morning so you don't have to worry about me."

No change of expression crossed Mitch's face, but there was a flicker of reaction in his eyes that said he would worry anyway.

"I have a new client tomorrow who will be making decisions about in vitro fertilization and a few follow-up appointments after that. So if you need anything, I can try to rearrange my schedule."

She jumped in. "No need. I'll be sorting baby clothes with Gina and hanging decorations on the nursery walls. I wasn't prepared for an early delivery, which isn't like me at all!"

Mitch set the duct tape he'd carried in on an end table. "You wanted to stay in the pregnant zone as long as you could."

Although diplomatic, what he wasn't saying was obvious. She'd wanted to put off the idea of becoming a mother without Troy by her side for as long as possible. For once in her life, denial had definitely been more palatable than reality.

But now reality had smacked her in the face.

"You look lost," Mitch said, with a gentle edge to his voice.

That gentleness fell over her like a warm cloak. But then she had to ask herself, *did* she feel lost? Adrift? Alone? But she wasn't alone when she had good friends helping her. "No, not lost. Just off balance. I hate the unexpected. And my life has been one unexpected crisis after the other."

Rounding the coffee table, he approached her and she wished he'd sit beside her on the sofa. But he didn't. "Sophie and Grace coming home will be grounding. You'll see."

His dark eyes didn't waver from hers and she felt sudden heat rising in her cheeks. Not from looking at Mitch! How many times had she looked at him in just that way?

No. Not just *this* way.

"The bedding for the sofa is upstairs," she said in a rush. "I'll get it."

"Are you staying up there?"

"I suppose." She produced a smile. "You'll have the downstairs to yourself if you want to watch TV or get a snack."

"I'll walk up with you."

There was no point in protesting. What would she do? Toss him the bedding over the banister?

When she swung her legs over the side of the sofa, Mitch was there, holding out his hand to help her up. She could be stubborn. Or she could accept a hand up when she needed it.

His strong fingers closed over hers, and her heart raced as her mind searched for something to say.

"Take it slowly," he reminded her as she rose to her feet.

Everything Mitch said today seemed to be full of deeper meaning. Although she longed to keep her hand in his, she slid it free and headed to the stairs.

A few minutes later in the hall on the second floor, Lily stopped by the linen closet and opened the door. Blankets lay folded on the shelf above her head. She reached up but she shouldn't have bothered. Mitch was there, behind her, easily pulling a blanket from the closet. His superior height and strength was obvious. She could sense both, even though he wasn't touching her. Jittery, tired and anxious about what was going to happen next, she knew her hormones were out of whack. That was the best explanation she could think of to explain how she was feeling around Mitch.

He stepped away, bedding in hand. "This is great."

"Don't be silly. You need a sheet and pillow." And *she* needed something to do with her hands. She needed something to do with her mind. She needed something to *do*.

Choosing a pale blue sheet, she yanked a matching pillowcase from a stack. "The extra pillows are way up on the top shelf," she explained, moving away, letting him reach.

He easily removed one of those, too.

"I wish the sofa pulled out. You're going to be uncomfortable all scrunched up."

He laughed. "Believe me, I've slept on a lot worse. You worry too much, Lily. Did anyone ever tell you that?"

Her husband's name came to her lips, but she didn't say it. She didn't have to. Mitch knew.

He looked disconcerted for a second—just a second—but then he took the sheets from her arms. "Do you have a phone in your room?"

"My cell phone is in my purse. You brought that up with my suitcase. Why?"

"If you need something, call me. You might go to bed and an hour from now figure out you want a pack of crackers or a glass of milk."

There was only one way to answer with a man like Mitch. "I'll call you if I need you."

But somehow they both knew she wouldn't.

She went to the door to her room, which was only a few feet away. He didn't move until she stepped over the threshold and murmured, "Good night."

He gave her a slight nod, responded, "Good night, Lily," and headed for the stairs.

As she closed her door, she leaned against it and sighed. She wanted to make up the sofa for him so it would be comfortable.

How silly a notion was that?

* * *

"What do you mean you sent Gina home?" Mitch de-manded as he stood in Lily's living room the following evening, a gift-wrapped box under one arm.

"She arrived before I was up this morning, as you know. She helped me ready the nursery. She took me to see the babies, and then I told her she should go home to her husband and son."

"And she just went?" He seemed astonished by that idea.

"She protested, but I plopped here on the sofa, told her I'd stay here, and she saw I meant it."

Lily was one exasperating woman! There was no doubt about that. But he had to admire her in spite of himself. "What did you do for dinner?"

"What is this, the third degree?"

He just arched a brow.

"Gina made a casserole for lunch and I had leftovers, with a salad and all that. What did *you* have?" she re-turned, almost cheekily.

All day he'd thought about eating dinner with her last night…saying good-night at the end of the day, spending the night on her couch in the strong grip of an insomnia he knew too well. Yet that was better than waking up in a sweat after too-real flashbacks or nightmares. Mo-ments of sensual awareness when Lily had come down-stairs this morning had been unsettling enough to push him on his way as soon as Gina had arrived.

Answering her, he said, "I went to the drive-through at my favorite burger joint." At her expression, he laughed. "Don't look so outraged. I have to do that once a week to keep fit."

Lily laughed then, even though she tried not to. That

was the first real laugh he'd heard from her since before—even he had trouble saying it sometimes—since
before Troy had died. He wanted to keep her spirits up.
"So…how are Sophie and Grace?"

"Sit down," Lily said, motioning to the sofa. "I hate it
when you loom. What's under your arm?"

"We'll get to that." He considered her comment. "And
I don't loom."

"Whatever you say," she said too quickly, with a little smile.

Shaking his head, he set the box on the coffee table
and lowered himself to the sofa. Not too close to her.
Before he'd driven over here, he'd warned himself about
that.

"The babies are so small," she explained, worried. "I
can touch them but I can't hold them, and I'm dying to
hold them."

"You'll soon be able to hold Sophie, if not Grace.
How's their weight?" he asked, digging for the bottom
line like a doctor.

"They're holding their own. My milk should be in
soon and I'm going to pump it—" She stopped as her
cheeks turned more pink.

"Don't be embarrassed. I'm a doctor, Lily. We talk
about this all the time with our patients." Right now he
had to think of her as a patient so other images didn't
trip over each other in his head.

"I know. But it seems different with…us."

Yes, something *did* seem different. Her perception of
him? His of her? The fact that they'd been friends and
maybe now something more was going on?

Nothing should be going on. It was way too soon for
her. Maybe way too late for him.

"Can you tell them apart?" he asked, knowing conversation about her little girls would be comforting for her.

"Of course. Sophie's nose is turned up a little bit more at the end than Grace's. Grace's chin is just a little daintier, a tad more refined. They both have Troy's forehead and probably his eyes. It's a little too soon to tell. Sophie's a half inch longer than Grace, but Grace could catch up if she gains weight."

"She'll gain weight. They both will."

"Grace is still on the ventilator." Lily's voice trembled a bit.

Needing to fortify her with the truth, he asked, "What does Francesca say?"

"Francesca insists they're doing as well as can be expected and I have to give them time. I just feel like I should be doing something. Do you know what I mean?"

"Oh, yeah. Sitting still isn't easy for either one of us." He patted the box. "That's why I brought this along. Doing is always better than worrying."

"A gift?" Lily tore the wrapping paper off and read the information on the outside of the box. "Oh, Mitch, this is one of those new baby monitors."

"It is. The screen is small, but there's a portable handset you can carry with you to another room. So I'm also going to hook up a larger monitor you won't need binoculars to see. It's in my car."

"I can't let you—"

He shook his finger at her. "Don't even say it. You're going to be running yourself ragged when those babies come home. Having cameras in their cribs and a monitor down here so you can see them will help save a little bit of your energy."

"It will save a lot of my energy. Thank you."

Her blue eyes seemed to try to look inside him, into his heart…into his soul. That unsettled him. His soul was tormented at times by everything that had happened in Iraq. He hadn't been able to save his friend, and that, along with the PTSD symptoms, clawed at his heart. He quickly replied, "You're welcome. Why don't I get this hooked up? That way it will be ready whenever you bring the babies home."

"The cribs were delivered this morning. Gina supervised so I didn't have to run up and down the steps. But I don't know if she put the bedding on."

"Don't worry about it. I can position the cameras with the bedding on or off."

"Do you need my help? I can come up—"

"No." If Lily came upstairs, she would definitely be a distraction. "I brought along a toolbox and everything I might need. You drink a glass of milk and crochet or something."

"Drink a glass of milk?" She was smiling and her question was filled with amusement.

That smile of hers packed a wallop. It turned up the corners of her very pretty mouth. It seemed to make the few freckles across her cheeks more evident, her face actually glow.

Had he been attracted to Lily before Troy's death? If he was honest with himself, he had to say he had been. But attraction was one thing, acting on it was another. He'd shut it down when he'd learned she and Troy were to be married. He and Troy had become good friends and he'd congratulated them both at their wedding, always keeping his distance from Lily.

Being colleagues at their practice had been difficult at times. But not impossible. He kept their dealings strictly professional. They'd been cohorts, interacting on an intellectual level. He and Troy had been close. He and Lily? They'd just existed in the same universe.

Until…after Troy had died. When Mitch had hugged Lily that day after her ultrasound, he'd experienced desire and felt like an SOB because of it. That day, Mitch had realized that if he was going to keep his promise to Troy, he couldn't deny his attraction any longer. At least to himself. *She* didn't have to know about it.

But now—

Now nothing had changed. He had baggage. She had a world of grief and loss and new responsibility to deal with.

Turning away from her smile, which could affect him more than he wanted to admit, he muttered, "Milk's good for you and the babies. You've got to keep your vitamin D level up, along with your calcium. I'll go get what I need from the SUV and be right back."

Sometimes retreat was the best part of valor. Remembering that might save them both from an awkward or embarrassing situation.

Lily was emptying the dishwasher when Mitch called her into the living room. She'd been aware of his footfalls upstairs, the old floors creaking as he moved about. She'd been even *more* attuned to his presence when he'd come downstairs and she'd heard him cross the living room. She'd stayed in the kitchen. Somehow that had just seemed safer…easier…less fraught with vibrations she didn't want to come to terms with.

Hearing her name on Mitch's lips was unsettling now, and she told herself she was just being silly. Yet, seconds later when she stepped into the living room and found him taking up space in his long-sleeved hoodie and jeans, she almost backed into the kitchen again.

Making herself move forward, shifting her eyes away from his, she spotted the twenty-inch monitor on a side table. One moment she glimpsed one white crib with pink trim and green bedding. The next he'd pressed a button and she spotted the other crib with its pink-and-yellow designs. She could watch both babies by changing the channel.

"The wonders of technology." A smile shone in his voice.

She knew Mitch was good with electronics and especially computers. He was the first at the office to understand a new system, to fix glitches, to teach someone else the intricacies of a program.

"Are systems like this a side hobby for you?"

"Always have been. I'm self-taught. The skills come in handy now and then."

As long as she'd known Mitch, he'd downplayed what he did and who he helped. "You're a good man, Mitch."

He looked surprised for a moment.

She added, "If you can do something for someone else, you do."

"Lily, don't make so much of setting up a monitoring system."

Telling herself she should stay right where she was, she didn't listen to her better judgment. She advanced closer to Mitch and this time didn't look away. "You're not just helping *me*. It's sort of an attitude with you. If someone has a problem, you take time to listen."

Maybe he could see she was serious about this topic. Maybe he could see that she was trying to determine exactly how much help she should accept from him. Maybe he could see that this conversation was important to her.

Nevertheless, by his silence he seemed reluctant to give away even a little piece of himself.

"Does it have something to do with being in Iraq?" she asked softly.

The flicker of response in his eyes told her she'd hit the mark. She saw one of his hands curve into a fist and she thought he might simply tell her it was none of her business. Instead, however, he lifted his shoulders in a shrug, as if this wasn't important. As if he didn't mind her asking at all.

"I survived," he told her calmly. "I figured there was a reason for that. I returned home with a new understanding of patience, tolerance and simple kindness."

Although Mitch's expression gave away nothing, Lily knew he was holding back. He was giving her an edited version of what he felt and what he'd experienced.

"Have you ever talked about Iraq?"

"No."

"Not even with your buddies?"

"They know what it was like. I don't have to talk about it."

She supposed that was true. Yet from the tension she could sense in Mitch, she understood he had scars that were more than skin deep.

With a tap on the control sitting next to the monitor on the table, he suggested, "Let me show you the remote and what the lights mean."

Discussion over. No matter what she thought, Mitch was finished with that topic, and he was letting her know it. She could push. But she sensed that Mitch wasn't the type of man who *could* be pushed. He would just shut down. That wouldn't get her anywhere at all. Why was she so hell-bent on convincing him that the bad stuff would only damage him if he kept it inside?

She'd let the conversation roll his way for now. For the next few minutes she let him explain the lights on the remote and how she could carry it into the kitchen with her and upstairs to her bedroom. When he handed it to her, their fingers skidded against each other and she practically jumped. She was so startled by the jolt of adrenaline it gave her, she dropped the remote.

She stooped over to retrieve it at the same time he crouched down. Their faces were so close together… close enough to kiss…

They moved apart and Lily let him grasp the control.

After Mitch picked it up, he handed it to her and quickly stepped away. "I'd better get going," he said. "Do you want me to turn off the system?"

"I can do it."

He nodded, crossing to the door, picking up the toolbox he'd set there.

She followed him, feeling as if something had gone wrong, yet not knowing what. "Thank you again for the monitoring system. I really appreciate it."

"Are you going to be alone tomorrow?"

"No. Raina's coming to visit. She's going to drive me to the hospital so I can spend time with the twins while she makes rounds."

"That sounds like a plan. I'm glad you have friends you can count on."

"I am, too."

As their gazes found each other, his dark brown eyes deeply calm, Lily felt shaken up.

"If you need help when you bring the babies home, you have my number."

Yes, she did. But the way she was feeling right now, she wasn't going to use it. She couldn't call on him again when she felt attracted to him. That's what it was, plain and simple—attraction she was trying to deny. Oh, no. She wouldn't be calling his number anytime soon. She would not feel guilty believing she was being unfaithful to her husband's memory.

Maybe Mitch realized some of that, because he left.

Even though a cold wind blew into the foyer, Lily stood there watching Mitch's charcoal SUV back out of the driveway. When his taillights finally faded into the black night, she closed the door, relieved she was alone with her memories…relieved she might not see Mitch for a while.

Then everything would go back to normal between them.

Over the next few weeks Mitch didn't see much of Lily, though he stopped in at the hospital NICU almost every day. A few days ago, the twins had been moved to the regular nursery. This morning he'd run into Angie, who told him they'd gone home. Lily hadn't called him. Because she was overwhelmed with bringing the twins home and everything that entailed? Or because she wanted to prove to herself she could be a single mom and manage just fine?

He was going to find out.

When Mitch reached the Victorian, he scanned the house and grounds. Everything *seemed* normal—until he approached the front door. Although it was closed, he could hear the cries of two babies inside. New mothers had enough trouble handling one, let alone two. But where were Lily's friends?

With no response when he rang the doorbell, he knocked. When Lily still didn't answer, he turned the knob—no one in Sagebrush locked their doors—and stepped inside.

Immediately he realized the wails were coming from a room down the hall from the living room. Turning that way, he found the room that had been the women's exercise room. Now it looked like a makeshift nursery. There were two bassinets, a card table he assumed Lily used for changing the twins, and a scarred wooden rocking chair that looked as if it could be an antique. His gaze was quickly drawn to her. He knew he should look away from Lily's exposed breast as she tried to feed one baby while holding the other. Respectful of her as a new mom, he dropped his gaze to an odd-looking pillow on her lap, one of those nursing pillows advertised in baby magazines. But it didn't seem to be doing much good. Lily looked about ready to scream herself.

When she raised her head and saw him, she practically had to yell over the squalls. "I couldn't come to the door. I can't seem to satisfy them," she admitted, her voice catching.

Without hesitating, Mitch took Sophie from her mom's arms, trying valiantly to ignore Lily's partially disrobed condition. He had enough trouble with the visions dancing through his head at night. Concentrating for the moment on Sophie, he flipped a disposable diaper from a stack, tossed it onto his shoulder and held the infant against him. The feel of that warm little girl on his shoulder blanked out any other pictures. Taking in a whiff of her baby lotion scent, he knew nothing in the world could be as innocent and sweet as a newborn baby. His hand rubbed up and down her little back, and miraculously she began to quiet. In a few moments, her sobs subsided into hiccups.

Lily, a bit amazed, quickly composed herself and tossed a blanket over her shoulder to hide her breast. Then she helped Grace suckle once more. This time the baby seemed content.

"Did your friends desert you?" He couldn't imagine them doing that.

"No, of course not. Gina and Raina were here most of the day. When Angie got ready for work and left, Sophie and Grace were asleep."

Mitch watched as Lily took a deep breath and let it out slowly. "But they woke up, crying to be fed at the same time."

"Do you have milk in the fridge?"

"Yes, but—"

"Breast-feeding two babies is something that's going to take practice. In the meantime, I can give Sophie a bottle." He gestured to her lap. "Nursing pillows and experts' advice might work for some people, but you've got to be practical. There is no right way and wrong way to do this, Lily. You just have to do what works for you and the babies."

"How do you know so much about babies?" Lily asked in a small voice, looking down at her nursing child rather than at him.

His part in the practice was science-oriented and mostly behind the scenes. "Training," he said simply, remembering his rotation in obstetrics years ago.

That drew her eyes to his. He added, "And…sometimes in the field, you have to learn quickly." In Iraq, he'd helped a new mother who'd been injured, returning her and her newborn to her family.

Before Lily could ask another question, he gently laid Sophie in one of the bassinets and hurried to the kitchen to find her milk. A short time later he carried one of the kitchen chairs to the nursery and positioned it across from Lily. Then he picked up Sophie again and cradled her in his arm. They sat in silence for a few minutes as both twins took nourishment.

"What made you stop by today?" Lily finally asked.

Lily's blond hair was fixed atop her head with a wooden clip. Wavy strands floated around her face. She was dressed in a blue sweater and jeans and there was a slight flush to her cheeks. Because he was invading private moments between her and her babies?

"I was at the hospital and found out they were discharged today."

Lily's eyes grew wider. Did she think he was merely checking up on her so he could say he had? He wished! He was in this because she'd gotten under his skin.

"Feeding these two every three hours, or more often, could get complicated. What would you have done if I hadn't arrived?"

"I would have figured something out."

Her stubbornness almost convinced him to shock her by taking her into his arms and kissing her. Lord, where had that thought come from? "I'm sure Gina and Raina never would have left if they knew you were so overwhelmed."

"Raina and Gina have families."

"They also both have nannies," he reminded her.

"They also both have—"

Mitch knew Lily had been about to say that they both had husbands. Instead, she bit her lower lip and transferred Grace to her other breast, taking care to keep herself covered with the blanket.

"I'm sorry I just walked in on you like that." He might as well get what happened out in the open or they'd both have that moment between them for a while.

"I'm going to have to get over my privacy issues if I intend to breast-feed them for very long. I sat down with the accountant last week. I can take a leave for seven or eight months and be okay financially. My practice is important, but I really feel as if I need to be with them to give them a good start in life."

Since she was the only parent they had, he could certainly understand that.

"Do you think the practice can do without me for that long?"

"We can manage. You know our client list is down because of insurance issues. This could work out to everyone's advantage. We can always consult with you from home if we need your expertise."

Suddenly remembering the need to burp Sophie, he set the bottle on the floor and balanced the tiny baby on his knee. His hand was practically as large as *she* was. What would life be like taking care of them every day? Being able to watch their progress and all the firsts? Keeping his palm on her chest, he rubbed her back until she burped.

Smiling at Lily he said offhandedly, "She's easy."

Lily smiled back.

In that moment, he knew being here with Lily like this was dangerous.

What he was about to suggest was even *more* dangerous.

Chapter 4

"Do you want me to sleep on the couch again tonight?" Mitch asked as he cradled Sophie in his arm once more and offered her the bottle again. He couldn't help studying her perfect baby features. He was beginning to recognize a warm feeling that enveloped his heart when he was around Sophie and Grace.

After a lengthy pause, he cast a sideways glance at Lily to gauge her expression. As long as she was upstairs and he stayed downstairs, he wouldn't worry her with the restlessness that plagued him at night.

She looked somber as she debated with herself about what to say. He could almost hear her inner conversation because he'd already had the same one. If he stayed, they'd connect more. If he stayed, they might get to know each other better.

Quietly, she responded, "If you stay, I think I can keep

Sophie and Grace happier. The two of us are obviously handling them better than *I* was handling them alone. I have to learn what works and what doesn't. That will just take time. In the meantime, I want to stay calm. I want to enjoy both of them. I can't go into a panic just because Grace and Sophie are crying at the same moment."

"Why *did* you panic?" Extreme reactions weren't at all like Lily. But she'd never been a mom before. She bit her lower lip and he found himself focused on her mouth much too intensely.

"I have these two little beings depending on me twenty-four hours a day, seven days a week," she attempted to explain. "I don't want to let them down. I don't want either of them to feel neglected."

It was easy to see Lily had already bonded with her daughters and she wanted nothing to interfere with those bonds, not even another willing pair of hands giving her aid. He attempted to be reasonable, realizing he wanted to stay more than he wanted to go. "Right now, they need to have their basic needs met—feeding, changing and cuddling. They'll learn to know you," he reassured her quickly. "They won't mind if someone else gives them what they need. In a few months, they'll both be more particular. They'll want you when they want you. So for now, take advantage of the fact that someone else can help."

"You make it sound so simple," she said with a wry smile. "And we know it isn't."

No, nothing was simple. Besides the sheer enormity of the twins' birth, other feelings besides affection for Sophie and Grace were developing between him and Lily. However, neither of them were going to mention those. No. They wouldn't be having that discussion anytime soon…which left the door wide open for his desire to cause trouble. Yet he still wanted to be close to her.

As he set Sophie on his knee to burp her again, he asked, "Will you take the babies upstairs to sleep tonight?"

"Yes. I want them to get used to their cribs. I've got to get the hang of breast-feeding both of them, but that might be easier to juggle during the day. I thought I might put a small refrigerator upstairs for night feedings."

"That sounds like a good idea. Maybe I can go pick one up for you tomorrow."

"But I'm paying for it."

"Okay, you're paying for it." He knew better than to argue.

With her gaze locked on his, he felt a turning so deep inside of him that he had to stand with Sophie and walk her back and forth across the room. She'd drunk three ounces of the bottle and that was good. Taking her to the card table, he unsnapped her Onesies so he could change her.

"Mitch, you don't have to do that."

He glanced over his shoulder while he held Sophie with one hand and picked up a diaper with the other. "I don't mind changing her. But if you'd rather I didn't, I won't."

Mitch guessed Grace was still locked on Lily's breast. Just imagining that—

"As long as *you* don't mind," Lily finally said.

He seemed to be all thumbs with the small diaper, but he hoped Lily wasn't noticing. The tiny snaps on the Onesies were a challenge, too, but his left hand had almost become as proficient as his right hand had once been— before shrapnel had torn into it.

Finally Sophie was ready for bed. Her little eyes were practically closed and her angelic face was peaceful. "I'll carry her upstairs and lay her in her crib. You can come up when Grace finishes."

"I have receiving blankets up there on the side of each crib. Can you swaddle her in one? They're supposed to sleep better if I do that."

"I'll try it."

"And you have to lay her on her back."

"I know, Lily."

She flushed.

"After I put her to bed, I'll pull out a blanket and a pillow for the sofa. I remember where you got them."

Lily nodded, but dropped her eyes to Grace and didn't look at him. If they didn't admit to the intimacy developing between them, then the intimacy wouldn't exist, right?

Right.

They were tiptoeing along a line in the sand, hoping neither one of them fell onto the other side.

He let out a pent-up breath he didn't even know he was holding when he left the downstairs nursery and headed up the steps, Sophie sleeping against his shoulder. The hall light guided him into the babies' room, where he grabbed the blanket and carefully wrapped Sophie in it on the changing table, murmuring softly to her as he did. Then he gently laid her in her crib and switched on the monitoring system.

After turning on the castle night-light by the rocker, he went to the hall for his bedding. At the closet, he glanced back at the room, almost ready to return and wish the little girl a good night. But he knew he couldn't become attached, not to the babies any more than to Lily. Nothing was permanent. Everything ended. He had no right to even think about Lily in a romantic way. He had no intention of making life more complicated for either of them.

After Mitch went downstairs, he made up the sofa and sat on it, staring at the monitor. Sophie did look like a cherub with her wispy blond hair, her blue eyes, her little body that seemed more heavenly than earthly. Her tiny face turned from left to right and he wondered if she missed Grace already.

He was so engrossed in his reflections that he didn't hear Lily come into the living room until the floor squeaked. She was holding Grace in a sling that kept her nestled against her chest.

"Is Sophie asleep?" Lily asked.

"Come see."

"I have to put Grace down, too."

"A couple of minutes won't matter. Come here."

Lily just stared at Sophie, her sweet sleep as entrancing as her little nose, long eyelashes and broad brow. "The monitor is wonderful, Mitch," Lily said in a low voice. "But they're so small. I'll probably be going in every fifteen minutes to check on them."

"You need your sleep. I'll be watching from down here. How about if I stay awake until the first feeding?"

"You need your sleep, too."

"I'm used to not sleeping. I was a trauma surgeon, remember?"

She remembered and unintentionally her gaze went to his arm and his hand.

Self-consciously, he moved it and balled it into a fist. Though he expected her to move away, she didn't.

"Do you think about what you used to do very often?"

"Often enough. But that was then and this is now.

Why don't I walk you upstairs? We'll make sure both babies are settled."

Lily took one last look at the image on the monitor and then crossed to the stairway. Mitch waited a beat or so and then followed her.

Upstairs, by the glow of the night-light, Lily took Grace from her carrier and wrapped her in a blanket as Mitch had done with Sophie. After Lily laid Grace in her crib, she stooped over the baby and kissed her forehead. "I love you, sweet girl. I'm glad you're home."

Then she moved to Sophie's crib and did the same.

Aware Mitch hadn't come far into the room, Lily glanced at him as he stood by the chair, his arms crossed over his chest—watchful and distant.

When he'd arrived at the house earlier and come into the downstairs nursery, she'd felt so many emotions that they'd tumbled over each other. Yes, she'd been embarrassed. But she'd also felt a little proud. Only a few moments had passed until she'd realized she *should* feel embarrassed. And then she had.

As they'd put the babies to bed, though, the situation had seemed right. Mitch handled them so well… so comfortably…so like a father. Sometimes she could see the affection he felt for them. But other times, he removed himself.

Like now.

He fell into step beside her as she left the nursery and walked down the hall to her bedroom. At her door, she was ready to say good-night, ready to fall into bed, exhausted from the stress, the worry and the joy of bringing the babies home today. Yet a simple good-night didn't seem adequate and when she gazed into Mitch's eyes, she couldn't look away.

He seemed to have the same problem.

There was something about him standing there, perfectly still, his shoulders wide enough to block the doorway, his height filling the space. Maybe it was the sight of him without his tie and with the first few buttons of his white shirt open. Maybe it was her reaction to the black chest hair peeking out. Maybe she thought about all he'd done for her. Maybe, for just a short time, she gave in to the thought that she might *need* someone to watch out for her. She only knew that thoughts weren't running through her brain as fast as heat was flashing through her body. She wasn't thinking at all when she leaned forward. Rather, she was feeling and wishing and hoping and remembering what it had felt like to be held by a man.

Her babies were so little. Her life had been torn apart. In the midst of caring for her girls and forging ahead, her attraction to Mitch seemed to be a living, breathing entity that at that moment she couldn't deny.

When his strong arms enfolded her, she felt safe. As he murmured her name, she felt cared for. He lowered his head and she lifted her chin. Their lips met.

Lily's senses whirled and she couldn't deny a longing that came from deep within. As Mitch's mouth opened over hers, she lost all sense of time and place. All she cared about was now, the rush of wanting, the scent of Mitch that was new and exciting, the thrill of feeling like a woman again.

Suddenly her womb tightened as it did when she nursed the babies. Troy's daughters.

What in God's name was she doing?

As suddenly as the kiss began, she tore away. The expression on Mitch's face told her he knew why. She clamped her hand over her lips and tears rushed to her eyes. She saw that determined look come over Mitch and she couldn't face it, not tonight.

"Talk to me, Lily," he coaxed gently.

She shook her head. "I can't. Not now. Maybe in the morning."

"Do you want to let us both stew all night when what you need is sleep?"

"It was a mistake."

He sighed. "Maybe that's one of the things we need to talk about."

When she remained silent, he stroked a tear from her cheek, finally agreeing. "All right. Go to bed. I'll be here if you need help with the babies during the night."

"Mitch, I'm sorry."

He put his finger gently over her lips.

Backing into her room, she closed the door. She heard his boots on the wooden floorboards, his tread as he walked down the stairs. Then she collapsed on her bed, not even taking her clothes off, shutting her eyes and praying sleep would come quickly.

The following morning, Mitch made scrambled eggs while Angie and Lily fed the twins in the upstairs nursery.

He'd crossed the line last night. He'd known physical contact with Lily was taboo. But it hadn't been until his lips had touched hers that he'd realized how truly vulnerable she was.

He'd damaged their relationship and he didn't know if

he could fix it. But he had to get the old one back—he'd made a promise to Troy.

When Angie had arrived home after midnight, the twins had been starting to stir. She said she'd help him feed them so Lily could sleep. But Lily had heard them, come in, taken Grace from Angie and told her to go to bed. She'd hardly glanced at him.

They'd fed Grace and Sophie in silence. When the twins woke again at four, they'd both fed them again. Mitch had never actually appreciated how complicated this was for women. They hadn't recovered completely from giving birth and they had to use reserves they didn't know they had to combat sleep deprivation, fatigue and chores that seemed to multiply with each hour.

And what had he done? Stirred up something that was better left alone. He didn't know if Lily was ever going to look him in the eyes again.

He'd just switched off the burner when she and Angie rolled in a double stroller. Grace and Sophie looked as if they were content and almost asleep.

Crossing to the refrigerator, Angie pulled out milk and orange juice, snagging the coffeepot and bringing it to the table. "You should go back to bed," Angie told Lily as they pulled out their chairs.

"I have laundry to do, and I want to make up a couple of casseroles and freeze them so we can just pull them out this week if we need them."

Although Mitch sat at the table with them, Lily glanced down at her plate. She picked up a slice of toast, took a bite and set it down again.

For the next ten minutes, the lump in Mitch's chest grew as he and Angie made conversation.

Finally, his breakfast eaten, he asked Lily, "Can I talk to you for a minute before I go?"

Her attention automatically went to her daughters, but Angie reassured her quickly. "I'll watch them. Go ahead."

There were so many things he wanted to tell Lily as they stood in the foyer. But he couldn't think of one. She was wearing jeans and a pink sweater and looked as if she were going to face the new day with determination and courage, the way she always did.

He knew what she wanted to hear from him, so he said it. "You were right. Last night was a mistake. I was out of line."

"You weren't the one who started it," she admitted honestly. "I don't know what got into me."

"You were grateful for a little help," he said with a smile that didn't come from inside.

"A *lot* of help," she returned, gazing into his eyes like she used to.

"Are you going to be okay when Angie leaves for work?"

"I'll be fine. It's Raina's day off. She's coming over."

He nodded, sure her friends would give her any help she needed, at least for a while. But he also knew Lily wouldn't want to burden them and she'd soon be taking all of it on herself.

They couldn't get involved for so many reasons. What if Lily ever saw his scars, learned his fears? The last relationship he'd tried a few years ago hadn't worked because of all of it. Nothing had changed since then, and on Lily's part, her grief and her connection to Troy was sustaining her in some ways. Missing and longing for him meant loving him. She wasn't ready to let go of that.

Still, Mitch didn't know how to walk away from her. He couldn't because he'd promised he wouldn't.

"I'll call you in a couple of days, just to see if Grace and Sophie are settling in. If you need anything, you have my number."

She reached out and touched his arm, probably feeling the same wall he did, a wall they were both standing behind so they wouldn't get hurt.

"Thank you," she said softly.

He left the Victorian again, realizing he didn't want her thanks. What he *did* want was still a mystery to him.

A few weeks later, Mitch was driving home from work when he decided to call Lily. They'd had a *brief* phone conversation last week because neither was comfortable with what had happened and they couldn't seem to get back on that "friend" footing. Now her cell phone rang and rang and rang until finally—a man picked up.

"Who is this?" Mitch asked, surprised by the male voice. A repairman, maybe? But why would he have Lily's cell phone?

"This is Craig Gillette. I'm the manager of Sagebrush Foods."

"Sagebrush Foods? I don't understand. Where's Lily Wescott?"

"Mrs. Wescott had an incident in our store. She's okay now but…"

An incident? What the hell was that? "Put her on," Mitch ordered.

Apparently speaking to the authority in Mitch's voice, the man said, "Sir, I can't right now. We've got two crying infants and she's feeling a little dizzy."

Dizzy? "You tell her not to move. I'll be there in five."

Mitch didn't give the manager time to protest or approve. He stepped on the gas.

Minutes later Mitch rushed into the store, scanning the produce area. Rounding a corner, he spotted Lily in the canned goods aisle, holding a paper cup. There were cans of green beans all over the floor around the folding chair where she sat. The twins were ensconced in their stroller. Sophie's little face was screwed up in displeasure, but Grace seemed content for the moment to stare at the bright lights and rows of colorful cans.

Mitch let his training prevail rather than the fear that threatened his composure. In as calm a voice as he could muster, he asked, "What happened?" followed by, "Are you all right?"

Lily looked so pale, and all he wanted to do was lift her into his arms and carry her somewhere safe. But the twins were a concern, too, and he had to get to the bottom of what had happened.

"I just felt a little dizzy, that's all," she said in a soft voice, taking another sip of water. "I haven't gotten much sleep lately and I ran out of diapers…" Grace reached out a little hand to her and Lily reached back.

He got the picture much too well and he didn't like what he saw. His guess? She'd felt faint and she'd run the stroller into the corner of the green beans display.

"Did she pass out?" he asked Gillette.

"No, sir. We wanted to call an ambulance, but she said she just needed to put her head down between her knees for a while—" He stopped when Lily gave him a scolding look as if he were divulging too much information.

Mitch went to Lily and crouched down beside her, looking her over with a practiced doctor's eye. "Be honest with me. Do I need to call an ambulance?"

There were deep blue smudges under both of her eyes. Her hair was a disheveled ponytail and she wore a sweatsuit. This wasn't the Lily he was used to, with her composed attitude, neat hairdos and tailored clothing.

Looking up at him, she forced a smile. She was clearly exhausted.

With his fingertips to her neck, he felt her pulse beating fast.

"Mitch," she protested, turning her head.

His fingers stayed put. "Quiet for a few seconds," he suggested.

Her pulse was definitely racing.

"No ambulance," she said.

"Then tell me what's going on. But drink that water before you do." He guessed she was dehydrated.

"You're acting like a doctor."

"I'm also acting like a friend."

Their gazes met and Mitch could see she was remembering their kiss as vividly as he was, even in these circumstances. Just friends? Not likely.

She didn't argue with him, but rather drank the cup of water.

"Are you still dizzy? Should I call Hillary?" Their colleague was her OB/GYN.

"No. I'm seeing her in a few days for a follow-up. I know what's wrong, Mitch. Not enough sleep, not enough liquids, probably not enough food. I forget to eat when I'm busy. Please don't scold."

He would have, but he could see she realized what he'd known could happen all along—she was overwhelmed.

"Let's see if you can stand on your own."

He held her around the waist and helped her to her feet. She felt slight to him. She'd definitely lost weight.

He should have been checking in with her daily, no matter how uncomfortable things were between them. So much for looking after her.

His body was responding in ways it shouldn't as he kept his arm around her waist and they walked a few steps down the aisle.

"Do you think you can walk to your car on your own steam? I'll drive yours then walk back here for mine."

"I drove over here for the diapers because I didn't want to bother anyone," she muttered, then added fiercely, "I'm capable of walking to the car."

At least she wasn't protesting him driving her home. He wanted her to understand the seriousness of what was happening to her. But that discussion would have to wait until she was on the sofa with her feet up and Sophie and Grace were fed and diapered.

In the house a while later, they sat on the sofa, hips practically touching, watching the babies in their cribs on the monitor. Mitch had found laundry in the washer and dryer, bottles in the sink, and had coaxed a little information from Lily. The babies now had a fussy spell that lasted from after Angie left in the evening until well after midnight. And they were nursing at least every three hours. She *was* exhausted and dehydrated and had to do more to take care of herself. But she couldn't do that unless the twins needs were met first.

Mitch began, "You need help, Lily, and you've got to get it before you can't take care of Sophie and Grace. Hire an au pair who will stay at the house for free rent."

He shifted so they weren't quite so close as he expected Lily to protest. She didn't. Rather, she just looked pensive. "I really hadn't thought about doing that. I don't know if Angie would like having a stranger move in."

"She can probably see you need help, too, but doesn't know what to do about it. Talk to her. Talk to Raina and Gina. Maybe they'll know of someone who needs a job and is good with children. But you can't go on like this."

"I know. Believe me, Mitch, I do. What just happened scared me. I just wish—" She swallowed hard. "If Troy were here—"

Mitch watched as she blinked fast and faced the cold splash of reality once more. He didn't know whether to cover her hand with his or move even farther away. Everything had become so complicated between them.

After a few moments of silence, Lily seemed to pull herself together. "Thinking about Troy…" She stopped. "His sister Ellie might be the perfect person to help me."

"Isn't she in Oklahoma?"

"Yes, but Troy's mom and Ellie have wanted to visit. Maybe they could come and help out and maybe…" A smile bloomed on Lily's lips. "Maybe Ellie could stay! She could set up her web business from here. I'm going to call Angie first. If she's agreeable, then I'll phone Ellie."

Lily picked up the handset from the end table.

As she dialed a number, Mitch realized he should be happy she was going to get the help she needed. Yet part of him knew that if Troy's sister came to assist her, Lily could stay entrenched in the past instead of moving on.

That shouldn't matter to him. But it did.

Chapter 5

Lily hung up the receiver and glanced at the glass of juice Mitch had brought her, now empty. She knew better than to let herself become dehydrated. She knew better about a lot of things. She should be grateful Mitch had called right when he had. Troy had always maintained, *There are no coincidences.* She'd always laughed when he'd said it, but maybe he was right.

She found Mitch in the laundry room, pulling baby clothes from the dryer. "You don't have to do that," she said.

He just arched one heavy brow at her and removed the last of the Onesies, settling them in the wash basket.

"I ordered takeout from the Yellow Rose." He glanced at his watch. "It should be here in about fifteen minutes."

"Takeout? But they don't deliver unless—"

"I ordered two dinners for tonight, and three more.

You should have enough for a few days so you don't have to worry about cooking."

She knew better than to protest. She should have ordered food herself. She'd intended to cook, but with Angie on the late shift, it had seemed a bother when she had so many other things to do. Still, almost fainting had scared her. She had to eat, drink and get some rest.

"That was a long phone conversation," Mitch commented, carrying the laundry basket into the kitchen and then the living room.

"Just set it on the coffee table," she said. "I have to divide the clothes. I keep some down here, and the rest upstairs."

After he set it down, he asked, "So is the cavalry coming?"

She smiled. "Troy's mother is going to stay for a week. She doesn't want to leave his dad for longer than that. But Ellie will drive her here and stay as long as I need her. She said she could use a change of scene, and Texas seems like a good spot. She's going to bring her sewing machine and make baby clothes and get her website up and running while she's here. If the three of us get along well, she might stay indefinitely."

"I assume since she makes baby clothes, she likes babies."

"She worked at a day-care center for a while, so she's had more practical experience than *I* have."

"I'm glad that's settled. When are they coming?"

"Next week."

"And in the meantime?"

"In the meantime, I'll get by. But I'll take better care of myself."

"That's a promise?"

"It's a promise."

There was about six inches of space between them that seemed to be filled with all kinds of electricity. Lily couldn't understand why, when she was around Mitch now, every nerve in her body tingled a new message.

"Why don't you take out the clothes you want to keep down here, and I'll carry the rest upstairs."

She took a few outfits from the basket and laid them on the coffee table. As Mitch lifted it again, she found her hand going to his forearm.

He pulled away and she realized she'd clasped his scarred and injured arm. "I'm sorry," she said.

He put down the laundry and took a step closer to her. "There's nothing to be sorry about. I'm just not used to having anyone touch me there."

"Does it hurt?"

"No."

"Do you ever let anyone see it?" She didn't know why the personal question had rolled off her tongue so easily, but what had happened at the grocery store had solidified the bond between them.

"Do you?" she prodded. "You wear long sleeves, winter and summer."

"Why does it matter?"

"Because we're friends and I'd like to know."

His expression remained steady, his voice steely. "Most people can't handle seeing scars. They're fascinated by them, but they're afraid of them. They want to ask questions, but they turn away."

"Do you think I'd turn away?"

The two of them were breathing the same air, standing in the same space, but a shield went up in Mitch's eyes that sent him somewhere apart from her. Suddenly she suspected why.

"Have you been in a relationship since you returned from Iraq?"

He started to swivel away from her to go into the kitchen. She wouldn't let him evade her that easily. She didn't touch him this time, but just slipped in front of him so he couldn't take another step without running into her.

"Lily," he said with exasperation. "I don't want to talk about it."

"Have you ever talked about it…talked about *her?*"

"No."

"Just as you haven't talked about Iraq."

"That's right."

Men! Lily thought. Troy had been the same way. He hadn't spoken to her about his earlier deployments, and she hadn't pushed. She had imagined that he'd eventually confide in her. But they hadn't had time. And maybe if he had confided in her, she would have been more prepared—

"So don't talk about Iraq," she conceded.

"But tell you about my love life?" Mitch asked, almost amused.

She realized how ridiculous she was being, when Mitch was a private man who didn't reveal much at all! "I guess I just need something to think about besides my own life right now."

That shield was still in his eyes but his face took on a gentler look.

"Okay. I'll do this once." He jammed his hands into his trouser pockets. "I was back over a year. I'd gotten a fellowship in endocrinology in Dallas and met Charlene, who was a reporter for the local news. She wanted to do a story about my new specialty and why I was changing, but I told her no. After a few tries and a few conversations, we started going out. I wore long sleeves most of the time then, too. One night I took her out to dinner. Afterward, things progressed naturally but when we got to the bedroom and I took off my shirt— She couldn't bear to see my scars, let alone touch them. That's when I realized reality was just a little too difficult for most people to handle."

"Most *women,*" Lily murmured, realizing how little emotion Mitch had put into that recital. "That's what you meant to say."

"Maybe I did."

"Not every woman is the same." She could see right away that he didn't believe that. "The scars are more extensive than on your arm and hand," she guessed.

"Yes. They're on my shoulder, back and side, too."

Lily thought about what he'd said but kept her gaze from falling to his shoulder, or to his flat stomach. She was feeling almost dizzy again. Could that be from imagining Mitch without his shirt? Was she different from that reporter? Would extensive scars make her want to turn away?

The doorbell rang.

Mitch took a step back, looking…relieved? Was *she* relieved that the personal conversation was over? Or did she *want* to delve deeper? Somehow she knew Mitch wouldn't let her do that. At least, not tonight.

"So what's for dinner?" she asked brightly, knowing the Yellow Rose delivery had arrived at the door.

Getting to know Mitch any better would mean ties she might not want…problems she didn't need. Getting to know Mitch better could lead to another kiss.

Neither of them wanted that—right?

* * *

Lily's cavalry arrived and Mitch stayed away. He knew it was best for both of them.

Almost a month after the grocery store incident, he received a call as he sat at the desk in his spare bedroom, ready to check email and eat dinner—a slice of pizza and a beer. When he recognized the number on his cell phone, he quickly swallowed his mouthful of pizza and shut down his email program.

"Hey, Lily. How's it going?"

When he'd called to check on her a couple of weeks before, Troy's mother had just left Lily's home and Ellie was settling in. Mitch had known Lily didn't need him there, or even want him there. He knew what had probably gone on while Troy's family was with her—lots of remembering.

It was best that he stay on his side of town and not interfere.

"Darlene and Ellie have been wonderful. They gave me a chance to pull myself back together, get my diet straightened out and find a sleep schedule. And Ellie's definitely going to stay. Angie really likes her, and we all get along great."

After a long pause, she asked, "Why haven't you been over lately?"

"I really didn't think you needed another visitor. Besides, the practice is picking up. I've been working late many nights."

"The beginning of May is a time for growth and thinking about the future. I can see why the practice picks up this time of year. I miss it."

"I thought you might."

"Don't get me wrong, I love taking care of Grace and

Sophie. Doing that, even with Ellie here, is enough to keep me busy all day. But working with you and Hillary and Jon and the staff is part of my life, too."

"So you're coming back?"

"I have to, Mitch. I'm going to see how the summer goes with Ellie, then I'll give you all a definite date."

Lily sounded less frazzled, more peaceful, maybe even a bit happy. He guessed the babies were bringing her joy, not just work, and that was lifting her up, fulfilling her in a new way.

She went on, "They're both cooing. And they're fascinated by their mobiles. You've got to come see them, Mitch, and meet Ellie."

Ellie was Lily's family now, along with her friends. He would bet a week's pay that their first meeting was going to be…uncomfortable. He thought about what type of visit this should be, how much time he should spend with Ellie and Lily, how much time with the twins.

"Have you been out of the house much?"

"Nope. The twins keep me a prisoner," she said with a laugh. "Seriously. I went to the grocery store again last week. This time I made it without knocking anything over. But that's been about it."

"Would tomorrow night be convenient?" he asked. "I could meet Ellie, see how the babies have grown, then take you for a drive. In fact, we could drive to the lake to hear the outdoor concert. How does that sound?"

"That sounds wonderful! But you realize, don't you, I'm going to have to call back here every fifteen minutes to see what the twins are doing."

"That's a mother's prerogative. Why don't you check with your housemates to see if they mind your leaving, then give me a call back. I think the concert will be a nice break for both of us."

"Your idea sounds perfect. I'll get back to you shortly."

"I'll talk to you soon," Mitch said and hung up.

He didn't know whether to hope for this idea to go through or not. It could become more than a casual outing. Then he grabbed hold of reality again. Not if they *wanted* only casual. After all, it would be easy to stay casual. Lily could tell him all about the memories she and Troy's mother and sister had stirred up during their visit.

Casual would be the theme of the evening.

"How long have you been working with Lily?" Ellie asked on Saturday evening.

He'd arrived a short time before and looked in on the twins, who'd been finishing their supper. They were asleep in their bassinets now and Lily had gone upstairs to change.

Studying Ellie, he noticed she wore her light brown hair in a short, glossy bob that swung against her cheek. The style accentuated her heart-shaped face. At twenty-six, she was ten years younger than the brother she obviously missed.

Mitch tried to answer her question without becoming defensive. After all, who could blame her for watching out for her sister-in-law. "We've worked together for two and a half years."

"Troy mentioned you," she admitted. "Something about playing pool at the Silver Spur Grill."

"We did."

"He said you were in Iraq and had to leave the Guard for medical reasons." She looked him over as if expecting to find his injury and her gaze settled on his hand. She quickly looked away.

"I did," he answered crisply, not intending to go into *that,* even for Troy's sister. The screws the doctor had put in his shoulder and leg, his missing spleen, never mind the damage to his arm and hand, had shut down his ability to serve. Most of the time, no one could tell he'd been injured.

It was time to go on the offensive with Ellie. "Lily tells me you worked in a day-care setting."

"For a while," she responded.

If he got her talking, she might relax. "But you like to sew?"

Looking surprised that he knew a detail like that, she responded, "I started making customized outfits for gifts for friends and relatives. They became so popular, I was getting orders. That's when I decided to open the store. At first I did pretty well, but then when harder times hit, even folks who had the money for those kind of clothes decided to spend it elsewhere."

"I hope your web-based business takes off for you."

"I hope so, too. But in the meantime, I'm going to enjoy taking care of Grace and Sophie. Did you spend much time with them when you brought Lily home from the hospital?"

She clearly wasn't giving up on turning over every leaf of his association with Lily. But he didn't have anything to hide—not really. "Two babies are a handful. That's why I think it's important Lily get away for a bit tonight."

Ellie's green eyes canvassed his face as if searching for motives. Finally, she admitted, "I'm glad the weather turned warm enough."

At that moment, Lily came down the stairs.

Automatically, Mitch turned her way. She was wearing blue jeans and a red blouse with a yellow windbreaker tossed over her arm. She'd fashioned her hair with a clip at the nape and she looked…fantastic. Her blue eyes seemed even bluer tonight as she gave him a tentative smile. He couldn't look away and she seemed to be as immobilized as he was…

…Until Ellie cleared her throat and asked, "How long do you think the concert will last?"

Lily burst into motion, as if in denial that the moment of awareness had ever happened. "Oh, we won't stay for the whole concert, and I'll call in to check with you. That's the nice thing about going to the lake. I don't have to worry about anybody being bothered if I make phone calls during the concert. Since this is the first concert of the season, the audience will be sparse. So call me if the least little thing is wrong, or you think I should come home."

Lily talked very fast when she was nervous, and that's what she was doing now. Her last comment led him to wonder if she was looking for an excuse not to go. Was it because she was still uncomfortable since their kiss? He'd find out shortly.

Lily gave Ellie a list of instructions along with phone numbers, then hiked the strap of her purse over her shoulder, took a last look at the monitor, blew a kiss to the image of her daughters and went out the door.

On the drive to the lake they didn't talk, but rather enjoyed the peaceful scenery—ranches and cotton fields that spread as far as the eye could see, tumbleweeds rolling by.

After he turned off the main road, down a gravel lane, and bumped over a dusty area used as the parking space for the concert, Lily finally said, "I think I'd forgotten how green everything is at this time of year, how spring smells, how the sky turns purple and orange at sunset. In some ways, I feel like I've been locked in a closet since last summer, not really seeing what was around me. Except the twins, of course."

"You've faced a lot of change in the past ten months."

She lowered her window and took a huge breath of outside air as the May breeze tossed her hair. "I don't want to go back into that closet again."

"Then don't. You have help now. While you're on leave, take some time for yourself, too. Figure out who you are again in your new life."

Turning to him, she reached for his arm, and he guessed she didn't even realize she'd done that. "You've been through this, haven't you?" she asked.

Her fingers on his forearm seemed to send fire through his body. Trying to smother it, he responded roughly, "You know I have. I'm not sure major life change is anything anyone welcomes, especially when it's borne from tragedy."

He gently tugged away from her touch. "Come on. Let's go to this concert."

His body still racing with adrenaline from their contact, Mitch pulled a blanket from the backseat. They headed toward the people gathering in a large pavilion. They didn't see anyone they knew as Mitch dropped the blanket on one of the park benches facing the bandstand. The sides of the pavilion would block the wind and Lily could always wrap herself in the blanket if she got cold.

Their shoulders brushed. Mitch considered moving away, but didn't. Still, he was glad they hadn't recognized anyone. He didn't want Lily having second thoughts about coming. Something told him Ellie would be grilling her when she got back, and she'd have plenty of second thoughts then. He was just glad she'd accepted his invitation tonight, even if it was only to escape her figurative closet for a little while.

The quartet that performed with oboe, bass, clarinet and guitar played instrumental versions of popular songs. The crowd didn't grow much larger as Mitch was sure it would have if this had been a country-and-western or bluegrass band, or even an oldies night. But it suited his purpose to be here tonight with Lily, to listen to calm and easy music so she could relax. Even when she called home, no worry lines fanned her brow as Ellie reassured her that her girls were fine.

When Lily recognized a song, she hummed along. Her face was in profile as she gazed toward the lake, and he could study her without being afraid she'd catch him. Her hair waved in gentle curls under the barrette. Her turned-up nose was so recognizable on Sophie and Grace. Lily's bangs were long, brushed to one side, her brows a shade darker than her hair as they drew together when she concentrated on the music. She'd never worn much makeup, but tonight he noticed a sheen of gloss on her lips.

He could watch her all night and not tire of her expressions, the tilt of her head, the slant of her cheeks. He felt desire grip him again.

At that moment, she turned away from the music toward him…as if she wanted to sneak a peek at *his* expression. They both froze, their gazes locked, their bodies leaning just a little closer until the press of their shoulders was noticeable. Mitch reminded himself that there were so many reasons to keep away from Lily.

The music ended and the quartet announced a break.

Not moving away, Lily asked, "What do you think?"

About her? About the night? About the music? Which was the question to answer?

"My mother would have called them a dance band."

Lily blinked as if she hadn't expected that at all. But then she rallied. "Did she like to dance?"

Letting out a silent sigh of relief, Mitch leaned back so the pressure between their shoulders eased. "She didn't go out dancing, if that's what you mean. She didn't date. She always told me she didn't have time. She'd say, 'Who could work and have time for a man, too?'"

"A modern philosophy if I ever heard one," Lily joked.

Mitch chuckled. "Maybe so. But once in a while, she'd put on the radio and I'd catch her dancing around the kitchen. She always got embarrassed, but I could tell that if she'd had the time and a partner, she'd be good at it."

To his surprise, Mitch felt his phone vibrate against his hip. When he checked the caller ID, he recognized the number of a friend, Tony Russo. "I should take this," he said.

"Go ahead. We can go back to your SUV. I really should be getting home."

Because of that pulsating moment when he'd almost kissed her again? "You're sure?"

"Yes."

The certainty in her answer told him she didn't want to take the chance of staying longer, the chance that darkness and a starry sky might urge them to become more intimate.

A few minutes later, Lily stood beside Mitch at his SUV, wondering why she had agreed to come with him tonight. This seemed so much like a date and it just couldn't be! She'd known right away Ellie didn't approve when she'd told her where she was going.

She had to ask herself…would Troy approve of her being here with Mitch tonight? Troy's approval still mattered to her. She fingered her wedding ring, still feeling married.

Inhaling the scents of spring on the wind, she attempted to stay in the moment. She exhaled confusion and loss, in favor of life and music and the sliver of moon above. She was aware of Mitch's conversation, his deep laugh. He asked about someone named Jimmy and reported he'd gotten an email from Matt last week.

She was learning Mitch had more facets than she'd ever imagined. He had depth she'd never known about. He had a past he didn't want to talk about.

Now, however, when he ended his call, he smiled at her. That smile both comforted her and made her breath hitch!

"An old friend?" she guessed, taking the safe route.

"Yes, Tony served with me in Iraq."

Surprised he was forthcoming about that, she asked, "Is he coming for a visit?"

"You heard me mention the bed-and-breakfast."

She nodded.

"Every year, the first weekend in December, I get together with servicemen I knew in Iraq. We alternate locations and their families come, too. This year it's my turn to host."

"What a wonderful idea!"

"We usually start planning this time of year to get the best airfares and accommodations. We have a money pool so if someone can't afford to come, the cash is there to draw on."

"How long does your reunion last?"

"Friday to Sunday. My house will be home base on Saturday. Do you have any ideas to occupy kids?"

"Besides enlisting someone to play Santa Claus?" she joked. "I used to do some face painting."

"You're kidding."

"No. I'm *not* just a doctor. I have an artistic bent."

He laughed. "That would be perfect."

A bit of moonlight drifted over them as they stood close. The look in Mitch's eyes was recognizable to her. He'd had that same look before he'd kissed her outside her bedroom.

When he reached out and stroked her cheek, she didn't pull away. She couldn't. There was something about Mitch that drew her to him, that made her want to forget her inhibitions, her idea of propriety, her sadness and loss.

"Lily," he murmured as the stars bore witness, as the moon seemed to tilt, as the ground trembled under her feet. The touch of his fingers on her face was filled with an aching longing.

But then he dropped his hand to his side and opened the passenger door. He didn't have to say anything and neither did she. They knew they couldn't kiss again. If they did, they might not stop there.

Ellie, Sophie and Grace were waiting for her. She didn't want to be any more confused when she walked in that door than she already was now.

Chapter 6

Time rolled by so fast, Lily could hardly count the days. She spent a lot of time thinking about Mitch, of how he'd touched her face at the lake. That night they'd silently but tacitly backed away from each other. Because of Ellie? Because they both feared their feelings were inappropriate?

The last week in May, Lily pushed Sophie and Grace's stroller into the office suite that was still familiar to her. Yet when she looked around at the sea-foam-green furniture, the rose carpeting and the green-and-mauve wallpaper, she didn't feel as if she *did* belong any more. She'd only been away three months, yet it seemed like a lifetime.

"This is where I work," she told Ellie, motioning to the reception area, the glass window behind which their receptionist Maryanne sat, the hall leading to exam rooms, office suites and the lab.

"It's really kind of…cozy," Ellie remarked as if she was surprised. "I think I expected white walls and tile and a sterile atmosphere."

"We try to keep it relaxed," Lily explained. "The couples and women who come to us are stressed enough. The more relaxed we can keep the process, the better."

"How many doctors work here?"

"Four, as well as two nurse-practitioners, two techs and our receptionist."

Lily rolled the stroller up to the receptionist's window.

Maryanne slid the glass open and grinned at her. "We miss you, Dr. Wescott," she said to Lily.

"I miss all of you, too," Lily returned, meaning it. Helping other women have babies was important to her, and even more so now, since she knew the joy of her twins.

She introduced Ellie.

Maryanne came out of her cubicle to coo over the babies. "They're adorable. I'm so glad you brought them in. And at just the right time. Everybody's on their lunch break. Go on back to the lounge."

Ellie took a peek down the hall. "Maybe I shouldn't go with you. I don't want to interrupt anything."

"Don't be silly," Lily said. "The practice is usually closed from twelve to one every day. That's why I was glad when we finished with Tessa right on time. I know Hillary will want to meet you. When I had a checkup with her, I told her about your baby store and your customized outfits. She has a one-year-old. She could be your first paying customer in Sagebrush."

Although Lily had attempted to prepare herself to see Mitch again, she didn't feel ready. Not after their awkward parting the evening of the concert.

As soon as she pushed open the door to the lounge and saw Mitch sitting at the table with Hillary and Jon, she was tossed back to that night, standing close to him by his SUV, the heat of his fingers a scalding impression on her cheek.

Mitch stood as soon as he spotted her and Ellie, the white lab coat he wore giving him the professional appearance that had been so familiar to her before the night of the banquet, before Grace and Sophie had been born.

The twins were the center of attention now as everyone crowded around. Lily was glad for that, relieved to be able to introduce Ellie to her colleagues, grateful that no one could see how being in the same room with Mitch affected her. Lily couldn't believe it herself. Maybe she just didn't want to believe it.

What kind of woman was she? She'd loved her husband, loved him to the moon and back. He'd only been gone for ten months. Many nights she still cried herself to sleep, missing him, needing him, longing for him. Her reaction to Mitch didn't make sense. Not at all. Before the twins were born, she'd never looked at him as anything but a colleague. But now, as everyone babbled to the babies and chatted politely with Ellie, Mitch's gaze passed over Lily's lilac top and slacks then swiftly returned to her face. His appraisal left her a little short of breath.

Hurriedly, she ducked her head and bent to scoop Sophie from the stroller. "I don't know what I'd do without Ellie," she told everyone. "I seem to need six hands when these two are crying at the same time."

"So when are you coming back?" Hillary asked, her short chestnut hair fringing her face.

"Probably in November," she answered, not knowing what the next months would bring.

"You take your time deciding," Jon said. He was tall and lean with narrow black glasses that made him look scholarly.

Hillary asked, "May I hold Sophie?"

"Sure."

Hillary took the baby and settled her in the crook of her arm, looking down on her with the affection moms feel for kids. "I believe these little girls are going to be petite."

"Maybe. Or they could eventually grow as tall as Troy." Lily felt the need to mention his name, to bring him into the conversation.

Jon leaned a little closer to her. "How are you doing, really?"

"I'm okay. It's just the world's very different without Troy in it. Some days I expect that. Other days I expect him to come walking through the door, pick up Grace and Sophie, to figure out which one will look for his approval and which one won't."

Hillary had obviously overheard. She said, "I'll always remember Troy, Lily. I really cherish the table he made for me. It's absolutely beautiful craftsmanship."

Lily vividly remembered the piece of Troy's unfinished furniture still in storage. In fact, he'd been in the last stages of completing the plant stand she'd asked him to make when he was deployed. So much was unfinished and Lily didn't know how to complete the tapestry of the life that had been hers and Troy's.

Mitch had heard their conversation, too, and turned away, crossing to the refrigerator, closing the top on a juice bottle and setting it inside. His actions were slow and deliberate. She knew she'd brought up Troy to put a boundary around herself again, a boundary that would keep Mitch out. Why had she dropped in today? To catch up with old friends? Or to see *him?*

As Hillary moved away, rocking Sophie and cooing to her, Lily's gaze landed on Ellie, who was glancing toward her and then Mitch. No one else seemed to notice the vibes between Lily and Mitch, but apparently Ellie did.

Lily hung out with her colleagues in the lounge for a while. They all wanted to take turns holding the twins and see if they could distinguish between the two. As Lily had suspected, Hillary asked Ellie to tell her all about the clothes she created.

Stepping away from the group with Grace in her arms, Lily went in search of Mitch. He was her friend, and they would be working together when she returned. She had to keep communication open between them. She had to know what was going on in his mind. Maybe it had nothing to do with her. If it didn't, she'd be relieved. At least that's what she told herself.

She found him in his office, at his computer. She stood there for a few moments, listening to Grace's little soughing sounds, studying Mitch's profile. Her gaze went to his hands as his fingers depressed keys. His left hand was faster than his right and she wondered if the fingers on his right hand hurt to use. What kind of pain did he experience on a daily basis? With what he'd told her, she guessed his injuries had left repercussions. On the other hand, were the memories in his head more painful than anything physical injuries could cause? She wished he could talk to her about all of it. She wished—

Moving into the room, she said, "You should still be on your lunch break."

"A fertility specialist never sleeps," he joked. "I have

a couple coming in this afternoon because the time is right."

"They're going the artificial insemination route?"

"For now. In vitro doesn't fit into their budget." His gaze went from Lily to Grace. "She seems content."

Lily checked her watch. "Probably for about fifteen more minutes."

Rolling his chair back, Mitch stood and approached her. His large hand gently passed over Grace's little head, his thumb brushing her strands of cotton-soft blond hair. "So you just decided to stop in or did you and Ellie have errands in the area?"

"Sophie and Grace had appointments with Tessa. Since we were in the building…" She trailed off.

"You wanted to stay in touch."

"I think it will be easier for me to come back to work in the fall if I do."

He nodded.

"Mitch…" She didn't know what she wanted to say, or how to say it. "I need to talk about Troy."

"I know you do. That was another good reason for Ellie coming to stay with you."

"You left the lounge and I thought—"

"I told you I have clients coming."

"I know." She felt so stymied for the right words to say. She could say, *I want to be around you, but when I am, I feel guilty.* Yet that couldn't come out because she and Mitch were both fighting becoming any closer.

She bowed her head, placing a tiny kiss on Grace's forehead, trying to figure out what she was doing in this room with Mitch and why she had actually stopped in today.

Yet Mitch wouldn't let her stand there, stewing in her

own confusion. He slipped one knuckle under her chin and lifted it. "I think we're both feeling things we don't believe we should be feeling. You don't know whether to run in the other direction or pretend we're just friends."

"I don't want to pretend!"

His brows arched as he gave her a crooked smile. "That *is* the crux of it."

"Lily." Ellie was standing in the doorway with Sophie, studying the two of them standing close, Mitch's finger under her chin.

He quickly dropped his hand to his side while Lily turned to face her sister-in-law. "I know. They're both going to start crying for lunch soon."

"If you'd like to use my office, you can," Mitch offered. "I have work to do in the lab."

Crossing to his desk and reaching for a file folder, he picked it up, then stopped in the doorway. "It's good to see you again, Ellie."

"You, too," she said politely.

Mitch stood there for a few moments as if waiting to see if Troy's sister had something else to say. But she didn't. After a last glance at Lily and the twins, he strode down the hall.

Lily waited, not knowing if Ellie might have something to say to *her*. But her sister-in-law just moved toward the door. "I'll get the diaper bag." Then she was gone, too, leaving Lily with Grace in Mitch's office with very chaotic thoughts and feelings.

"They sure like those swings," Angie observed a week later as Lily came into the kitchen and watched her putting together a casserole for lunch.

Lily stirred the white sauce she was cooking and

glanced over at her content daughters. "They're settling into a real schedule."

"Where's Ellie?"

"She went shopping to get material she needed."

Angie poured herself a cup of coffee and took a seat at the kitchen counter. "Mitch hasn't been around for a while. Did you two have a fight or something?"

Or something, Lily thought. "I saw him when I visited everyone at the practice."

"That was a week ago. He stopped in to see Sophie and Grace every day when they were in the hospital and he worried about you. It seems odd he hasn't called or dropped by more."

"I think he's giving me space."

Angie studied Lily over her mug. "Do you want space?"

"We're just friends." If she repeated those words often enough, she might believe them.

"I know that. And I know he's watching over you because Troy asked him to."

Lily found herself wanting to protest, to say that wasn't the only reason. Yet she wasn't sure she should. She didn't know what was in Mitch's mind. "I feel I owe him so much for everything."

"So why not call him and ask him to dinner?"

Angie made it sound so simple. On the one hand, Lily would love to do that. But on the other, she wished she and Mitch could have a little time alone, maybe straighten out everything between them.

"I could go to his place to cook dinner," she said aloud, testing the idea.

From the doorway, several bags in her arms, Ellie

asked, "You want to cook dinner for Mitch?" There was wariness in her tone and an element of disapproval.

"He did so much for me, including encouraging me to call you. I'd like to thank him."

Ellie came into the kitchen and dropped her bags on the table. Then she went to the twins and crouched down, greeting both of them.

"I'm off for the weekend," Angie offered. "I could watch Sophie and Grace if Ellie has plans."

"No plans tomorrow. Just the concert with you in Amarillo on Saturday," Ellie said to Angie, without looking up. "I can watch them."

"Are you sure?" Lily asked. "Because I could invite Mitch here instead."

"No," Ellie responded, standing. "It's fine. Angie and I and Sophie and Grace will have a girls' night together. It will be a blast, even if the babies can't eat popcorn yet."

"Before we make too many plans, I'd better find out if Mitch wants me to cook for him. I'll leave a message on his cell phone." She picked up the cordless phone in the kitchen before she lost her nerve.

An hour and a half later, when Mitch returned her call, Lily had just finished breast-feeding both babies. It was much easier now than when she'd first tried to juggle their needs.

"I got your message," Mitch said. "Is everything all right?"

Lily looked down at her sleeping daughters. "Everything's fine. I…" She cleared her throat. "If you're going to be home tomorrow evening, I'd like to cook you dinner."

"Home? As in at my house?"

She laughed. "Yes. Angie and Ellie offered to watch Sophie and Grace, and this would be my way to thank you for everything you've done."

He didn't say, "You don't have to thank me," because they'd gone through that routine before and he probably knew it would fall on deaf ears. "A home-cooked meal would be a nice change," he agreed noncommittally.

"What's your favorite meal?"

"Why don't you surprise me."

"You're not going to give me a hint?"

"Nope. I like everything."

"Okay, I'll stop at the market and then come over."

"I'm taking off tomorrow afternoon to meet with the couple who own the bed-and-breakfast around three. But I should be home by four. I can tape a spare key under the garage spout in case I'm tied up longer."

Lily was surprised Mitch was taking off, but she knew planning the reunion was important to him. "That's perfect. I can get started and then when you arrive, we can really catch up."

"Catching up sounds good," he responded, as if he meant it.

Lily's heart seemed to flutter but she told herself it was just her imagination.

After she ended the call, she wondered if she was doing the right thing. But showing her appreciation was important to her. No matter what Mitch said, she believed it was important to him, too.

She'd find out tomorrow night.

Lily found the key behind the spout on Friday and let herself into Mitch's brick ranch-style house situated on the outskirts of Sagebrush. She liked the looks of the outside with its neat plantings and tall fencing, and the protected entrance where she'd set the grocery bags on a wooden bench that perfectly fit the space. Slipping the key into the lock, she pushed open the door and stepped inside.

To the right of the small foyer, a door led into the garage. Beyond that lay a rambling living room. It was huge, with a fireplace, tall windows and a cathedral ceiling with a fan. The comfortable-looking furniture was upholstered in masculine colors, navy and burgundy. Distressed-pine tables and black wrought-iron lamps sat in practical positions around the furniture. She was surprised to see only a small flat-screen TV in the entertainment center rather than a larger model. But then maybe Mitch didn't spend much time watching TV.

The kitchen was straight ahead and she eagerly picked up the bags, took them in and set them on the counter. Stainless steel appliances looked shiny and new. An archway opened into a sunroom where French doors led outside to a large rustic brick patio. A round table and four chairs nestled in a corner of the dining area of the kitchen under a black wrought-iron chandelier. She liked the clean lines of the house, its spaciousness, its practical floor plan.

She was unpacking the groceries when her cell phone rang. She thought it might be Mitch telling her he was on his way. Instead, she recognized Raina's number and happily answered. "How are you?"

Her friend said, "I'm in labor!"

"You're not due till next week," Lily said practically.

Raina laughed. "Tell that to our son or daughter."

"Where are you?"

"At the hospital. Emily is with me."

Lily knew Raina was comfortable using a midwife, but her husband hadn't been so sure. "How is Shep handling this?"

"Let's just say he drove here under the speed limit but that was a struggle. Now he's pacing while Emily's trying to keep the mood relaxed."

Raina had wanted to have a home birth, but she'd compromised with Shep. Since Emily and Jared had managed to bring about changes at the hospital to include a midwife in the birthing process, there were two suites there now that were supposed to simulate the comforts of home. The birthing suites provided the advantages of delivering a baby in a more natural setting while having a doctor nearby should any complications arise.

"How are *you* handling labor?"

"I can't wait for this baby to be born. Wow," she suddenly exclaimed, "I'm starting another contraction and it's stronger than the last one. Either Shep or I will let you know when the baby's born. Talk to you later."

Lily thought about her own contractions, how they'd come on so suddenly, how Mitch had helped her. In some ways, that night seemed eons ago.

After considering her options, Lily had decided to make Mitch something she had never cooked before. She'd found the recipe for chicken in wine in her favorite cookbook. It wasn't complicated. It just required a little time to prepare. Today she had the time. She'd brought along her favorite pan and started bacon frying in it. Rummaging in Mitch's cupboard, she found other pots and pans she could use. After she sorted her ingredients, she prepared the chicken to fry in the bacon drippings.

A half hour later, the chicken was browning nicely when she heard the garage door open. She took a quick look around the kitchen. She had managed to set the table before she'd started the chicken. She'd brought along two place mats, matching napkins, as well as a vase filled with pretty, hand-carved wooden flowers. Mitch's white ironstone dishes looked perfect on the dark green place mats.

Lily heard the door from the garage into the foyer open then Mitch's deep voice calling into the kitchen. "Something smells great."

And then he was there in the doorway, tall and lean, his almost black eyes taking in everything at a glance. He wore blue jeans, black boots and a navy henley. Skitters of sensation rippled up and down her spine.

They just stood there for a few moments, staring at each other. He assessed her white jeans and pink top with its scoop neckline. "Shouldn't you be wearing an apron?"

"The clothes will wash."

"Spoken like a mom."

Moving forward into the kitchen, he caught sight of the table and stopped. "You've gone to a lot of trouble."

"Not really. You're just not used to a woman's touch." As soon as the words were out, she knew she should have thought first before speaking. Letting the thoughts in her mind spill free could land her in deep trouble.

Mitch didn't react, simply hung his keys on a hook above the light switch. "I don't know how long it's been since I walked into a kitchen with something good cooking. Do you want me to help with this?" He motioned to the stove and the sink. "Or do you want me to get out of your way?"

"You're welcome to help, but if you have something more important to do—"

"Nothing that can't wait," he said, washing his hands. "I worked in the yard earlier this afternoon."

"I like your house, and the way you've decorated."

His brows drew together as he dried his hands on the dish towel. "Maybe you can tell me the best way to set it up to entertain twenty to twenty-five people for the reunion weekend. I'm afraid space will be tight."

"What about a fire pit on the patio, depending on the weather, of course. It might draw a few people out there to toast marshmallows."

He studied her with one of those intense looks again and she knew it wasn't just the heat from the stove that was making her cheeks flame. "What?"

"You have great ideas."

Smiling to herself, she turned back to the chicken, deciding it was browned just right and that she had to concentrate on the meal so she wouldn't focus too much on Mitch. "My next great idea is that I'd better watch what I'm doing or your kitchen could go up in flames."

He chuckled. "What do you need help with?"

"Can you open the wine? I need a cup. I have everything else ready to simmer." She dumped in onions and celery, stirring to sauté them a bit, added carrots, chicken broth and the crumbled bacon. After Mitch loosened the cork and poured out a cup of wine, she took it from him, their hands grazing each other, hers tingling after they did.

Moving away from him, she poured the wine into the pot, put the lid on and set it to simmer, glad the major part of the meal was finished.

"Now what?" he asked.

"I need three apples peeled and sliced into that pie plate. I'll make the topping while you're doing that. Tell me about your meeting. Will you be able to reserve rooms at the bed-and-breakfast?"

When Mitch didn't answer, she looked up at him and saw him staring down at the apples. At that moment, she realized the request she'd made, as well as the mistake of asking him to do that kind of task.

"I've learned to do a lot of things with my left hand," he said matter-of-factly, "but using a knife to slice apples isn't one of them."

"Mitch, I'm sorry. I wasn't thinking."

"There's nothing to be sorry about. Why don't I look through my collection of DVDs and find something we would both enjoy?"

She wanted to put her arms around Mitch. She wanted to breathe in his scent and kiss him, letting him know the use of his fingers wasn't an issue between them.

"Okay," she said lightly. "I'll be there in a few minutes." That was all the time she'd need to slice the apples, mix them with cranberries and pour on a topping.

Then she might have to decide just where she stood where Mitch was concerned.

Chapter 7

Mitch knew he shouldn't have reacted as he had. It had been a very long time since something so simple had pushed his buttons. After Iraq, he'd been grateful he'd survived. He'd been grateful he could retrain in another specialty. He'd been grateful he had a life.

The truth was, he could have peeled an apple with his left hand, but those slices would have been chunky and choppy, maybe still bearing some skin.

At the practice, he spoke with couples, analyzed their needs, helped them decide which process was best. He calculated cycles, administered drug regimens, analyzed test results, sonograms, fluoroscopic X-rays. He could facilitate artificial insemination procedures. But he couldn't peel and slice an apple to his liking.

He could help bring life into the world, but he couldn't perform surgery to save a life.

Why had that fact hit him so hard just now?

He shuffled through the DVDs lying on the coffee table without paying attention to the titles. He was vaguely aware of the scent of cinnamon and apples baking, adding to the aroma of the chicken and wine. But when Lily stood in the doorway for a couple of moments before she took a step into the living room, he was elementally aware of her.

As she sat beside him on the sofa, only a few inches away, he wanted to both push her away and take her into his arms. It was the oddest feeling he'd ever experienced. Desire bit at him and he fought it.

"Dinner will be ready in about twenty minutes," she said, as if that were the main topic for discussion.

He could feel her gaze on him, making him hot, making him more restless. Facing her, he concluded, "Maybe this wasn't such a good idea."

"Eating dinner?" she asked, a little nervously, trying to make light of what was happening.

"Cooking together, eating together, watching a DVD together."

"I want to be here," she assured him, her eyes big and wide, all attempts at teasing gone. It was as if she were inviting him to kiss her.

He balled his hands into fists. "Lily—"

Reaching out to him, she touched the tense line of his jaw. "I don't know what's happening, Mitch, but being here with you is important to me. Maybe that first kiss wasn't as intense as we both thought it was. Maybe it was just an outlet—"

He was tired of analyzing and debating and pushing away desire that needed to be expressed. His hands slid under her hair as he leaned toward her, as he cut off her words with his lips. For over two years, he'd kept his desire for her hidden, locked away. Now, unable to resist, he set it free.

Passion poured out. Lily responded to it and returned it. For that reason, and that reason only, he didn't slam the door shut. He didn't throw the combination away again. She was softness and goodness and light in his hands. When his tongue swept her mouth, she wrapped her arms around his neck and held on. He was caught in the storm that had been building between them since the day he'd first held her. Warning bells clanged in his head, reminding him he should stop kissing her and pull away. But those warning bells seemed distant compared to the hunger that urged him on.

He sensed that same hunger had built in Lily. She wasn't holding back. Nothing about her was restrained.

The sounds of satisfaction Lily was making were driving Mitch crazy. His hand slid from her hair and caressed her shoulder. He could feel the heat of her skin under her knit top. Was she on fire for him as he was for her? Would she consider this kiss another mistake?

His hand slid to her breast. He knew if he didn't breathe soon, the need inside him would consume him.

Lily leaned away just slightly, as if inviting him to touch her more. His control was in shreds. He tore away from the kiss to nuzzle her neck as his hand left her breast and caressed her thigh.

When she turned her face up to his again, her eyes were closed. At that moment, Mitch knew this could be a very big mistake. What if she was imagining Troy loving her? What if she just needed someone to hold her and any man would take the form of her husband?

He leaned back, willed his heart to slow and found his voice. "Lily, open your eyes."

The few seconds it took for Lily to find her way back to the sofa seemed unending. She'd been so lost in pleasure that the sound of Mitch's voice—the request he'd made—seemed impossible at first.

When she did open her eyes, she was gazing into his. They were so dark and simmering, filled with the questions that took her a moment to understand. Until he asked, "Were you here with me?"

Her reflexive response was, "Of course, I was here with you." But as soon as she said it, she had to go back and think and feel. She had to be honest with Mitch and herself. As he didn't move an inch, she whispered, "*Mostly* here with you."

While she was kissing Mitch, had she been longing for Troy to be the one making love to her? Shaken by that question, as well as the aftermath of the passion that had bubbled up inside her like a well waiting to be sprung, she jumped when the cell phone in her pocket chimed.

Mitch seemed just as jarred. The resigned look on his face told her he knew she had to take the call. After all, Sophie or Grace might need her.

She checked the screen and then glanced at him. "It's Raina. She's in the hospital in labor. I have to find out if everything's okay."

Just then, the timer went off in the kitchen. Mitch rose to his feet. "I'll check on dinner," he said gruffly.

Lily closed her eyes and answered Raina's call.

Swallowing emotion that was confusing and exhilarating, as well as terrifying, Lily cleared her throat. "Raina?"

"It's a girl, Lily! We had a *girl*." Her friend's voice broke.

"That was pretty fast."

"Once we got here, it was like she couldn't wait to

get out. You've got to come see her, Lily. I know you… understand."

Lily did understand Raina's history, the loss of her husband and dreams unfulfilled. Now she'd captured those dreams again. "I'm at Mitch's."

Raina didn't miss a beat. Her joy was too big and broad. "Bring him, too. Shep could use a little distraction. He's hovering over both of us. Eva's here with the boys but she's going to leave in a few minutes. They're so excited about their new sister that they're getting a little rowdy."

"I'll call you back after I talk to Mitch."

"If I interrupted something, I'm sorry. You can wait to visit tomorrow."

Yes, she could. Yet she knew the joy Raina was feeling. She knew this was a once-in-a-lifetime experience for her.

After she and Raina ended the call, Lily went into the kitchen, where Mitch had taken the apple dessert from the oven and set it on the counter.

"Raina had a baby girl," she announced brightly.

"I bet she and Shep are ecstatic."

She remembered Mitch had met Shep the night of the awards dinner that now seemed forever ago. "She'd like us to come see the baby."

"Now? She wants company?"

"You know how it is with new moms. They're so proud, so full of life. And Raina and I, we have a special bond. She says we can wait until tomorrow, but I don't want to let her down. The chicken should be finished. Do you want to have dinner first?"

Mitch glanced at the kitchen clock. "Visiting hours

will be over soon. Let's put it in a casserole. We can warm it up when we get back."

"I can go alone."

"Would you rather go alone?"

Their intimacy on the sofa was still fresh in her mind and in her heart. She wanted to stay with him…*be* with him a little longer.

"I'd like you to come along."

He gave her a hint of a smile. "Then let's put this away and get going."

Lily thought she'd jump out of her skin every time Mitch glanced at her in his SUV. Their awareness of each other was so acute, it was almost uncanny. She suspected Mitch was feeling the same way when he flipped on the CD player. Both of them had agreed to go to the hospital because that was the easier thing to do. She'd almost gotten naked with Mitch, almost let him make love to her. Then what would they have had to say to each other?

At the hospital, alone in the elevator as they rode up to the maternity floor, Mitch turned to her. "I don't feel as if I belong here."

"Here?"

"The maternity floor. With your friend."

"My guess is Shep will be glad to see a friendly male face. He's not real comfortable with the softer things in life, if you know what I mean. But I think Raina's changing that."

"Softer things in life, meaning women having babies, pink blankets, nurses cooing?"

"You've got it."

Mitch almost smiled. "That does take some getting used to."

"I guess the transition from trauma surgeon to fertility specialist wasn't always easy for you."

"Fortunately I was able to rely on some of the research skills I'd acquired while I was in med school. I was a teaching assistant for a professor studying T cells, so analyzing data and studies wasn't foreign to me. I think the hardest part was learning to act as a counselor sometimes to couples who were stressed out because they'd been trying for years to have a baby and couldn't. All kinds of things popped up. I suppose that's why we have Dr. Flannagan as an adjunct."

"Vanessa is good. I've sent couples to her who are indecisive or who can't agree on what they want to do. Do you know Vanessa well?" Lily asked.

"No. We had lunch together once to discuss a case. She doesn't like to skate on the surface and I didn't want to be psychoanalyzed, so let's just say we didn't socialize after that—we stuck to business."

Lily was surprised to find herself relieved that Mitch hadn't gotten on well with the pretty psychologist. She admonished herself that she had no business being possessive. She had *no* rights where Mitch was concerned.

After Lily and Mitch signed in at the desk, Lily caught sight of Shep in one of the family waiting rooms. Joey and Roy, Shep and Raina's older boys, stood in the doorway as if ready to leave. Eva, their nanny, had one arm about each of them while Manuel, Shep and Raina's almost three-year-old, was throwing a tantrum, his arms tightly holding Shep around the neck, his tears as heartbreaking as his sobs.

"Daddy, you come home, *too*," he wailed.

Shep spotted Lily immediately and said above Manuel's wails, "Don't you tell Raina about this."

"She'd understand."

"Hell, yes, she'd understand. She'd want me to bring them all into the room so they could sleep with her."

Lily had to chuckle because she knew Shep was right. "She'd call it a birthday sleepover," Lily joked.

Mitch groaned. "I think you're going to have to do better than that to cheer this little guy up. So your name's Manuel?" Mitch asked, bending down to him, looking into his eyes.

At first Lily thought the little boy would play shy. Instead of hiding in Shep's shoulder, though, he pulled himself up straighter and studied Mitch. "What's your name?"

"My name's Mitch." He pointed to Lily. "You know her, don't you?"

Manuel nodded vigorously. "She and Mom are BFFs."

The adults all looked at each other and broke out into laughter.

"Who'd you hear that from?" Shep asked.

"Joey. He knows."

"Yes, he does know lots of things," Shep agreed with a grin he couldn't suppress.

"Maybe you should go home and make sure everything's ready for tomorrow when your sister comes home," Mitch suggested. "I bet your mom and dad would both be surprised."

Eva stepped in. "We could cut some roses and put them in pretty vases. Your mom would love that. We can make sure everything in the baby's room is just right."

Manuel stared at Eva.

Adding another incentive, she offered, "I can turn on the new baby monitor and you can watch the lights flicker when we make noise in the room."

Swiveling toward his dad again, Manuel screwed up his little face. "Okay."

Shep tapped the pocket of his shirt. "I'll give you a call before bed and you can say good-night to Mom. How's that?"

"That's good," Manuel assured him, climbing off his dad's lap and taking Eva's hand.

After hugs and kisses from all his boys, Shep watched them leave the maternity floor with Eva.

"Man, that's tough," he muttered. "It breaks my heart when they're sad."

Lily patted Shep's arm knowing that before he met Raina, he never would have been able to admit that.

"I'm going to visit the new mom," Lily said.

Shep studied Mitch. "You want to get a cup of coffee with me?"

"Sure," Mitch answered, exchanging a look with Lily that told her she'd been right about Shep needing a break.

"See you in a bit," she said with a wave, and headed for Raina's room.

When she entered her friend's room, she stopped short. This was a woman who had her world together.

The head of the bed had been raised and Raina was holding her infant daughter. She looked absolutely radiant and Lily almost envied her calm sense of satisfaction.

"Hey, there," she called softly from the doorway.

"Hey, yourself. Come on in. Meet Christina Joy McGraw."

"What a beautiful name! Did you and Shep decide on it together?"

"He just said he wanted something pretty and a little old-fashioned. I added Joy because that's what she's going to bring us." After passing her hand over her baby's head, Raina looked beyond Lily. "Where's Mitch?"

"He's keeping Shep company for a cup of coffee."

"This is a rough day for Shep, but if he drinks more than two cups, he's not going to sleep tonight."

Lily laughed. "I don't think he's going to sleep anyway. You *do* know he's going to stay here with you."

"He said something to that effect, but I thought he was kidding."

"Uh-uh. He's not letting you or that baby girl out of his sight for very long."

After they both stared down at the infant, Lily taken with her raven-dark hair and eyes, Raina asked, "Did I interrupt something when I called? I never imagined you'd be with Mitch."

"Oh, I just decided to make him a thank-you dinner. It was easier to do at his house."

"Did you eat?"

"No, we put it in a casserole for later. It will be fine."

"I have lousy timing," Raina murmured.

"No, actually you have very good timing."

The two women exchanged a look.

"Do you want to tell me what's going on?" Raina asked.

"Not here. The men could come back. Besides, I'm not sure anything is going on. Nothing should be going on, right?" If there was one person to ask about this, that person would be Raina.

"I waited nine long years to find love again. You don't have to wait that long."

"But what if it isn't love? What if I just miss Troy so much, long to be held so much, that I mistake something else for real emotion?"

"Is that what you think is happening?"

Lily sighed. "I don't know. When I'm with Mitch, I

actually can't think sometimes, let alone figure out the best thing to do."

"Then don't do anything until you're ready to do whatever's right for you."

"You make it sound so easy."

"Yeah, I know," Raina said with a wry smile. "If I'd taken my own advice, I wouldn't have this little girl in my arms right now. Do you want to hold her?"

"You bet I do."

Shep sat across from Mitch at the cafeteria table, staring down into his coffee. "When Raina went into labor—" He shook his head. "I don't think I've ever gone into such a panic."

"I know what you mean," Mitch said, thinking about that night at the banquet, Lily's contractions, knowing the twins would be premature.

Shep didn't say anything for a moment, but then remarked, "So you felt that way when Lily went into labor?"

What kind of trap had Mitch just walked into? He kept silent.

"You being a doc and all," Shep went on, "I would think you'd be more matter-of-fact about it."

He would have been with anyone else, but not with Lily. No way was he going to admit that out loud. Then it didn't seem he had to. Shep was giving him a knowing look that made Mitch feel uncomfortable. One thing Mitch never thought he'd be was transparent. He expected another question, but it didn't follow.

Instead, Shep took another sip of his coffee and set it down again. "Raina and Lily have become really good friends. They have a lot in common."

"Raina's been a great support for Lily since Troy

died." He might as well just get the subject out there so they weren't trampling around it.

"I heard you've been, too."

"You heard?" Mitch tried to keep the defensiveness from his voice, but he was worried that gossip was spreading about him and Lily.

"That night at the banquet when you carried Lily off. Raina told me Troy had left a letter asking you to look after her. That's why you're with her again tonight, right?" Shep inquired blandly.

Lily had told Mitch about Shep's background and why he'd wanted to adopt. She'd always spoken admiringly of him and Mitch knew her to be a good judge of character.

So when Shep stopped beating around the proverbial bush and added, "When I met Raina, nine years had passed since her husband died. Even so, we had a few bumps in our road because of it."

"Lily and I aren't—"

"Aren't serious? Aren't involved? Only friends? I get that. No one's judging you…or Lily."

"Maybe *you're* not, but Troy's sister is and I can't blame her for that. Even *I* know Lily's still vulnerable and I should watch my step. But how do you keep a promise to protect someone and step back at the same time?"

"That's a tough one," Shep admitted. "But if you care about her, you'll figure out the right thing to do, without interference from anyone else." Shep drank the last of his coffee. "Thanks for coming down here with me. I want to be with my wife and baby, but I needed a little break just to settle down a bit."

"I understand."

Shep nodded. "So are you ready to meet my daughter?"

* * *

When Lily and Mitch returned from the hospital, they warmed up dinner and ate at the table Lily had set. She called Ellie to see how the twins were doing and to give a report on Raina.

After she closed her phone, Mitch asked, "Ready for dessert?" and brought the apple crumble to the table.

"I have to get back home. Sophie and Grace are okay but I don't want Ellie and Angie to feel as if I've abandoned them."

"You haven't. A couple of hours away will do all of you good."

"I know, but—"

"You don't have to run off because you think I might kiss you again. I won't, if you don't want me to."

Lily felt her heart start hammering. "That's the problem, Mitch. I think I want you to."

Although another man might have acted on that subtle invitation, Mitch didn't. He set the dish on the table and started scooping dessert out for both of them.

"You don't have anything to say to that?" she asked quietly.

"Shep thinks we're involved."

Lily felt rattled that the subject had come up between the two men.

"I didn't start that conversation, if you're wondering," Mitch assured her.

"No, I wasn't. I guess I was just surprised."

"Everyone who cares about you is worried about you. It's natural that they're going to watch what you're doing."

"I hate to think I'm being watched," Lily murmured.

"In a good way."

After Mitch took his seat again beside her, she confessed, "Raina thinks we're involved, too."

"And what do *you* think?" he asked, his dark gaze penetrating, assessing, questioning.

"I think I'm scared. I think a kiss means more than I want it to mean with you."

"We did more than kiss," he reminded her.

She couldn't look away, didn't look away, wouldn't look away. She had to be as honest as she could with him. "I'm not sure where we're headed, Mitch. A lot of hormones are still driving me. What if we go up in flames? How much damage will that do to either of us? I've never had affairs, even before Troy. I was always in committed relationships. So what's happening between you and me—"

"Isn't a committed relationship."

"We're really on sandy footing," she said with a shake of her head.

He didn't disagree.

"But I like being with you," she continued. "I feel so alone sometimes, but not when I'm with you."

"We're back to the friends-versus-more question," he said.

Suddenly Lily was tired of the seriousness of it all. She was a widow with two babies to raise and sometimes she just wanted to scream. "Why do we even have to decide? Why are we worried about affairs and committed relationships? I mean, why can't we just enjoy being together?"

A light smile crept across his lips. "You couldn't be saying we're analyzing too much."

"I'm saying I need to take some deep breaths and not worry so much, and maybe *you* do, too. Yes, I think about Troy all the time, and how much I miss him, and how much the babies would love to have him as a father. But he's not here, and I can't pretend he will be again."

"You still love him a lot."

"Yes, Mitch, I do. But that love can't fill up my life twenty-four hours a day anymore. I have to start making room for a different life."

"And?" Mitch prompted.

"And," Lily repeated, then hesitated a moment.... "And Ellie and Angie are going to a concert in Amarillo tomorrow. They're going to stay overnight. So why don't you come over around four and we'll take the babies for a walk. Then maybe we can toss around some ideas for your Christmas weekend. That will be looking ahead and it should be fun. I can plan a menu. You can decide who will be Santa Claus. We'll just hang out."

His gaze was still on her, seeing into her and through her. They had to both figure out what they wanted and maybe the only way to do that would be to spend some time together.

"You just want some help with Sophie and Grace," he teased.

After considering what he'd said, she shook her head. "No, I want to hang out with you."

If she thought Mitch had ignored her invitation earlier, she could see in his eyes now that he hadn't.

Leaning toward her, he reached out and moved a stray wave from her cheek. Then he rubbed his thumb over her lips, leaning even closer. "Does hanging out involve kissing?"

"Maybe," she said with a little uncertainty.

His lips came down on hers and the rest of the world fell away.

Chapter 8

Mitch pushed the double stroller down the street, noticing the darkened gray sky and the storm clouds that
had gathered. He felt a similar storm inside of himself,
agitating to be set free.

We're just going to hang out together, he repeated in
his mind like a mantra.

Strolling beside him, Lily bent to make sure Sophie
and Grace were happy under their canopies. Lily wore a
yellow sundress with strawberries appliquéd around the
hem. He wondered if she'd dressed up for him or if he
was reading too much into her choice of a simple dress
on a warm June day. She'd tucked her hair behind her
ears and held it in place with two pretty mother-of-pearl
combs. She was a vision that plagued his dreams and
unsettled his days.

When she straightened, she flashed him a quick smile.
"You're staring."

"Caught in the act," he joked. "You look pretty today. But more than that. Freer somehow."

"It was nice being in the house alone with the babies the few hours before you came. Don't get me wrong. I'm so grateful for how Angie and Ellie help. I love being housemates with them. But I also like the feeling that I'm Sophie and Grace's mother and no one means as much to them as I do. Isn't that silly?"

"Not at all. But you don't have to worry. Their eyes are starting to follow you. They know you're their mother, no matter who takes care of them. You have an innate bond with them, just as they do with each other. Nothing will change that."

"Not even me going back to work?"

"Not even."

The breeze suddenly picked up, tossing Lily's hair across her shoulders. "Uh-oh," she said, looking up. "We might not make it back before it rains."

"The rain could hold off," he assured her, yet he knew it probably wouldn't. Once the weather cycle was set in motion, nothing could stop it.

"I'm not wearing running shoes. *You* are."

"I promise I won't race ahead of you. Sophie and Grace are protected by the state-of-the-art stroller your friends gave them. So I don't think we have to rush on their part."

Still, he rolled the stroller around in a half circle and headed back the way they'd come.

Lily stepped up her pace beside him. "I don't like sudden storms."

"You'd rather have planned storms?" he asked, amused.

She cast him a sideways glance. "I know you think that's funny, but just imagine. What if you knew ahead of time about the crises in your life? You could prevent them."

"Maybe. Or maybe fate would just find another way to get you to the same spot so you'd have to make the same kind of decisions."

"Oh my gosh! You're a philosopher and I never knew it."

Mitch had to laugh. "That's one title I've never been given."

"It's a compliment," she assured him, with a teasing tone in her voice that made him want to tug her into his arms and kiss her right there and then on the street. But in Sagebrush, that would almost be a spectacle.

She must have guessed what he was thinking because she slowed for a moment. He didn't stop, and she took a couple of running steps to catch up.

The wind buffeted them with a little more force now and large, fat drops of rain began to pelt them. Lightning slashed the sky not so far away and thunder grumbled overhead. The flashes and booms reminded Mitch of faraway places. He fought to keep memories at bay. Even though he was practically jogging with the stroller, he took deep, even breaths, reminding himself where he was and what he was doing.

A half block from the Victorian, the rain became steadier, rat-a-tatting on the pavement, pelting the leaves of the Texas ash trees blurred in Mitch's peripheral vision. The thunder became a louder drumroll.

Mitch blocked the sound as best he could.

Almost at the front yard of the big, blue house with its yellow gingerbread trim, Lily's sandal caught on the uneven pavement. Mitch sensed rather than saw what was happening and training took over. He reached low for

Lily, catching her around the waist before she fell. Her body was warm, her shoulders slick with the rain dripping down. One of her arms had surrounded his waist as she'd steadied herself to keep from falling. His face was so close to hers he could almost feel the quiver of her chin as emotion and desire ran through them both.

Yet they seemed to recognize where they were and what they were doing at the same time because in unison, they murmured, "The twins."

Mitch tilted his forehead against hers for just a moment then released her and pushed the stroller up the walkway to the porch.

Lily unlocked the door while he easily lifted the stroller, carrying it up the steps and into the foyer.

Moments later she switched on the Tiffany light to dispel the shadows while he rolled the twins into the living room and stooped down at Sophie's side of the stroller to see if any pelts of rain had made their way to her.

Lily did the same on Grace's side. "They're dry," she said with amazement.

"At least their clothes are," he returned with a wink.

When Lily laughed, he felt as if he'd done something terrific. He also felt as if the lightning strike had sent supercharged awareness through *him*. When his eyes met Lily's, he knew she felt the same way.

Ducking her head, she lifted Grace. Her pink-and-yellow playsuit with the dog appliquéd on her belly was a little big. It wouldn't be long until she grew into it, Mitch knew.

Grace cooed at Lily and Lily cooed back. "You're a happy girl today. How would you like to sit in your swing?"

Grace's little mouth rounded in an O and her very blue eyes studied her mom's face.

Mitch held Sophie in the crook of his arm. "Do you want to join your sister?"

Sophie's outfit was pink-and-green with a cat appliquéd on the bib of her overalls. When she waved her arms and oohed and aahed in her baby language, Mitch chuckled.

He and Lily set the girls in their swings and wound the mechanism that would start the motion. Then of one accord, she and Mitch seemed to come together, standing close behind the twins.

He brushed his hand down her arm. "I think you need a towel." She was wet from the rain and he was, too. The result of that seemed to be steam rising from both of them.

"I need to change," she murmured but didn't move away.

He fingered one of her combs. "I like these in your hair."

"They were my mother's," she replied softly. "I haven't worn them very much. I was afraid something would happen to them. Suddenly today I realized she wouldn't want me to just leave them in my jewelry box."

Lily's skin was lightly tanned as if she'd taken the babies for walks many days in the sun. He clasped her shoulders and ran his thumbs up and down the straps of her dress. "I've been wanting to kiss you since I got here."

"I've wanted you to kiss me since you got here."

She tilted her head up and he lowered his. He told himself to go easy, not to scare her with too much need. He didn't want to need her at all. But the moment his lips settled on hers, he couldn't keep the hunger at bay.

The feel of her in his arms was exquisite, the soft pressure of her lips was a temptation that urged him to claim her. When his tongue thrust into her mouth, her gasp was only a preliminary response. She followed it with a tightening of her arms around him. A return taste of him became a chase and retreat that had them pressing their bodies together.

Outside, a bright flash of light against a darkening sky was soon followed by thunder that seemed to crawl up one side of the roof and down the other. The crackle and boom sounded very close.

All at once the light in the foyer went out and the hum of the refrigerator ceased.

Mitch held Lily tighter, ended the kiss and rubbed his jaw against her cheek. "The electricity." Huskiness hazed his words. "The lightning must have hit a transformer."

After a few moments, she leaned away from him. "I'd better find the oil lamp in case we don't have power for a while. I had a stir-fry planned for supper."

"We'll have to make do with lunchmeat and cheese."

"I made a coconut cake. We don't need power to eat that."

"You have flashlights and candles?"

"I think they're under the kitchen sink. The oil lamp's upstairs. I'll get it when I change."

"Go ahead. I'll watch Grace and Sophie until you come back down. Then you can stay with them while I rummage."

After a last longing look at him, sending the message their kiss had ended much too soon, she ran upstairs.

Mitch took a hefty breath.

Sandwiches eaten, candles and oil lamp lit, Lily forgot about time and just lived in the moment. She and Mitch had talked as they'd sat on the sofa and exchanged fussy babies. They'd played patty-cake and peekaboo with Sophie and Grace in between talking about books they had read, movies they'd seen, first experiences swimming, diving, surfing, hiking. There seemed to be so much to talk about. Yet underneath it all, whenever their gazes met or their fingers brushed, memories of their kisses danced in her mind.

After a few hours, Lily breast-fed Grace while Mitch bottle-fed Sophie. Sophie finished first, and he laid her in her crib, starting her mobile.

They'd brought the oil lamp to the babies' room while they fed them. A flameless candle Mitch had found in a cupboard glowed in place of a night-light. Shadows were heavy in the room and Lily could see Mitch caring for her daughter, gently making sure she was settled, watching her for a few moments, then touching his fingers to her forehead.

He would make a wonderful father.

Turning from the crib, he stooped to pick up the bottle he'd set on the floor. "I'll wash this out."

Grace had stopped suckling and her eyes were closed. Lily raised her to her shoulder until she heard a little burp, and then she carried her to her crib, settling her in for the night, then she took the oil lamp to the bathroom where she set it on the vanity. A small candle burned next to the sink where Mitch was rinsing the bottle. He'd rolled up his shirtsleeves and for the first time, Lily saw the scars on his right forearm. She didn't look somewhere else, but studied the lines that still looked raw... the gashes that had healed but would never fade away.

Slowly she raised her eyes to his.

He turned off the spigot and blew out the candle.

He was about to roll down his sleeve when she stopped him, her hand clasping his. "You don't have to hide them from me."

"They're ugly."

"No, they're a badge of honor." Without thinking, only feeling, she bent and kissed one of the welts.

"Lily." He said her name in a way he never had before. His words were thick with need, with desire that needed to be expressed.

Her lips lingered on his skin for a few seconds, maybe because she wanted to anticipate what might happen next, maybe because she was afraid of what might happen next.

When she straightened, he took her face in both of his hands. "Do you know what you're doing?" he asked, his voice raspy.

"I'm feeling," she said without apology.

"Damn," he growled, wrapping his arms around her, possessing her lips with his.

His kiss was long and hungry, wet and wild. Lily felt like someone else, like a woman who could throw caution to the side and be free from the chains of what she should and shouldn't do. She kissed Mitch with a fervor that shocked her, yet gave her hope.

Lily's breasts pressed into Mitch's chest. Instead of trying to touch her with his hands, he let their bodies communicate. His breathing was as hot and heavy as hers. They fit together with perfect temptation, perfect anticipation, perfect exhilaration. He seemed to wait for some sign from her that she wanted more and she gave it, pressing even closer. She felt his hardness, the desire he'd been controlling up until now. There would be no turning back from this.

She didn't want to turn back. She wanted tonight with

Mitch. Did he want her as badly? Would he let his scars be an issue?

She lowered her hand from his shoulder and insinuated it between their bodies, cupping him, leaving him with no doubt as to what she was ready to do.

Still holding her securely, Mitch backed her out of the bathroom…across the hall…into her bedroom. The area was pitch-black, the glow from the oil lamp in the bathroom the only light, reaching just inside the door. But that didn't stop them. The dark seemed to hold some comfort for them both. Once they were enveloped by it, their mouths sought each other, their arms embraced, their fingers touched. The dark held more excitement than anything else.

Mindlessly, Lily reached for Mitch's shirt buttons.

He searched for the edges of her top and somehow managed to pull it up and over her head.

After he'd tossed it, she asked, "Do you have a condom?"

His hands went still on her waist. "Yes, I do." He reached into his pocket, pulled out the foil packet and dropped it on the nightstand.

They'd both known this night was coming, hadn't they?

"I'd hoped," Mitch said honestly. "That's why I brought it."

His hands slid to her bra and unhooked it. She shrugged off the straps quickly and leaned forward, kissing his chest. She couldn't see but she could feel hot skin against her lips. Her hands became her eyes as she ran them down his flat abdomen and stopped at the waistband of his jeans. His belt was pliant but fought her hands as she tried to unfasten it. He helped her with it. A few moments later, he'd shed his sneakers, jeans and briefs. She'd flicked off her sandals. Now he slid his hands into the waistband of her shorts, sliding them down her hips along with her panties.

She knew he couldn't see much more than shadows, either, and she asked, "Should I light a candle?"

"No time," he muttered as he pushed her hair aside and kissed her neck, trailing his lips along her collarbone. His foray to her breast made her restless, flushed and needy.

"Mitch," she moaned, but he didn't stop. He just kept kissing lower, down her belly to the mound between her thighs. She couldn't let him be that intimate. She just couldn't. The reason why eluded her.

She grasped his shoulders and said again, "Mitch."

This time she felt him shift, felt his head tilt up. He straightened, flung back the covers, and climbed into bed, holding his hand out to her.

Thunder grumbled again outside and she thought fleetingly of Grace and Sophie and whether or not they'd awaken. She listened as the sky rolled but heard nothing from the babies' bedroom.

As if he read her mind, Mitch asked, "Do you want to check on them?"

She knew she'd hear them if they awakened, even without the monitor. "They'll let us know if they wake up," she replied, crawling in beside him, moving closer to him.

He wrapped his arm around her and stroked her back. "You'll have to tell me what you like."

She suddenly couldn't speak and didn't know why. So she tilted her head against his and finally managed, "I want *you,* Mitch. Kiss me and everything else will be okay."

His lips were searingly hot, his tongue an instrument

of pleasure that urged her to caress his back, his sides, his manhood.

"Lily," he gasped. "Are you ready?"

"Yes, Mitch. I am."

Reaching to the nightstand, he grabbed the packet and ripped open the foil. After he slid the condom on, he stretched out on top of her, letting her feel his weight. He spread her legs and lay between them. As he braced himself on his elbows, she tensed a little. He must have felt it because he kissed her again until all she wanted was him filling her, giving her pleasure, helping her to forget.

Forget what? a little voice inside her head whispered, but she ignored it, not bothering to find the answer.

When Mitch entered her, she *was* ready. Each of his thrusts made her call his name, asking for more. Mitch's body was as slick as hers with their passion. His chest slid against her breasts as they rocked, tempting each other, provoking each other to the next level of pleasure. Lily held on tightly as a strong orgasm overtook her, shaking her world until it was upside down. Mitch's shuddering release came moments later.

She felt as if the storm had somehow come inside. Stunned by the pleasure still tingling through her, she also felt overwhelmed by the intimacy she'd experienced with Mitch. She wobbled on the verge of feelings that terrified her and she didn't know whether to run or to hold on to Mitch for dear life.

After Mitch collapsed on top of her, he whispered in her ear, "Are you okay?"

She didn't know how to answer him, but gave him the response that would be easiest. "Yes, I'm good."

He kissed her cheek then rolled onto his side, taking

her with him, their bodies still joined. "Do you want me to check on Sophie and Grace?"

"In a minute." She was still catching her breath, still trying to absorb what they had done, what she had done.

"Talk to me, Lily."

"Just hold me, Mitch. Just hold me."

"I shouldn't fall asleep with you. I could have a nightmare."

"It doesn't matter, I don't want you to leave."

So Mitch stayed and she held on, unsure what morning would bring.

Lily snuck glances at Mitch as they made breakfast the next morning. The night before, the first time the twins had awakened, Mitch had climbed out of bed quickly. Lily wondered if he'd slept at all because he'd seemed so wide awake as they fed Sophie and Grace and settled them once more. Afterward, Mitch had kissed her and she thought they might make love again. Instead he'd said, "Get some sleep. I'm going to bunk on the couch. When the electricity clicks back on, I'll make sure everything's working okay."

"Mitch, you could sleep with me."

But he'd shaken his head and she'd known better than to argue.

The twins had slept later than usual this morning, so it was almost ten o'clock as she scrambled eggs and Mitch fried bacon. Sophie and Grace faced each other and babbled in their swings.

She hadn't talked to Mitch about last night. They'd been too busy changing, dressing, diapering and now making breakfast. What she wanted to ask most was, *What did last night mean to you?*

However, as she was about to begin the discussion, the front door swung open and Angie and Ellie charged in, overnight cases in hand. They gave some attention to the babies and then stopped short when they saw Mitch.

Cheerfully, Angie tried to set the tone. "Good morning."

"I didn't expect you back so soon," Lily remarked. "How was the concert?"

"It was wonderful," Angie replied. "I felt like a teenager again. Brad Paisley is one hot dude."

Lily forced a laugh because Ellie was being so quiet.

Angie slipped a CD from her purse. "I got his new one."

"Did you have a good time?" she asked Ellie. Mitch silently listened, forking the slices of bacon.

"Yeah, it was great. But we heard you had storms last night and a lot of the electricity was out. We were worried. That's why we got up early and drove back. I tried to call but the phone must not be working. It just kept ringing and you didn't answer your cell, either."

"Oh, I'm sorry you worried," Lily apologized. "My cell was out of power when the electricity went down and I unplugged the charger so it wouldn't get damaged if there was a surge." She felt as if she were overexplaining and Ellie was eyeing her and then Mitch. Lily felt uncomfortable.

"Did you have any trouble getting back?" Mitch asked. "Trees down? That kind of thing?"

"Just a tree down on Alamo," Angie answered when Ellie didn't. "Branches here and there. We heard a tornado went through Odessa. That's why we were worried. How did Sophie and Grace do with the storm?"

"They didn't seem to mind," Mitch said with a smile.

"How long have you been here?" Ellie inquired.

Mitch looked to Lily, obviously deciding to let her answer. She felt suddenly unsettled, as if what had happened with Mitch last night was definitely all wrong. She was the mother of three-month-old twins. What was she doing having an affair? What was she doing making love with a man when Troy hadn't been gone a year? What was she doing trying to find a life when her old one still seemed so real?

Suddenly plagued by doubts, she answered, "Mitch came over last evening to visit. While he was here, the electricity went off. He stayed to make sure we were all safe. He slept on the couch and when the power came back on, he made sure everything was working right again."

She sensed Mitch's body tense. With a sideways glance at him, she saw his jaw set and his mouth tighten. She didn't dare look into his eyes.

"I see," Ellie responded.

Silence shrouded the kitchen until Angie broke it. "We bought donuts at the convenience store. I left them in the car with the souvenirs. I'll go get them."

"I can throw more eggs into the pan," Lily offered. "We have plenty of bacon and toast."

Mitch switched off the burner, fished the bacon from the pan and let it drain on a paper towel on a dish. But then he said, "I think I'll be going. Everything's back to normal here and the three of you can catch up."

Lily reached out a hand to him. "Mitch, you don't have to go."

His gaze locked to hers. "Yes, I think I do."

Lily felt her heart drop to her stomach. The look on Mitch's face told her that her explanation to Ellie hadn't been what he'd expected her to say. She slid the eggs from the pan onto a serving dish and set it on the table.

"I'll be right back," she told Ellie. "I'm going to walk Mitch out."

Mitch stopped by Sophie and Grace, jiggled their feet, gave them a last long look, then went to the living room. Making sure the timer on the swings would keep the babies content for a little while longer, Lily bent down and kissed them both. She passed Angie in the living room and saw that Mitch had already gone out the door.

"What's up?" Angie whispered to her.

"We'll talk later," she told her friend, not knowing what to expect when she went outside.

Lily had never seen Mitch angry. A sense of calm always seemed to surround him. But now, even though he was still, he wasn't calm. His brown eyes simmered with an emotion she didn't understand. She thought he was accusing her of something and she went on the defensive.

"You could stay for breakfast."

"If I stayed and Ellie asked what happened last night, what should I tell her?"

Maybe the emotion she was witnessing in Mitch's eyes wasn't anger. It was something worse. It was betrayal.

Her hands suddenly felt clammy. "I couldn't tell her what happened."

"I understand you want to keep your life private. I understand you're afraid you'll hurt her feelings. I understand that you feel she'd be upset if she thinks you're moving on. What I don't understand, especially after last night, is that you gave her the impression I was like a security guard seeing to your safety. Why are you afraid to admit to yourself what happened last night. We were *intimate,* Lily, as intimate as two people can be. Do you want to erase that from your memory?"

The breeze tossed her hair across her cheek as she self-consciously looked around to make sure no one was walking anywhere nearby. Glancing over her shoulder, she needed to be certain neither Angie nor Ellie were in the foyer, listening.

"I don't know what to think about last night," she admitted. "I'm not like that, Mitch. I don't seek pleasure to wipe out—"

"Loss and grief and memories?"

"Why are you so angry?"

He ran his hand over his face and considered her words carefully. "I don't think I'm as angry with you as I am with myself. I should have known better. I should have known you weren't ready."

She remembered him asking her last night, "Are you ready?" He'd meant so much more than the physical. Deep down, she'd known that.

"The dark made it easy," he decided. "The dark let you think, subconsciously at least, that you were with your husband again."

She wanted to protest. She wanted to scream that he was wrong. Yet how could she? She didn't know if he was wrong or right. She didn't know if last night had been about her and Mitch, or if it had been about her needing a man to hold her. She felt awful. She felt as if she *had* betrayed him.

"I'm going to leave before I say something else I shouldn't," he muttered. "It's probably better if we don't see each other for a while."

For a while? How long was that? She'd be going back to work in November. He didn't mean that long, did he?

But she had her pride and he had his. She'd hurt him badly and now she had to suffer the consequences.

He took his car keys from his pocket. "Take care of yourself, Lily."

Moments later, he was driving down the street away from her.

Taking a deep, shaky breath, she tried not to think or feel and went inside to Grace and Sophie.

Chapter 9

Lily sat across from Mitch in his office, hardly able to bear the awkwardness that had developed between them.

She'd been back at work for two weeks and had only caught glimpses of Mitch. He had definitely made himself scarce. The only reason they were in the same room together now was because they had to discuss a patient. "Joan Higgins has high levels of FSH, which definitely lowers the quality of her eggs. I think further testing is indicated."

Mitch nodded, keeping his gaze on the notes on his desk.

After he'd left the Victorian that morning in June, he'd emailed Lily every few weeks to inquire about her health and her daughters'. *Emailed.* He was doing his duty and keeping his promise to Troy without truly getting involved.

Could she blame him?

Lily desperately wanted to blurt out to Mitch, "I miss you," yet she knew she couldn't. She'd hurt him greatly by making love with him while she grieved for her husband. But he'd hurt *her* by walking away as he had. If he could leave her life so easily, what had that night meant to him? What if they'd continued the affair? Would he eventually have opened up to her? Would he have been ready to care for her and the twins out of more than duty?

"I'll order further tests," he agreed, ending their discussion of the patient.

They sat in awkward silence.

Finally Mitch laid down his pen. "How does it feel to be back at work?" His expression was neutral and he could have been making polite conversation with any of their colleagues.

"It feels good to be back. But I miss Sophie and Grace," she added honestly, as if he were still the old Mitch. "I miss not being able to hold them whenever I want. I mostly miss not hearing every new baby word first."

"You could come in part time," he suggested, as an employer might.

"I might be able to do that for a month or so, but I need my salary. I can't just think about the moment, I have to think about the future."

When their gazes collided, they were both thinking about taking pleasure in the moment, and the night neither of them would forget. At least, Lily hoped Mitch wouldn't forget it. She knew *she* never would.

Mitch pushed the papers on his desk into a stack, clipped them together and tossed them into his in-box.

"It's getting late. I won't keep you any longer. I know you want to get home."

"Sophie and Grace are really growing and chang-ing."

He looked surprised she'd started up the conversation again.

Reaching into her lab coat pocket, she drew out a small picture portfolio. "These are the latest pictures... if you'd like to see them. I can't believe they're already nine months old."

Maybe she was making it difficult for him to refuse to look, but right now she needed to see emotion from him, something more than a polite facade meant just for her. She'd ached for him all these months, but she hadn't been able to do more than answer his emails in the same tone he'd sent them—politely and with pertinent information. Yet seeing him and working with him again, she realized how much she'd lost when he'd walked away.

As she slid the little booklet across the desk to him, she confessed, "I need to keep their faces close by."

He stared at the small album for a couple of seconds and then picked it up. After he leafed through it, he stood and handed it back to her. "They're beautiful kids, Lily. I imagine in a few weeks, you'll have their picture taken with Santa Claus."

Yes, the holidays were coming and she found she didn't want to celebrate them without Mitch. Did he feel anything when he looked at Sophie and Grace's photos? Did he wonder if the monitor was still working? If the sun rose and set now without her feeling grief twenty-four hours a day? What could she say to him to bring warmth back into his eyes?

She returned the photos to her pocket and rose to her feet. Obviously, he wanted her to leave. She could feel the figurative miles he was trying to shove between them. She'd let him do that for the past five months because she hadn't known what else to do, what was fair, what was necessary. But she couldn't merely leave things like this, emotions all tangled up, words gone unsaid, desires left unfulfilled.

"Mitch, what can I do to fix this?"

He didn't pretend to not know what she was talking about. "I don't think there's anything to fix."

It had taken courage on her part to bring it up, but he had shot her down without a glimmer of understanding...without a glimmer of hope that they could reestablish the connection they once had. She felt foolish and embarrassed. She should just go home to the people who loved her and wipe from her memories everything that had happened with Mitch.

She'd almost reached the door when she felt his hand on her shoulder. That simple touch brought back everything—the long, wet kisses, his hands on her body, the orgasm that had swept her to another realm. She hoped the naked feelings weren't showing in her eyes.

"I don't know how to fix it," he admitted. "We crossed the line and we can't go back."

The five months that had passed had seemed like a lifetime. If she told him she was ready now, would it be the truth? Would he believe her?

"We could start over," she suggested.

"As what? Colleagues who once had sex and now are trying to renew a friendship?"

His words hit her solar plexus squarely, just where he'd intended. Yet she couldn't give up. "Maybe," she answered truthfully. "We can't deny what happened, but I hate this...wall between us. You were there when Grace and Sophie were born, and now you've just dropped out of their lives."

"I thought the emails—"

"Mitch, you sent them from a sense of duty, because you made a promise to Troy. I didn't know if you really cared. I didn't know whether to email you pictures or describe how I rolled their strollers through the sprinkler and they loved it, or how their hair was finally long enough to put little bows in."

He dropped his hand from her shoulder as if he could see the pictures, too, the pictures of *them* as they'd been, not just the twins. "I walked away because it was the right thing to do."

"For *me* or for *you?*"

"For both of us."

He didn't look or sound as if he had any regrets. That hurt—a lot. She shook her head and accepted what seemed to be inevitable. "If you want to just be colleagues, that's fine. We'll figure out eventually how to relate on that level."

She would have gone again, but this time the huskiness in his voice stopped her. "Lily."

When she swung around suddenly, she saw a flicker of something on his face…and she waited, hoping.

"What did you have in mind?" he asked.

If that wasn't a loaded question! But she did have something in mind. She just didn't know if he'd go for it.

"How are you celebrating Thanksgiving?" Lily asked. It was only three days away. If he had plans, so be it. She'd figure out something else.

"I plan to pick up a turkey dinner at the Yellow Rose."

She noticed the lines around Mitch's mouth seemed deeper. "And take it home and eat it alone?"

"I guess that's not how most people celebrate Thanksgiving, but afterward I was going to make some phone calls, to make sure everyone was still coming next weekend."

His reunion weekend. The one she'd thought she'd be involved in. "Would you like to come along with Ellie and me to Raina and Shep's?"

Considering that for a few heartbeats, Mitch finally answered, "Are you sure they wouldn't mind having an unexpected guest?"

Her heart seemed to jump against her chest. "Shep said Eva bought a turkey big enough to fill the entire oven. I'm sure they won't mind."

"You already checked this out with Raina, didn't you?" he asked suspiciously.

"Actually, it was her idea. I mentioned things were strained between us here."

"Women," he said with a bit of exasperation. "Do you have to tell each other *everything?*"

"Not everything," Lily assured him quickly.

There was a darkening of Mitch's eyes and she knew he'd caught her underlying meaning.

"Ellie might not like the idea," he pointed out.

"No, she might not. And for her sake, it might be better if we meet at Shep and Raina's ranch."

"Doesn't this take us back where we started?" he asked with such soberness she realized much more was going on under the surface than he was revealing.

"No, it doesn't. Because I'll tell her I invited you. I'll make that clear."

It was easy for her to see that Mitch was debating with himself.

Although she didn't want to say acceptable words just

because he wanted to hear them, she did. "If you don't want to come, that's okay. I understand. I just thought maybe we could ease back into…friendship."

"With a crowd around?" he asked, the corner of his lip quirking up.

"Sometimes conversation comes more easily that way."

"And kids are always great buffers."

"Yes," she agreed, now holding her breath, waiting for his answer.

He gave it in the form of another question. "What time does Thanksgiving dinner start?"

When Raina pulled Mitch into a bedlam of bubbling voices, running kids and chattering adults, he knew he must be crazy. He could be sitting home alone, in front of a takeout turkey dinner—

His gaze found Lily right off. At the stove, she was testing the boiling potatoes. Her hair was arranged in a wispy version of a bun that made his fingers tingle to pull it down. She was wearing a calf-length suede skirt with tan boots, and a long multicolored blouse with a concho belt slung low on her slim waist. When she turned to wave at him, he could read her apron that proclaimed in block lettering, I'd Rather Cook Than Clean.

As Shep came toward him, Mitch offered him a bottle of wine. To Raina, he handed a bouquet of colorful mums.

"You didn't have to do that," she said.

"I wanted to." He really had. It was nice of them to include him.

How much did Lily want him here? Maybe she just wanted them to work together without snubbing each other. That would be a far cry from becoming friends again. Friends like before Troy had died? Or friends like after the twins were born?

Lily's babies were sitting in play saucers in the kitchen so she could keep her eye on them. Eva was conversing with Ellie as they made a salad together. Ellie had given Mitch a glance and lifted a hand in his direction, but that was about all.

This could be one interesting Thanksgiving dinner.

Although he knew it wasn't in his best interest, he did want to see how Sophie and Grace had grown.

It had been more than difficult to stay away from Lily and her daughters all these months. But he'd felt it was the right move to make. She'd needed time to recover from Troy's passing. And even now he doubted enough time had passed. But today was about getting a real look at her life again. If he had to try to watch over her without getting involved, then somehow he'd manage that.

He hunkered down at Grace's play saucer, helping her ring a bell, spin a wheel and study her face in the mirror. She giggled at him and reached out to touch his jaw. That tiny hand on his chin made his heart squeeze uncomfortably, so he gave it a gentle pat and moved on to Sophie, who seemed a little more sedate. After all, she was the older sister, even if it was only by two to three minutes. She was slower to let Mitch join in her private game, but eventually she welcomed the intricacies of his set of keys and would have kept them if not for her mom intervening.

"She'll put them in her mouth," Lily said. "I try to keep her toys as sterile as possible, but you know how that is."

"Actually, I don't, but I can imagine with their crawling all over the floor." He looked around at the saucers and stroller and the high chairs. "You must have brought a truck."

Lily laughed.

"The high chairs and stroller fold. Ellie stowed them in the back of her car." She glanced back at the potatoes. "I'd better finish those if we want them ready with the turkey."

"Do you need help with the pot?" It was huge and, he imagined, quite heavy.

"Sure. That would be great."

As he stepped around her, his hip brushed hers. That minor connection of their bodies threw him more than he wanted to admit. He stood in front of the stove and reached for the pot. As always with Lily, physical contact sent his system into a rush forward toward something out of his reach. He thought that might have diminished in their time apart.

It hadn't.

Coming here today had been stupid. He avoided her gaze as he drained the potatoes into a colander in the sink, steam billowing up all around them. *This isn't the first time,* he thought ironically.

"Into the mixing bowl?" he asked, looking at the bowl on the counter.

She nodded, avoiding his gaze, too.

They were a pair. No, *not* a pair, he corrected himself. Just two individuals with wants and needs that couldn't be fulfilled.

He saw Lily go over to her daughters and consult with Raina, who was playing with them, her own five-month-old cuddled close on her lap. Then Lily returned to the mixer.

"Raina said I could put in whatever I want, so here goes."

"Whatever you want?" he asked. "I thought they just got butter and milk."

"That's the plain version," Lily explained with a smile, starting the mixer. "I like to add a little pizzazz."

She added pizzazz all right. With fascination, he watched her add sour cream, milk, chives and a blob of butter for good measure.

"No cholesterol there," he muttered.

She jabbed him in the ribs. "It's Thanksgiving."

He liked the feel of her friendliness again. He'd missed her a lot over the past five months. In his email inquiries, he'd wanted to ask question after question—about the babies and about her. Yet he'd known he had to, in large part, leave her alone. He should have done that to begin with. Today, however, with her close by his side, within kissing distance, inhaling the familiar scent of her perfume, he saw keeping a wall up between them was either very smart…or very stupid. What would an affair do to them? Was she even open to one? Were either of them really ready to move on?

After whipping the potatoes into a delicious white frenzy, Lily stuck in a spoon, took a fingerful and poked it into her mouth. She rolled her eyes. "Just right. Try some?"

He'd watched that finger go into her mouth. He'd watched her lips pucker up. He'd watched her lick it. If there weren't so many people in the big kitchen, he'd kiss her. But there were and he didn't. Instead he put his finger on the spoon, curled potatoes onto it and popped it into his mouth.

"Just right," he agreed, his eyes locking to hers, his gut telling him they weren't finished and might never be.

Mitch barely heard the sound of scraping chairs and laughter and the clatter of silverware.

He *did* hear the doorbell ring. Soon after, the door opened and he heard a woman's voice call, "We're here."

Shep picked up the turkey on its platter and carried it to the table, explaining to Mitch, "It's Raina's mom and brother. Ryder just got off his shift."

Mitch knew Raina's brother was a cop.

Ryder and Sonya Greystone came into the kitchen and were introduced to Mitch. Sonya said to him, "I hope you're a big eater, like Shep. I made pumpkin, apple and cherry pies, and I don't want to take any home."

Shep gave her a bear hug. "You don't have to worry about that."

Mitch had never experienced anything like this Thanksgiving celebration—so many people who seemed like family and really cared about each other. Then he realized that conclusion wasn't true. When he and his buddies and families got together, it was a similar feeling. Family meant something different to everyone, and he was suddenly glad he hadn't stayed home today and eaten dinner in front of a football game.

In the next few minutes, he helped Lily transfer the potatoes from the mixing bowl to a beautiful serving dish embellished with roses and gold trim. He stared at it for a second and Lily asked, "Mitch?"

In the midst of the holiday chaos, he said in a low voice, "This dish reminds me of one my mom used when she tried to make the holidays a celebration for the two of us."

"Holidays are supposed to be about memories and

traditions and loved ones, even when they're not still with us."

He'd walked into that one. When his gaze met Lily's, he expected to see sadness on her face. Instead, he saw an emotion more poignant.

She said, "If you'll put those on the table, I'll set the twins in their high chairs."

In the next few minutes, everyone was seated around the huge, rectangular table. Even Joey and Roy seemed awed by the amount of food in front of them.

In the moment of quiet, Shep said, "Let's all give thanks for being together today."

Mitch didn't know where the chain started—maybe with Shep's children—but everyone held hands and bowed their heads, remembering Thanksgivings past, grateful for the opportunity to be together like this with more than enough food for everyone to eat.

Lily had taken Mitch's hand. He intertwined his fingers with hers and she looked over at him, her eyes questioning. He didn't have the answers to those questions. They'd have to just see where today took them.

After dinner, Mitch and Shep played a board game with Roy and Joey while Eva recorded everything she could on a video camera. Every once in a while Mitch glanced over at Eva, who was sitting on the floor beside Manuel as he rode a high-tech rocking horse. The letters of the alphabet appeared on a little screen in front of him the longer he rocked back and forth. Grace and Sophie crawled around Lily and Ellie's feet, while Raina played with her daughter in one of the play saucers.

Roy shouted, "I won," and everyone cheered as he moved his marker into the winning block.

Mitch moved to the sofa while the boys ran to the playroom for another game. Aware of Grace crawling over to him, he smiled when she sat before him and raised her arms. He knew what that meant. It had been a while since he'd held one of the twins, a while since he'd felt as if he should.

A baby's needs always trumped overthinking, so he bent and lifted her up to his lap. At nine months she was a heartbreaker. He could only imagine how beautiful she'd be as a teenager, when someone would have to protect her from overeager guys who would date her.

Grace grinned up at him and snuggled into his chest as if she were just waiting for a place to enjoy a comfortable nap.

Ellie, who'd been talking to Raina's mother and Eva across the room, came to sit beside him. She patted Grace's leg. "Tired, little one?"

"The day's celebration has wiped her out," Mitch said amiably. He didn't know what Ellie thought about his being here today.

"She only had a short nap this afternoon before we came."

Mitch touched Grace's name embroidered on the front of her pale green overalls. "Did you make this?"

"Yes, I did. I finally got the website up and running last month, and I have orders."

"So you're thinking about staying in Sagebrush?"

"That depends on Lily. Mom asked her to come back to Oklahoma and raise the twins there. That way she and my dad could see them more often and give her all the help she needs."

Mitch remained silent. Finally he said, "Lily seemed happy to get back to work. She'd have to find a practice in Oklahoma City or start her own."

"That's true. But Oklahoma City is a medical center. I don't think she'd have a problem starting over there."

Grace's tiny fingers rubbed up and down against Mitch's sweater as if it were a security blanket.

"What if Lily decides to stay in Sagebrush? Will you support that decision?" Mitch asked.

"Do you think you can convince her to do that?" Ellie asked in return.

"This isn't about convincing. It's about what Lily wants and where she wants to raise her daughters."

"You sound so removed from it. Don't you care?"

Oh, he cared. More than he wanted to admit—more than he dared to admit. "I won't persuade Lily one way or the other. She has to make up her own mind. If she doesn't, she'll have regrets."

"She asked you here today." Ellie's voice was almost accusing.

"I'm not sure why she did. As you know, we haven't seen each other for a while." Ellie was the type of woman who wanted the cards on the table, so he might as well put them there.

"You two have a connection," Ellie said softly. "One anyone can see."

"Anyone can?"

"You can't hide it, even though you both try."

Mitch smoothed his hand over Grace's hair, tweaking the little green bow with his finger. "And how do you feel about that?" he asked Ellie.

"I don't think it matters how I feel."

"Yes, it does." Mitch could tell Ellie that she was the reason he and Lily hadn't been in real contact since June. On the other hand, she wasn't actually the root of the problem.

"Lily asked you here today without my input," Ellie confided.

Mitch gave Ellie a regarding look. "What would your input have been?"

Ellie kept silent.

So he said something he probably shouldn't have. "I think Lily feels she needs your permission to move on."

That widened Ellie's eyes. "You're not serious."

"Yes, I am. We probably shouldn't even be having this conversation, but I thought it would be better if we cleared the air. I don't know what's going to happen next, but I do know Lily deserves to be happy."

He'd said too much. He'd tried to take himself out of the equation as much as possible, but that was difficult when he thought he had a stake in it. It was difficult when he felt as if Lily and the twins owned a piece of his heart.

Seeing them talking, Lily crossed to the sofa with Sophie in her arms. Sophie was rubbing her eyes and her face against Lily's blouse. "I think we'd better get these two home. In a few minutes they're either both going to be asleep or fussing because they're tired."

Mitch carefully picked up Grace and stood with her. "I'll help you pack the car. I should be going, too."

"I can take Grace," Ellie said, reaching for the little girl.

Mitch aided in the transfer, wondering just how seriously Lily might be thinking about moving to Oklahoma City.

While Ellie watched the twins, Lily and Mitch took baby paraphernalia outside to Ellie's car. The weather had turned colder. The late-November wind blew across the parking area and through the corral across the lane. Lily opened the car door while Mitch slid the high chairs inside, along with a diaper bag. At the trunk, he adjusted the stroller to lay flat.

After he shut the lid, he regarded Lily in the glow of the floodlight shining from the back of the house. "Ellie tells me Troy's mother wants you to move to Oklahoma City." He'd never intended to start like that, but the question had formed before he could think of anything else to say.

Although she wore a suede jacket, Lily wrapped her arms around herself as if to ward off a chill. "I'm surprised she told you that."

"Were *you* going to tell me?"

"I don't know. After the past few months…" She trailed off. "If I went to Oklahoma City, you wouldn't have to worry about your promise to Troy."

"Is *that* why you'd move?"

She turned away, as if making eye contact was too difficult, as if she couldn't be as honest if she did.

But he clasped her arm and pulled her a little closer. "What do you want, Lily? A different life in Oklahoma?"

"I'm thinking about it. I have good friends here, but Troy's parents are Sophie and Grace's grandparents. I'm not sure what the right thing to do is."

"Whatever makes you happy."

She gave a short laugh. "And how do we ever really know what that will be?"

He'd meant it when he'd told Ellie he wouldn't try to persuade Lily one way or the other. They'd have to set aside the question of her moving…for now. "I'm glad you asked me to come today," he said after a long pause.

"Are you?" Lily's voice was filled with the same longing Mitch felt. They'd been apart and he'd hated that. He just didn't know if they should be together.

"I never experienced a holiday quite like it," he explained. "I haven't had a place to go for holidays in a long time."

"I think Sophie and Grace remember you. They're so comfortable with you."

"And how comfortable are you with everyone watching?" He swore under his breath. "That didn't come out right."

"Yes, it did. I know what you mean. But we weren't really together today, were we?"

He had to make a decision now, which way was he going to go with Lily. He could just cut her out of his life. But wasn't that in itself making a decision for her?

"How would you like to go to the tree-lighting ceremony on Sunday at the library? We can show the twins all the lights and let them listen to their first Christmas carols."

She only hesitated a few moments. "I'd like to do that."

He didn't ask her if she'd ever been to the tree-lighting ceremony with Troy. He didn't want to know. Although he longed to take her in his arms and kiss her, he didn't. This time, they were going to take small steps toward each other to find out if that's where they wanted to be.

Maybe Sunday would be a beginning. Maybe Sunday would be an end.

At least he'd know one way or the other.

Chapter 10

"It pays to have connections," Mitch said with a grin as he stood inside the library, peering out the long window with Sophie in his arms. Raina's mother was the head librarian and had told them they could settle inside for as long as they wanted.

Lily was holding Grace, peering outside beside Mitch. Her arm was brushing his. Every time it did, he remembered everything about their night together—everything about her hands on his body and the shake-up of his soul. Not for the first time he wondered if he wanted Lily simply because he shouldn't have her.

Mitch suddenly felt a hand on his shoulder and tensed. As he turned, he relaxed. "Hello, Mr. Fieldcrest. Are you and your wife going to enjoy the tree-lighting ceremony?" Tucker Fieldcrest and his wife owned the B&B where his friends would be staying this coming weekend.

"We surely are. I was going to call you this week, but now I don't have to. I just wanted to tell you, we're all ready for your guests."

Mitch introduced Tucker to Lily. They all chatted for a few minutes and then Tucker motioned to the crowd gathering outside. "They're almost ready to light the tree. You'd better get your place. I'll see you Friday night." With a wave, he left through the library's huge wooden double doors.

"He seems very nice," Lily said, after the older man had gone outside.

"He and his wife Belinda are good people. They're cutting us a break, only charging half the normal room rates. They insisted they'd be empty this time of year anyway, and our veterans deserve more than reasonable room charges."

"Absolutely," Lily said emphatically, and Mitch knew what she was thinking about. Yet she surprised him when she asked, "So, do you still need activities for the kids? Would you like me to come over and paint faces?"

"I roped Matt into playing Santa Claus and I was hoping that would take up the whole afternoon. But if you're still willing, I'm sure everyone would appreciate it."

"I'm still willing."

To do more than face paint? he wanted to ask. All the words that passed between them seemed to have an underlying message. When he'd asked her to come along tonight, he'd thought of it as a sort of date. But did she think about it that way, too? Did having the twins along make it merely an outing they could enjoy together?

He'd drive himself crazy with the questions, especially when Lily looked at him with those big, blue eyes and a smile that again brought back their night together in vivid detail. It was ironic, really. They'd had sex in the dark but every moment of it was emblazoned in his mind in living color. Sometimes he thought he could see those same pictures running through Lily's thoughts, but that could be wishful thinking.

"Let's get Sophie and Grace bundled up so we don't miss their expressions when the tree lights glow. Do you have your camera?"

Lily patted the pocket of her yellow down jacket. "Right here. But I don't know how we're going to hold them both and take their picture at the same time."

"We'll figure out something," he assured her. Sophie suddenly took hold of his nose and squeezed it a little, babbling new consonant sounds as she did. He laughed. "Getting impatient, are you? Come on, let's cover that pretty blond hair with your hat and hood so you stay warm."

Once the girls were dressed, Mitch and Lily pushed the stroller down the side ramp to the sidewalk. A fir tree stood on the land in front of the eighty-year-old, two-story brick library. The storefronts farther up the street were all lit up with multicolor lights, more than ready for Christmas shoppers. Grady Fitzgerald owned a saddle shop in the next block and Mitch thought he caught a glimpse of him and Francesca with their little boy on the other side of the tree. Lily waved to Tessa and Vince Rossi, who'd brought their children, Sean and Natalie, to watch the ceremony.

"Gina and Logan are here somewhere," Lily said to Mitch, leaning close to him so he could hear her amidst the buzz of people talking.

She pulled the camera from her pocket. "You hold the stroller and I'll take your picture."

"Lily, I don't think—" But before he could protest, before he could say he hated to have his picture taken, she'd already done it. Turnabout was fair play, so he motioned her to the back of the stroller, snagged the camera from her hand and took more than one of her with her girls. Sophie and Grace seemed to be mesmerized by the people passing by, the stand with the microphone where the mayor stood, the wind carrying the smells of French fries, corn dogs and hamburgers from the food cart parked not far away.

As the mayor, Greta Landon, came to the mike and started her remarks, Mitch handed the camera back to Lily. He swooped Sophie out of the stroller and said, "If you hand me Grace, I can hold them both up, and you can take their picture when the lights go on."

After Lily lifted Grace from the stroller, she transferred her to Mitch. As she stood close, she tilted her chin up and was almost near enough to kiss. She said, "This was a great idea. Maybe we'll start a tradition."

If you don't leave Sagebrush for Oklahoma City, he thought. He believed he was so good at not giving anything away, but he must have been wrong about that. Because Lily backed away as if she couldn't reassure him she would be staying in Texas. Her impulsive exclamation had been just that—impulsive.

Just like their night together.

At that moment, the mayor announced, "Let this year's Christmas tree glow brightly for all the residents of Sagebrush."

The tree came alive with blue, red, green and purple balls. Strand after strand of tiny white lights twinkled around those. Mitch witnessed the expression on Sophie and Grace's faces, and their wide-eyed awe was priceless.

Instead of looking at the tree when the Christmas carols began playing, Lily's face was Madonna-like as she gazed at her girls. Then her eyes locked to his. Something elemental twisted in his chest.

The twins already seemed to be developing their own language. They babbled to each other and the gibberish was almost in a cadence that Mitch thought of as language.

Lily leaned in and kissed both of their cheeks, then snapped a picture of Mitch holding them. "What do you think of all those lights?"

They waved their hands at each other and at her.

All of a sudden, Hillary was at Lily's side, carrying her own daughter. "Look who's here," Hillary said, taking in Mitch, Lily and the twins. "Since when are you two seeing each other outside of the office?"

"Since tonight," Mitch answered, matter-of-factly. "We're sharing some Christmas cheer. How does Megan like all this?" If there was one thing Mitch knew, it was that talking about someone's children always took their mind off anything else.

Still, Hillary gave him a knowing look. "She loved it, but now I think she's ready for bed. Besides, I don't want her out in the cold too long. How about you? Are you going to go back into the library for some complimentary hot chocolate?"

He and Lily hadn't discussed that, but he imagined what her answer would be. "We're headed home, too."

Hillary shifted Megan to her other arm. "Well, it was good to run into you without your lab coats on. I'll see you tomorrow." Then as quickly as she'd appeared, she was gone.

If Lily was going to take issue with what he'd told

Hillary, this wasn't the time or place. He said, "Let's get them into the stroller and roll them to the car, unless you really would like some hot chocolate first."

As Lily took Sophie from him, she replied, "We can make hot chocolate back at the house."

Hmm. They just might be in for that discussion after all.

Lily had been surprised tonight at what Mitch had said to Hillary. For all those months he'd seemed as far away as the North Pole. But when he'd asked her to come along with him tonight, he seemed to have established a now-or-never attitude. However, everything was unsaid. Everything was up in the air. Everything was up to them.

How should she feel about his proprietary statement? Were they going to be a couple? Could Mitch make a lifelong commitment if that's where they were headed? What if she decided she shouldn't stay in Sagebrush? All the questions were terrifying, along with the life changes they could provoke.

But for tonight?

The warm and fuzzy feelings from the tree-lighting ceremony lingered as they drove home.

After they pulled into the drive, gathered the girls and the stroller and rolled them up the front walk, Mitch asked, "How will your housemates feel about us coming back here?"

"I guess we'll find out."

Her flippant reply almost seemed like a challenge.

Once in the living room, he found Angie and Ellie watching a forensic drama on TV while they strung popcorn to use as garlands.

"You're getting ready for Christmas?" he asked as a hello.

Ellie looked up, shot him a forced smile, then went back to stringing.

Angie responded to his question. "We all like to do home-crafted decorations, so it can take a while."

Without thinking twice, he took Sophie from her stroller, unzipped her coat, took off her mittens and hat and picked her up.

"Ma-ma-ma-ma," she said practically, as her sister chimed in with the same syllable.

He laughed and asked Lily, "Two bottles upstairs?"

She nodded.

"If you need some help…" Ellie called.

"You look like you're busy," Mitch said. "We'll be okay." Taking the lead was second nature to him. Would Lily mind? She didn't give any indication that she did.

"I put bottles together," Angie said. "They're in the refrigerator in their bedroom."

Mitch glanced over his shoulder as he carried Sophie upstairs, right behind Lily with Grace. He wasn't surprised to see Ellie's gaze on them.

In the twins' bedroom, Mitch and Lily stole glances at each other while they fed the girls and readied them for bed. They'd been super-aware of each other all night, but hadn't been able to act on that awareness. Now they still couldn't, with Sophie and Grace to care for and Ellie and Angie downstairs. The whole situation was frustrating, titillating and exciting. Mitch knew he'd thrown down a figurative gauntlet tonight, and Lily had to make the decision whether or not she wanted to pick it up. She could deny their bond as she had once before. Maybe he was just waiting for her to do it again. Maybe he wanted the safer route. Maybe living alone was preferable to caring about a family. Maybe he didn't think he deserved a family. Because he had come home but others hadn't?

It was a lonely route, yet he was used to it.

Once the twins were comfortably settled in their cribs, once Lily had kissed them both and he'd simply laid a protective hand on each of their foreheads, Lily and Mitch left them to sleep by the glow of the night-light and stepped into the hall. This was about the most privacy they were going to have.

At least that's what he thought until Lily said, "I need to turn on their monitor in my bedroom."

Lily's bedroom. Visions raced through his mind.

Lily went ahead to her nightstand and switched on the monitor. He stepped over the threshold and shut the door.

She didn't move and neither did he for a moment. Then he saw that flicker in her eyes, the memory of what it was like when they were together. He covered the two steps to her, lifted her chin and looked deep into her eyes. "I told Hillary we were dating."

"I know."

"Do you have an opinion about that?"

"I didn't protest."

"No, mainly so you wouldn't embarrass us both."

"That wasn't the reason."

"What was?" he demanded, tired of waiting, yet knowing that with Lily all he could do was wait until she was truly free of yesterday.

"Because I want to spend time with you, Mitch—*with* the twins…*without* the twins. I can't tell you everything's going to go smoothly. I still miss Troy." She looked down at her hand, and he did, too. Her wedding ring glistened there, as real now as the day Troy had slipped it on her finger.

"And *I'm* used to being alone," he admitted.

"Do you like that?" she asked with the spirit that was all Lily.

He almost laughed. Almost. But the question had been a serious one. "I used to think being alone was the only way I could deal with my life on my terms."

"And now?"

"I'm open to finding out differently. That's all I can give you right now."

The expression on her pretty face said she didn't know if that was enough. He didn't, either. But as he bent his head, kissing her seemed a lot more important than the future.

He brushed his lips against hers, maybe to test her, to see how much she wanted. But the test became his to pass or fail. She responded by twining her arms around his neck and slipping her fingers into his hair. He'd wanted to take everything slowly with Lily. This time they'd take it easy. This time he'd make sure she knew what she was doing. This time, she wouldn't want to deny what was going on between them.

But the moment her fingers tugged at his hair as if she wanted more, undeniable desire rushed through his body.

Making himself slow down, he kissed her neck, and asked, "How much time do you think we have?" He leaned back to check her expression, to see if she felt guilty about being in her room with him, to see if what her housemates thought mattered.

"A few minutes," she responded. "Ellie and Angie will wonder if everything's all right."

A few minutes wasn't enough time. So he didn't waste

a moment more of it. His mouth came down on hers possessively, coaxing, teasing, plundering. Still the moan that came from Lily's throat gave the kiss more power as they both gave in to the primal quality of it. He thrust his tongue into her mouth, felt her soft, full breasts against him, and knew he was more aroused than he'd ever been. His hands slid down her back and he pressed her into him. She shivered and the trembling of her body made him wonder what he was doing. Their kisses awakened him to the raw need inside him. What if that need could never be satisfied? What if Lily, too, turned away from his scars? After all, the last time, they'd made love in the dark. What if he had a nightmare while he was lying beside her? How would she react?

The questions flooding his brain doused the far-reaching, fiery tendrils of his desire. A good thing, too, because he might have pulled her onto that bed, undressed her and joined their bodies no matter who was downstairs.

Tearing himself from her and the kiss, he stood away so he wouldn't reach for her again.

Looking a bit dazed, she said, "Wow! Those few minutes sure went fast."

He rubbed his hand over his face. "You get to me."

Smiling, she replied, "*You* get to *me*."

What bothered Mitch was that, despite the rush of passion that had enfolded them, the smile on Lily's face and in her voice didn't touch her eyes. Neither of them seemed happy about it.

"I'm looking forward to this weekend, Lily, but if you don't want to take the time away from Sophie and Grace, I'll understand. I'll be busy playing host, so I don't know how much time I'll have for…us."

Her hands fluttered as if she didn't know what to do with them, so she stuffed them into her front jeans pockets. "Why don't we just play it by ear? I'll see what kind of day the girls are having and then decide."

"Fair enough," he responded. Yet what he'd suggested didn't seem fair at all. He'd just given her an out, and she might take it…just as she might still move to Oklahoma City and leave her life in Sagebrush behind.

Midweek, Lily softly descended the steps into the living room, not wanting to awaken anyone. Sophie and Grace were snuggled in for the night. Angie, on day shift now, had turned in around the same time as Ellie after the evening news.

But Lily couldn't sleep. The decision whether or not to go to Mitch's on Saturday was gnawing at her. Every time she ran into him during the course of the day, she knew he was wondering if she'd be there or not. She felt that if she decided to go, she would be making a commitment.

A commitment to Mitch when she still wore her wedding ring?

She'd had lunch with Raina today, who had given her a DVD copy of the video Eva had recorded on Thanksgiving. Lying in bed, feeling more alone than she'd ever remembered feeling, Lily decided she needed to watch that DVD.

After she inserted the disk in the machine, she sat on the sofa, perched on the edge of the cushion, pressing the buttons on the remote. The video sprang to life and she watched Thanksgiving Day come alive for her all over again. The living room at Shep and Raina's had been full of lively chatter. Mitch sat on the floor with Joey and Roy, his long legs stretched out in front of him, crossed at the ankles. The boys said something and Mitch laughed. He had such a deep, rich laugh and she rarely heard it. But he'd laughed often on Thanksgiving Day. Because he'd been relaxed? Because kids surrounded him? Because the two of them were together with friends in a way they hadn't been before?

The moment Grace raised her arms to Mitch and he'd lifted her onto his lap brought tears to Lily's eyes. He was so caring and gentle with the girls. Yet Lily sensed he still withheld part of himself. He didn't want to get too attached. Because in being attached to them, he'd be attached to her?

"You should be asleep," a soft voice scolded.

Startled, Lily dropped the remote.

"Sorry," Ellie said, coming to sit beside her. "I didn't mean to scare you."

Bending to the floor, Lily found the remote and hit the stop button.

"This is Thanksgiving," Ellie noticed, staring at the freeze frame on the TV, the still image of Mitch holding Grace.

"Raina gave me a copy today. She thought I'd like to have it for posterity," Lily said with a small, short laugh that she had to force out.

"You don't have to stop it on my account. I was there, remember?"

"I know, but I thought—"

"Stop tiptoeing around me, Lily. You don't have to. I know how I reacted at the beginning of the summer when Mitch was around. I'm sorry for that."

"You had every right to feel whatever you were feeling."

"I had no right to dictate who you should or shouldn't see."

"You didn't."

"Then why didn't I see Mitch around for almost six months?"

"That was *my* fault, not yours. I wasn't ready to open my heart to another man."

Ellie pointed to the screen. "It looks as if you're trying to figure out if you're ready now."

"If I have to figure it out, that means I'm not?" Lily asked, in turmoil about it. Yet that's what she was feeling.

"I don't know, Lily. Troy is still real to me. He's still my brother. I talk to him, and I listen for his advice. Is that crazy or what?"

"I don't think that's crazy at all. I still do that, too."

"Then maybe you should ask him about this," Ellie advised her.

The two women sat there for a few moments in the dark, with the silence, staring at the frozen picture on the TV in all its color and high definition.

Now that she and Ellie were having an open talk about this, Lily went to her purse on the foyer table and removed her camera. It had been in there since Sunday night.

"I want to show you something," she said to Ellie, sitting beside her sister-in-law again.

She switched on the camera, pressed the review button and brought up a picture. She was standing in front of the town's Christmas tree with the twins in their stroller. Then there were a few shots of Sophie and Grace by themselves, their faces filled with awe, the excitement of their first Christmas shining from their eyes. The miracle of Christmas was starting to unfold for them. She wanted the holiday to be filled with kindness and love and sharing so they'd never forget the importance of giving all year.

The final picture was Mitch holding Sophie and Grace, gazing into the camera with the intensity that was all his. Even though he was smiling, she knew he had questions about what the future held for all of them. Their attraction to each other couldn't be denied. But it muddied the already stirred-up waters. As Lily studied his face, her heart tripped. Her gaze fell to his smile and her stomach somersaulted. Staring at him holding her twins, she felt as if she could melt.

Lily flipped again to the photo of herself with Sophie and Grace, then the other one with Mitch. She said in almost a whisper, "I'm falling in love with him, and it terrifies me."

"Why?"

"Because I've lost everyone who loves me. Because Mitch has an area of his life he won't open to me. Because I'm still attached to Troy and afraid to let go."

"So what are you trying to decide?"

"Mitch's reunion with his buddies from Iraq is this weekend. Saturday they'll be at his place most of the day and he asked me to come over. I'll be setting foot in an area of his life he kept closed off to me. He said we won't have much time alone, but after everyone leaves, we might."

"Are you asking my permission?" Ellie asked with a hint of a smile.

"No. I guess what I'm asking for is your blessing."

Ellie's gaze dropped to the end table by the sofa where a picture of Lily and Troy stood. Then she lifted it to the TV screen. "Go, Lily. You have to. It's the only way you'll know for sure if you're ready to move on. That's the best I can do."

Lily switched off the DVD player and set the camera on the coffee table. "Let's have a cup of hot cider. I want your opinion on what I'm thinking of giving to Angie and Raina for Christmas."

"You want to be distracted from what's really going on in your mind."

Ellie knew her too well because she was right.

Chapter 11

Mitch opened his door to Lily, trying to adjust his thinking about today to include her in it. His gut always twisted a little when he saw her...when her blue eyes looked at him with so many questions he wasn't sure he'd ever be able to answer. "I wasn't sure you'd come."

She had a cake holder in one hand, a paint case in the other. "I told you yesterday that I'd come to help."

Yes, she had. They'd been passing in the hall and she'd stopped him with a touch of her hand on his elbow. He'd felt the heat from it the rest of the day, though he'd told himself that was impossible. Had his caresses branded her the same way?

Stepping aside so she could enter, not sure what her presence meant, he pointed to the far end of the kitchen. "I put the desserts on the table. The deli trays are in the fridge and the barbecued beef is in the slow cooker."

"It sounds as if you have all of the bases covered."

Except the base with her on it. He nodded to her carrying case. "Paints?" The mundane conversation had to get them through, although the question he wanted to ask was—would she stay the night? Too much to expect?

"Yep. And I have some board games and puzzles in the car. Along with Santa Claus, you should have the kids covered."

"I have a table set up for you in the sunroom."

After she unzipped her parka, he moved behind her, taking it from her shoulders. He hadn't been *this* close to Lily all week, though each time he'd passed her in the hall he'd wanted to haul her over his shoulder, carry her to a closet for privacy and kiss her. She'd left her hair loose today and he caught the scent of it as his hands closed over her jacket and red scarf. She was wearing a Christmas-red sweater with black jeans, dangling gold earrings and black shoe-boots with tall heels. She looked incredible.

When she glanced over her shoulder, their gazes collided and he bent his head to kiss her.

But that kiss wasn't to be. His doorbell rang and he swore under his breath. Not that he didn't want to see his visitors. But every private moment with Lily was precious.

"I'm nervous," she admitted with a shaky smile, as he hung her jacket and scarf over his arm.

"Why?"

"Because these are your friends and I'm not sure I belong here."

"I felt that way at Thanksgiving until Raina and Shep made me feel comfortable. Relax, Lily. These are just families who share a common bond. *You* share it, too."

His words didn't seem to reassure her. He wanted to wipe the anxious look off her face with a touch…with a few kisses. But he couldn't. His guests were arriving and he had to play host.

The next half hour passed in a whirlwind of guests entering and introductions being made. Lily had no trouble making conversation, as Mitch had known she wouldn't. She was easily drawn to the moms with kids, and to one of Mitch's best friends, Matt Gates, who was an ER doctor in Houston. After everyone else had arrived, Jimmy Newcomb's wife, Robin, drove their van into a space the guests had left for them in Mitch's driveway. All of the guys went outside in case Robin needed help. But the Newcomb's van was equipped with a wheelchair lift and, fortunately, Mitch's house had only one step to navigate to push the wheelchair inside.

"I don't want to make tracks in your carpet," Jimmy said to Mitch as he wheeled into the kitchen.

"You can go anywhere you want to in my house," Mitch assured him.

Robin and Maya, Tony Russo's wife, set up the kids in the sunroom with games and puzzles, drawing paper, pencils and crayons, while Lily arranged her face paints on a small table. The children began asking questions right away and she explained what she could do. Soon they were lined up, pleading with her to paint a Christmas tree or an angel, a reindeer or a butterfly on their faces. Once when Mitch looked in on her she was telling them about Christmas traditions around the world. Another time, the children were explaining how they celebrated Christmas. He realized how much he wanted Lily to stay tonight. It had to be *her* decision. As she took a few breaks, he suspected she was calling Ellie to check on Sophie and Grace.

In the course of the afternoon, he attempted to spend time with everyone. He lit a fire in the fireplace, pulled bottles of beer from a cooler, made pots of coffee. When darkness fell, he set out the food. He'd ordered more than enough, and he was glad to see all his guests looked pleased to be there, sitting near the predecorated Christmas tree he'd bought at the last minute. Reunions could bomb. But this group had too much in common. Feelings ran deep and so did loyalties.

Matt had brought his Santa paraphernalia and stowed it in a spare bedroom where Mitch had stacked presents for the kids.

As most of the guests enjoyed dessert and Lily sat on the couch deep in conversation with Robin, Matt beckoned Mitch to follow him into the hall.

"Ready to sweat in that Santa suit?" Mitch asked with a grin.

Matt grimaced. "You're going to owe me for this one."

"Not if I can help it. You're going to love doing this so much you'll want to do it every year. If the gifts are too heavy in that flannel sack—"

"Do you think practicing in the ER is making me soft?" Matt inquired with a raised brow.

"Not for a minute," Mitch assured him.

"Before I forget, I want to give you something," Matt said, taking out his wallet and slipping out a business card.

"What's this?" Mitch glanced at it and saw the name, address and telephone number of a doctor—the head of the Hand and Trauma Surgery division at the hospital where Matt practiced.

"Eric Dolman is good, Mitch. The best I've ever seen. He's performed nerve grafting and conduits, as well as nerve transfers, with success. If you want to return to surgery, you might want to fly to Houston to see him. I could probably get you in on short notice."

Mitch's gut tightened. "I have a new career now. I was told surgery could cause more damage than I already have." He flexed his fingers just thinking about it.

"Look, Mitch. I know about survivor guilt. Most of us carry it. Maybe it's time to lose it and reach out for something you deserve to have. If you don't want to go back to trauma surgery, that's your decision. But Eric might be able to restore full use of your hand."

Mitch heard a noise and swung around. Lily was standing there and had obviously cleared her throat to make her presence known. She was holding her cell phone and probably looking for a quiet place to make her call.

"I didn't mean to interrupt," she told both of them. "I was just trying to find—"

"A little quiet?" Matt filled in with a smile. "That's hard to do around this crowd." His grin faded, then he became serious. "Tony's wife told me you lost your husband to Afghanistan. I'm sorry."

"Thank you," Lily replied, looking down at her phone where a picture of her twins stared up at her.

Matt tapped the card Mitch was still holding. "Don't lose that. Call him anytime. Just mention my name." Then he strode down the hall to the bedroom.

Lily's blue eyes found Mitch's. "I really didn't mean to interrupt. I overheard a little. This doctor could repair the damage to your hand?"

If Mitch was going to even think about doing this, he

had to run it through his own mind first. "The risk could be greater than the rewards."

"But if you could return to surgery—"

"Lily, I don't think this is the time or place to have this discussion. Can we just table it for now?"

"Does that mean you'll want to talk about it later?" she challenged.

Not only was Mitch hesitating to start a serious relationship with Lily because of her memories...but also because of his. She might want too much from him, a closeness he didn't know how to give. She was pushing him now, and that made him restless and uncomfortable. So he was honest with her. "I don't know. I need some time to think about what Matt said. I might want to research this doctor. I might not want to discuss surgery at all."

He saw the hurt on Lily's face, and he knew he was closing her out. But this was sacred territory to him. She didn't understand the ramifications of everything surgery could stir up. Not only memories of his time in the hospital and rehab, working to change his specialty to endocrinology, but also the cause of it all. He didn't talk about *that* to anyone.

More gently, he told her, "I'm going to set up the kindling in the fire pit. After Santa leaves, we can toast marshmallows with the kids."

"I'm sure they'll like that," Lily said, much too politely.

He left her in the hall, believing that after the marshmallows were toasted, she would leave.

Lily opened one side of the French doors and stepped outside onto the red-and-gray brick patio. It was huge, running along most of the back of Mitch's house. But three high stone walls framed the outside of the patio, giving it a protective feel. Mitch, Jimmy and Matt sat by the fire, talking, mugs of hot coffee in their hands.

She walked over to them, zipping her parka. "The kids want to come out and sing Christmas carols before they all go back to the bed-and-breakfast."

"Tell them to come on," Mitch said, rising to his feet.

Lawn chairs were scattered across the bricks, where after Santa's arrival and departure some of the older children had toasted marshmallows for the younger ones under their parents' watchful eyes. Now the fire had died down and short flames licked at the remaining logs under the mesh fire screen.

Lily didn't have to convey Mitch's invitation to the guests inside. As soon as she turned toward the door again, all the children and adults who had gone for their coats poured out. Light from inside shone on the closest section of the patio. The rest was lit by a half moon and so many stars she couldn't count them all if she tried. For Mitch's guests who lived in cities, this had to be a treat. Those who lived in more rural areas knew how to appreciate the beauty of the winter night.

Jimmy's little boy, who was eight and had Rudolph painted on one cheek, grabbed Lily's hand and pulled her toward his mom and dad. "Stand over here," he told her.

She did and found herself beside Mitch.

The night was turning colder and a light wind blew over the stone walls, but she felt protected in the cocoon of the patio, although her breath puffed white vapor in front of her.

Beside her husband, Robin suggested, "Let's take hands."

A hush fell over the group and even the little ones reached for a hand on either side of them. Lily found one of her hands in Mitch's, the other holding Jimmy's. She was emotionally moved in a way she couldn't even begin to express, especially when Maya's sweet voice began "Silent Night." Lily's throat closed as she tried to sing along with the words.

All is calm. All is bright.

How these men deserved calmness and bright.

Instead of holding her hand now, Mitch swung his arm around her shoulders.

What was he feeling at this moment? What had this night meant to him? Would he talk to her about it? Would he talk to her about the possible surgery?

Sleep in heavenly peace. Sleep in heavenly peace.

She suspected all the men were thinking about fallen comrades and maybe how lucky and grateful they were to be alive…to be here together. She thought about the Purple Heart medal tucked away in her jewelry box and how well Troy would have fit in here tonight.

After the last verse of the Christmas carol, moms and dads herded up children and one by one thanked Mitch for his hospitality. She heard him say, "It'll be your turn sometime. Then I'll be thanking you."

He'd gone to a lot of trouble to put this weekend together and it showed.

Inside the house again once more, Mitch saw his guests to the door. Lily stowed food away while he made sure Jimmy accessed his van without difficulty.

"You don't have to do that," Mitch told Lily when he returned to the kitchen.

Actually she'd been grateful for something to do. She knew what *she* wanted to happen next, but she wasn't sure how Mitch felt. "There's not much left. A few pieces of chocolate cake, a half dozen cookies. Some guacamole and a bag of corn chips."

She covered the remainder of the cake with plastic wrap and set it on the counter. "Matt was a great Santa."

"He's always the life of the party," Mitch replied.

The echo of "Silent Night" and the picture of the group gathered outside would be lasting. "Jimmy's a remarkable man. Robin explained a little of what their life is like since he became paralyzed. They're both courageous people."

"She stuck by him when he wasn't sure she would."

"She loves him."

"Sometimes love isn't enough."

Mitch's decisive words seemed to echo in the kitchen. Lily didn't know if he was going to ask her to stay the night, but if he wasn't, she wanted to discuss the surgery on his hand.

He was standing by the counter perfectly still as she moved closer to him. "Nothing can change what happened to Jimmy in Iraq." She took Mitch's hand and ran her thumb over the top of it. "But maybe you can change some of what happened to you."

Mitch pulled away from her, his expression closed. "I told you—surgery could have repercussions."

"I understand that. But a consultation would do no harm."

"I'd have to take time off."

"The practice slows down over the holidays," she reminded him.

His jaw became more set. "I don't want to be a guinea

pig. I don't want to be given false hope or become a statistic."

"You haven't even *met* this doctor. You don't have the information you need to make an informed decision."

He blew out a frustrated breath. "Lily, I don't want to argue about this."

"Fine," she said agreeably. "We don't have to argue. I'm merely making a few observations." Then stepping even closer to him, laying her hand gently on his tight jaw, she whispered, "I care about you."

The tension in his body was obvious in his granite-like expression, the squareness of his shoulders, his legs defensively widened. Did it come from more than this interchange between them? After all, although he'd never admit it, this had to have been an emotional day for him.

Looking deeply into her eyes, he seemed to try to see to her very essence. She stood silent, holding her breath.

Then he covered her hand with his. They stood that way for what seemed like hours. The ice maker in the freezer rumbled as it made new ice. The heating system pinged as it battled against the cold night. Lily could feel the pulse in Mitch's jaw jumping under her palm.

Finally he dropped his hand and wrapped his arms around her. When he kissed her, his raw hunger excited her need, ratcheted up the desire that had been building between them, told them both that coming together again would be an explosion of passion.

After Mitch broke the kiss, he leaned away slightly and asked, "Will you stay tonight?"

"I thought you'd never ask," she replied a bit shakily.

Moments later, sitting on the corner of the bed in Mitch's room, her earrings in her palm, Lily ended her call with

Ellie. She'd switched on one of the dresser lamps when she'd entered. Now as she glanced around, she saw Mitch's minimalist taste reflected here, too. The bed's headboard was dark pecan, as were the dresser, chest and nightstands. The lamps were a combination of wood and black iron, with the dresser top uncluttered. Yet the multicolored rug beside the bed looked handwoven. The afghan on top of the brown suede-like spread seemed to be hand-knitted.

Rising to her feet, she walked to the dresser and laid her phone and earrings there. She hadn't packed an overnight bag. Because she hadn't wanted to think tonight was a sure thing?

When Mitch entered the room, her body knew it. She didn't turn around but rather raised her gaze in the mirror.

He came up behind her, his eyes on hers. "Everything's okay at home?"

She nodded.

Sliding his arms around her, he pulled her tight against him. "We both smell like wood smoke," he growled against her ear.

Feeling him strong and hard against her body, excitement coursed through her. Her breaths became more shallow, and already she was tingling in the places she imagined he might touch.

"Wood smoke can be sexy," she teased lightly.

"*You're* sexy," he returned, his hands covering her breasts.

Lily trembled from head to toe. At that moment her need for Mitch was go great, she felt she could melt in his hands. Even though she'd stopped breast-feeding, her breasts had remained larger than they once were. Now as they lay cupped in Mitch's palms, she was grateful for every sensation, every nuance of feeling. Yet she understood that feeling would be so much greater with her clothes *off*.

"Undress me," she requested with an urgency that Mitch could obviously hear.

His low chuckle vibrated against her back. "Sometimes making out can be more scintillating with your clothes on." His hands moved down her stomach to the waistband of her jeans.

"Aren't we going to do more than make out?" she asked.

His answer was rough against her ear. "Eventually."

Mitch's foreplay was driving her crazy. All she wanted to do was crawl into bed with him, their bodies naked and exposed to each other's hands and mouths.

Before she realized what Mitch was going to do, her jeans were around her hips, held up by his thighs. His hands slid inside her panties and cupped her. She'd never felt like this—on the verge of an orgasm without even a kiss.

"Do you know how often our first time together plays in my mind?" he asked with an erotic rasp to his words.

She had those same pictures in her mind. The continuous loop the visions made came to her at odd times and could make her blush.

His finger slipped inside of her and she moaned, needing to turn and face him.

But he wouldn't let her. "Watch in the mirror," he commanded.

There was something so sensual about what they were doing, and the way they were doing it. She'd never watched herself enjoy pleasure. When she lifted her gaze to his and stared at their reflection, his fingers started moving again. Her breath caught. She stared into his eyes as her body tensed and then released in swirls of muscle-melting sensations.

After the orgasmic release, she lay her head back against his shoulder. He held her tightly.

After a few moments of letting her catch her breath, he said, "Let's take off those boots. They make your legs look like a million bucks, but I think they could be dangerous in bed."

They undressed each other beside the bed, and this time—unlike the first—they did it by the glow of the lamp. If Mitch had given her pleasure to blunt the experience of what she was about to see, it hadn't worked. All of her senses seemed even more sensitive to everything that was revealed. His body was hard and muscled and strong, attesting to his workouts. Silky black chest hair formed a Y, arrowing down his flat stomach, around his navel. But red scars from surgery streaked his side. The heel of her hand slid over them as she sifted her fingers through his chest hair.

"Lily," he breathed, "we can just get in bed—"

"No."

She wanted to see. She wanted to know. She needed to feel.

His shoulder and arm were mottled with zigzagging scars, bumps and ridges, and she could only imagine the pain of his injury. She kissed the arm that he kept covered the whole way down to his wrist. Then she took his hand in hers and brought it to her lips.

He again murmured, "Lily—"

He'd undressed her first, but now she finished undressing him. When he kicked his jeans and briefs aside, she rested her hands on his hips and gazed up into his eyes.

Then he was kissing her and his tongue was in her

mouth and hers was in his. She couldn't seem to reach far
enough to explore or hold him tight enough against her to
hear the beat of his heart. She wasn't even sure how they
managed moving, but they fell or rolled onto the bed, so
hungry for each other they didn't have enough words or
touches to express it. Mitch's fingertips stroked her face.
Her hand passed down his thigh and cupped his arousal.
They were frantic to kiss each other all over, to explore
erogenous zones, to stoke their desire to the limit. Mitch's
scent had become familiar to her and now it was like an
aphrodisiac she couldn't get enough of. The intensity of
their foreplay made her body glisten, her heart race, her
limbs quiver in anticipation of release. She didn't want to
admit how, at that moment, Mitch blotted out everything
else in her world. She didn't want to admit to having this
mindless passion she'd never felt before. Yet she had to
face what was happening, how deeply she was falling,
how inexorable their attraction was.

"I need you," she confessed with sudden tears closing her throat.

Mitch reached for a condom, prepared himself, then
rose above her. He took her hands, one on either side of
her head, and interlocked his fingers with hers. When
she raised her knees, he entered her with a thrust of pos-
session that made her gasp. Her climax began building
from the first stroke. She wrapped her legs around him,
swimming in pleasure that was bigger than the ocean,
wider than the universe, higher than heaven.

"Open your eyes and look at me," Mitch commanded,
and she knew why. He wanted her to make sure she knew
who he was.

"Mitch," she cried, assuring him she did.

His rhythm became faster. She took him deeper. The

explosion that rocked them both should have blown the roof off the house.

But it didn't. It simply left them both breathless and gasping and exhausted from a union that had been months in the making.

Lily lowered her legs, loving the feel of Mitch's body on hers. She wanted to postpone the "where do we go from here" moment for as long as she could.

At first, Lily didn't know what had awakened her. A shout. Groans.

Mitch wasn't in bed with her.

Another shout and she finally was alert enough to know what was happening.

She grabbed Mitch's flannel shirt from a chair and slipped it on as she ran from his bedroom to the guest bedroom next door. Mitch was thrashing in the bed, calling a name—Larry. He was drenched in sweat, breathing hard, eyes open but unseeing.

Lily had learned about post-traumatic stress disorder but didn't know whether to awaken him, or whether to get too close. She'd read about the cut with reality that occurred when flashbacks became more real than life itself. What had triggered this? Being with fellow servicemen who knew what war was about? Sitting around the fire? Talking about surface life yet never going too deep?

Grabbing the metal waste can, she banged it against a tall, wrought-iron floor lamp. The noise was loud and seemed to penetrate Mitch's nightmare. He sat up, eyes open with awareness now, and stared at her still holding the waste can.

When he passed his hands down his face, rubbed his eyes and forehead as if to try to erase everything he'd just seen, she slid into the bed beside him and attempted to fold her arms around him.

He prevented her from doing that and pushed away.

"Everything's fine now, Mitch. I'm here."

"Your being here doesn't change what happened over there." His voice was gravelly with regret, sadness and too many memories.

"Maybe it's time you tell me about it."

"You don't want to hear this, Lily."

When she clasped his shoulder, he flinched, but she didn't remove her hand. "I might not want to hear it, but you need to say it out loud. You need to talk to somebody about it, and right now I think I'm the best person. Just stop fighting your subconscious, Mitch, and let it out."

"Do you think talking about it is going to take away the nightmares? Get *real,* Lily."

"I don't know if talking about your experience will take away anything. I suppose it could make memories worse for a while. But suffering in silence isn't the answer, either."

In that silence Lily could hear Mitch's breathing, still not quite as regular as usual. She could feel his doubt, as if revealing *anything* could make his nightmares worse. But she sat there steadfastly, her hand on his shoulder.

His voice was detached when he said, "I got used to the scud alerts, the bunkers, the MREs. It's amazing what can become normal. I not only cared for our soldiers, but for Iraqis too, many of them children with shrapnel injuries. The sound of artillery shots and mortars coming back at us became a backdrop."

Stopping, he seemed to prepare himself for remembering. Sending her a look that said he didn't want to do this and he was going to get it over with quickly, he continued, "We had spent a couple of days cross-training with ambulance teams, going over procedures. We slept when we could catch minutes, sometimes an hour."

After a quiet so prolonged she didn't know if he'd continue, he did. The nerve in his jaw worked and she could hear the strain in his voice when he said, "I was traveling in a convoy when RPGs came at us. The next thing I knew we'd hit an IED."

Lily was familiar with the military speaking in acronyms. RPG stood for rocket propelled grenade... IED, improvised explosive device.

Mitch's face took on a gray pallor as he forced himself to go on. "Blood was *everywhere*." His voice lowered. "The man beside me was…gone. At that point I didn't realize the extent of my injuries, because adrenaline raced so fast I didn't think about anything except helping anybody who was hurt. My ears rang, though. And rounds were still bouncing off the Humvee even though it was burning. I helped two men from the vehicle, but I saw others who'd been tossed out by the explosion. There was fire all around. I spotted Larry and somehow reached him. He had a hole in his thigh—the femoral vein—" Mitch closed his eyes. "Tony covered me with an M16. All I could think of was that I had to stop the bleeding. I *had* to stop it. What seemed like wild shots zinged over my head. Everything was on fire," he said again. "So I threw my body over his. I heard a muffled yell. I finally saw part of the Humvee had been blown away from the fire. I dragged Larry behind it. Someone handed me a piece of a shirt. I tried to staunch the blood. Then I… must have blacked out."

Mitch took a deep breath…stared away from her… into the past. "I had recollections of the medevac, but other than that, the next thing I knew I was waking up in a hospital in Germany, my spleen gone, internal injuries repaired, a pin in my shoulder and another in my leg."

By the time Mitch finished, tears ran down Lily's cheeks. She hurt *for* him and *with* him and couldn't even fathom living with his memories. She wrapped her arms around him, and he was rigid with resistance. Yet she kept holding on and wouldn't let go.

"Larry died," he said, his voice rough. "Larry died."

Leaning her head against his, she didn't even breathe. After what seemed like an eon, she murmured, "Don't send me away. Let me sleep here with you."

Whether Mitch was too exhausted to protest, too awash in the past to care, he slid down under the covers, letting her hold on.

She didn't fall asleep again until she heard the deep, even rhythm of his breathing. Then she let herself slumber with him, knowing morning would come sooner than they both wanted.

Chapter 12

In the morning everything always looked different.

That's what Lily thought as she awakened, reached across the guest room bed and found that Mitch was gone.

He'd slept in the bed with her most of the night. She'd awakened a couple of times and cuddled close to him with her head on his shoulder. He'd been asleep then... she could tell. But something had made him leave now and she had to admit to herself that that was her biggest fear—that he would leave. If not physically, then emotionally.

Their physical reunion last night had been spectacular. What he'd shared with her about Iraq had been wrenching. Did he have regrets about that now? Was that why he'd left the bed?

She glanced at the clock and saw that it was 7:00 a.m. She knew he was meeting his friends at the bed-and-breakfast for brunch, but that wasn't until ten o'clock. She caught up the flannel shirt she'd discarded last night and slipped it on. She'd shower and dress after she found out where Mitch had gone.

After she buttoned his shirt from neckline to hem, she realized how silly that was. She certainly hadn't been so modest last night. She'd never felt so wanton or so free... so hungry or so sexual.

Sunlight poured in the hall skylight, a new, bright December day with Christmas right around the corner. What gift could she get Mitch?

She hated feeling uncertain like this. She hated not knowing how deep his feelings ran. Were they just having an affair?

That possibility made her heartsick.

She smelled the aroma of coffee and heard Mitch's voice before she saw him. He was pacing the kitchen, talking on his cell phone. He went to the French doors and looked out as he listened.

Spotting his jacket around the kitchen chair, a mug of coffee half gone, she wondered if he'd sat outside this morning in the cold before he'd come in to make his phone call. Who was he talking to? Jimmy? Matt?

Then she heard him say, "Dr. Dolman, I appreciate what you're saying. I searched your articles online this morning." There was a pause. "Yes, that too. I trust Matt. But I wanted to check out your credentials for myself."

Dr. Dolman. The surgeon who could possibly repair Mitch's hand. If Mitch was going to talk to him, why hadn't he discussed it with her? Why had he disappeared from the bed without a "good morning" or a kiss? Last night had meant the world to her. Decisions they each made would affect the other's life. Unless they weren't really "together." Unless last night hadn't meant what she thought it did.

She felt hurt and knew she shouldn't. This was *his* life. This was *his* decision. But she did feel let down. She'd thought last night they'd gotten closer than any two people could get.

Mitch sensed her presence and turned, finding her in the doorway. For a moment their gazes met, but then his mind was on the conversation again and he looked away, shutting her out.

At least that's the way it felt. She wouldn't eavesdrop if he didn't want her there.

She returned to the master bedroom and bath, catching the scent of Mitch's soap still lingering in the shower. She'd thought maybe they could shower together this morning. She'd thought—

Stop it, she chastised herself. Disappointment pressed against her heart as she showered quickly, found a blow dryer under Mitch's sink and blew most of the wetness from her hair. She'd dressed and was picking up her own phone to call the Victorian when she heard Mitch coming down the hall.

She closed her phone and waited.

He saw her standing there with it in her hand. "How are the twins?"

"I don't know. I haven't called yet."

The intimacy they'd shared last night seemed to have been lost. The electric buzz between them was still there, but there was nothing comfortable about it. She kept quiet to let him choose the first topic for discussion.

He asked, "You overheard some of my conversation?"

"Not much. Just the name of the doctor Matt told you about last night."

"Dr. Dolman."

She nodded.

"I was up early, went outside and did a ton of thinking."

She wanted to ask, *About us?* But that obviously wasn't what was on his mind.

"I thought about everything Matt said. He thinks I have survivor guilt."

"Do you?" she asked.

"Hell, I don't know. But I did think about why I wouldn't want to get my hand fixed. Yes, there could be more damage. But it also has to do with the life change I made."

"In other words, why rock the boat?" she inquired.

"Exactly. Yet I've never been a half-measure person. Why in this?"

There were only about three feet between them but it seemed like so much more.

He went on. "Dr. Dolman's success rate is outstanding. I made an appointment with him for Tuesday afternoon."

Tuesday was Mitch's day off. He could reserve an early flight and be in Houston before noon.

"I see," she said.

Tilting his head, he studied her. "I thought you'd be happy about it."

She *was* terrifically pleased he'd made the decision. "I am. But why didn't you wake me up to talk about it? Why did you leave and cut off the closeness we'd shared? Why didn't you think I'd want to be part of whatever you decided?"

His back became straighter, his stance a little wider, as if he had a position to defend. "Why do you think?"

"I'm not at all sure."

"You're insightful, Lily. Take a guess."

"Mitch…"

"No woman has ever touched my scars. *You* did. No woman has ever seen me in the throes of one of my nightmares. *You* did. I never told a civilian back here what happened over there. But I told *you*. If I had stayed in that bed this morning and you'd opened your eyes and I'd seen pity or worse yet, dismay, that even after all these years I still haven't gotten a handle on my own subconscious—" He stopped abruptly. "I just didn't want to have to deal with that."

She didn't know what to say. There were so many levels to his statement. She didn't know how to separate it into all the aspects they needed to examine.

So she stated what was obvious to her. "Why would I feel pity? Mitch, you're a decorated hero. You were awarded a Silver Star, a Purple—"

"I'm *not* a hero. I didn't save Larry's life."

"No, but you tried. You risked *your* life."

"Results matter…in surgery, in helping couples conceive, in life."

Shaking her head, she sank down onto the corner of the bed, hoping he'd do the same. "You expect too much of yourself. And maybe you don't expect enough of me."

"Maybe that's because I think in your mind you're still married."

His words struck her hard and stole her breath. "Did I act like I was still married last night?"

"Did you feel guilt afterwards?"

"No, I didn't," she said almost angrily.

Then he looked down at her hand in her lap. "Then why are you still wearing your wedding ring?"

"This is about my *ring?* You're jealous because I can't forget my husband?"

"I'm *not* jealous," Mitch protested with a vehemence she almost believed. "It's not about that," he concluded. "It's about your ability to let go of Troy so you have something with me."

The thought of letting go of Troy absolutely panicked her! If she let go, didn't that mean their love hadn't been very strong? If she let go, didn't that mean Sophie and Grace would never know their real dad? If she let go, and Mitch left, what would she have then?

He must have seen the color drain from her face. He must have seen how shaken she was, because he covered the few feet between them and clasped her shoulder.

But his touch, which still sent scalding heat through her body, activated her. She stood and pulled away from him. "I have to go home to Sophie and Grace."

"I know you do." His voice had lost its edge and was gentler than she expected. "But this is something we've needed to discuss and haven't."

"I thought we were discussing your surgery." Her feelings for Mitch had been simpler when the focus was on *him*.

"If I have surgery, I'm doing it to move on. You say you want to move on, but I don't know if that's really true."

She was stymied for a response and didn't know what he wanted from her.

"Why don't you go home, get the twins and meet me at the bed-and-breakfast for brunch?"

"I don't think that's a good idea." The words reflexively spilled from her.

"Why not?"

"Because…because I don't know what kind of night they had. I don't know if they're fussy or content. I should have called first thing and I didn't."

"Why didn't you?" he probed.

Because you were on my mind, she thought. "Because you left and I didn't know why."

"I only went as far as the kitchen."

Maybe that was true, but it hadn't felt that way at the time.

"I need to go," she whispered. More than anything, she needed to hold Sophie and Grace. To kiss them. To feel the bond she had with them.

Seeming to understand that, Mitch nodded. "Okay. I'll help you carry your things to the car."

Lily felt shell-shocked…as if her whole world had just crashed in. Mitch had turned the tables so effectively she didn't know who was more conflicted…or which one of them could figure out where they could go from here.

On Tuesday evening Lily sat at the kitchen table with evergreen boughs, ribbon and gold bells spread across newspaper. She was making a wreath for the front door while Angie and Ellie added more Christmas touches to the rest of the house. The last time she'd looked they were arranging a nativity set on the table by the sofa.

When the phone rang, she called into them, "I'll get it," went to the counter and picked up the cordless. The caller ID simply read Out of Area without a number.

"Hello," she answered, afraid to hope the caller was Mitch. Yesterday he'd been busy at the office tying up loose ends, cramming appointments together, going over histories of his patients with Jon and Hillary in case he got tied up in Houston. When she'd asked him about the brunch, he'd said everyone hated to leave the bed-and-breakfast, but they all had to get back to their lives. He'd given her one of those "Mitch" looks that was intense and full of meaning.

But then Jon had buzzed him and he'd rushed off. He didn't seem to be shutting her out, yet he didn't seem to be waiting for anything from her, either.

Before she'd left for the day, she'd placed a note on his desk, wishing him luck.

"Lily, it's Mitch. Are you tied up?"

She wanted to say, *Yes, my stomach's tied in knots and I'm worried about you.* Instead, she replied, "Sophie and Grace are sleeping. Ellie, Angie and I are decorating."

"I wanted to let you know Dr. Dolman believes I'm a good candidate for surgery. He has a slot open on Friday afternoon, so I'm going to stay, have some tests and then let him operate."

"That soon?" she murmured.

"I had to make a decision, Lily. This surgery will either work or it won't. One way or another, I'll know, and I'll adjust my life accordingly."

That's what Mitch did. He adjusted his life to fit whatever happened to him. His history had shown her that. He was a decisive, confident man who didn't stall or procrastinate or wait…unless waiting fit into the big picture. How long would he wait for her? Maybe his patience had already come to an end.

"Anyway, I'm staying at the Longhorn Inn. Matt said I could crash at his place, but he's starting a three-day rotation and will be tied up. I wanted to give you the number where I'll be in case my cell is out of reach. Got a pen and paper?"

She grabbed a pen and tablet from the counter. "Go

ahead." She jotted down the number he gave her. "How long will you be in Houston after your surgery?"

"I'll be discharged the next day, but Matt wants me to give it forty-eight hours until I fly. If all goes well, I'll be back Monday. I can do physical therapy in Lubbock."

If all goes well.

"What about after you're discharged? Doesn't someone have to be with you?"

"I'll be fine, Lily. Matt said he'll have one of his doc friends check on me."

She hated the fact Mitch was going through this practically alone. Like most men, he probably didn't want anyone to see him when he wasn't at his best. But she didn't like the idea he'd be alone after surgery. She didn't like the idea that he was in Houston alone now.

After a long silence, Mitch asked, "So, did you put up a Christmas tree?"

"Yes, we did. Complete with a lighted star on top. Sophie and Grace haven't seen it yet, though. When they wake up they won't know what to think."

"You're lucky they're not walking yet. You can still keep most things out of their reach."

"Except for the tree. Angie hung ornaments that wouldn't break on the bottom. I have a feeling they'll have a few tantrums until they realize they can't touch it."

"They have to learn boundaries."

There was a commotion on Mitch's end. "Someone's at my door, Lily. It's probably room service."

"You're just having dinner?"

"After the consultation, I talked to Matt and then drove around for a while. I needed to…think. I wasn't hungry then. But after I got back and showered, the idea of food sounded good."

"I won't keep you then."

"I'm sorry you're going to have a heavier load this week because of my being away."

"Don't be concerned about that, Mitch. Hillary and Jon and I will be fine."

"Okay, then. If you need anything, or have any questions about my patients, just call."

"I will. And Mitch, I'll be praying for you…that everything goes well."

"Thanks, Lily."

When his phone clicked off, she set down hers, the hollow feeling inside her seeming to echo with Mitch's voice.

Angie came into the kitchen and saw Lily standing there, staring at the phone. "What's going on?"

Lily told her about Mitch's consultation and surgery. "He shouldn't be there alone," Lily murmured when she was finished.

"Who should be with him?" Angie asked.

Lily knew what Angie was suggesting. "I have Grace and Sophie to think about. And the practice."

"Take them with you."

Suddenly Lily heard a cry from the baby monitor. "That's Grace," she said. "I'll find out what's wrong." On her way out of the kitchen, she glanced back at Angie. "I feel pulled in so many directions. I can't think about going to Houston. At least not tonight."

"Tomorrow will come soon enough," her housemate suggested.

Lily knew she was right.

On the way home from the office on Wednesday, Lily took a detour. After arriving at the outskirts of Sagebrush, she turned down a road where she hadn't driven for over a year…almost sixteen months. Mid-December darkness had already fallen and she glimpsed farms along the road with Christmas decorations and lights twinkling from eaves, gables and shrubs in front yards.

Eventually Lily reached an illuminated lane where a security guard was housed in a cupola before a high fence. She presented ID to him and a key. After a few taps into his computer, he okayed her, opened the gate and let her drive inside.

She passed row upon row of storage compartments, some looking more like closets, some the size of a garage. The area was well lit and there were no other cars around. It didn't take her long to find the row, and then the storage compartment that she was looking for. She didn't think as she parked in front of it. She tried not to feel. If she let herself feel now, what would happen after she went inside?

She did check her watch and knew she couldn't spend a whole lot of time here. Not today anyway. Sophie and Grace were waiting for her.

After she unlocked the combination, she inserted the key into the padlock. Two levels of security. Now both were just barriers, locking her out of memories that she'd stored because they were too painful to see, listen to or handle.

The roll-up door stuck and she wondered if she'd have to call the security guard to help her heave it up. But then it gave way and rolled open, revealing the remnants of her marriage. At least the physical ones.

Stepping into the past, she looked around and her eyes burned. It was the cold, the staleness of the compartment, the boxes upon boxes that almost sixteen months ago she couldn't bear to donate or toss away. Moving to the Victorian had accomplished more than giving her an economical place to live, friends to support her, room for her twins to grow. Moving there so quickly after Troy had died had removed her from a good dose of the pain of losing him. She'd been nearly numb when she'd packed up her belongings and his. She'd sent a lot of Troy's things home to his mother, knowing she'd treasure them. But the rest was here in front of her, making her eyes go misty with the remembrance of what was inside the boxes.

She could sit here and go through them one by one. They were labeled and she knew what she'd find. But she hadn't come here to open a box with souvenirs from her Caribbean honeymoon with Troy or CDs they'd once listened to together. She'd come here to find something that would tell her whether she could meld the past with the present…if she *could* really move on. Besides cartons, she had to step over and around Troy's saws and metal boxes that held sets of chisels or a Dremel tool. Finally, after she'd moved a circular saw housed on its own table, she found what she was looking for in the corner.

She had asked Troy to make this for her. It was a multi-tiered plant stand fashioned in oak. Almost finished, it simply needed a last smoothing with fine sandpaper, polishing and then a coat of acrylic.

At least three feet high, the plant stand was bulky as she pushed it from its protected place to the front of the storage compartment and ran her hands over it, imagining Troy doing the same. Now tears really pressed against her eyelids. Giving in, she let them come and didn't even try to brush them away.

When she heard a sound, she realized an airplane was buzzing overhead. At the edge of the compartment, she lifted her gaze to the sky. The moon was bright, almost full, and brought back the memory of standing at the fire pit on Mitch's patio singing "Silent Night." Her nose was numb. Her fingers were stiff. Her feet were cold in her high-heeled pumps. But the cold didn't matter now as she stood still, just letting every feeling in her life wash over her.

Her gaze lifted to the moon and she suddenly saw something to the east of it—a shooting star. It glowed, streaked, then vanished.

Like Troy?

Turning away from the sky, she ran her hands over the solid wood again. She heard the question in her head as if someone were standing in the compartment speaking to her. *Do you love Mitch?*

Searching for the answer here, in the midst of her past life, she knew she did.

Why? that little voice asked again. *Because I asked him to look out for you?*

Reverently she slid her hands over the oak grain, straight and crooked, with imperfections and beauty despite that. She and Troy and Mitch had imperfections and beauty, too. No, she didn't love Mitch because Troy had asked him to watch over her. She loved Mitch because of who he was, and who she was when she was with him. She loved him because he was passionate and intense, and tender and caring. She loved him differently than she'd loved Troy. Whether or not that was because of Sophie and Grace, she didn't know. All of a sudden she just knew her love for Mitch was right.

Yes, it had come along at a time when she was still grieving. And maybe she'd miss Troy for the rest of her life. Loss wouldn't go away merely because she wanted it to. But Troy had so often told her, *There are no coin-*

cidences. On and off, over the past nine months, she'd tested what she'd felt for Mitch. And every time, the desire, the aching to be with him, the dreams that appeared when she let herself think about the future couldn't be denied.

With one hand on the plant stand, she looked down at her other hand, where her wedding ring gleamed in the white moonlight. She slipped it off her finger and set it on the top shelf of the stand.

It was then that she felt warmth seeping into her body, as if someone had given her a giant hug. The sensation only lasted a matter of moments. Then once again she felt her cold nose, her stiff fingers, her numbing feet. She picked up the ring and slipped it into a zippered pocket in her purse. Then she pushed the plant stand out of the storage compartment, determined to fit it into her car.

She had to get home to Sophie and Grace and make an airline reservation to Houston.

Chapter 13

The nurse ran the IV and Mitch watched the drip. This surgery was really going to happen.

Although Matt had stopped in a little while before, the one person Mitch wanted to talk to was Lily. But she was back in Sagebrush.

When the nurse left Mitch's cubicle, he flexed both hands, staring at his right one. Someday in the future, if not able to perform surgery, he might have fuller use of his fingers. Would he feel whole if he did?

He doubted it. Because he realized now he didn't need the use of his fingers to feel whole. He needed Lily. That need had been supremely evident the night of the reunion when they'd made love. Somehow, on that night, attraction and chemistry had transformed into something else entirely.

It had transformed into love.

He hadn't had the courage to admit it or the courage to feel it until he'd awakened the following morning holding her. Yet at that same moment he'd had doubts about Lily's ability to love again…doubts about her ability to freely make any kind of commitment to him. If he pushed her, he'd lose her.

He'd almost lost her when his ego had slid between them in June and his pride had convinced him to put time and distance between them. He'd almost lost her again when he'd prodded her about her wedding ring on Sunday morning.

Would she cut and run? Would she decide loving Troy for the rest of her life was enough? Were her feelings not deep enough to allow a future to develop between them?

He wanted her here to talk about all of it—his past mistakes, his future possibilities, her independence, their passionate hunger that went deeper than pheromones. He hadn't asked her to come, because she had Sophie and Grace to consider first. He hadn't asked her to come, because he knew if he pushed too hard she'd slip away entirely.

Turning away from the IV stand, he closed his eyes and tried to blank his mind.

Lily rushed down the hospital corridor hoping she wasn't too late. She had to see Mitch before he went into surgery. She *had* to.

The past three days had felt like a global marathon.

When she'd returned from the storage unit, Ellie had helped her carry in the plant stand. She'd also noticed the absent wedding ring. When Lily had explained what she wanted to do, Ellie had offered to take care of Sophie and Grace while she went to Houston. Angie had been at home, too, and when Lily couldn't find available seating on a flight, she'd called her brother-in-law, billionaire Logan Barnes. He'd booked Lily first-class seats. Both Angie and Ellie convinced her the twins would be well taken care of. Lily didn't have to worry about anything... except what Mitch was going to say and do.

Now as Lily headed for the information desk in the surgical wing, she was afraid. She loved Mitch Cortega with all her heart. But what if he'd lost patience with her? What if she was too late? What if he rejected her and she'd made a fool of herself?

She kept going anyway, almost at a jog. If she made a fool of herself, so be it.

When she reached the desk and inquired about Mitch's whereabouts, the woman asked, "Are you family?"

Lily said blithely, "I'm his fiancée."

Narrowing her eyes, the clerk asked if Lily knew his date of birth.

"I do. It's January twenty-first."

A tad less warily, the gatekeeper of this surgical unit next asked for his home address and telephone number.

Resigned to this delay, Lily rattled them off.

Finally the clerk pointed her in the direction she should go, advising, "Follow the yellow floor line."

Doing so, Lily almost ran toward the surgical waiting area, found cubicle number six and peeked around the curtain.

There Mitch was, lying on a gurney, an IV line attached to the hand that wouldn't be undergoing surgery.

She wondered if he'd already been given medication to relax, if he'd even be aware that she was here.

Crossing to the bed, she stood beside it and asked softly, "Mitch?"

His eyes opened. They were clear, alert and totally flabbergasted. "Lily? What are you doing here? My surgery was delayed an hour and they haven't given me anything yet. So I know you can't be a hallucination." He sat up and looked ready to climb out of the bed.

She laid a hand on his shoulder, stood as close as she could without jumping into bed with him, then plunged in. "I had to see you in person. I had to tell you before you went into surgery."

"What? Did something happen to Sophie or Grace?" The lines on his forehead cutting deep, his expression showed his extreme worry.

"They're fine. Ellie and Angie are taking good care of them."

Now he just looked totally perplexed.

She took his hand, stroked the scars on his arm and gazed deeply into his eyes. "I love you, Mitch. I couldn't let you go into surgery not knowing that. You've been so patient and I don't know if that patience has run out or not. But I do love you. I want to be with you. I want a future with you."

He didn't look as ecstatic as she thought he might, as she'd *hoped* he might. Instead, he looked troubled. "What happened, Lily?"

He didn't believe her! In fact, he seemed to consider her appearance as impulsive, that she might change her mind tomorrow. She stayed close to him, her hand still on his arm. Somehow she'd make him understand. "I went to the storage compartment where I kept everything I didn't move into the Victorian. Troy's tools are there, and the plant stand he made for me before he was deployed."

Mitch began to say something but she didn't give him the chance. She rushed on. "The stand isn't finished and

I'd like to finish it. And then I want to put it in your sunroom where it can hold plants or flowers and remind me
of the love Troy gave me. It's part of my past, Mitch.
Troy is part of my past. And I'll always hold his memory dear in my heart. I don't think it was a coincidence
he chose you to look after me. He used to say, 'There
are no coincidences,' and I believe he was right. When
I was standing there looking at the moon and spotting a
shooting star—I'd never seen one before in my life—I
remembered standing by the fire pit with you and singing
'Silent Night.' My whole being just understood I should
finally admit what I've been feeling. I *do* love you, Mitch
Cortega. I'm ready to commit to you for the rest of my
life. If you aren't ready, that's okay. We'll figure things
out as we go. *Together.*"

She could see that what she was saying and feeling
and meaning took a few moments for Mitch to absorb.
But then he opened his arms to her. "Come here."

She didn't hesitate. If someone came in to take him to
surgery, they could just take her along, too!

On his lap, with his arms around her the best he could
manage it, he kissed her with such soul-stirring passion
she thought she'd melt right into him.

But then he broke the kiss and lifted his head. "When
we made love Saturday night, I was forced to admit to
myself I was doing a hell of a lot more than watching
over you. I hadn't tried the word *love* on what I felt. But
on Sunday, I did. I guess I was embarrassed after the bad
dream. I woke up thinking I had to do *something*. If you
weren't ready, then I had to prepare myself for whatever
life dealt. The best way to do that was to see if I could
have my hand repaired."

"I was hurt you didn't talk about it with me," she admitted, knowing she had to be honest with him about everything.

"I'm sorry. I guess I thought I'd given you too many pieces of myself and this was one I had to take control of."

Stroking his face, she said, "I want all of you, Mitch. Not just the strong parts or the perfect parts. I'll support you no matter what happens, whether we return to our practice or whether you want to go back to trauma surgery. And I have no intention of moving to Oklahoma. I'm staying in Sagebrush with *you*."

Taking Lily's hand, Mitch smiled. "This isn't the place I'd imagined we'd be talking about this. I want to give you romance and flowers and music to remember the day by, not the clanging of hospital trays. But it seems like I've waited for you for so long, and I don't want to wait a second longer. Will you marry me?"

"When?" She'd be ready today if that's what he wanted.

"Soon. As soon as we can fly back to Sagebrush and arrange it. I don't want to wait a minute more than I have to to be your husband. And," he hesitated, then continued, "a stepfather to Sophie and Grace."

"You're not going to be a *step*father. You're going to be their dad. Troy would want that. I know he would."

Mitch kissed her again, just as the nurse swung back the curtain.

They were oblivious, lost in passion and promises they yearned to share.

Epilogue

"This is as unconventional as it gets," Mitch murmured to Lily, folding his arm around her in her cream wool cape. As long as she was in his arms, the world was good and he slept peacefully during the deep night hours. Marriage would gift them with the future they both wanted and needed.

Twinkle lights were strung around the border of Mitch's patio. The fire pit was lit, giving off warmth. The minister from Lily's church had agreed to perform the service. He'd told her early evening was fine. Afterward, he could return to his congregation for Christmas Eve midnight service.

Fortunately, the weather had cooperated and even Mitch had to admit his patio looked wedding-ready. The stars were crystal clear and the slice of moon glowed with silver-white light. An arbor, also decorated in evergreens and twinkle lights, housed the minister as Lily and Mitch stood before him, ready to say their vows.

Lily cast a glance at Ellie, who was holding Grace, and at Angie, who was carrying Sophie. The twins were bundled up in their pink snowsuits and mittens, their noses barely peeking out from their hoods. Gina had dressed Daniel similarly in blue, and Logan held his son so he could see what was going on, too, as Eva stood with Hannah ready to help with the kids. Shep and Raina had brought along Joey, Roy and Manuel. Tessa and her husband, Vince, held their children's hands, while Francesca and Grady as well as Emily and Jared stood by with their children. Within driving distance, Tony and Jimmy had brought their wives, children and Christmas along with them. Beside them, Lily and Mitch's colleagues watched from along one stone wall where the twinkle lights flickered high above them.

Lily had wanted them all here to witness this joyous celebration. She loved Mitch so much she wanted everyone who could to share their joy. They'd only be outside for about ten minutes and then they'd go inside for their reception, which would be homey and all theirs.

In a low voice beside Mitch, Matt said, "You two couldn't wait until spring, could you?"

Mitch shook his head. "Not a chance. You and I both know each day is a precious gift, and I want to spend them all with Lily."

Lily cuddled closer to Mitch, not at all cold, just wanting to feel him near. He was wearing a black, Western-cut leather jacket. His hand and wrist were still bandaged. After Christmas they would fly back to Houston for an exam by the doctor and decide whether Mitch was ready for physical therapy. The surgery had gone well, but it might take time for him to have use of those fingers again.

Reverend Allbright made some opening remarks and then said, "I understand the two of you have vows to make to each other."

"We do," they said in unison.

"Whoever wants to go first," the kindly older man invited.

Lily took Mitch's hands, one bandaged and one not, in both of hers. "I know how important vows and promises are to you. I promise to love you from morning till night and every minute in between. I vow to be your partner, lover and friend and I will always respect your opinion in raising our girls. Each and every day, I will try to bring happiness into your life and will be proud to call you my husband."

Mitch cleared his throat and held on to her as tightly as she was holding on to him. "I was broken when I met you, in ways I didn't even understand. Your acceptance, passion and caring have changed that. Having you and Sophie and Grace in my life has healed past wounds. I want nothing more than to be your husband and their dad. You are everything I've ever wanted, the woman I didn't even know I hoped to find. I love you, Lily, and I will cherish you, protect you, honor and respect you every day of our lives."

The minister opened his hand to Lily. Raina handed her a wide gold band and Lily placed it in the minister's hand. Matt handed Mitch a circle of diamonds and Mitch placed that in the minister's palm, also.

Reverend Allbright said, "These rings embody the circle of love that you have promised each other. I give them to you now to slide onto each other's fingers in memory of this night, the vows you have made and the love you will share."

Lily took the ring again and slid it onto Mitch's finger. "I thee wed," she said solemnly.

Mitch took the ring from the minister's hand and slid it onto Lily's finger. "I thee wed," he echoed, just as solemnly.

They held hands and faced forward again.

Reverend Allbright smiled. "I now pronounce you husband and wife."

Mitch took Lily into his arms and she lifted her face to his. Their kiss was an embodiment of everything their ceremony had entailed.

When Mitch raised his head, he said loud and clear, "I love you."

She kissed him again and buried her nose by his ear. "I love you, too."

Everyone around them was applauding and they realized they weren't alone in the universe. With her husband beside her, Lily went to Grace and lifted her into her arms. Mitch did the same with Sophie and they came together for a group hug.

"Can we cut the cake now?" Joey asked.

"We can cut the cake," Mitch announced happily, tickling Sophie.

After more hugs all around, they headed into Mitch's house, ready to begin their lives and the future they would build together.

* * * * *

Love Harlequin romance?

DISCOVER.

Be the first to find out about promotions,
news and exclusive content!

Facebook.com/HarlequinBooks

Twitter.com/HarlequinBooks

Instagram.com/HarlequinBooks

Pinterest.com/HarlequinBooks

You Tube YouTube.com/HarlequinBooks

ReaderService.com

EXPLORE.

Sign up for the Harlequin e-newsletter and
download a free book from any series at
TryHarlequin.com

CONNECT.

Join our Harlequin community to
share your thoughts and connect
with other romance readers!
Facebook.com/groups/HarlequinConnection

HARLEQUIN

Heartfelt or thrilling, passionate or uplifting—Harlequin is more than just happily-ever-after.

With twelve different series to choose from and new books available every month, you are sure to find stories that will move you, uplift you, inspire and delight you.

HNEWS2021

Get 4 FREE REWARDS!

We'll send you 2 FREE Books plus 2 FREE Mystery Gifts.

Harlequin Special Edition books relate to finding comfort and strength in the support of loved ones and enjoying the journey no matter what life throws your way.

FREE
Value Over
$20